Praise for
Love Lethal, Death Divine

"An intricate dance of love, loss, grief, and cold gods. Dunato's *Love Lethal, Death Divine* casts a dark magic all of its own."

—Angela "A. G." Slatter, award-winning author of
A Forest, Darkly

"*Love Lethal, Death Divine* is a brilliant dark fantasy, with a fascinating premise, nuanced characters you can't help but root for, and a story that will keep you up at night. I devoured it."

—Millie Abecassis, author of *A Legacy of Blood and Bone*

"In a tale about many forms of love and death, Jelena Dunato explores the selfishness and the sacrifice of both. Against a backdrop of folklore, fickle deities, and centuries of conflict, she paints a story of political intrigue and desperate attraction that will have your heart racing from the opening page through to the final twist. The beautiful prose will draw you in, but the characters will ensnare you forever."

—Alethea Lyons, author of *The Seer of York* books

"Both a pulse-pounding time travel thriller and an emotionally gripping tale of the cost of true love in a land of smart women up against cruel gods and crueler fate. Dunato's intelligent, stunning dark fantasy tale is everything unmissable about this genre. I may never recover from this book, and I'm not sure I want to."

—Ed Crocker, author of *Lightfall*

Love Lethal, Death Divine

Edited by Maddy Leary
Book Design and Layout by Rob Carroll
Cover Art by Mona Finden
Cover Design by Rob Carroll

Library of Congress Control Number: 2026935169

ISBN 978-1-958598-99-3 (paperback)
ISBN 979-8-9933676-5-1 (eBook)

darkmatter-ink.com

Love Lethal, Death Divine

Jelena Dunato

DARK MATTER INK

To those who left too soon.

Till
Virion
Myrit
Amrath
Leven
Larion
Abia
Svr
Elmar
AMRIAN
KINGDOM

Even now if I saw you
only once,
I would long for you
through worlds,
worlds.

—Izumi Shikibu

Liana

A white stag stood in the middle of the clearing like a harbinger of fate. Plumes of milky vapor rose from its nostrils, while the setting sun gilded its pristine coat and wrapped the magnificent animal in a luminous cloud.

Liana reined her horse in. Her throat tightened in a painful spasm, while the icy claws of panic gripped her chest. "No," she whispered.

They were less than thirty paces apart, yet the stag stood perfectly still, undisturbed by Liana's bow and arrows, its dark eyes fixed on her face.

She knew that stag. She remembered the silken caress and musky smell of its coat, the hard, velvety touch of its antlers when her fingers gripped them, the raspy wetness of its tongue when it licked her tears. She had slept beside it on the bed of dry leaves for so many nights, wrapped in its safe warmth, her small head resting on its massive flank.

They went back a long way, the stag and Liana.

It was the last creature she wanted to see now.

The winter forest around them fell silent. Liana's breath froze into a still white cloud. The pale orange sun hovered a finger's breadth above the snowy peaks in the west. In the winter afternoon, it should've been sinking like lead, pulling the shimmering train of light behind it, revealing the night sky studded with brilliant lights.

Time slowed down, and then stopped, freezing the air around her, replacing it with the cold nothingness of the spaces between the stars.

Liana swallowed the rising dread and took a deep breath of the deathly still air. "Go away!" she shouted. Her voice, high and resonant, shattered the unnatural chill. She spurred her horse and charged towards the unmoving stag as the sun finally dropped behind the mountains. Instead of crashing into the mighty animal, they ran through a cloud of white mist.

A lonely bird cried from the bare bough; the magic was broken. No trace of divine presence remained in the winter forest. The stag was no more than a wisp of fog, a trick of the dying light.

Liana rode on, drenched in cold sweat. This forest of gnarly old oaks—this lone, wild, wooded hill in the landscape of olive groves—used to be her refuge, her safe place. But now, as the shadows crept down the mountains and the night rolled over the winter landscape, she dared not look back.

The shard of fear in her heart moved a fraction, and the cold light glinted off its deadly edge. Gripping the reins so hard her fingers turned white, she rushed down the winding king's road that lead from the hills to the deep bay and the walled town of Abia nesting there.

Liana's brain writhed in panic, struggling to explain away the divine omen. It was a coincidence, an echo, surely. There was no one to see her cry among the dark, craggy hills, but still she bit on her leather glove as the salty wind tugged on her braid and froze the tears on her cheeks. Fate was catching up with her. She should have been more careful, she should have known.

She should have never let Amron out of her sight.

The walls of Abia rose before her. The massive gates were locked for the night, the torches above them lit. She paused on the drawbridge to compose herself, exhaled slowly, rubbed the tears out of her eyes. Then she whistled a short tune once, twice, three times.

"Who goes there?" A familiar voice; she knew all the guards at this gate.

"Liana."

"My lady, you're late tonight." The sound of bolts lifting and a key turning in the lock.

Cold wind howled behind her, lashing the deserted hills, calling her to turn and ride back. There was no respite for her behind these walls tonight, no solace brought by the light, warmth, or human kindness.

"I was delayed," she said as a small door opened in the big gate. She dismounted and led the horse through the narrow opening, turning her head away from the guard's torch. "Has anyone come today?"

He knew what she meant. "No, my lady."

"Thank you." She threw a silver coin to him. A spark of hope tried to ignite in her lungs, foolish and futile. No news was not good news, not anymore.

She led the horse down the cobbled street. The winter evening chased people away from the windy corners and squares, but warm light seeped through closed shutters and the smell of fried fish and boiled kale wafted from kitchens. Tall, narrow stone houses huddled together for warmth and company.

The closer she got to the seafront, the more inviting the taverns looked, overflowing with music, wine, and chatter. For a few reckless heartbeats, she was tempted, craving a distraction, a fleeting feeling of safety, but whenever her footsteps slowed down, the darkness inside her swelled and the wind pushed her onward, towards the main square, towards the palace.

She entered through a side door: another guard unlocking it just for her, another silver tossed for the trouble. She left the horse in the stable, in the safe hands of the grooms, and climbed a narrow wooden stairway. She gave a wide berth to the offices on the first floor, where busy clerks scribbled in their books regardless of the hour, and reached the private apartments on the second floor, where another guard just nodded, accustomed to her unpredictable comings and goings.

"Any visitors?" she asked him.

"No, my lady."

The palace in Abia had been the grand seat of the lords of Larion for centuries, an image of power and wealth conjured up in white stone, with elegant arches, high vaulted ceilings, and stained glass windows, but it reminded Liana of nothing so much as a tightly run ship, a living mechanism where everybody knew their place.

Everybody but her.

She was the intruder, a creature of the woods, neither a clerk, nor a soldier, nor a servant. A lady who was not a lady, and a wife who was not really a wife.

She entered a string of rooms, empty and yet murmuring with other people's lives, glowing with the silvery imprints of their footsteps; the warm, wooden chairs worn out by their touch; the glass panes breathed on by so many mouths. A continuity which had nothing to do with her. She had no family, no venerable ancestors, no name beside the one her mother had carelessly flung at her. Her bedroom with large windows overlooking the sea, her massive walnut bed with green brocade curtains, her mirror in its gilded frame—all of it was just borrowed. She had slid into this life sideways, a shadow, a traveler just passing through.

Liana sighed and took off her muddy riding boots, leaving them by the door, threw her cloak over a chair, and walked barefooted across the woolen carpet to the bathtub waiting for her by the fire. The palace did not agree with her tonight, but it was not the palace's fault.

Every evening, the maids filled the bath for her with warm, fragrant water. But when Liana touched it to check its temperature, her hand sank into a gray, ice-cold sludge. The pungent odor of decay hit her nostrils. Dark and deadly, like the sacrificial pond in the heart of the woods where they used to drown people to placate the hungry goddess. A white hand emerged from the depths, grabbing at her fingers.

Liana jumped back with a yelp, tripped over the edge of the carpet, and fell. Not waiting to see what would crawl out of the bathtub, refusing to even look at the cursed thing, she scurried to the nearest wall and lifted a corner of a tapestry, revealing a small door. She clawed at the latch and threw herself into the darkness on the other side, slamming the door shut behind her.

Sprawled on the carpet, breathing hard, she waited for the wet lurch, the scratching, the creak of hinges. But the soft silence was interrupted only by her thunderous heartbeat.

Stagnant waters were the realm of Morana, the Goddess of Death. Ponds, moats, abandoned wells. And bathwater, apparently.

Liana hadn't been hallucinating up in the hills and she wasn't hallucinating now. Something was wrong. The world had become thin like a painted porcelain vase, she could see the shadows moving behind the fragile surface. The gods were knocking, looking for a weak spot.

"Damn you," she whispered. "Damn you."

Time trickled in the darkness. Her heart struggled to find its beat while her eyes searched for comfort in the snug familiarity of the room. Books and papers were stashed precariously on the large desk, under the silver moonlight that poured through the window. A canopied bed dozed in the corner like a massive animal. Wind whispered in the empty fireplace.

Liana took a deep breath, reached for the tinderbox, and lit a candle. The light flickered, emphasizing the darkness rather than driving it away. Shadows danced across her hands and pooled in the creases of her shirt. The fear, the feeling of wrongness, grabbed her again.

The world was cracking around her. The stag, the bath water, this empty room that still smelled of frankincense and bergamot, as if Amron had stepped out a moment ago. The desk where he used to sit and where she liked to sneak up on him, the bed where he held her in his arms while the waves murmured outside, the window where he loved to watch the clouds roll over the sea. His lingering presence in all things.

"What happened? Why didn't you come home?" she asked.

Instead of an answer, she heard commotion in the other room.

"My lady, where are you?" Nina called with shrill urgency.

Liana opened the door and stepped back into her room. "Here."

"My lady—" A soft linen bathrobe shook in Nina's white-knuckled grip. Liana glanced at the bath, expecting some new horror, but the bathwater was clear and still, steaming gently. The darkness had retreated, there was nothing in there to scare the girl. And yet...

"At least you're not in the bath." Her maid chuckled, and that sound, broken and ill-suited, snapped Liana back into this moment, into this room. She barely had the time to register the panic on Nina's face when a chorus of male voices boomed in the corridor.

"In the name of the king," someone shouted, and a group of soldiers barged in, crowding together like a pack of curs in a dark alley. Five young men reeking of sweat, their boots leaving dirty footprints on the carpet.

Liana lifted her chin a little, a barefooted lady hiding her trembling hands. "What is the meaning of this?"

Their eyes widened when they saw her face.

"My lady, I tried to stop them," the maid stammered, still holding the bathrobe, "but they claimed they were here on His Majesty's orders."

"It's fine, Nina," Liana told her. "You can leave us." Then she turned to the men. This breach of her privacy was calculated, surely, to catch her unawares. In bed, in the bath, alone and vulnerable. "What do you want?"

Finally, one messenger, lanky, liveried, cleared his throat and said, "Mistress Liana?"

Mistress, not *lady*. King's instructions, surely, petty and disrespectful like the man who issued them. For dynastic and legal reasons, for her own unwillingness, for the king's objection, Amron had never married her.

Liana let the insult slide like water over glass.

"I'm here to bring you the news." He paused and Liana could discern a faint swamp-green outline around him, invisible to his companions. Time slowed down again, and for a moment she hoped it would stop completely. But then the young man cleared his throat once more, and said, "His Royal Highness, Prince Amron, is dead."

There it was.

Right there.

The news she'd dreaded, slamming into her chest like an arrow.

She took the blow standing, even though every bone inside her body turned to dust. Her hearing betrayed her, drowned by the exploding silence. Her sight followed, filling her vision with darkness, and for a heartbeat she thought she would faint.

But no, she would not faint before these men. She would not disgrace herself. Clenching her fists so tight her nails bit into her palms like claws, she willed her face to remain perfectly still.

"How did he die?" she asked.

"He was kil—" Whispers, shuffling.

Another man stepped out, older, with a dark beard. "We're not here to discuss that," he said. "We're here to inform you that, since the prince had no heirs, the city of Abia and the province of Larion revert to the Crown immediately."

Liana nodded. She'd expected as much: the king's greedy, impatient little paws. She didn't care, she had never wanted any of it. She'd been bound to Larion, to Abia, to this palace, by one reason alone, and that reason was Amron.

"I understand," she said, keeping the tremor out of her voice. "Thank you for bringing me the news. I'd like a moment of privacy now."

They hesitated, exchanging looks, but then the bearded man spoke again. "You must leave immediately. We're here to escort you out."

Liana had always known the king disliked her, but she'd never thought it was this personal. The calculated disrespect was nothing compared with the pain the news of Amron's death caused her, yet it left her speechless. After more than a decade, after the immense service she had done for the king, after Amron had given everything, including his life, she was going to be thrown out like a beggar.

They came to hurt and humiliate her, believing that she was as attached to shiny trinkets as that spoiled brat who sat on the throne. They forgot that for the first twenty years of her life she'd possessed nothing but the clothes on her back. All she ever cared about was Amron; without him, this palace was just a shiny husk, an empty shell echoing the voices of the dead.

Gritting her teeth, she pulled her riding boots on and wrapped herself in her woolen cloak. Then she walked to her desk and took a bundle of letters Amron had written her over the years.

The young man who had spoken to her first cleared his throat again. "You are not to take anything with you."

She had her cloak, her boots, her dagger. She had a silver medallion tucked safely under her shirt, with a lock of Amron's hair inside it. She had her memories.

"I wasn't planning to take them," she said and threw the letters into the fire.

The bearded man roared and jumped at her, grabbing her braid and pulling her away, even though the letters were already turning to ash. She twisted in his grip and hit his face with the heel of her palm, registering a satisfying crunch when his nose broke.

He screamed and fell to the floor, bleeding all over the carpet. His men pulled their swords. At that moment, a handful of palace guards stormed into the room, Nina at their heels.

"My lady, do you want us to throw them out?" the captain asked.

Liana blinked and assessed the scene. The angry messengers bent on revenge, the furious guards ready to defend her with their lives, the blood soaking into the carpet as the injured man writhed in pain, and altogether too much sharp steel for such a small room. One word and it would turn into butchery.

Amron would never want that.

"No, stop." She turned to the bleeding man. "I'm sorry I hit you."

He spat out a glob of blood and shot her a venomous look.

"I'll go in peace," she said. "Escort me out."

A strange procession formed in her room and walked down the corridors: Liana leading, followed by the king's men, who were in turn followed by the wary palace guards and Nina, silently crying, at their heels.

The word must have spread because, even though it was past midnight, the doors opened as they passed and people—clerks, maids, pages, guardsmen—watched her go. Some nodded or raised their hands in farewell, but most stood in shocked silence.

She walked, avoiding their eyes, head held high, tears frozen on her eyelashes. When they reached the palace yard, she turned to the stable. "May I take my horse?"

The king's men exchanged glances. The one with the broken nose spoke. "His Majesty said you were to take nothing from the palace."

She bit her lip and let the insult go. It didn't matter, none of it mattered. The guards opened the gate for her and she walked out of her old life without a backwards glance, poorer than she was when she arrived thirteen years before.

~Chapter 2~

Melia

The acrid ash from her brother's funeral pyre still hovered in the air when a maid brought a note summoning Melia to her father's study.

Death never left Melia's side. Its high voice rang with the desert winds blowing through the empty corridors of Syr, its shadow stalked her through the abandoned rooms, its shape materialized in the dust rising on the empty plains. Melia let it engulf her, for the idea that she still existed, took up space, breathed, ate, drank, felt like an offense. Her survival felt like an insult to Rovin, burnt to dust, blown across the sky by the wild wind.

She made herself invisible in her grief, perfecting her shadowy existence, praying her father would forget about her.

It was a futile hope.

Roderi of Elmar lifted his head when his daughter entered his study and looked at her with eyes that were as cold and dead as two shards of black marble.

"Melia," he said, and there was no warmth, no hope, no affection in his words. Between them, invisible but forever present, lay her brother's bloody remains. "It's time to discuss your future."

Future? *Discuss?*

"What do you have in mind, Father?"

"You will wed Prince Amron."

The winter sky outside bled the colors of the sunset. The massive desk, looming on the frayed carpet, threw long shadows, reaching for Melia. Her fingers twitched in an involuntary reaction; she tucked them behind the folds of her skirt.

"I thought I was promised to Cousin Maren," she said softly, not as a contradiction, but a gentle reminder.

Her father scoffed. "That was when you were a nobody, a spare daughter whose dowry I could not afford. Now your dowry is the whole of Elmar and you deserve a prince."

Melia wasn't sure what she deserved. Since Rovin's death, all the eyes in Elmar had been turned to her, the lord's only child, the heiress. Her destiny had suddenly become greater than the confines of her person. And yet, she felt like a cold shadow, a skulking bad omen, a handmaid to death.

Her father had always worn mostly black, but since Rovin died, he took pains to wear no other color. Even his linens were dyed black. Servants whispered and rumors spread: Melia had heard people in Syr calling him the Black Lord. The name fit him, surely. Looking at him, she could see nothing but darkness, even greater than her own. He'd aged ten years in one month. His olive skin used to have a golden glow, now it looked deathly sallow. His eyes were dead and cold, and the corners of his mouth now rose only in derision.

"I talked to the king," her father said, measuring her up. "You're the greatest heiress in the kingdom now, so I offered your hand to the crown prince. Do you know what the king replied?"

That she was an empty husk, unworthy of his son. Melia shook her head, trembling. She was supposed to be insignificant, invisible, not a bargaining chip on the king's desk.

"He said," her father continued, "that the peace talks with the Empire were almost done and that, if everything goes according to their plans, the crown prince will marry one of the emperor's daughters."

Those words shook her out of her self-loathing stupor. "Peace with the Seragians?" she asked, careful to keep her voice flat, to hide any morsel of hope she might feel.

"Imagine that." Her father's lips twisted into a grimace of disgust, as if he'd bitten into a rotten plum. "So much blood spilled and he thinks he'll solve it with a wedding."

Melia looked at the sky, now the deepest purple of the imperial banners, behind his head. So much blood had been spilled, so naturally, more blood should be spilled to avenge it. Rivers of blood, flowing from here to eternity, mountains of bleached bones, thousands of lost souls, whispering about lives that had been cut too short, too soon.

Death was her father's horizon, all that he could see.

"The king offered me his younger son instead," her father said. "It's barely a suitable match for my heir. But I accepted. Do you know why?"

She could guess, and had she still cared about anything at all, she'd have been furious. But she'd long stopped caring, about herself, about Elmar, about the whole kingdom and their endless war. So she shook her head and waited for her father to say it out loud.

"Because I want you to go to court," Roderi of Elmar said. "I want you to watch them for me." His eyes glinted with dark fire. "That peace treaty would be a dagger stuck in the back of every man in Elmar. A betrayal of every life lost on the border. It must never transpire."

His Royal Highness, Prince Amron of the House of Amris.

The name meant little to her. She'd seen him once, a couple of years before. He'd spent six months on the border with Rovin, and they showed up one evening for dinner, laughing all the way through it at their end of the table, with that easy companionship young men sometimes shared. The prince was fair where Rovin was dark, soft-spoken where her brother was loud, and pleasant enough to look at. She'd felt a spark of interest, but Rovin and he were thick as thieves, inseparable throughout the evening. Melia left them to their boyish antics that night, and never thought about the prince again.

She hardly ever thought about men at all. She had no beauty, no cheerfulness or sweetness men found attractive. In any other city, at any other court but her father's, she would've been unremarkable. Black hair and dark eyes, a slightly crooked nose and lopsided smile, a body composed of sharp angles, lacking grace. But in Syr, where women were scarce and noblewomen rarer than hen's teeth, men noticed her. Soldiers followed her with their eyes as she passed.

For a brief period of time, before Rovin died, she'd imagined meeting someone interesting—more interesting than her moody cousin Maren, twice her age, holding a border fort even more desolate than Syr—and doing something with her life other than quietly fading away. After all, she was young and strong and healthy, a resilient desert breed, reared for survival. There was a spark of life inside her that refused to go out, a streak of stubbornness pushing her forward. She imagined that there could be a different kind of life outside the massive red walls of Syr, slowly crumbling to dust. A life that didn't necessarily include weapons and horses and men endlessly waging war.

But now, as she walked through the empty corridors, marrying a prince didn't seem like an opportunity to escape—quite the opposite. It seemed like the dark desperation of Syr spreading out, pouring over the border like thick mud, drowning everything before it.

She knocked on a low wooden door tucked away in a dark alcove.

"Come in," a voice said.

A pungent herbal scent hit her in the face as soon as she entered. Ferisa was in practical garb, hair tucked beneath a scarf, leather apron protecting her clothes. She looked up from the granite mortar filled with crushed leaves, and her eyebrows—two thick charcoal strokes emphasizing her onyx eyes—shot up when she noticed the look on Melia's face.

"Tell me the news," she said.

The smell made her dizzy in a good way, so Melia took a deep breath and walked further into Ferisa's orderly realm, where potions were kept in neatly labeled bottles and vials stacked in cabinets, and herbs were dried and packed in little bags, hidden in the deep drawers. She gently patted the shell of a taxidermied turtle.

"Father is marrying me off," she said.

"To Maren?" Ferisa was incredulous. "Now? That doesn't make any sense."

"No." She approached the worn wooden desk where Ferisa was working and laid her trembling hands on it. They looked like dry twigs, thin and knobbly. "To Prince Amron."

"Oh." Ferisa laid her pestle down. "That's a major match. The highest one can get."

"So high up the air is thin and freezing." Melia inched her hand forward until the tips of her fingers touched Ferisa's.

Their eyes met. There had been few secrets between them before Rovin died, and none since.

"You are strong enough, I know you are," Ferisa said.

"No, I'm not. I'm weak and afraid." She squeezed Ferisa's hand. And then, acting on pure, desperate impulse, in a move that spat in the face of cold darkness, she pressed her lips to Ferisa's, tasting the bitter arrowfoil that kept her alert. It was an act of defiance, a gossamer bridge that led from nothingness to life.

"No, little raven, not like that." Ferisa pushed her away gently.

"I love you," Melia said. "Only you."

"I know." Ferisa wrapped her arms around Melia. "I know."

Three months later, Melia watched from the battlements of Syr as the royal procession meandered up the road. It the afternoon sun, it glimmered like a fairy-tale serpent, an explosion of gold and blue. Three hundred people, knights and ladies, courtiers and clerks, soldiers and servants—more than her father had in the keep on a good day. A river of people in splendid attire, cheerful and noisy, crashing like a colorful tidal wave over the dour red stones of Syr.

The procession was an affront, a slap in the face of the heavy silence that ruled the corridors. Melia watched it pour through the main gates of the city like the breath of a glorious spring in this place where all seasons looked the same. It climbed up the narrow streets, followed by thousands of curious eyes, greeted by the rusty, half-hearted cheers of the people who'd forgotten how to celebrate in public. It flooded the inner courtyard of the keep, bringing clamor and disorder and pure, unbridled life.

Melia rushed down the stairs, exhilarated against her will, picking up the skirts of her new gown, careful not to tear it. Heavy silk, in a moss green hue that favored her complexion, the finest fabric and cut her father's money could buy. She'd thought she didn't care about clothes, lurking in the empty chambers in her dark wools and worn-out linens, but it was only because she'd never seen clothes like this before.

Through the dark corridor and into the arched gallery, straight above the noisy crowd of light-skinned people, speaking in accents as far and foreign as the snowy mountains of Virion. She was not allowed to come down and show her face before the signing of the contract, but no one had forbidden her to look from the safe shadow of a massive pillar. She spotted her father, wearing black silk, of course, but a fine, heavily embroidered black silk, his hair neatly tied back, his face cleanly shaven, looking almost welcoming. Melia wasn't looking for him, though, so she turned to where the crowd was thickest, into the tangle of guards and banners and huge snow-white horses.

While her eyes flew over the faces, young and old, handsome and homely, her fingers played with the thin golden bracelets around her wrist and she wondered if she'd be able to recognize him again in that sea of strangers. Then, as if on cue, the crowd parted and the noise died down. A rider sat alone in a circle of courtiers as the light bent towards him and the shadows scurried away. The illusion lasted half a heartbeat, barely enough to make her gasp, and then he dismounted, greeted her father, and followed him inside.

Up close that evening, when they signed the wedding contract, there was no magic to him. Like every child in the kingdom, Melia had heard the legend of Amris the Golden-Haired a hundred times, but the young man who walked in her father's great hall, surrounded by an entourage whose jewels were worth more than all the precious things in Syr heaped together, had nothing divine about him. She remembered his lean frame and his sharp face, slightly more mature now, and his quiet, measured voice. Back straight as a rod, every hem and fold on his attire perfectly sharp, every step carefully choreographed. He spoke with a precise, haughty diction strange to her ears; with the clear, clipped words of someone used to giving orders.

Roderi of Elmar smiled, but Melia recognized disdain in the curve of his lips. She read her father's thoughts easily, his contempt for the arrogant Northerners, for their lavish ceremonies and indulgent ways, for their inability to survive on the barren, windswept soil of Elmar.

If he'd felt that burning derision, the prince did nothing to reveal it during that long, unbearably dull ceremony of presenting the bloodlines of their families ten generations back, of reciting the endless clauses of their wedding contract, of reading aloud every detail of her dowry and displaying and describing every royal gift she would receive. He barely looked at her throughout the evening, and they got no chance to speak in private.

Melia tried to read him, to see if he remembered her, if he liked her, but his face revealed nothing, and his eyes, blue-gray like rainclouds, remained cold.

It was almost midnight when the formalities ended and the tide of people drew them apart. They were not allowed to be together yet, not before the binding ceremony, so she let a group of women she barely knew lead her to her chambers, where she muttered "I want to be alone," and slammed the door in their faces.

She sighed and leaned on the carved wood, grateful that the long day was over.

"So, do you like him?" Ferisa asked.

She sat in a dark corner of Melia's room in her somber priestly garb, her face unreadable.

"You shouldn't be here," Melia whispered.

"Who's going to notice?" Ferisa scoffed. "So, do you like him?"

"He's cold and distant and I don't know what to think." Melia sat on the bed. "Come sit beside me."

When Ferisa joined her, Melia rested her head on her shoulder and closed her eyes. "Have you ever done it with a man?" she asked. There was no possessiveness, no jealousy—no relationship to speak of—just careful curiosity.

"Yes." Ferisa didn't elaborate.

"What's it like?"

"Brief and unpleasant," Ferisa said. "If you lie still and do what he says, it will be over soon enough."

𝕿𝖍𝖊 𝖓𝖊𝖝𝖙 𝖒𝖔𝖗𝖓𝖎𝖓𝖌, Melia was little more than a doll to dress and paint. Dozens of hands touched her, scrubbing her, combing her hair, wrapping her in layers of fabric like a precious gift. She chose a red gown, for luck, and wove blood-red roses into her black hair. Women lined her eyes in black, painted her eyelids gold and her lips dark red. They rubbed perfumed oil into her skin and polished her nails, bitten down to raw flesh, until they shone like alabaster. A gold necklace with six dark rubies as big as hazelnuts, Amron's wedding gift to her, hugged her neck.

Yet, when she looked at herself in the mirror, all she could see was a scrawny, overdressed girl with a wreath of roses too beautiful for her on her head. An apparition dragged out in the sun against her will, exposed before curious, unfriendly eyes. Suddenly, she yearned for silence, for her shabby wool, for the dark, empty corridors.

Women crowded around her—her late mother's ladies, smelling of dust and old leather; her maids, giggling behind her back; the pale courtiers from the prince's entourage, with their derisive eyes. They made her feel more alone, exposed and raw.

Melia wished Rovin was there, and her mother.

She descended into the courtyard, blinking away tears. The binding ceremony was always performed out in the open. Their only garden was a dried-up wasteland of thorny shrubs, so her father decided the courtyard was more appropriate. Carpets were brought out and laid on the dusty flagstones and someone had erected a wooden arch and adorned it with garlands of fresh leaves and flowers. A sweet, melancholy tune floated in the air as she descended the stairs and all eyes turned to her.

She saw the prince, in somber blue and gray, waiting beside a priestess in a flaming red robe. The color of the Goddess of Love. It felt like a mockery, to drag Lada's priestess to perform a ceremony so blatantly devoid of love. The God of War would've been more fitting.

Her father caught her hand when she descended. "You look like a princess," he whispered in her ear, leading her through the crowd. His words stuck to her skin like oily residue, tarnishing her. His kiss on her forehead, before the altar, seared her skin like a flaming curse.

"I give her to you," her father told the prince.

Prince Amron took her hand with an unreadable expression on his face, serene and unblinking. His skin was warm and dry, and there was a faint scent of bergamot about him.

As the priestess tied their hands together with a red ribbon, Melia watched his profile, wondering what thoughts filled his head.

"I join you before the eyes of gods and people, from now until death," the priestess said, and offered him a silver chalice.

He took a sip. "Melia, I take you to be my wife, from now until death," he said in a voice clear enough to reach the far corners of the courtyard.

She took a sip. It was overly sweet and very bitter at the same time. "Amron, I take you to be my husband, from now until death," she said.

He bowed down and kissed her: a quick dry brush of his lips against hers, over in a heartbeat.

The crowd cheered. She looked up as the sun dipped behind the battlements. The dusk in Syr always smelled like blood.

There was a feast afterwards, with mountains of food and rivers of wine, and music and dancing. And still, the prince eluded her, surrounded by other people, dragged this way and that. He danced with her once, gliding across the floor while she struggled to keep up, feeling clumsy and provincial. The dress constrained her, the roses scratched her scalp, the gold paint burned her eyelids.

The evening slid out of her hands, shattered like a crystal vase on the flags. Melia didn't want to be there, she knew she would mess everything up, grind it into fine dust the wind would blow away. She was a creature of death and grief; no silk nor paint nor fresh flowers could change that.

The odor of blood lingered in her nose, the light flickered, and all she could see in the great hall were the dead, whirling to the fast tune, toasting her, their decomposing faces grinning like outlaws swinging on the gallows, staring at her with their empty sockets. A terrified sob escaped her lips, her hand jerked, pushing her glass over, a bloody stain splashed the white cloth—

"Melia." Prince Amron touched her hand. "It's time."

And still they were not allowed to be alone. Men gathered around him, women grabbed her and dragged to her chambers, laughing and squealing. It took almost as much time to unwrap her as it took to deck her out. Off went the red silk and the roses, the golden necklace, the face paint. She was washed, again, more perfumed oil was rubbed into her skin, a gossamer-thin embroidered nightgown was pulled over her head.

As if on cue, he walked into her room when the women finished combing her hair. "Out," he said, and they scattered like a flock of birds.

He was casually disrobed, out of his formal attire, but still in his shirt and trousers. He walked to the small round table in the corner. "They left us nothing but wine," he said, "and I've had too much already."

The first words her husband said to her in private, and she didn't know what to reply.

He opened the door and peered out. "Tea," he said in that clear, measured voice of his, and tea materialized in an instant, mint with lemon, chilled, with two cups glazed green and white beside it. He poured one for her and she took it, to have something to hold on to.

The swollen red moon hung in the night sky, the faint echo of music seeped through the cracks in the floor. Her room was scrubbed clean, every piece of wood polished, every scrap of material washed. Its austerity now looked almost deliberate, almost elegant. A subtle scent of roses engulfed her in a soft cloud.

They were alone, finally, but as Melia sipped the tea, Ferisa's words about men made her skin crawl. She'd had a small vial of potion, something to make her numb and sleepy, in the pocket of her wedding gown. She'd been touching it for reassurance the whole day, and yet when the time to swallow it came, she hadn't done it. She'd been numb for too long; a doll moved by her father's wishes. She wanted to feel something, even if it hurt.

"What's wrong?" Amron asked.

His words startled her and she lifted her eyes, looking at him—really looking at him—for the first time. He sat on the edge of the bed, studying her. The candlelight was kind to his fair skin, his golden hair, the clean, sharp angles of his face. The arrogance was gone, and so was the severity. When he smiled at her, he looked young.

She exhaled slowly and put the cup down on the table. "I don't know how to do this." Her voice trembled.

He patted the bed. "Come, sit beside me."

She approached carefully, like a wary cur. He didn't seem dangerous like the men she knew: rash, violent, cruel. But there was something about him, some heaviness bending the world and everyone in it towards him, that frightened her.

She perched on the edge of the bed.

"Are you afraid of me?" he asked.

She bit her lip. Was she? "A little," she admitted.

Someone had strewn rose petals on the bed. She picked one up, crushing it between her fingers. Candles flickered in the warm midnight breeze that blew in through the open window.

"I'm not going to—" He paused, looked up, and brushed a lock of hair behind his ear. "I wanted to say I wasn't going to hurt you, but what kind of madman would say such a thing? Of course I'm not going to hurt you." He waved his words away. "You know what happens now? Someone's explained it to you?"

She swallowed the nausea down with difficulty. "Yes," she said, and blushed.

The tips of his fingers touched her cheek, outlining her features.

The only person who'd touched her face since her mother died was Ferisa, and her hands were firm, thorough, coarse— nothing like this slow, light touch. She leaned into his hand. He traced the line of her mouth with his thumb and angled towards her slowly until their lips met. His kiss was cautious and gentle, gradually growing deeper until she moved her body to accommodate his.

As his hands slipped under her nightgown, pulled it over her head, and caressed her bronze skin, she felt the slow tide of desire warming up her limbs, pooling beneath her ribs and trickling down her stomach. His shirt followed her nightgown; he was lean and hard beneath, nothing but muscle and bone, a body almost as sharp as hers. No cushioning between them, not even her breasts, so small they offered hardly any yield before his fingers met her ribcage.

He kissed her collarbone, traced the shape of her nipples with his mouth, brushed the soft skin of her belly with his warm breath. She closed her eyes, waiting for the roughness, the pain, but instead he opened her legs with a light push and his fingers slid between them, stroking her. His tongue followed, with a quick, fluttering touch that made her hips rise towards him.

She gasped in shock. It was pleasure without pain, pure and unbridled. It was a betrayal, a lie that left her raw and exposed, her body reacting to him intuitively.

"Please don't," she breathed. "Please."

He stopped, raised his head. "You don't like it?"

"I—" She liked it. But it was a trick, a ruse to make her vulnerable, to trap her in an intimacy so naked and defenseless there could be no lies, no dark places between them.

"Melia?" His hands rested on her thighs. He had the fingers of a musician, long and skillful, and she wanted them to slide inside her and—

"I can't," she said. "I'm sorry, I'm so sorry. I can't."

He withdrew immediately, rolling to the other side of the bed, grabbing his shirt.

She wrapped herself in the sheet, her cheeks burning. The red petals looked like drops of blood, mocking her. "I'm sorry," she repeated.

He stood up, somewhat disheveled, but already fully dressed. She expected him to cajole, push, threaten, do anything but retreat with such speed. She stared in wonder as he rubbed his temples and composed himself, becoming the perfectly poised stranger again.

Only then did it occur to her that there might be serious consequences. "I didn't mean—"

"It's fine," he cut her off. "It's been a long day and we're both strained and weary."

"I'll do whatever you want me to do," she said very softly, trying in vain to catch his gaze. All she could think about was her father's fury. A marriage that remained unconsummated was void. She'd failed to do her duty.

Amron didn't look angry, though. "There's no rush, and I won't tell anyone," he said. "But also, I won't take what is not willingly given. There are very few choices I can make freely and this is one of them. If you want me, you know where to find me. Good night, my lady." With that, he bowed curtly and walked out of her room.

~Chapter 3~

Liana

The streets of Abia were empty when Liana stepped out of the palace. The wind howled, banging unlatched doors and rattling wooden shutters as the first raindrops hit the cobbles. Liana's courage wavered, faced with the winter night. Grief softly fell into step with her as she walked, whispering how easy it would be to turn towards the harbor, climb the breakwater in the darkness, and dive into the freezing waves. The sea-maidens would pull her down into the depths, where everything was dark and peaceful and no pain could touch her ever again. Her ties to the world of humans were cut now. She had no one to love here, nothing to hope for.

If she disappeared, not a single soul would mourn her; it wouldn't even cause a ripple in the fabric of the world. She only had herself to blame for it: the reclusive, selfish, solitary Liana.

I hoped you'd join me in Myrit, Amron had written in gentle rebuke in the last letter that reached her, the one from some hunting lodge in Leven.

She paused on a street corner. A silver thread of cause and effect led from that moment to this one. She hadn't joined Amron, hadn't gone to the royal court in Myrit to meet him.

If she had, she would have ridden out with him on his last journey, and then…

What happened on that journey?

Amron's last letter was strange, filled with bitterness because the king had sent him on yet another onerous mission. Amron wrote about a young man he had to escort to Abia, about disobeying the king, about the rift that had grown between him and his royal nephew over the subject. He had planned to leave Leven and ride towards the White Mountains before turning south to Abia—a journey that should have taken his small company nine or ten days across a lonely, wooded, sparsely inhabited landscape. There was nothing particularly dangerous about that route, nothing deadly.

And yet he died on that journey.

Liana shook her head and massaged her temples. The king's men wouldn't tell her how he'd died, but there must have been someone who'd witnessed it. Even if she couldn't do anything about it, even if she had nothing to live for, she wanted to know the truth. Amron didn't just die, he'd been killed, that was what the messenger had said. Someone was responsible for his death.

"Liana!" A voice cut through the darkness, followed by the beat of heavy boots hitting the cobbles. A dark figure ran towards her. "Liana, wait!"

She knew the voice and she knew the man who emerged from the shadows, short and rugged, dressed in filthy riding gear.

"Telani!"

"Liana—"

Instead of a greeting, Liana pushed him so hard he slipped on the cobbles and fell.

"Tell me you're dead," she growled. "Tell me you're an apparition, you faithless bastard."

"Wait, let me—"

"How dare you come here without him? You swore to protect him with your life!"

The man wheezed on the ground, shaking. She almost pushed him again, but then he raised his face to her, unshaven, haggard, pale as a three-day-old corpse. "I deserved that," he said.

"Get away from me." She spat and turned on her heel, too engulfed in rage to think clearly.

"I deserved that," he repeated. "But I didn't choose who lived and who died. The gods did."

Liana froze mid-step. "What? What did you say?"

He got up slowly. "It was a trap. She lay in wait for him. There was nothing I could do."

Liana wished she could hate Telani, she wished she could believe it was all his fault, but when he mentioned the goddess, she knew he was telling the truth. All the fight drained out of her, only the cold remained, and the incessant rain. Her husband's secretary, his bodyguard, war comrade, and loyal companion stood before her, his eyes raw with grief. "Telani," she said, "what happened?"

"He's gone. I'm so sorry. I should have been the one to bring you the news, but I was delayed on the road, so the king's men got here before me. I rushed to the palace as soon as I reached Abia and heard they kicked you out."

"Screw them," she said. "I want to know everything."

"Let's get out of this rain first. They keep a room for me at the Boatswain's Sweetheart, we can have some privacy there."

Liana nodded. "I'm sorry I pushed you."

"As I said, I deserved it. Come, it's freezing out here."

They walked together towards the harbor. The air smelled of brine and rotting fish. The narrow, cobbled streets were deserted, most taverns had already closed their doors, and the icy rain chased away the drunken revelers. Streetlamps were few and far between. Alley cats ruled this dark kingdom, stalking their prey, watching them pass with curious, glowing eyes.

The Boatswain's Sweetheart was a filthy little tavern in a ramshackle two-story house on a street inhabited by fishermen and netmakers. Rickety wooden stairs were stuck to the side of the house, leading to the second floor. Telani unlocked the door and Liana climbed up, following him into the dark interior. He lit an oil lamp and the flickering light revealed that the room was tiny, with uneven floorboards and bare, whitewashed walls. A narrow bed was crammed into one corner, while a makeshift desk—two crates stacked on top of each other—occupied another. No fire was lit in the fireplace, but the warmth from the downstairs tavern seeped through the floorboards, together with the muffled noise of the last desperate drunks who had no home to return to. There was just one chair; Telani motioned for her to sit down while he settled on the bed.

"I've seen battlefield corpses who looked better than you," she said.

They had a tolerant, casual relationship most of the time, like two cats in the same kitchen, clever enough to realize their feelings about each other were irrelevant because they were both tied to the same man for good. A southern soldier turned secretary and a northern huntswoman turned a reluctant companion, they were like two moons orbiting a planet, always on the opposite sides of Amron.

"I had two hours of sleep in a ditch last night." He rubbed his face, which looked ten years older than she remembered it, and a good deal thinner. "What happened at the palace?"

"The king sent five men to throw me out immediately and make sure I don't steal anything," she said. "What did Amron do to irritate him so?"

The corners of Telani's lips curled into a wan smile. "What's the last you've heard from him?"

"I got a letter from some hunting lodge in Leven. About the task the king had given him, and a ward he had to escort to Abia."

"That brat." Telani rummaged through his pockets and offered Liana a flask. "You'll need this. Don't worry, it's the good stuff."

She uncorked it and took a sip. The brandy burned her throat and lit a flame in her stomach. It might have restored a spark of her bravado, because she said, "I want to know what happened."

Telani cocked his head and measured her up, as if he were trying to decide how much pressure she could take before she broke. Liana held his gaze without a blink. Ever since she'd heard the news, she felt a part of her was detached. Grief, sharp like a glass shard, was wrapped carefully in cloth and set aside for the day when she could allow herself to mourn her husband. Not today, though. Today she had to find who was responsible for his death.

"A blizzard hit us on a deserted road and our ward ran into a forest. We followed and stumbled upon a forsaken castle." Telani shifted his weight, and the straw bed beneath him rustled. "The gods stepped in. I can tell you what I saw, but don't expect me to explain any of it."

Telani possessed no trace of divine blood, no talent for divination. All he could see was the surface of the world, not its background.

"A cursed castle?" Liana asked.

"A trap, set by *her*. Preying upon unfortunate travelers."

He knew enough about invocation to not carelessly say Morana's name aloud, but Liana knew he meant the Goddess of Death. The dread she had felt seeing the black bathwater crept back through her veins. "Amron must have seen it."

"He did. But there were other people trapped there, so he refused to run away from it and abandon them." He hesitated, creasing the rough woolen blanket. "Many things happened that night. I don't pretend to understand all of them. I promise you, though, if there'd been any other way out, if I could've done it instead of him—"

"I understand," she cut him off. He'd never given her any reason to question his loyalty. "Tell me what happened."

"His ward, the boy we were supposed to escort to Abia, was manipulated by the gods to duel my lord. And my lord deliberately lost, to spare him."

Liana shivered, imagining the glint of steel, the cloying odor of blood. "And the gods came?"

"They came, and they took him away."

She breathed in sharply, fighting the spasm in her chest. "So there's no body? You didn't bury him?"

"No, but I saw him die."

"That's not the same," she said. "That's not the same at all."

She got up and paced around the tiny room, her head almost touching the beams. Amron wasn't rotting in some hastily dug grave, then. He was dead, but Liana knew that, when the gods were involved, dead didn't always mean gone. There had to be a way to bring him back.

"I have a letter for you, he wrote it a few hours before death. Read it before you decide what to do," he said, eyeing her, reading her thoughts. He pulled a small bundle of letters tied with a blue ribbon out of his doublet, three or four folded sheets, no more. "These are the letters he wrote on our way home. The last one is on top." He delivered them into her shaking hands.

"Thank you." She removed the ribbon, unfolded the last letter, a crumpled sheet of paper. Unlike his usual tidy lines in black ink, these were written in broad charcoal strokes. *I'm sorry I'm leaving you like this. Take care of yourself and don't fight the gods. I love you. A.*

Her heart sank. It wasn't enough, it wasn't what she wanted to hear. She handed the letter to Telani without a word.

Telani's dark eyes flew over the lines and then fixed on her. He must have registered the frustration on her face. "I saw your mother on my way here, too. She chose to appear before me, the white stag and silver bow and all. She wants you to join her."

A welcome surge of fury drowned Liana's frustration. That was what the stag had been about. A demand, a divine wish. Delivered by a messenger because Lela had known her daughter wouldn't see her. She'd just wanted to upset her, to frighten her, to warn her she was being watched.

Liana let out a choking sound, halfway between a chortle and a wail. She crashed on the bed beside Telani. "Damn them all," she said. "My mother, the king, the gods. Damn them!"

The tears finally came then, and she pushed her face into a crumpled pillow and cried. But the deluge didn't last long. She was no frail lady in distress, and Telani was no chivalrous hero. He did manage to find a clear scrap of linen somewhere, though, and offer it to her to wipe her face with.

"I must leave Abia," she said, sniffing.

"If you wish so," he said. He let her have the bed and moved to the chair, which he straddled backwards. "There are people all over the kingdom who'd be happy to receive you. But I think you could do more than that."

"More?" She blinked away the last tears.

"I imagine things will get unpleasant for the king soon. My lord protected him even when the king schemed against him. Now that protection is gone, and Abia has no lord, Larion has no ruler."

She and Amron had never had children and, incredible as it seemed now, he'd never mentioned heirs to her.

"It reverted back to the crown," she said. "Those were the conditions of Queen Orsiana's dowry."

"And you are fine with that?" He frowned, a flash of annoyance twisting his face. "You're fine with leaving Abia to the king, who deliberately sent us on that depraved mission, or to some upstart bastard who will rise to claim it?"

"I don't see what you expect me to do," she said.

His annoyance turned into exasperation. "You've lived in Abia for thirteen years, you've had access to every nook and cranny of the palace, to every clerk, soldier, and diplomat who entered it, to every administrative decision my lord made. Don't tell me you haven't learned anything."

His words poured over her like a bucket of icy water. Watching Amron all those years had been a lesson in ruling, indeed. People crowded around him, seeking help, advice, favors. The palace was always filled with nobles, soldiers, merchants, artists, and petitioners of all kinds. She could have played the role of the lady, she could have stepped into the public life and helped him carry that burden, she could have learned how to govern.

But if she had, she would have been someone else, a different, unrecognizable creature, a hawk pretending to be a parrot to placate the visitors. The divine blood that ran through her veins was as much a curse as it was a blessing. It gave her youth and strength and hunting skills second only to her mother's. But it also gave her the ability to see how thin the world of humans was: like a silk scarf stretched in front of a fire, she could see right through it. She saw things as they were, and people too. She'd never learned how to weave a web of words, how to move through the meaningless structure of norms, expectations, traditions, and outright lies the society was built upon.

"I'm not fit to rule Abia," she said. "I don't want it. I want to find a way to bring him back."

"Why?"

"What do you mean why?" She shot him an incredulous look. "Don't you want him back?"

"He expressly asked you not to fight the gods," Telani replied, motioning at the letter that lay unfolded on the blanket.

"Don't you want him back?" she repeated.

The question cut through the stuffy room like a gust of northern wind. A sharp, metallic echo rang in Liana's voice. Telani froze on the chair and gripped the wooden back so hard his knuckles turned white.

"Of course I want him back," he said, his southern vowels stretching into a soft growl. "But have you paused to think what he might have wanted?"

She stared at him, his words reaching her ears but not her mind.

"He went willingly," Telani continued. "With courage and determination. And there was something else, too." His expression turned harsh and spare, like a craggy side of a mountain. "He was tired. I followed him around for almost twenty years and I've never seen him shirk his duty. Every task, no matter how difficult and unwelcome, he never said no."

"He didn't want it any other way."

"He couldn't do it any other way. But, Liana, he was exhausted, he was bone-tired and fed up with his duties. This was supposed to be the last mission, he wanted out."

"He wrote about returning to Abia and staying here," she said, remembering his words. "He said it was time the king took responsibility for the kingdom. But he wanted to retire, not die."

"I don't think you understand what I'm saying." Telani shook his head. "If he miraculously returned this very moment, all his plans for a peaceful life in Abia would shatter. There's trouble brewing in the kingdom. There always is. He would just go back to doing whatever was necessary to keep the peace."

The never-ending echoes of war, spreading like tendrils of mist over a graveyard, waking the dead.

"I'd rather have him running around the kingdom than not at all," she retorted.

"Yes, but this is not about you, is it?"

She opened her mouth to say something, but his words left her speechless. He sounded reasonable and fair. He made her look selfish.

"I've known him for a long time, and I think if he had a choice between being dragged back here to do even more until it killed him again, or having someone work for the benefit of the kingdom using what he taught them, he'd choose the latter."

His sharp words were meant to shake her, to make her question her choices, but instead they helped her make up her mind. For the first time that evening, her thoughts were settled, her goal clear.

"You knew him well, but not as well as I did," she said. "What does a secretary know about his master's heart?"

Her words landed like a slap.

"You may care about the politics, about the kingdom, about which spoiled young man is going to rule this city," she continued. "I don't give a damn about it. But I do care about Amron and I'm not going to allow the gods to decide his destiny on a whim."

"But, his letter—"

"What about it?" she cut him off. "If I'd said to him, *don't go to Myrit*, do you think he would've listened? It's a wish, not a command." Hollow, bleak laughter rasped in her throat. "Of course I'm going to fight the gods for him. If I could make them bleed and burn, I'd do it. It's my choice to make."

He stared at her in silence. It was strange how they couldn't really be allies, not even now. She did not question his grief nor doubt his will to do something. They just couldn't agree on what it should be.

Perhaps her idea was selfish. She was a selfish person, that's how she survived.

"You always do whatever you damn please," he said.

"Is there any other way to get what you want?"

"You know," he said, "I've watched you get what you want every time, and I've watched him forgive you. Your stubbornness, your inflexibility, your unwillingness to accept the rules of the world you chose to inhabit. It hurt him, because that world you rejected was his birthright and duty. And you left him to face it all alone."

She stared at him, too shocked to reply. She thought Telani's disapproval of her was general, since he was as immune to her as he was to any other woman. Apparently, it wasn't.

"And if you get to him, he'll forgive you that as well," he continued. "But you won't be doing it for him, you'll be doing it for yourself."

"That may be true," she shot back. "And yet, you'll be the coward who stayed here and wasted your time on politics, and I'll be the one who went and tried to get him back. Thank you for your advice, I'll be leaving now."

"Don't be rash, Liana. At least wait until the morning, it's miserable weather outside."

The patter of rain on the roof emphasized his words.

"My mother likes miserable weather," she said, "and the sooner I get to her, the better. I have some accounts to settle."

𝕷iana abandoned 𝕿elani with his schemes, left the town that had been her home for over a decade, and climbed the steep road in the darkness, oblivious to the rain and cold. She hiked through the forest of evergreen oaks as the moonlight pierced the canopy, speckling the brown carpet of leaves with silver. Hands raised, palms turned outwards, she touched the curtain of the mortal world, the gossamer reality that bound every living creature to its fate, and pulled it aside. Time slowed down, impotent and ignored in this place where fate was created rather than endured.

Weight fell off her shoulders, tiredness evaporated as the divine blood in her veins sang with joy. A strong sense of belonging filled her with warmth. This was the realm of the beautiful, immortal, and strong. This was home.

A blazing lick of fire singed the soft skin between her breasts. She yelped and tugged at the chain around her neck, pulling out the silver medallion.

"Liana, you dolt," she whispered to herself. Silver burned her fingers, reminding her that she was a half-breed. Human enough to fall under the spell of this place, divine enough to get burned.

"Mother, I'm here," she called.

The stag did not make a sound as it approached, moving as softly as a cat on thick carpet. One moment, all Liana could see were the dark trunks and the dappled shadows, and the next, the majestic Lord of the Forest stood before her.

"Come," she whispered and offered her hand. A cautious sniff, and then a hot tongue licked her singed fingers. "You remember me, don't you?"

The stag pushed its nose into her hair, rubbing its cheek against hers in mute greeting. She patted its large head, relishing the silky touch of its coat.

"I need you to take me to my mother."

The stag knelt down before her, allowing her to climb onto its wide back. As Liana gripped its antlers, a memory hit her: She had been a tiny thing, light as a leaf, flying through the forest faster than a gale, holding on for dear life, shrieking madly with terror and excitement.

"Go now," she said, and the stag moved, smoother than any

horse. "Faster." It broke into a trot. "Faster!" The leaves and branches melted into a blur. "Faster!"

She laughed in exhilaration. It was like running in a dream, an effortless, mad, horizontal fall, until the woods fell away and nothing but darkness surrounded her, speckled by a myriad of stars.

Liana shut her eyes and the sense of movement disappeared. Had they flown at all?

"Liana?"

Liana sat on the back of the unmoving stag, deep in the ancient forest. Her mother stepped out from the shadow of a tree with the deadly grace of a panther. It shocked Liana how inhuman Lela looked. She'd never noticed it as a child, perhaps because at that time she had known no mortal women to compare her with.

"Mother."

Liana slid off the stag's back and stood still, keeping the distance. Lela made no move to approach her, measuring her up instead.

"So, you finally decided to visit me."

A hundred furious replies bloomed in Liana's head and she swallowed them all. "I got your message," she said, barely keeping her voice from cracking.

"And?" Lela moved so fast Liana saw a flash of her black hair, and then sensed the goddess behind her, lithe and predatory. "Have you come to join me at last?"

Liana swallowed a volley of possible answers, reminding herself that the gods felt no empathy and it was futile to expect it from them. "I've come to ask you to help me bring Amron back."

"Oh, not that old story again." The goddess now stood beside her, features melting into something softer. Not motherly, definitely not, but unthreatening. A hand, deceptively human, no claws in sight, touched Liana's cheek. "I don't understand why you like to pretend you're human and play wife to one of them."

"Because he was kind to me when nobody else was," Liana

said so softly the sound hardly crossed her lips. "Because he loved me."

The goddess chuckled, which sounded more like a growl, coming from a mouth full of sharp teeth. "I don't see how you can find someone so weak, so vulnerable, so quick to age, desirable?"

The corners of Liana's eyes itched with angry tears. She blinked quickly, then lifted her gaze to her mother's mocking face. "Just tell me where Amron is. Please."

The goddess flicked her question away with a sigh. "Gone. As you knew he would be, eventually."

Liana grabbed her mother's wrist. "No." It was like a kitten trying to fight a cat, but Lela paused nevertheless. "That's not the whole truth. His man told me he saw him die, but there's no body. What happened to him, Mother?"

"Perun took him."

"Then he is…not dead?" Liana's patience was wearing thin, yet she forced herself to remain calm, to focus on her goal. They were in the wild and unbridled territory of legends now. The Father-God raising heroes, welcoming them into his hall. Lela had her hunt, Morana had her cursed souls at the bottom of the lake, and Perun had his warriors. "Is he in a place where I can reach him? Maybe you could lead me—"

Lela's sinister chuckle interrupted her. "That's nonsense. You cannot go where you're not invited, and I've never heard of Perun inviting a woman to join him."

"I don't want to join Perun," Liana snapped. "I want Amron back. Here, with me."

Her angry words turned Lela's chuckle into full-blown laughter. It echoed among the trees, mirthless and threatening like a leopard's growl. "Oh Liana, oh child, you didn't come all this way to ask for this. You avoid me for years and years, and when you finally appear, you come with this ridiculous, puny, utterly human request."

"What is it to you?" Liana asked. "If it's so small and insignificant, why can't you just grant it? I promise I'll repay you in any way you see fit."

Lela's image flickered once more, and she became something sharp and savage again, all claws and fangs and carnivorous grace. "Is that a promise?"

"Yes," Liana said. "You have my word."

Chapter 4

Melia

Three days after the wedding, Amron's retinue was getting ready to leave. He watched them, leaning on the window frame in Melia's room, the morning sun gilding his hair. Melia's meager possessions had been packed and loaded on one of the carts. Having nothing useful to do, she paced to and fro on the carpet worn to a threadbare rag, her feet itching to run downstairs.

"Shouldn't we get ready?" she asked.

"As soon as they leave."

"What?" She paused mid-step. "Aren't we going with them?"

"No."

"Are we staying in Syr, then?"

"With your father?" He scoffed softly. "No."

She approached the window, biting her lip, and laid her hands on the warm wood. After that first night, he treated her in a polite, distant manner. They took their meals together, walked on the battlements, discussed life at court. His company was unobtrusive and calming, but now she wasn't sure if he was teasing her or treating her as an object to be wrapped and stuffed in a saddlebag.

"Where are we going?" she asked.

He didn't reply immediately, focused on the colorful chaos below. Then he said, "We're going to the border. I promised my father I'll personally visit the forts."

Despite the sunlight pouring in, she felt cold. There was nothing there but the barren wasteland. "I don't want to go," she said, her voice barely audible.

He turned to her and frowned, looking pensive. "Why not?"

Because the red sand was drenched in blood and the dry trees lifted their branches to the sky like skeletons in agony. Because something had been broken there and never got better. But she couldn't explain that, she couldn't put it in words before his pale, calm face, his cold, sharp eyes. Therefore she shrugged, feigning nonchalance. "Can't you send someone else?"

"My father wouldn't trust anyone else."

It was about the peace with the Seragian Empire, then. The king did not trust Roderi of Elmar, and rightly so. She slowly breathed in, wishing her life could remain small, insignificant, far from intrigues and other people's ambitions.

"Do I have to go with you? I could stay here and—"

"What do you think about the peace treaty?" he interrupted her.

She opened her mouth to say something, but there was nothing she dared to say to his face. So she mumbled, "I don't know."

No one had ever asked her opinion before. She was not a player in this game, she was a prize. Still, Amron refused to let it go.

"That's not good enough," he said. "One day you'll inherit Elmar, you should understand it. I'm aware of your father's opinion on the treaty, but I want to hear yours."

She shook her head, looking over the plains and the mountains in the distance. "What do you want me to tell you? That it hurts to think about it? That it feels like a lie, mocking all our sacrifices? Every inch of this soil is soaked in our blood."

"Every inch, yes." He crossed his arms, following her gaze into the distance. "But I'd think three hundred years without peace would be enough to make everyone wish for it."

He'd gotten on his high horse, she could see that.

It was his direct ancestor, Amris the Golden-Haired, who had decided to conquer the borderlands after Abia surrendered to him. He defeated the tribes that freely roamed Elmar, and laid a bloody, two-year siege to Syr, a city under the protection of the Empire, before slaughtering its population and turning it into a ghostly fortress. It was Amris and his heirs who profited from the blood spilled on the border, from the men and women who died protecting the kingdom. To hear Amron talk about peace was like hearing a wolf talk about grazing after he slaughtered the whole flock.

"Two signatures on a piece of parchment will hardly make it better," she said. "It's not over just because you say so."

"No," he said. "And that's why I'm going there, to see what it takes for it to really be over."

He'd spent six months there with Rovin. There was a chance—weak and tiny—that he understood what he was talking about. But it still sounded like gibberish to her. What could a smug, patronizing princeling understand about the border?

"You're just going to give them hope," she said.

"Is that a bad thing?" The corners of his mouth twisted in a wry smile. "Have you ever seen how they live? Do you claim it's better to be locked in endless bloodshed than to hope something might change for the better?"

Nothing ever changed in Syr, she wanted to tell him. But he didn't want her opinion, he wanted her approval. So she shut her mouth, packed warm, sturdy travel clothes, and followed him into the wasteland.

She thought life in Syr had made her tough, but three days of riding on the dusty roads under the merciless sun battered her into humility. She was unused to the saddle, to being in the open all day. She thought she would feel fine among the soldiers—she'd grown up among them, after all—but not a single one of them dared to look at her, let alone talk to her, wrapped in her dark cloak. Amron had fallen quiet as soon as they left the walls of Syr behind, and she realized his earlier polite chat had been just another court ruse, like fine clothes or dancing. Under the vast red sky of Elmar, he turned into a taciturn, self-contained stranger.

She gritted her teeth and refused to complain, terrified that she would look weak, defeated by the land she was supposed to rule. She was embarrassed of her saddle sores when she disrobed in the first room they shared at an inn, but he bid her good night without so much as a glance, and left to join his escort. When he tiptoed back late that night, and slipped beside her in silence, she expected his hands on her body, but he turned his back to her instead and fell asleep. He repeated this routine every night after that, as an unspoken deal between them. She lay awake on various hard, dubiously clean beds, her skin bruised and scratched raw, her muscles cramping, her body crying for rest, and tried to convince herself she wasn't insulted by his disinterest. The opposite would have been worse.

She missed Ferisa, her firm hands, her brusque words, her friendship.

On the fourth day, the border mountains loomed high on the horizon, their sharp peaks piercing the heavy clouds above them. The lay of the land, the lonely crossroads they chanced upon, stirred something in her memory. A nightmare she had as a child: a horse lying in the middle of the road with its entrails spilled, an overturned carriage with dead men strewn around it. Blood soaking into the dust, a bloodstained female hand reaching for her. A sudden wave of terror gripped her, her vision darkened and she would have slid out of her saddle had Amron not caught her.

She came to on the ground, her head in his lap.

"Here, take a sip of water," he said.

Her head must have still been muddled, otherwise she wouldn't have said, "I thought I saw something on the road." She sat up and swallowed the tepid water. "A dead horse. Dead men."

Amron studied the empty landscape, the lonely fig tree beside which their escort waited. "Is this where—" he started and paused, clearing his throat. "Have you ever seen the border forts?"

She shook her head. It was uncanny, the thought that he knew this land better than her, that he'd spent six months here with her brother.

Was the carnage she'd seen connected with her brother? But no, he'd been wounded closer to Syr, and she had no idea what the attack had been like.

"Do you ever think of Rovin?" she asked.

"Out here?" He looked over the dry red plains to the stony foot of the mountains and up towards the snow-topped peaks. "All the time."

She could almost see Rovin then, the black-haired youth on his swift horse, the warm rays of the setting sun burning red on the bronze and steel of his armor.

"I miss him," she said, and it was a strange statement, because she didn't really miss the reckless, fiery boy fascinated by the stories of blood and steel, eager to throw himself in the path of the Seragian arrows. She missed the man he might have become, the man who had a spark of cleverness and a morsel of love inside him that would have made him a good lord one day, and a good brother to her. She missed the future she imagined he would have given her.

Amron helped her get back on her horse and motioned at their retinue to keep moving. "I'm sorry he died," he said. Then, as if reading her thoughts, he added, "And I'm sorry his death left you with such a heavy burden to carry."

A sharp blade of grief slashed her from the inside just when she thought she was safe. She squinted into the sunset, again wishing that Ferisa was here with her. She understood her rage and sorrow, knew how to fight them away with rough, insatiable fire. Melia had no use for kindness. This scathing sympathy, this arrogance of her soft-spoken husband, made her furious.

"I don't need your pity," she snarled and spurred her horse.

She spent the afternoon angry, though she wasn't sure who she was angry with. Her father, for his schemes; her brother, for dying; Amron, for being polite? Herself, for failing to control her emotions?

As they approached the mountains, the air turned crisp and the sharp wind brought the scent of snow from the peaks. The six border forts lay like a long necklace along the mountains, guarding the passes and the roads that led from them. The stories Melia heard as a child had turned them into legendary places in her mind. She expected huge castles with massive walls and tall towers, but instead the first one she saw was an ancient rectangular fortress, crumbling under the relentless attacks of ice and wind, garrisoned by the tired men whose uniforms were so worn out she couldn't tell their original color.

They all seemed to remember Amron, though. They opened their gate with welcoming cheer, and their captain hugged Amron like an old friend.

She dismounted in the small courtyard. The deep shade of the late afternoon was so cold she shivered. She thought she knew what spare meant, but she'd never seen such austerity in her life. A wooden shed that could hardly be called a stable. Bare, freezing corridors poorly lit by smoking rushlights. One large room with a massive fireplace and straw on the floor that was used by everybody for eating and sleeping. A few women crossed her path and scurried away like mice when they saw the prince and his retinue. Maids, wives, bed-warmers—who knew?—none of them deemed appropriate to be introduced to her.

The dinner was old, chewy mutton, stale rye bread, and sour wine. Melia sat through it with downcast eyes, her hands folded in her lap. She could feel the men gazing at her; she could read their thoughts without lifting her head. On her right, Amron talked with the captain about the peace treaty, the size of the garrison, and the idea that the mountain passes will be open to everybody one day, and she pricked up her ears, knowing that her father would have wanted her to listen.

"How soon?" the captain asked.

"This autumn, probably," Amron said. "Most of it is already negotiated and drawn up. We're waiting for the emperor to sign."

Overwhelmed by the whole day of riding and the dull pain in her muscles and joints, Melia had to force herself to focus, staring at the congealed fat on her chipped plate.

"The border tribes won't know that and won't care about it," the captain said. "We'll still have to be here to stop them."

More fighting, more blood. The captain knew nothing ever changed.

"The Empire tolerates the tribes for now, even supports them, because it suits them to have endless skirmishes on our border," Amron said. "But after the treaty, they'll stop sending help. And once the caravans start crossing the border again, do you think the Empire will tolerate the passes to be unsafe?"

The captain paused before he answered, laying down his knife on the table. "No. They'll protect their own." He dragged his words. "The merchants will pay for armed escort, and the imperial army will patrol the imperial roads."

"To protect trade, yes."

Melia pushed her chair away from the table, tired of listening to men, tired of their endless talks of weapons, armies, conflicts. "Excuse me," she said.

Amron turned to her. "You didn't touch your food. Are you unwell?"

"No, I just need some fresh air." She rose and all the men jumped to their feet.

"I'll come with you," Amron said.

"No, please, I'm sorry I interrupted your dinner." Her cheeks burned under the weight of so many eyes. "I'm capable of taking a walk on my own."

She fled the hall before he had the time to stop her. The corridors were cold and deserted, but she knew where she'd find more people, the people who hadn't been invited to sit at the table with the prince. The women of the fort.

The kitchen was a badly lit place in the bowels of the castle, with a low, vaulted ceiling, long shadows, and the enduring stench of boiled cabbages and old grease, but it was blissfully warm. A dozen women moved around it, scrubbing the pots, eating, feeding small, squirming children. They all froze when she walked in.

"Good evening," she said, hoping that the shadows hid her intense discomfort. The few women in Syr were used to her presence, they'd known her since she was a girl. Here, she was the lord's daughter, the prince's wife, a highborn intruder. "Please, carry on," she said, but they remained still, staring at her.

The awkward moment was threatening to stretch into eternity when one woman, gray-haired, gaunt, gathered the courage to address her. "Is there anything you need, m'lady? Can we help you?"

Melia shook her head. "I don't need anything. I just....May I sit with you? I'm tired of being surrounded by men all the time."

There were blank stares and there were smirks, but no one objected. She found a free spot on the bench at the corner of the long table. Someone poured her a mug of beer; she wrapped her hands around it to stop them from shaking and watched the woman sitting across from her feed a small boy with morsels of bread soaked in milk.

"How old is he?" Melia asked.

"Sixteen months, m'lady."

The other women had gone back to their tasks. Melia sipped the beer, trying to look casual. "And you live here with him?"

"Yes."

The boy seemed healthy and well-fed, but the young woman looked haggard.

"And the boy's father? Is he garrisoned here?"

"Dead," the young woman said, not lifting her eyes from her child.

Loss was something Melia could understand, something they shared. But the young woman remained focused on her son, unwilling to look at Melia.

"Half of us are widows here, m'lady, and the other half are waiting for the axe to fall." An older woman with a plate full of something hot and unappealing sat beside Melia. "Those who have family to go to when their husband is killed, leave. Those who don't, stay here and find another man to take care of them. There's a shortage of women, I'm sure you noticed, m'lady."

Melia stared at the woman in awe. She looked shriveled and hard like a smoked fish.

"He was Danka's first, so she's still grieving." The woman nodded towards the young mother. "I'm on my fourth now."

Melia swallowed another sip of beer. "And do you hate the Seragians for killing them?"

"The Seragians?" the woman asked, and several heads turned to them. "What do they have to do with us?"

"I thought…" Melia paused, unsure. "Seragians and Elmarrans, we fight each other, don't we?"

That caused a few snickers around the table.

"M'lady, there's just the garrison men and the bandits here," a fair-skinned woman that didn't even look like a Southerner said. "The men choose their path and we follow them."

"But…the border?" Melia stammered and provoked some deep chuckling.

"We all have family on both sides of the border," another woman said.

"I was born on the other side."

"I have a sister married there."

Melia sat in silence, feeling outrageously dumb, while the women's words battered her beliefs. When she couldn't tolerate it any longer, she rose. "Thank you for your company," she said. "I must go before my husband comes looking for me."

It was unseasonably cold in the small circular chamber she shared with Amron in the tower, as if the stones oozed the icy fog of winter. It whirled around Melia's feet, slipping under her skirts, touching her bare skin with its frosty fingers. The fire in the fireplace looked as if it were painted on the logs, a blob of orange and yellow emitting no heat. Goosebumps rose on Melia's arms, and for the first time in her life, she envied the soldiers and women sleeping in a thick cluster of warm bodies in the great hall.

"I'm so cold," she said, sitting on the edge of a narrow bed with a straw mattress. "Will you stay with me tonight?"

"I can't," he said. "We're leaving tomorrow and I still have questions for the garrison." He unclasped his fur-lined cloak and wrapped it around her shoulders. "This should keep you warm. I'll try to be back soon."

Melia had no talent for divination, but as the coldness filled her from the inside despite the warm fur wrapping her body, she was absolutely sure something bad was coming. Death passing by once more, white flowers of frost blooming where her robe touched the ground. Melia opened her mouth to utter a warning, but she and Amron were still strangers, there was no trust between them, no intimate language of couples that could transmit her fear without sounding dramatic and ridiculous.

In the end, all she managed to say was a feeble "Take care."

She mulled over the kitchen conversation, wondering if the women had reason to lie, until sleep defeated her. She dreamed of cold watery depths where no ray of sunlight ever pierced the darkness. She struggled to move through it, her limbs leaden, her lungs screaming for air, until the pressure abated and she found herself in an unfamiliar courtyard. The flagstones were slick with blood, the people around her pushing, fighting, crying for help in the flickering light of the burning buildings. Amron stood before her, smeared with blood and ash, with a bemused expression on his face. Her eyes slipped down to his hand pressing his belly, black blood pouring through his fingers, soaking into the blue silk he wore, dripping on the flags. He opened his mouth to tell her something, but no sound came out as his legs folded and he fell.

She screamed and woke up. A lonely bell was tolling outside. At first she couldn't recognize the freezing room with the fire burnt down to ashes, but then she remembered the fort, the border, their journey. She was alone in the bed, Amron hadn't come back.

The bell tolled again: a cold, desolate sound in the dark. Whatever she'd feared earlier that night had reached them now.

She jumped out of the bed, fully clothed, and unlocked the door, unwilling to remain trapped in that small room with no way out. She rushed through the abandoned corridors to the great hall. The fire was still burning there, but there was no man in sight, just a scruffy girl sleeping in front of the fireplace.

Melia shook her awake. "Where is everybody?"

"Out," the girl muttered in her sleep. "It's the bloody smugglers again."

Melia jumped away from the girl as if she were cursed. Panic grabbed her and squeezed all the air out of her lungs. Images rushed through her head: the brigands with their blades, the red dust soaking in red blood. She looked around for a weapon. There were some battle axes stashed in one corner, old and probably blunt. She had no idea how to wield them, she had no idea how to use any weapon but a dagger. Years ago, Rovin showed her how to defend herself, but it had been against one man with a short blade, not a horde of killers with swords and spears.

She ran into the courtyard looking for a way out just as the gate opened and men poured in. She ducked into the shadows, trembling, before realizing it was the garrison men and the king's guard, with torches, shouting. The women and the ragged boys hurried out, bringing more light as the men dismounted, revealing the blood and grime on their faces and uniforms.

Melia saw it then: a horse with a motionless man thrown across the saddle, a wisp of fair hair catching the light. The hairs on her neck rose as a cold gust of wind touched them with the icy kiss of death. Old nightmares rushed in to bury her, guards bleeding out on the ground, Rovin begging for mercy.

"Amron!" she screamed, running towards the unmoving man. "Amron!"

"I'm here," a voice said. A hand caught her, turned her

around, and she found herself facing her husband.

"You're alive!" Her hands flew to his face, wiping off the dirt, and slid down his armor, looking for holes, dents, blood.

"Very much so." He laughed and she caught the bitter aroma of arrowfoil on his breath. His connection to the men at the fort went deeper than she'd assumed if they'd shared it with him. "It was just a group of smugglers, nothing serious."

"And what about him?" She craned her neck, motioning towards the unconscious soldier.

"Knocked out. He'll be fine by the morning."

The cold lingered, the sharp shards of the dream still cut her from the inside with the image of Amron's wide-open eyes, the blood pouring through his fingers. Death was still too close, the whole courtyard filled with it.

"Come," she said.

"No, I must—"

"Come," she insisted, pulling his hand, her eyes burning. She felt sharp and spry as if she were the one who'd swallowed the bitter herb.

She led him upstairs and locked the door. He radiated the energy of the skirmish, the elation of survival. As she removed his armor, as deft as any squire after years spent in Syr, she soaked in the heat of his body. They kissed in silence, urgent, hungry, unwilling to waste their breath on words. He unlaced her dress without breaking the kiss, unwrapped her from the burdensome layers of clothing. She couldn't discern what moved her, a sudden surge of desire or some primal lust for life, but when his fingers reached between her thighs, she moaned and leaned towards him.

They crashed onto the bed, the ancient wooden frame creaking in protest. He opened her legs; she pulled him close, her limbs wrapped around his body, her mouth on his, stealing his breath. No words, just two bodies moving together in a desperate need to prove they were here, unscathed, chasing pleasure as if their lives depended upon it.

The cold disappeared as he pressed her down, his hips grinding against hers in a rhythm that made her cry out. She pushed him over then, straddled him and rode him as beads of sweat formed on her skin and her bruised thighs screamed in protest. When he closed his eyes and bared his teeth, when the breath caught in his throat in a silent scream, she was already there, suspended in a moment of pure bliss, bright white and searing hot, filling her body from the tips of her toes to the roots of her hair.

They remained embraced, reluctant to let go as their bodies cooled and their breathing slowed down. Melia outlined the shape of his face with her fingers, memorizing the contours—the high cheekbones, the sharp nose, the long curve of his mouth, the angle of his chin—turning this stranger who lay beside her into someone she knew.

He remained quiet, watching her, his hands stroking the soft skin of her back. Up close, she liked him. If this room and this bed were their whole world, they would've been fine. His gentle distance, his controlled intensity, made her feel safe.

And yet, even as he lay beside her, his gaze seemed distant, his thoughts far away from her. He would become a stranger again as soon as he put on his uniform, his leathers and steel or his silks and fur, his soldier's ruse or his courtier's mask. A volatile ally in a tangled web of other people's interests.

"I must go," he said, pulling away from her, leaving her bare skin exposed to the freezing air. "A message from the king arrived during the night."

"Why? What happened?" she asked, a note of panic seeping in her voice.

"The peace treaty," he said. "The emperor signed it. It's finally done."

A world-shattering moment, and she was curled up in a rickety bed in a crumbling border fort. "What now?" she asked.

"Now we pack and go to Abia. The final clause of the treaty is my brother marrying the Seragian princess."

His words dissolved in the shadows as she waited for something to fill the emptiness inside her—anger, or disappointment, or betrayal.

"Sleep now, I'll take care of the rest," he said.

Begging him to stay would be a weakness, a disadvantage. So she shivered under the covers, watching him hastily pull his clothes on as the first light of dawn appeared in the window, and she said nothing. When he bent to kiss her, she offered him her cheek, and when he left, she remained silent. Whatever happened between them was over now, a lapse of reason fueled by danger and fear, a reckless slip, a mistake.

~Chapter 5~

Liana

The deep, clear sound of the bell pierced the darkness. The Fat Odo above Abia's Northern gate was striking the hour of dawn. Liana opened her eyes.

She lay in a ditch beside the road. A dry ditch, and reasonably clean, no refuse piling around her. She took a deep breath, and a splitting headache bloomed between her temples. Her mouth was dry and filled with the residue of something awful; her stomach churned, brimming with angry acid. A massive hangover surged through her body like a swarm of angry eels.

She sat up and promptly retched a thin stream of sickeningly sweet slime. The stench of alcohol mixed with the odor of vomit.

Mead, she'd drunk mead to seal the deal in the smoke-filled hall of the Father-God. He'd promised to send her back.

Liana jumped to her feet and swayed. Her head spun, filled with the shards of memory. She took another deep breath, wincing. The world came into focus and with it, her memory. She'd made a deal with Perun to try and win Amron back.

Above her, a deep indigo sky faded towards the east, where the first light of dawn gilded the mountain peaks. It was so warm she was sweating in her hunting leathers and her woolen cloak. The last thing she remembered was Perun on the snowy mountaintop, shaking hands with her.

She scrambled out of the ditch. The road led to Abia, hunkering like a torchlit beast in the distance, still wrapped in the cloak of the night. She knew where she was, she just didn't know *when*.

In the past, the god had said.

Liana unclasped her cloak and shook it, scrunching her nose at the unpleasant smell. She removed the twigs and dried leaves from her plait and smoothed it down, trying to look less like a vagrant even though she reeked like one. That was a problem she would have to solve later, after she'd answered the more pressing questions.

She shuffled towards the town, unsteady on her feet. Dozens of torches flickered on the city walls, illuminating the colorful standards. The northern wall had no moat, but it was thirty feet high, built of massive stone blocks, with a double gate made of wood and iron that led into the dark tunnel that passed under the wall. Despite the early hour, it was already open. The royal banner of the House of Amris—the golden sun on the blue field—hung above the gates, signaling that the king was in town. A crowd of people with donkeys and carts blocked the entrance: farmers rushing to sell fresh fruit and vegetables at the market.

Liana pulled her hood up, lowering her head as she snuck up to them, trying to look insignificant enough that no one would question her presence. Her hunting garb blended with their leather and linen, and the smell of donkeys and live chickens masked her odor. No one paid any attention to her, she was just a scruffy girl in a group of peasants.

She stepped through the dark tunnel, followed by a rooster's crow greeting the new dawn. In the early hour, the streets of Abia were quiet, but the street vendors were already stacking their wares and the taverns had opened their doors to sweep out the previous night's dirt. The mood, subdued by the lingering darkness, was nevertheless festive. Banners crisscrossed the streets above her head, garlands of flowers poured from the balconies, and every square and street corner was lit. The irresistible scent of fresh bread wafting on the morning breeze made her mouth water.

But Liana had no time to waste, no curiosity to spare. Ignoring the early birds, she took the shortest route through the streets to the palace. She had one goal and one goal only: to see if Amron was there.

By the time she reached the palace, the first rays had already touched its red roofs, rendering them aflame with the sunlight. The elegant arches and ornate facade caused a sharp pang between her ribs. She'd left the palace only yesterday—or whenever it was from this point in time—like a heartbroken beggar. Yesterday, she'd had nothing. But today, somewhere inside these walls, Amron was alive.

The main gate, the one facing the square, was open, but Liana didn't intend to negotiate with the guards. There were other ways in for someone who knew the palace like the back of her hand. She climbed over the garden wall in a back alley, where the stones weren't as smooth and a fig tree grew on the other side. She slid among the trees and bushes, their flowers opening to greet the light, and then ran through the corridors, registering the changes in the familiar layout. It was the same palace, and yet, nothing was the same. It felt more crowded, filled to the brim, not just with the regular palace staff, but with royal servants, clearly signaling the king was there. More eyes to see her, more suspicious people to stop her. She found a dark alcove near the stairs that led down to the kitchens and hid there, breathing hard. She needed to think.

Her impatient heart urged her to run to Amron immediately. She didn't know which rooms were his, but they had to be somewhere on the second floor. How hard could it be to find a prince? *He doesn't know you.*

She clawed at her mud-splattered clothes, at her tangled hair. Amron had always been a kind man, willing to listen to anyone who threw themself at his feet. Still, how likely was he to pay attention to a dirty waif spewing nonsense?

She bit her lip. The day had barely begun, the sun had not fully risen yet; she had a little time to spare. Amron was an early riser, but he was probably still asleep. Pouncing on him in bed wouldn't make him warm up to her.

No, she needed to look decent enough. The future could wait until she'd washed herself.

With a sigh, she descended into the basement of the palace. The laundry rooms and the baths were in the same place, no amount of shuffling around could move those. She first slunk to the room where the clean laundry was folded and stored to be taken upstairs by the maids. Time was a luxury, and so was choice; she didn't want to be caught borrowing clothes and interrogated by the head laundress who would surely see through her excuses better than any guard. The simple, pale-yellow linen dress folded on a shelf near the door would suffice—no fancy embroidery or lace someone would make fuss about. And a light chemise, a little worn and mended a few times. She didn't have to look highborn, just decent.

Liana folded the clothes into a tight bundle and rushed to the servants' communal bath. In the changing room, she slipped out of her riding gear, leaving it in a messy heap on the shelf, too unappealing for anyone to pilfer, and grabbed a clean towel and a sponge. The silver medallion lay between her breasts, and she touched it with the tips of her fingers for luck before entering the steaming pool room, where two girls soaked in the warm water, chatting.

The stones were pleasantly warm under her feet as she walked to the cubicles in the back, where buckets of hot and cold water and bars of lavender-scented soap waited for those who needed a more vigorous wash. She scrubbed her skin until it turned pink and rinsed every last speck of dust out of her hair. She wrapped it in a towel, trying to squeeze out as much water as possible, and combed it with a wooden comb. She didn't have enough time to let it dry—that took hours— but she braided it and wrapped the braid around her head to prevent it from dripping on her clothes.

The linen dress fit her loosely and barely reached to her ankles, but at least it was clean and pretty. With much regret, Liana left her sturdy riding boots in the changing room and borrowed a pair of leather sandals which were about her size.

A small circle of polished metal serving as a mirror told her she was as beautiful as always, her divine blood making her look not a day over twenty—the curse and blessing of the children of gods, who did not age, but faded away at the end of their long lives. For a lonely girl raised among the hunters of Till, it had been a liability. It meant she had learned to fight men off when she was twelve and still pretend to be grateful and humble, careful not to provoke them into rage.

Liana sighed and grabbed a basket of clean towels—if she kept her head down and looked busy, she might be mistaken for some lady's companion and left alone.

Using the hidden servants' staircase, she climbed to the second floor. A large arched corridor opened on the one side, overlooking the main yard. From there, doors led to a labyrinth of interconnected chambers. The colorful terrazzo floor echoed the gentle tap of her sandals. It was quiet here and the few sleepy guards paid no attention to the lonely girl.

She walked to a guard in the blue royal livery and, eyes cast down, she said, "Could you please help me? I think I'm lost."

"What are you looking for?"

"I have to deliver something to Prince Amron's chambers."

"Through this door, turn left, and you'll get to the next guard. Wait." He stopped her when she tried to slip beside him. "Let me see that basket." He stuck his hand in, and when he found only soft fabric, he nodded. "Alright, go."

In the palace she knew, the rooms she now entered were reserved for high guests, and usually closed off. Their large windows overlooked the city and colorful floral tapestries covered their walls. They always made her think of summer meadows and disappointed her with their odor of wool and dust instead of the sweet scent of flowers.

She ran over the soft carpets and polished wood to the next guarded door. "Delivery for Prince Amron's chambers," she said.

"Wait," the guard said, peered through the door and called for someone.

A moment later, a sleepy, irritable chamberlain appeared at the door. "Towels? What am I supposed to do with towels? I sent for his shirts."

"I'm sorry, sir, but the mistress gave me this—"

The chamberlain grabbed the basket. "I'll take it. Go tell Mistress Sariza to send me those shirts." And he slammed the door into her face.

"Do you want something else?" The guard smirked.

She turned on her heel. She didn't get in, but now she knew where he was. She retraced her steps to an empty room with red poppies and blue irises on the wall and found a hidden door behind the tapestry. A narrow corridor between the panels led to a small study, empty and dark. She opened the window and slipped to the balcony which connected to the next room. The bedroom.

One large window was open to let the morning breeze in. She thought he'd be asleep at this hour, but as she approached the sill, words floated out, spoken by the deep, smooth voice she knew so well.

"Did you get the protocol for today? We start off together, and then I must join my brother, receiving the guild masters, then lunch with the councilors and the ambassadors. In the afternoon, you're with the queen. In the evening, Amril has his…*thing*, and I must be there."

She dared to peer in. In the hazy light, his face was younger than she'd ever seen it, without a single line of worry or pain the war would etch on it. He sat in a high-backed chair, frowning at a sheet of paper, his long limbs tucked at sharp angles, sunlight dancing in his hair.

A wave of yearning hit her so hard her knees buckled.

"Amron," she whispered.

"Amron," echoed another voice, "I'm sure you've already memorized it. Let's go, they're waiting for us."

A young woman in a sunflower-yellow gown appeared behind him, thin and raven-haired, standing in her own pool of darkness, like a wisp of the night that had forgotten to retreat before the morning sun.

"I hope I'll see you tonight, before I leave with Amril," he said, rising and offering her his hand.

"I don't know when my father plans to arrive." She took his hand.

Together, they left the room.

Liana used to play a little game every time Amron was surrounded by people—which was often, because they naturally gathered around him, pleading, gossiping, demanding. She, always annoyed by the yapping crowds, would move out of earshot, retreat into the shadows, and watch him.

She'd imagine he wasn't hers, imagine he didn't know her: He was just a haughty prince in his palace, dispersing favors left and right, soaking in adoration, diluting malice, solving petty disputes. She watched his face, the way he looked straight at the people who spoke to him, the way he smiled at pretty women as they flocked like colorful birds. Her heart would tremble, the ache and the desire spreading through her chest, filling her with bittersweet longing.

Surrounded by people, he was as distant as a bright star in the sky. If she were a stranger to him, he would never find her in the crowd. But she would want him just the same: She'd stalk him like an infatuated shadow, glued to his heels, watching him as he moved, her fingers itching for a touch, her heart fluttering at the sight of his face.

She could keep it up for hours, letting the flowers of jealousy bloom like black dahlias in her heart, envying every woman, every charming man who brought the spark of animation to his face, who was awarded a brief flash of Amron's smile, his warm touch.

She'd push herself to the edge of despair, thinking how easy it would be to lose him. One day, the crowd would pull him like a strong current, drag him away from her, and she'd never be able to reach him again.

And then, just as she was ready to work herself into a frenzy, he'd stand on his toes, scanning the room. His eyes would find her, a mischievous smile would crack his princely mask, and he would wink at her above the heads of the crowd.

In an instant, he would be hers again.

𝕷ike a wet leaf sticking to the glass, Liana remained at the window until the buzz of the palace reminded her that someone might spot her on the balcony. Numb and clumsy, she retraced her steps through the rooms and corridors, down the stairs, and into the courtyard.

Amron was married.

She'd forgotten about Melia, she'd forgotten about that Elmarran snake Amron had been married to. In all their years together, Amron had never mentioned her, and why would he? It was an arranged marriage that fell apart when her father betrayed the king, and she disappeared from the kingdom forever. Liana had never found out if Melia was dead or alive and she'd never cared to ask. She was irrelevant, Amron had never loved her.

But she was not irrelevant now.

Paying no attention to the servants and clerks rushing around her, Liana walked out of the palace. Amron had never touched another woman behind her back, not when they flattered him at court, trying to sneak into his bed, not on the long journeys across the realm without Liana, when any kind of solace would have been welcome. He wasn't the unfaithful kind, he'd seen too much intrigue and drama in his everyday duties to seek them in his private moments, and his validation never sprang from what he did between the sheets.

He's twenty-three, you idiot.

It was entirely possible that he was a different person here, now.

Music floated in the morning air, a lively tune that wrapped itself around her ankles, inviting her to dance. The smell of food made her stomach churn: grilled meat, fresh bread, spices and herbs, fried fish and mussels with garlic and parsley. Someone tried to push a cup of wine into her hand, taking pity on her gloomy face.

She let the stream of people carry her forward, down the streets where she knew every stone, and yet where every detail she sought looked different. Very different. Enchanting scenes built of canvas and wood stood in the squares and on the street corners. Dramatic mountain landscapes of the north, the high towers of Myrit, the royal palace in Amraith laying like a bejeweled dragon beside the deep blue lake. It was like a walk around the kingdom and every turn revealed something new and breathtaking. It was as if every corner of the city, every street, every neighborhood tried to outmatch the next one. The whole city shone, bathed in the morning sunlight. Not even the narrowest alley, the humblest little passage, remained unscrubbed and unlit.

Liana's mind felt fuzzy and slow, but even the thick fog of shock couldn't hide that something important was happening. It dawned on Liana that she'd never seen Abia quite so pretty and festive.

"What's this all about?" she asked a woman selling fried fish on a street corner.

The woman gave her a strange look. "Which rock have you been living under, girl? It's the royal wedding. Our prince is getting married tomorrow."

The royal wedding?

Liana stopped dead in her tracks. Someone ran into her from behind and almost knocked her off her feet. "I'm so sorry," she muttered, moving out of the way.

The *wedding*!

Liana bit back a frustrated whimper, breaking out in cold sweat. Her memory was skewed, fragmented, and it wasn't the shock of seeing Amron with Melia, no. Liana could recognize a divine trick when she saw it.

The wedding had been a doorway to chaos, the start of a war that shattered the kingdom. She couldn't linger here, in this facsimile of the past, and wait for the bloodshed. She had to make Amron kiss her and get him out of here.

That was the reason the gods had sent her here, wasn't it?

She found a quiet alley where no one sang or tried to sell her beer and sat on a low stone ledge. Then she took off her medallion and held it dangling before her eyes. The silver oval caught the light, sharp and bright, impervious to magic, helping her tell memory from illusion.

Remember, she commanded.

Liana sifted through her memories. She had begged her mother in the heart of the divine forest to lead her to Perun. Grudgingly, for an extortionate price, Lela agreed.

Liana walked into a long, poorly lit wooden hall. The floor was beaten earth, strewn with old sawdust, the beds and chairs covered in animal furs. The air was close, reeking of ale and mead and piss. Enough weapons to set up a small army adorned the walls.

Liana expected the hall to be crowded, but the only movement she could discern was the shadows scurrying under the tables and close to the walls. Her footsteps and the crackling of the distant fires in two massive fireplaces at the opposite sides of the hall echoed in the eerie silence.

If this was Perun's legendary feasting hall, then it wasn't worth dying for.

She walked on, unable to judge the length. The shadows played with her: The longer she walked, the further the other end seemed. She tried walking faster; it didn't bring her any closer.

She paused, breathing heavily. "O Perun, the greatest of all gods, please allow me to speak to you," she pleaded.

"Come closer."

She stepped forward and the hall shrank. What she had mistakenly believed to be a heap of furs moved and revealed a huge man with a red beard, a war axe in his hand.

Liana fell to her knees and prostrated herself, spreading her arms, pressing her forehead to the floor, and waited. Fire crackled and shadows danced in the corners of her vision. Sawdust found its way into her nose and she held her breath to avoid sneezing.

"Lela's daughter," said the God of Sky and War, "get up. Let me see you."

Liana obeyed, wondering if she should have dressed more alluringly for this god who was fond of beautiful women. But the very thought made her stomach turn.

"Look up."

She banished her thoughts and lifted her eyes from the god's brightly painted boots, over his massive torso and long red beard, to his divine eyes, black with golden stars in them. They were just like Lela's, and yet they were completely different. Where Lela was furtive and unpredictable and cruel, Perun was cold and hard and cunning.

"I heard you have a request," he said.

She nodded, her teeth clenched so hard she could not open her mouth.

"Out with it. Don't waste my time."

Liana knew fear, she'd faced it many times, but it was her insignificance, not her fear, that paralyzed her now. This hairy mountain of a god, this dark, dirty hall, this stink that men left when they were crammed together. Somewhere, this hall was full; somewhere, Amron sat on a bench, unaware that she was steps away from him. She knew it. And yet, this wasn't like the mortal world, a curtain she could simply pull away. This was Perun's domain, and she was nothing but a beggar to him.

So she begged.

"My husband," she said, "Amron of the House of Amris. He was killed and you took him. I am here to beg you to give him back to me."

"And why would I do that?"

"Because I love him," she said, and it rang hollow and futile.

The god smirked. "Does that make you special?" He waved

his hand, the fire roared, shadows melted away, and for one brief moment, Liana could glimpse at the crowded tables, overflowing horns and cups, smiling faces, and—somewhere in the far corner—one golden head she knew so well.

She ran, but the table was empty, the hall was deserted.

Perun laughed. "He's out of your reach."

She turned back to him, furious and struggling not to show it. He read it on her face, nevertheless. It seemed to amuse him very much.

"Tell me," he said, "what makes your plea worthy? Lela has praised you so much, your beauty and courage and loyalty, but all I see here is an angry slip of a girl running after a man. What can you give him that he doesn't have here?"

"Why don't you ask him?" she said. "Why don't you let him choose?"

Perun laughed again. "He doesn't remember you anymore."

She looked down at her hands, trying to anchor herself in that place, for fear of dissolving into nothing. If Amron didn't know who she was…

But, "I don't care," she said. "It doesn't matter if he doesn't know who I am, because I know who he is. I love him. And I can make him love me again and again and again, as many times as necessary."

She must have said something right because the fire died down, the hall faded away, and she and the god were left standing on a bleak, windswept mountaintop.

"I propose a wager, then," Perun said. "I will send you into his past, before he met you. He won't know who you are. You'll have three days to make him love you. A kiss of true love will be required to prove it, before dawn on the third day."

"I agree," she said quickly.

"Wait, you haven't heard it all yet. Your mother wants me to tell you that if you fail, you will join her hunt, forget about your husband, and never return to the mortal world again."

"I agree," she said again, without hesitation. "Whatever you say."

"All right."

And on the lonely mountaintop, Perun and Liana shook hands and sealed the deal.

~Chapter 6~

Melia

Melia woke with a start, the remains of a nightmare rattling in her head: the dead horse, the entrails spilled in the dust. She reached across the bed for Amron, but his side was empty and cold, all the warmth long evaporated. The moon poured its silver light over the room's unfamiliar objects. Melia had her own room across the corridor, a tiny space with a bed, a chest, and a desk—the palace in Abia was crowded because of the royal wedding, they couldn't find anything better for her—but it felt so claustrophobic she preferred sharing Amron's bed.

The window was open, letting in the unfamiliar sounds of the palace that never slept and the cold night breeze. Melia reached for her silk wrap, her fur-lined slippers, and got up to close it. By the time she'd forced the heavy latch to slide into its place, she was fully awake and disgruntled with Amron's absence.

Where did he go in the middle of the night?

Melia tried to convince herself that he probably couldn't sleep and went for a walk to clear his head, but a small, nasty voice at the back of her mind called her a fool. The poison that cursed lady-in-waiting had poured into her ear was eating her alive.

She returned to bed, overwhelmed by the madness of the upcoming wedding, the high tension running through the palace like a ball of lightning, the sheer, infinite wickedness of the courtiers. Sleep evaded her as thoughts buzzed in her head.

She got up and opened the door, feeling foolish. There was no guard to see her, just a small page sleeping on a pillow like a scrawny kitten. Careful not to wake him, she slipped into the dark maze of corridors.

The palace was crowded, the queen and her ladies-in-waiting busy with planning the wedding. The idea that one of them could slip out to—no, it was ridiculous. And yet, Melia's feet kept moving, away from Amron's room, towards the royal chambers.

Melia was required to join the queen's ladies while the court was in Abia. She had no idea what was expected of her, there had been no gathering of women in Syr since her mother's death. The ladies who surrounded Queen Orsiana were refined, idle, and studiously ruthless. A lion's den padded with velvet and wool.

When she first arrived, they welcomed her with smiles and chatter, sweet wine and light gossip. For a heartbeat she balanced on the edge of hope that her status as a new bride, as Amron's wife, could protect her, that they would allow her to become one of them.

Her illusion came crashing down soon enough, as she discovered everything about herself was wrong. Her clothes were unfashionable, her manners provincial, her accent ridiculous. When she gathered the courage to utter her first full sentence, she saw how their eyes widened, how they exchanged long looks. One of the girls replied to her and for a moment Melia thought it wasn't so bad, because the girl's accent was also vaguely southern. In conversation with her, Melia didn't sound so hopelessly provincial. And then the girl's accent slipped, someone sniggered, and she realized the girl was affecting, mocking her.

They were bad when they were together, but they were even worse individually. And Vella was the worst. She ambushed Melia one afternoon in a cozy nook overlooking the garden. After trying to bait her with the most recent court gossip, she suddenly said, "And how is Amron these days?"

Melia stared at Vella's large blue eyes, her button nose, her stunning auburn hair, unsure what the question really meant.

"I thought you should know we had something going on just before he left for Syr," Vella continued, her smile wide and warm. "He was quite besotted with me, couldn't get enough. I taught him that trick with the tongue, you know, when—"

"I don't know," Melia interrupted her. "And I don't want to know."

"Oh, but you do." The girl's pale fingers wrapped around Melia's in an iron grip. "There are no secrets between friends, and I want to be your friend. I wouldn't dream of doing anything behind your back, so I wanted to ask you if you would mind us picking up where we left off?"

"I would," Melia said, tearing away from Vella. "I'd mind it very much."

"Oh, perhaps I was too direct, I'm sorry. You still have a lot to learn about court life. If not me, it will be somebody else, some girl who might not want to be your friend."

Melia wanted to tell her that no woman who ever slipped into Amron's bed could be her friend, but it felt too crude and provincial in that place where refinement comprised enchanting music, elegant poetry, glorious tapestries, and sleeping with other women's husbands.

Vella smiled and shrugged apologetically, but Melia hadn't been fooled. She knew with absolute certainty that this had been a duel, and that she had lost.

As she wandered through the dark corridors, Vella's poisonous whisper echoed in her ears. Melia was too much of a coward, too uncertain of her slippery position in the infinitely complicated court hierarchy to challenge Amron directly, although she'd watched him closely, looking for a morsel of proof. There was nothing to see. He didn't even come close to his mother's ladies: He moved almost exclusively among the men of the court, his brother's clique, his sparring partners and drinking buddies.

It might have been nonsense, a power move, but Abia had been so cruel to her since the day she arrived. Amron's cold, demanding mother; his disinterested father; his dangerous, intrusive brother. The courtiers, with their jokes about the Elmarrans' love for their sheep. The ladies, with their long stares and raised eyebrows. And even Amron, who'd seemed so large against the empty horizon of Elmar, suddenly shrank here to a cautious, taciturn shadow. He was kind to her—he'd always been kind, infallibly—but she feared the intimacy between them was too fragile to carry them through the court straits.

Wrapped in such dark thoughts, Melia startled when a door opened a few paces down the corridor from her. She barely managed to hide behind a column when a tall shadow slipped out. "Good night," a deep voice whispered.

A woman appeared in the yellow light pouring out from the room. She was practically nude, only a scrap of silk wrapped around her body, her dark hair tousled, her face flushed. Melia knew that face: It wasn't Vella, but another lady-in-waiting, a northern girl, spoiled and mellow, whose name escaped her memory. She reached for the man. "Wait."

Melia's heart stopped as the man turned; she expected to see Amron's face, just as flushed with lovemaking. The woman grabbed the man, pushing her fingers into his thick blond locks. He bowed down, his lips meeting hers, his hands pulling her close. Melia almost cried out, but then her brain finally registered what her eyes were showing her: The tall, golden-haired man kissing the lady-in-waiting in the doorway wasn't Amron. It was the king.

"Come back," the woman whispered, and giggled when he tore off the silk scarf and lifted her as if she weighed nothing.

"Your wish is my command, my lady." He carried her back into the room and shut the door behind him.

Melia waited to see if he would return, pressing her cold hands to her burning cheeks. When the soft sighs and moans slipped into the dark corridor, she turned on her heel and ran away. The king was plowing one of the queen's ladies, and she had almost walked into them like the most incompetent, most idiotic person in Abia.

They didn't see you, she consoled herself while she ran. *They couldn't have, they were too busy.*

Looking for fresh air, for an open sky, she ran into the garden. Only then did she allow herself to breathe loudly, moaning at her stupidity, clenching her fists in impotent frustration and embarrassment.

"Melia!" someone called.

And there he was, her missing husband, walking towards her, gravel crunching beneath his feet.

"What happened?"

She let him wrap his arms around her and lead her to a bench. She laid her head on his chest, wishing she could crawl under his arm and hide in the warm darkness. "Where were you?" she asked. "I woke up and you weren't there."

"I couldn't sleep, so I went for a walk. Did you go looking for me? Did someone scare you?"

"I went looking for you," she said. And then, feeling she would explode if she didn't share it with someone, she added, "I saw your father."

"My father? Where?"

"He slipped into a room with one of your mother's ladies, a dark-haired girl from North Leven, I can't remember her name."

"You mean Lenka?" He sneered. "That's hardly a secret. It's been going on for half a year or so."

The bluntness with which he said it surprised her, though she found it hard to pinpoint why. The image of the king kissing the girl was still etched on the insides of her eyelids. "How does your mother deal with it?"

The temperature dropped between them as his eyes studied her face in the moonlight. "I don't think that's a subject I want to discuss."

"But your father, why does he—"

"My father, as you have probably learned by now, takes whatever he wants, and what he wants is everything."

Melia nodded, silenced by the bitterness in his voice. She'd learned to stay as far away from the king as possible. From Amril, too, though the ladies talked about him all the time.

She bit her lip. It wasn't her intention to get Amron upset, quite the opposite. But the quiet garden wrapped in silver and black seemed to be the only place where truth could be spoken.

"And who is Vella?" she asked.

"Vella?" He was genuinely baffled. "One of my mother's ladies. I don't think she has anything to do with my father, though."

"But she has something to do with you, doesn't she?"

"What?" He moved away to the edge of the bench.

In some other situation, it would have amused her to see him lose his poise. But she was agitated and rash and the words spilled out of her mouth. "Vella took me to a quiet corner a few days ago and told me you were obsessed with her."

"That's ridiculous." He pulled at the collar of his shirt, creasing the fine fabric.

"Have you slept with her?"

That made him pause, avert his eyes to the sky. For a heartbeat she thought she'd crossed the line dividing his right to do as he pleased from her right to interrogate him; she thought he'd simply get up and leave. Abandon her in her nightgown and wrap, wild locks escaping her braid, an uncouth, pitiful savage, the laughingstock of the court.

"They like to draw blood, my mother's ladies, don't they?" he said slowly. "They'll stick their claws into your flesh to see where it hurts. Don't let them do it."

"But have you—" She tried to repeat the question, but the words stuck in her throat.

"They'll all tell you I have, and two or three will be telling the truth." He frowned and it seemed to her he was genuinely digging through his memory. "Vella? Yes, I believe I have, twice. Over a year ago, after some celebration when I was too irritable to be alone, and just before I left for Syr, when she cornered me with some wild talk about kindred spirits and I did it just to shut her up. Does that answer your question?"

"I didn't want you to tell me the details, I just—"

"Yes, yes, you did." He rubbed his temples. She'd noticed he did that when he was upset. "I'm not my brother, I don't have to lift every skirt that passes through this court, but I'm not a hermit either. I make mistakes, though I try not to make them with my mother's ladies because they scare the daylights out of me."

It sounded almost like an apology. So she gathered the courage to ask: "And will you be making more mistakes?"

"What?" It took him a second to understand. "Does it matter to you?"

She opened her mouth to answer him and found herself mute once more. It did matter to her, she realized, but she couldn't understand why. "I don't know the rules of this court," she managed to utter at last.

"Rules be damned," Amron said. "Does it matter to you?"

His unflinching gaze lay heavy on her, and it suddenly became too much to bear. Like that first night, she couldn't allow him to see her vulnerable. She turned her face away from him, gathering her wits and her dignity. "This is a political union," she said. "You are free to do whatever you please. I apologize for interrogating you."

A long silence followed. And then, after an icy eternity, he said, "I understand." He rose. "I'm going to bed. I'd prefer to be alone tonight."

The next day, a maid brought her the news while she was sitting in the garden with the queen's ladies, pretending to read a book of poetry just to avoid speaking to anyone. The sight of Vella made bile rise in her throat. She'd spent the long hours of the previous night tossing and turning, angry at herself for swallowing the bait, angry at Amron for being so stiff, angry at the whole world.

"My lady, the Elmarran delegation has arrived." The maid's voice cut her reverie.

"Did my father come?" she asked, jumping to her feet, but the maid shrugged. Abia was a barely controlled chaos, bursting at the seams. The guests had been pouring in throughout the whole week and the Seragians were expected to arrive the following day. Some overworked clerk probably had the list of every man, woman, and child who currently resided there, but it was too much to ask of a maid. "Never mind, I'll go and see for myself."

It was late afternoon, sunny and mild. The sun descending towards the White Mountains illuminated the Bay of Abia at an angle that turned the waves into liquid gold. Melia paused for a moment, breathing in the salty air, basking in the mellow light. She found it strange, this absence of harshness, a place that wasn't hostile to its residents. Her father had always claimed that such hospitable surroundings bred weak, spoiled people. But looking at Queen Orsiana, born and raised in Abia, as she sat on a wooden bench with her eyes closed, her face radiant in the sunlight, Melia thought that she looked neither weak nor spoiled, but peaceful and happy.

In the few precious memories Melia had of her mother, she never looked peaceful and happy. Her young face—she was not yet thirty when she'd died—was either a tight-lipped mask of worry or a frowning grimace of displeasure. No matter how hard she racked her brain, she couldn't remember one instance of her parents smiling.

"My lady." Melia curtsied. "The Elmarran delegation arrived. May I go and greet them?"

The queen opened her eyes. "Is Roderi with them? I'd like to see him."

Hearing the queen call her father by his first name surprised Melia, but there was no polite way of asking why she'd done it. "I'll check, my lady."

Sensing her curiosity, the queen added, "Has your father ever mentioned we knew each other when we were children?" She shaded her eyes, looking up towards Melia. "Our fathers were friends, I think they had plans for us."

Gentle melancholy dripped from Queen Orsiana's words. Melia's father had never mentioned the friendship or the betrothal plans, and she found it very hard to imagine this pale, delicate woman among the rough red stones of Syr. What kind of wife could she have been to Roderi of Elmar, what kind of mother to his children? She loved Amron, that much was obvious to Melia, and she wondered what it felt like to be loved by your parent.

"I don't think he mentioned it, my lady," she said.

"Oh well, it was thirty years ago," the queen said. "And it came to nothing."

Queen Orsiana's father was murdered in a bloody coup, which left her as the sole heiress of Larion. The king had scooped her up like a shiny prize in a shrewd political move that resulted—as far as Melia could understand—in a profoundly cold marriage.

"Don't let me detain you with my old stories." The queen waved her away. "Go greet your countrymen."

Melia rushed through Abia, followed by two guards and a surly maid, but instead of excitement, her mind was filled with the questions about the royal marriage. The image of the king with Lenka, the brutal, primeval desire he radiated with in contrast with his appearance at court, formal and distant, taking up all the space, all the air, all the sunlight like a massive oak tree. His presence dominated every corner of the palace—except for the queen's chambers. An invisible wall surrounded Queen Orsiana's world, and few men were allowed to enter it: the poets and musicians who entertained her and the little pages who served her, but no male courtiers, not even the princes. The ladies made up for this lack of men as soon as the queen retired, flocking like sparrows around Prince Amril and his pack, but the queen seemed quite happy to be left alone.

Melia wondered if she and Amron were heading in the same direction, towards a marriage which was nothing but a formal engagement that required her to stand beside him occasionally and smile. Although—the queen had produced two male heirs and a girl, which must have contributed to her current liberty. Melia had no such achievements.

It was a relief, in a way, because even the vaguest thoughts of children, of pregnancy, of childbirth, made Melia sick. Her monthly blood—irregular, painful, and black on her linen rags—disgusted her. It smelled of death and loss and grief; the chances of her body producing a life were about the same as the barren stones of Syr bursting in bloom.

Engulfed in such dark thoughts, she reached the house her father had in Abia, a small villa tucked away in a maze of narrow, winding streets and walled gardens. She'd never stayed there and she couldn't remember her father ever visiting Abia. It was a relic of another time, perhaps, of the childhood Queen Orsiana remembered, of the long-forgotten friendship between the two southern lords.

"Lady Melia!" someone called to her as she stepped in, and she turned to see men in her father's livery, red and black.

"Welcome to Abia," she said, and they moved to reveal a dark-haired woman standing in their midst. It took Melia a heartbeat to recognize her, so out of place did she look without the crumbling red walls and empty rooms of Syr behind her. "Ferisa," she blurted out.

She bowed. "I have a message from your father. We should talk in private."

Melia turned to her retinue. "Go back to the palace, you don't need to wait." Then she followed Ferisa into a sparsely furnished room that stank of ancient dust and winter damp. No one had scrubbed the floors, opened the shutters to let the sunlight in, or aired the carpets and pillows to prepare for the arrival of the master. No spark of life was ignited to wake the house up. Wherever her father went, the fog that quenched out all liveliness followed him. Preceded him.

And Ferisa, too, in her priestly colors: dark green, gray, and black. In Syr, she blended in. Here in Abia, compared to the gaudy court opulence, she looked like a scrap of misery, a poor cousin embarrassing everyone with her presence.

Ferisa was studying her right back. "You look pretty," she said.

Melia looked down at her dress, at the layers of sunflower-colored silk organza, at the fine embroidery studded with tiny pearls, at the amber-and-gold necklace the queen had given her, and cold unease twisted her stomach. She looked like an exotic bird.

"It's just court fashion," she stammered. "It's what all the ladies wear."

"It suits you well," Ferisa said, and again, although the statement was shaped like a compliment, there was broken glass waiting under a layer of honey. "You look like a princess."

I am a princess, Melia almost said, but then she checked herself. Why would she quarrel with Ferisa?

"My father is not here?" she asked.

"He's coming tomorrow."

"Tomorrow?" Tomorrow was important. Crucial, in fact. "So are the Seragians," she added guardedly.

The turbulent weeks after her wedding had been so hectic for Melia that she'd almost forgotten the reason her father had sent her there in the first place. The Seragians, the peace treaty, and Prince Amril's wedding all slipped her mind. In the lively streets of Abia, in the sunny gardens of the palace, the deathly silence of Syr seemed like a bad dream. She could have almost convinced herself it didn't concern her anymore. The sheer size of the court, the scope of the affairs so beyond her she might have been an eavesdropping pigeon on the windowsill, made her believe she was irrelevant. Her father's shadow didn't stretch as far as Abia, and the royal circle cared nothing about Elmar's feelings.

But now Ferisa was here, her dark fire burning, and Melia realized she'd been fooling herself. She could get out of Syr, but Syr would always be in her blood. The dark shadows of Elmar crept down the walls towards her.

"Your father wants you to help me," Ferisa said.

She reminded her of Rovin at that moment, not because she was rough and fierce like her late brother, but because she expected Melia to obey her without question.

"Help you do what?" she asked.

"Take me with you as your cousin and companion, show me the layout of the palace, get me the schedule for the wedding ceremony."

It was as if a stranger had stepped into Ferisa's skin, removed the priestess, the herbalist, the friend Melia had known, and replaced her with this brusque courtier.

"Why do you need it?" she asked.

"Oh, Melia, you know what your father wants."

This wedding must never transpire, he'd said.

That couldn't be right. That was just her father's grief speaking, his angry words. In Syr, he was the master of life and death, but here in Abia? He was a fragment of the queen's childhood memory, the uncouth southern neighbor, the surly father-in-law no one cared about. Melia had seen the scope of the wedding preparations. What could Ferisa do? Melia might as well show her everything, let her believe their mad schemes could change something.

With the shutters half closed, the shadows in the room pooled inside Ferisa's dark eyes as she lifted her hand to touch Melia's face.

It was a familiar touch, a comforting touch.

"How is it, with the prince?" Ferisa asked.

For the briefest of moments, Melia wanted to spill it all out: the hostility of the ladies, the broken intimacy, the occasional urgent lovemaking in the dark, the inability to express—or even determine—how she felt. But then, even though telling Ferisa everything had been an old habit, sharing details about Amron felt wrong. He wasn't a piece of gossip.

"It's fine," she replied.

Ferisa frowned. "Fine? That's all you have to say about your marriage?" Her eyes glinted with contempt. "He's already taught you to be like him? All proper and forbidding?"

Melia opened her mouth to explain that things were different here, that the coarse manners of Syr were unacceptable…and closed it immediately. There was nothing wrong with Ferisa, she was the same as she'd always been. It was Melia who'd changed covertly, unexpectedly.

"I'm sorry," she said, reminding herself that Ferisa was the one who knew her, the one who cared about her. The one who comforted her when there was no one else around. "I don't know what came over me. This place changes you."

"Resist it," she said, and this time, her grip on Melia's chin was firm, and she welcomed it. "Don't forget who you are and why you're here."

The shape of her, compact and firm, made Melia feel safe. "The people are so terrible here. The women are haughty and harsh. And the men are worse. Amril is a self-centered monster determined to make every woman who crosses his path uncomfortable. And the king, he sleeps with his wife's ladies and doesn't even try to hide it."

"Yes, I've heard," Ferisa muttered.

"I want to go away. I want to leave this place and never look back."

"Then we'll do it." Ferisa pulled Melia into a firm, sharp embrace. "As soon as our duty here is done."

~Chapter 7~

Liana

The villa stood on a quiet street surrounded by a blooming garden and a high wall. Liana knocked on the back door, tucked away in a narrow alley. She'd hidden her hair under a scarf, cast her eyes down.

"Mistress Sariza sends me. She said you're short of girls for tonight."

The woman at the door—short, gaunt, middle-aged—scrutinized Liana. "If all you do is pour wine for the high and mighty with that face, you're wasting your life, girl."

A genuine blush warmed Liana's cheeks. She could hardly escape her looks. "That's all I do, ma'am."

"Well, come in, then. What are you waiting for?"

She followed the woman through a cool whitewashed corridor, walking past a pantry and a bustling kitchen. The scent of hazelnuts and caramelized sugar made her breathe in deeply, imagining bittersweet brittle crunching between her teeth.

"Hurry up."

She followed the woman up the polished wooden stairs to the first floor. The house was decorated with superb taste in soft shades of mint and aquamarine, with glazed tiles on the floor, soft gauze curtains, and frescoed walls. The room at the end of the corridor was shaded, the wooden shutters letting in only a handful of slanting rays. Dust danced in the rose-scented air.

"My lady, a new girl from the palace arrived."

"Why are you bringing her to me? She should be in the kitchen." The woman lounging on a low sofa removed a cold compress from her eyes and looked at Liana. "Oh, I see. Come closer, please."

The woman was in her late thirties and pretty in a fragile way, with dark hair, pale skin, and large gray eyes which took in every detail of Liana's appearance. "Could you let your hair down for me?"

Liana removed the scarf, unbraided her hair, and let the honey-colored waves tumble down to her waist.

"She says she's just a server, my lady."

The pretty woman stood up and touched Liana's chin, urging her to lift her face. "Oh no, that's a complete waste."

"That's what I said, my lady."

Liana kept her mouth shut. She'd begged and bribed the maids at the palace to tell her where Amril would have his *thing*, as Amron had called it, that evening. A few girls mentioned an additional source of income, but only as servers. Lady Celandina had her own girls who entertained the visitors, she only needed the maids to bring food and wine and clean up afterwards.

"Show me your teeth."

Liana stretched her lips into a weak semblance of a smile.

"Perfect. Would you mind taking your clothes off for me?"

Liana kept her face as neutral as possible. She wanted a chance to get close to Amron without drawing attention to herself, not an audition for the most expensive brothel in the city. But refusing now would get her kicked out immediately, and anyway, it wasn't like she planned to stay here after tonight. She might as well play along.

"Oh, wonderful," the woman said when Liana let her chemise slip down to the tiles. "How old are you?"

"Nineteen."

"And you work in the palace as a maid?"

"Yes, my lady."

"And it never occurred to you to use your looks to get a better job?"

"I never thought I'd be any good at it." It was the truth. She'd done a fair share of hard, physically demanding jobs in her life, but none were as difficult as being groped by some horny animal reeking of sour wine and sweat.

"I can teach you to be good at it, it's a skill. What's your name?"

"Liana."

"Liana, have you ever been with a man?"

"Yes." She tried to remember how her nineteen-year-old self had felt about men. Tired of their relentless advances, wary of their possessiveness, bemused by their fumbling. That didn't stop her looking for the one that'd suit her, though. She'd always known that if she waded deep enough into the muck, she'd find the pearl. Now it was time for more muck, and she was old enough to handle it. She wanted the job. "I know how to make them happy, my lady. If that's what you want me to do."

"Hm." The lady lifted one eyebrow. "You're a rough diamond indeed, but that face of yours....I wish I had the time to teach you, but there'll be a crowd of restless young men here tonight, thirsting for a novelty. All you have to do is smile and be pliable. Can you do that?"

"Yes." Liana shot the lady her sweetest smile.

"Mera will give you something to wear and introduce you to the girls. I don't expect you to perform tonight, you don't have to sing or dance or even talk, just hover in the background and look pretty. If you catch someone's eye, I'll handle it. Do you understand?"

Liana nodded, and thus she was promoted from a maid to one of Lady Celandina's girls.

She had seen a fair share of brothels in her life—they were ubiquitous with both the army and the nobility. And she'd seen the whole palette of women who sold their bodies, from the most desperate camp-followers and half-starved waifs—selling a quick upright for two coppers—to pampered courtesans, singers, and actresses who could choose between the men who threw themselves at their feet. She knew she'd been lucky, in those early years of her life, to have had a grandfather who protected her, surrounded her with a close-knit group of people. If Lord Echton's hunters hadn't taken her as one of their own, she might have easily ended up in one of the inns along the northern road, sold like chattel, too young to set herself free.

Lady Celandina's girls didn't look like anybody sold them. When she joined them, dressed in a flowing, gauzy teal gown, her hair pulled away from her face and secured with pearl hairpins, she drew a few curious looks and quick nods, nothing else. She was pretty, yes, but so were they, as well as polished and businesslike.

"This is Liana," Mera introduced her. "She'll be joining you tonight."

A dozen cold, disinterested smiles.

"Show us what you can do," a blonde holding a harp said when Mera left. "What makes you special? Can you sing? Dance?"

"I can keep my mouth shut," Liana said.

~Chapter 8~

Melia

Once Ferisa switched her priestly clothes for a pretty wine-red gown, she became just another woman rushing through the busy palace. Melia didn't go so far as to introduce her to the queen—she had a disturbing feeling that Queen Orsiana saw people more clearly than she let it show. There was no need to risk a closer look or a deceptively gentle interrogation in the garden.

Apart from that, every corner of the palace was open to them. Their act required no special effort, they'd been playing this lady-and-her-companion game for years, and if it had passed the surly scrutiny of Roderi of Elmar, it was certainly good enough for the courtiers distracted with the royal wedding.

Prior to Ferisa's arrival, Melia had been afraid of the palace and avoided wandering through it alone. With Ferisa by her side, she felt giddy exploring the great hall as it was being made ready for the feast tomorrow, the busy kitchens and stables, the offices on the first floor where the overworked clerks and scribes went about their business trying to ignore the chaos, and the second floor, where the royal family and all the guests who didn't have accommodation in Abia now resided.

To a girl who grew up in Syr, where the only noise was produced by the wind howling through empty passages, this turmoil was overwhelming and scary. However, a strange surge of pride filled Melia while showing the magnificent floral tapestries in the long gallery, the marble sculptures and exotic flowers in the gardens and hidden terraces, the hand-carved furniture, the mirrors, the map room with maps of every corner of the world, the curious mechanisms and plants and animal specimens collected by the queen's late father, the library with thousands of books and rare manu-scripts. Showing it all to Ferisa was like seeing it for the first time, through the eyes of the girl who grew up surrounded by dust, rough-hewn wood, and threadbare carpets. It was a world neither of them was familiar with, but which now belonged to Melia.

She feared Ferisa would be bitter about it, dismissive of the opulence, resentful of the plunder on display. But instead, her companion watched in wide-eyed silence and nodded when Melia explained.

When they grew exhausted, Melia led Ferisa to her small room. "You can stay here if you like. I mostly sleep in the other room."

"The other room?" Ferisa lifted an eyebrow, but the question was teasing rather than hostile. Melia had done her best to make Ferisa know she was just as important to her as she'd always been. There was no reason for her to be surly or jealous.

As she fished for a neutral answer, a little page knocked on her door and said, "His Royal Highness, Prince Amron, requires your presence."

She shrugged apologetically to Ferisa. "I'll be back soon. He's joining his brother tonight."

"Where?"

"Oh, some lady's house. Her name is Celandina, I think."

"The brothel, right?"

Melia hadn't thought about it, but it was obvious. Only men were invited. How stupid of her to overlook that; Ferisa saw through it in an instant.

Melia checked her face in a mirror before entering Amron's room. Deception was written on it in bold brushstrokes. She tried to convince herself she hadn't been unfaithful, Ferisa wasn't a man, and yet the intimacy she shared with her felt dangerously close to betrayal. Her secrets, her dreams, her longing—it was all locked in a tight cocoon she shared with Ferisa. Amron was the one left out. But then, Amron had his ladies-in-waiting, and brothel girls, apparently. He had no need of Melia's affection.

"Wait," she barked to the page rushing before her. "I need water."

"Water, my lady?"

"I need to wash my face."

The boy looked at her as if she were mad, but ran off and returned with a jug and a small porcelain basin. Melia let him pour the cold water into her cupped hands and washed her face, scrubbing it with a handkerchief. When she looked in the mirror again, her face was red, her skin irritated.

"Good," she said to the boy. "Now get lost."

She knocked on Amron's door and entered. "It's me."

"Melia." He was already dressed for the evening, in cloudy gray hues that complemented his eyes, with his hair tied back and his face freshly shaven. Just like the interior of the palace, he looked like something you could show off, like a coveted prize, like the reason why the queen's ladies sighed into their pillows at night. No one in Syr, no one in Elmar, no one in the whole kingdom but her had a prince to parade with. A prince who smiled at her as she entered, and made her face burn even worse.

She checked herself. "You wanted to see me?"

"Yes. I must go with Amril tonight, but before that," he motioned to the window, "please sit down."

There were two chairs beside the window, with a small round table between them. Melia chose the nearer one and sat down, eyeing the flagon of red wine and two glasses, wondering what he was up to.

"I owe you an apology." He sat and poured the wine.

She accepted the glass and took a sip. With her father, this would be a trap, a false apology to draw out a confession. But Amron couldn't have known about Ferisa, could he? She studied his face. He looked sincere. "For what?" she dared to ask.

"For neglecting you," he said.

A part of her wanted to laugh at this. The men she grew up with hurt women without apologizing, without even noticing. They would have sneered at the idea of asking for forgiveness, they would have thought it weak.

But then, a part of her found his words curiously soothing, even if it was her who should be apologizing to him, for neglect and worse.

"I was rude to you yesterday," he continued. "And I've spent the last few weeks running errands for others, without pausing to check how you felt. My mother tells me you've found it hard to adjust."

She blushed. "Amron—" She cursed herself silently for reacting to him, and she cursed him for finding a way to get under her skin. She sipped her wine. "I'm not asking anything of you."

He drained his glass.

They spoke different languages, where the words were deceptively alike, but their meanings clashed.

"No one teaches you to do this," he said, looking out of the window. "There are no instructions for royal marriages. Oh, you see examples, but they are almost all bad." He rubbed his eyes with the heels of his palms, looking disheartened.

She was torn between the image of her father riding towards Abia, of Ferisa demanding her attention with soul-burning intensity, and this chance Amron was offering her, this miniature peace treaty of their own. No matter which side she chose, she'd be stabbing someone in the back.

"I sometimes don't know how to react to things and my body responds before my brain. That's why I tend to run away from situations that upset me, cut them harshly rather than engage in conflict. I'm sorry." He laid his hand on the table, palm up, like an invitation. "I've been trained for this life, and still I've found these last weeks trying. I can't imagine how it must be for you."

She reached across the table and caught his hand. She was tempted to tell him she was a worthless traitor, that she deserved his scorn, his punishment. And yet, something stopped her. Not fear, no—she had long stopped caring what would happen to her. It was only that she hated the idea of losing his kindness, of turning this gentle concern on his face into disappointment and disgust. She wanted him to look at her like that for just a little while longer.

"Read to me," she blurted out.

"What?" He blinked, but his fingers remained entwined with hers.

"I don't know how to talk to you and I'm not ready to discuss how I feel. This is too much, too hard. But if you read to me for a bit before you leave, it will be enough. I like the sound of your voice."

He raised his eyebrows. "Poetry?" he asked. "A six-tome history of Abia? A treatise on the wines of Larion?"

She chuckled against her will. "Poetry will do."

He shuffled through the books stacked on his desk and picked a hefty tome bound in dark leather and gold leaf, well-worn from use. "Mareo's posthumous collection," he said. "Any preferences?"

Her education was lacking: She barely recognized the name. "Anything you like."

He thumbed the pages and started reading in his clear baritone. The stress of the day evaporated from her limbs, leaving her heavy and pliable, her eyes half shut. He read about love and yearning and carnal pleasures, and the words ignited a small flame in her belly. When he closed the book after a dozen poems and rose to leave, she was sorry to see him go.

"That place Amril is taking you to, what is it?" she asked.

"Have the ladies been gossiping again?" he said. "It's just a place where men go together and encourage each other to behave badly. They'll get drunk and vulgar, and I'll get bored." He kissed the top of her head. "Good night."

When he left, she blew out the candle and sat in silence for a while, breathing in the scent of the room, the beeswax polish, the leather, the subtle notes of bergamot and frankincense, the salty smell of the sea that permeated everything. Then she got up and walked to her room, expecting to find Ferisa waiting for her. But instead of the priestess, she found an unsigned note. *Urgent business*, it said. *Meet me in the cherry orchard at dawn.*

Her mellow drowsiness hardened into anxiety in an instant. Ferisa had no other urgent business in Abia but the Black Lord's. Melia was stupid to believe that Ferisa was there for her. She was there for her father, to put into motion whatever he'd planned.

~Chapter 9~

Liana

The evening sky glowed purple, the lanterns in the trees spilled warm yellow light. Music whispered among the leaves and women glided through the garden, more women than Liana expected: maids in their dark aprons, Lady Celandina's girls in their diaphanous gowns, dancers in skin-tight costumes.

The men were already rowdy when they arrived, disrupting that harmony as soon as they entered. Laughing too loud, staggering on the grass, taking up too much space. The women scattered like a shoal of fish before them and then gathered again, forming new patterns, breaking the men apart, muffling their chaos.

Liana stood still in the shadows, watching. There was the crown prince, the bridegroom, the focal point of the evening. Amril, tall and golden, larger than life, like a fairy-tale hero, followed by his clique of sycophants. There were the high lords of the kingdom, the young ones, the fun ones, the ones who loved the prince. There were the accidental hangers-on, the ones who had to be invited, too important to be left out. And then there was a shadow, a gust of northern wind in the summer air, a face that made her chest ache.

The beautiful evening carried no ominous signs, no dark premonitions of war. Liana felt foolish thinking about it. Perun had muddled her memory, dropped her at a wedding she'd never seen because she'd been nineteen at the time, too unimportant to be taken to Abia to witness the glorious finale of the most difficult peace negotiations in history. The wedding of the Crown Prince Amril and Carevna Aratea of Seragia, where something went terribly wrong. The little she'd heard about it from Amron was a useless mush in her memory now. She did know, however, what followed afterwards: years and years of bloodshed, meager victories erased by staggering defeats, and death, so much death. Liana had to get to Amron before the bloody cleaver of destiny fell on Abia, had to get him out, away from the madness, back to the relative safety of *their* Abia.

She wanted to run to him but she couldn't. He wasn't alone, there were two dozen people between them. So Liana smiled, poured the sweet, iced white wine, and answered dull questions, lying and deceiving the guests into thinking they were interesting. A bearded man pulled her into his lap and she refrained from breaking his teeth, slipping out of his grasp like an eel. A young man, hardly more than a boy, asked for a dance, and then stood staring at her face, holding her wrists in his sweaty hands. She'd seen enough events at the palace to learn the art of light hovering, of making men feel like they had her full attention before disappearing from view.

The sky turned black and the night breeze cooled her hot skin. It felt like an eternity, but it couldn't have been more than an hour. She saw Amron chat with men and women; one of the girls made him laugh, another lured him into a dance, but he slipped away from them all in his gentle, unobtrusive manner, fading into the background. She lost him from sight for a moment and her heart stopped—she thought he'd left. Then she spotted him alone, sitting under a tree, a glass in his hand. She made a beeline for him this time, a huntress moving silent and unobserved through the forest of drunk men.

"Good evening," she said softly, sitting down beside him.

"Is it?" he said. "I'm not so sure. I feel mean, and drunk."

He was lying on both accounts. He'd never been mean and he was still on his first glass of wine. He didn't even spare her a look.

"Still, I'd like to join you, if you don't mind," she said.

"Did my brother send you?"

"What?" She glanced towards Amril, on the other side of the garden, in the spotlight, his arms around a girl. "Gods, no. Not him."

"Then why—" He turned his face to her and his words trailed off.

Many years ago, on a night when he'd drunk more wine than usual, when sleep eluded them both, and when she felt it was a good moment for foolish questions, Liana asked, "When did you fall in love with me?"

"The moment I first saw you." An immediate reply, without hesitation.

"I don't believe you." It was winter, and very cold. They were nesting among the down-filled pillows and quilts in his bed. A solitary candle burned on a nightstand, outlining his profile in gold. "You're not the type to fall for anyone quickly. And it took you months to say it out loud."

He laughed softly at that. "I didn't want to admit what it was, then. And I certainly didn't plan to do anything about it."

"So it was just a strange itch you ignored? A flea bite where you couldn't reach and scratch yourself?"

He turned to face her, upsetting the perfect cocoon of warmth. "Vivid, but untrue," he said. "No, it was love. You rode out of that snowy thicket, already wary of me although we'd never met, and you removed your hood and I thought, *This is who I'll dream of every night, for the rest of my life.*"

"**Oh**," **Amron said,** his eyes glued to her face.

Hope flickered in her heart. Some things were always true, even if he couldn't remember them.

"I don't think we've met." He frowned. "Yet you seem familiar."

"My name is Liana." It was all she could say, sitting so close to him she could feel the warmth radiating from his body. She hadn't prepared her words in advance; she'd thought it would be easy. She'd been talking to Amron for half her life. But she hadn't been talking to *this* Amron—this preoccupied young man, obviously attracted to her, but wary of strangers and still uncomfortable in his own skin.

The lanterns gave off a subtle golden light that warmed his pale complexion and flirted with the sharp lines of his face. His eyes, the color of the winter sea in daylight, turned nearly black in the pooling shadows. She wanted to touch him so desperately her fingers ached, but he hated being touched by strangers.

"Liana, I'm flattered, but you're wasting your time." He set his glass down, ready to flee. "You are beautiful, but I never touch Celandina's girls."

Of course he didn't, damn him. He avoided courtesans because their feigned willingness burned him like acid. Neither her beauty nor the sweetness of her smile would change that, not tonight. He abhorred it when people took liberties with him, he despised over-familiarity, he loathed advances. The situation slipped out of her grasp as he rose to leave.

"I'm not one of Celandina's girls," she said.

Any other man in that garden would probably laugh it off as a joke, but not Amron. He paused, his expression visibly cooling down. "Who are you, then?"

"I am—" *I'm your wife, dammit. I'd burn the world to ashes to get to you, why can't you see it?* "I'm your friend."

He raised his eyebrows as he sat back down beside her, and she could almost see the thoughts rearranging themselves behind his curious gaze. He was young, but he was not naïve. By this age, he'd already been well-versed in both fighting and diplomacy, he'd lived in every corner of the kingdom from the snowy mountains of Virion to the arid plains of Elmar, he was a courtier and a military commander. And if he still hadn't learned to trust his second sight, he was certainly not foolish enough to ignore a broken thread in the pattern of the world.

"Why are you here?" he asked.

She was here to kiss him and whisk him off as soon as possible, out of this place that vibrated with the low rumble of impending doom. But Amron wasn't willing to be whisked off, seduced, kissed in a dark corner until he moaned with desire. No, not him. He wasn't going to be feckless and frivolous, not even for one night at his brother's party, while everyone around him sank into a haze of wine-fueled debauchery.

No, Amron was not going to be coaxed into kissing a strange girl, no matter how much he liked her. And he was not going to accept lies.

"I need to warn you." She paused; she didn't want to sound like one of those crazy prophets on the street corners, foretelling doom. The idea of the catastrophe rolling towards them was vague in her head, she had nothing firm to grasp, no clear details to nail the story down. *Bloody Perun and his tricks.* "Your brother's wedding. Something will go wrong and there'll be bloodshed."

He blinked, weighing her words. "I don't know what to think about you, Liana. You look like a vision, you talk like a mad-woman. Is this some elaborate prank?"

"It's the truth, I swear."

Later in his life, Amron would hone his knack for reading people to a sharp, infallible blade. This Amron, though, was still learning how to wield it. "Why should I trust you?"

Why, indeed? She needed something true, and hidden, and shocking. Something intimate, something whispered in the darkness, his mouth touching her ear, his limbs entwined with hers. "If I tell you a secret, promise me you won't panic."

"Now you're just being dramatic."

She took a deep breath. "You have a crescent-shaped scar on your left thigh. Amril pushed you through a window when you were five, and a shard almost cut your artery and killed you. He claimed it was an accident. You know he did it on purpose, and yet you never told anyone."

Color drained out of his face. "Who are you?" he whispered.

"I am your friend," she said, covering his hand with hers, gentler than a butterfly landing on a blade of grass. "Bad things are coming."

Slowly, slowly—his gaze never leaving her face—he wrapped his fingers around hers into a tight grip. "Come." He rose to his feet, pulling her up. "Whatever you know, the captain of the guard needs to hear it."

To get to the gate, they needed to push through the well-lit crowd gathered around two girls who danced in a manner that left little to imagination. Liana kept her head down, trailing in Amron's wake, holding his hand.

But before they could slip away, a voice from the crowd said, "Where have you been hiding, Amron? People will think you're not happy for me."

Amron froze. Behind him, Liana peered around to see the unwelcome interruption. Amril blocked their path, flanked by a couple of young men. He'd drunk a lot that evening, and yet he stood firm, his eyes glinting with a mischief awfully akin to malice.

"I'm thrilled for you," Amron said. "But now you must excuse me, I have some urgent business at the palace."

"Urgent?" Amril stepped around his brother, his eyes finding Liana hiding in Amron's shadow. "Oh, I see now. You need to pin her down before she comes to her senses."

Amron didn't swallow the bait, didn't mention what Liana had told him. He just said, "We need to go."

Amril ignored him. "What do we have here?" He gripped Liana's arm and pulled her into the light. "Quite exquisite. I don't think I've seen you before."

"Amril, please," Amron said. "I need to talk to her."

"You don't want my brother." Amril's hand slid around Liana's waist. She'd never met him before: By the time Amron had found her, his brother was dead, his memory consecrated by his untimely demise, distilled into an image of a golden prince. The real Amril was as attractive as the story claimed: slightly taller than Amron, bulkier, flamboyant. His demeanor, though, oozed something small and mean, unfit for a prince. "Amron is a cold, dour fish. Come with me."

"Amril, for gods' sake, the garden is filled with girls. Leave this one to me."

"The other girls are boring, I've had them all." Amril caught Liana's chin, turned her face to the light. "But this one is new and fresh and gorgeous, and I choose her." His thumb caressed her lips. "This is my party, after all, and I get to pick first."

"Is there a problem, Your Highness?" Lady Celandina materialized beside them, shooting a cold, hard stare at Liana.

"No, we just had a small misunderstanding," Amril said. "I usually prefer to be more subtle and let certain things occur naturally, but this time I'm going to be perfectly clear. I want your new girl, I want her for myself, I want her for my friends, and I want her until dawn. My brother can watch, if he feels like it."

Lady Celandina bit her lip, obviously torn between her wish to please the prince and her conscience. "Your Highness, the girl is still new. She might not be ready."

"Are you running a whorehouse, Celandina, or a girls' school?"

Everybody in the garden gathered around them to watch the scene. All the while, Liana balled her fists in frustration, nails biting into the soft flesh, reminding herself that pushing Amril away would make everything infinitely worse. She shot a brief glance at Amron, registering the absolute horror on his face.

Amril scanned the crowd, challenge clear in his eyes. He was just waiting for someone to stand up to him. But all the high-and-mighty young bucks avoided his gaze, too cowardly to challenge him, too selfish to defend an insignificant girl.

Lady Celandina tried to disperse the tension. A discreet wink sent her girls to the men surrounding them to draw their attention away, diluting the crowd. She offered a fresh glass to Amril. "I'll prepare the girl if you want me to, but she's so new I haven't had the opportunity to teach her." She shrugged in a mock apology. "Knowing your tastes, Your Highness, you'll find her dull."

"Shut up, Celandina." Amril turned to Amron, the crown prince's smile shockingly ugly on his handsome face. "Amron, you're pale. Are you sure you're all right?"

Amron's voice was so quiet it barely reached Liana's ears. "No, I'm not. I'm angry and humiliated. Well done. Now will you please let her go and get back to your friends and your girls?"

Amril pulled Liana closer. "I'll let her go in the morning. I don't know what you're fussing about. There'll still be plenty left for you to enjoy. Celandina's girls are tougher than they look." He bowed down to kiss her.

Suddenly, it was too much for Liana to bear: the whiff of alcohol, his hard fingers on her back. She pushed him away. He grabbed her shoulder. Then Amron was between them, pulling her back, his fist a blur aimed at his brother's jaw. Amril's head flew back, spit spraying out of his mouth.

Silence dropped on the garden like a lead plate.

Amron grabbed her hand. "Run!" he said.

They ran to the gate just as Amril roared with pain and one of the girls screamed. Amron pulled her out onto the street and through a maze of dark alleys. Her heart beat so hard she thought her chest would explode. The silk slippers Lady Celandina had given her were ill-suited for running on the slippery cobbles.

"Stop!" she pleaded. "Stop!"

They stopped in the shadow of a large building, leaning on the wall, catching their breath. Amron shook his right hand with a painful grimace. His knuckles were bloody. "Ouch."

"Is it broken? May I see it?"

He let her take his hand, wincing as she inspected the bones.

"It's fine, I think. Just bruised a bit." She looked up. "I'm sorry I caused all that trouble for you."

"Don't be. I've been wanting to do that for a long time." He let out a surprised chuckle. "I feel drunk, light as a feather. I should hit my brother more often."

Liana smiled. "I'll make a ruffian out of you if you're not careful."

He laughed in earnest. "I'd let you do whatever you please with me." He paused, shocked by the words that had slipped out of his mouth, and looked down.

She laid her palm on his chest, feeling his heartbeat, his quick breathing.

"Liana," he said. He wet his lips with the tip of his tongue.

She let her body lean towards him until their hips met. He was hot with exertion, rigid with tension.

"Amron." His name rolled off her tongue, sweet like pomegranate syrup. Her fingers touched his cheek, guiding him to her.

Abruptly, he lifted his head, looking behind her, and his expression changed. "We're not alone," he said.

She turned to see half a dozen people materialize out of the shadows. At first she thought Amril's friends had followed them, but then her brain caught up and her stomach dropped. A long-forgotten terror sent a shiver down her spine as she recognized the embossed leather vests, the broad belts, the wide pants gathered at the ankles. The dark scarves wrapped around their heads and over their noses to stave off dust. Seragians. Each one of them brandished a long, curved blade. In Abia, where any weapon longer than a hunting knife was forbidden during the wedding celebrations.

"Get behind me," Amron whispered. He had nothing but a dagger on his hip.

The Seragians moved in a wide semicircle, cutting their route of escape.

"It's the wrong prince," someone said in the language Liana had hoped never to hear again.

Their leader appraised Amron and Liana with dark eyes gleaming under two exquisitely curved eyebrows. "He will do. His whore as well, don't let her get away."

Amron could speak Seragian, she knew. "I'll distract them," he whispered. "You go and get help. There's guards at every corner."

She nodded.

"Help!" he called. "Guards!" He lunged at the nearest man. The Seragian swung his blade, but Amron pivoted, stabbed the man between the ribs, and snatched his weapon.

Wooden shutters opened somewhere above their heads.

"Help!" Liana screamed. "Call the guards!"

Amron was armed now, but he was still facing five attackers closing in. Liana couldn't leave him alone. By the time she returned, he'd be dead.

She didn't know if she could die in this past the gods had sent her to, and she didn't care. She was faster than any mortal, and stronger than most of them; she'd been a huntress all her life. She ran into the melee kicking and biting like a rabid fox. She broke one man's nose, kicked another in the throat. A hand grabbed her hair, pulled her head back. A pair of coal-black eyes met hers, and darkness rushed at Liana, engulfing her in a cloud of miasma. She choked, unable to breathe.

Amron pushed between them, elbowing the leader in the chest. Liana jumped back, filling her lungs with fresh air, and kicked the Seragian approaching Amron from behind. The man swung his yatagan at Liana, forcing her to sidestep and narrowly avoid the blow. On her left, another Seragian lunged at Amron, but he was ready and knocked the attacker off-balance.

"On your right!" Liana screamed as the leader swung at Amron one more time. The Seragian's aura, darker than the shadows in the street, wrapped him like a cloak. His movements were strange, as if he wasn't—

A hard punch landed between Liana's shoulder blades. She fell and rolled on the ground to avoid the yatagan. Two attackers closed in, their movements practiced—these weren't some ragged bandits, but trained soldiers. One was limping, though, favoring the knee Amron had kicked.

Amron was still fighting the leader, locked in a deadly dance. Their blades flashed in the weak light. The Seragian whose nose Liana had broken was leaning on the wall, spitting blood, but the one she'd kicked in the throat was sneaking closer to Amron.

Liana kicked the limping man in the injured knee, sending him down, and grabbed his yatagan. She turned to face the other one, but at that moment, Amron cried out and stumbled. The leader swung at him. Amron parried and pushed him away, barely fast enough, just as the other Seragian rushed at him from behind. Liana roared and threw herself at the man, opening a deep gash across his arm. The man screamed and retreated from her furious attack.

Amron was fighting two men now, the wall at his back, his attackers closing in. Liana's last opponent was nursing his injured arm. The one Liana had snatched the blade from now rose and pulled a dagger, but instead of attacking her, he joined his comrades surrounding Amron. The prince was the main target, Liana was just a nuisance.

"No," Liana cried and ran towards them. She stepped in the dead man's blood, and her useless silk slippers slid on the wet cobbles. As she fell, Amron shouted her name.

They were going to get killed.

Above them, faces peered through the open windows, the good people of Abia always happy to watch a bloody show. Their doors remained firmly shut, though. No help was coming from that quarter.

Liana scrambled up, hands slick with blood, and charged at the leader, ignoring his putrid darkness. The Seragian's eyes were unnaturally bright, filled with murderous frenzy as he turned to face her.

"Stop right there!" someone shouted. A thud of heavy boots on the cobbles.

The Seragian leader risked a glance down the street, at the approaching guards. Calculation flickered in his dark eyes.

Behind him, Amron was still on his feet, doggedly fending off the blows.

"Come on, you coward," Liana challenged the Seragian, raising her blade. But he ignored her, turning away.

"Go!" A growled command in Seragian and their attackers dispersed, fleeing to the side alleys, leaving their fallen comrade on the ground.

In a heartbeat, Amron and Liana were alone again.

"Gods." Amron fell to his knees, catching his breath. His shirt was stained with blood.

Liana dropped her weapon and ran to him. "Are you wounded?"

"No, I don't think so."

The guards caught up with them. A handful ran after the Seragians. The rest moved aside to let a man in a slightly more elaborate uniform pass.

"Your Highness, I didn't expect to find you here. Are you all right?" the man said.

"A bit bruised and quite furious," Amron said. "Thank you for saving my skin, Captain. I was looking for you. This young woman has something to tell you."

The captain's gaze fell on Liana. "Well, I'll be damned," he said.

Melia

There was a time when Melia didn't speak.

She would sit still for hours on end. Her room had been spare: Not even the lord's daughter could expect much luxury in Syr. Whitewashed walls with hangings made by the local women, a bed with a sturdy frame, a carved chest for her clothes, a small desk with her spelling and grammar books, and stories.

At first, the real physicians came to examine her—the old, self-important men in long black gowns, pulling and prodding, staring into the whites of her eyes. One opened her mouth and poked at her tongue with a wooden stick, the other opened her legs and touched her with cold fingers. They conferred in low voices, using expressions Melia couldn't understand.

Her father came as well, sucking the air out of the room. Roderi of Elmar was not a particularly big man, but he somehow always towered above everybody else. "So?" he'd asked the physicians from the doorway, before he spared a single glance for Melia.

"There is nothing physically wrong with her, my lord," one of them said. "She is unharmed and untouched."

"I see." His eyes, so dark they looked black, focused on Melia.

She'd always been in awe of her father. On the rare occasions he entered the women's quarters, she would take cover behind a chair or under a desk, and watch him blaze like molten glass. His intensity left her frightened and confused.

He approached the bed and the physicians retreated, melting away into the shadows.

"They tell me you won't speak," he said.

Melia stared at him. It didn't occur to her to wish for kind words or gentle touch or any kind of comfort, because those were not things her father had ever bothered with. The sparse tenderness in her life had perished with her mother and her nurse.

"There's nothing wrong with you, though," he continued. "You're not injured or in pain, are you?"

Melia stared at him.

"Are you?" he repeated.

She managed to shake her head in response.

Her father's eyes studied her, assessing her scrawny body, her awkward limbs. "Then it's just a question of will, isn't it?"

Melia wanted to tell him he was wrong, but no words came.

"My lord, the child needs time," one physician dared to say.

"Time is a commodity," her father said. "This in no place for the weak and the self-indulgent."

"My lord—"

"Get out."

When the door closed behind the physicians, her father knelt by Melia's bed and lowered his voice. "You're no good to me weird or dumb. We're at war and I lead these men, they look up to me. I can't have weak spots. I can't allow you to be a burden, a living proof that it's easy to hurt me. I need you to pull yourself together. Do you understand?"

Melia nodded.

"Say yes."

Melia tried to obey, but no words came. Her father's eyes, two burning lumps of coal, bored into her mind, singeing her brain. The fog inside her hissed and evaporated, leaving behind the blood-soaked dust, the dead horse with his belly open, its entrails glistening in the dying light, and then the world went black.

Words abandoned her, and so did her father.

The servants had soon enough given up on her as well. The maids would talk openly about her in her presence, as if she were an object, as if she were deaf.

Only Rovin would come to try and talk to her. "Are you alright?" he would ask, his blushing cheeks revealing he was aware how stupid that question was.

And Melia would blink, keeping her silence. What good was talking? There was nothing she wanted to communicate. There was nothing left inside her, she was filled with gray fog, a cloud of miasma that extinguished all life.

It went on for months, the silence, until one day Melia's father walked into her chamber, followed by a young woman dressed in gray and dark green with a mass of black curls spilling from under her kerchief.

"If you can make her act normal, you can stay," he said, "but she hasn't uttered a word in over two years."

The young woman nodded. "My lord, may I examine her in private?"

"You may do whatever you think is necessary. I've wasted enough time on her already."

When the door closed behind her father, Melia expected the woman to act like so many physicians, healers, and charlatans before her. She expected to be examined, prodded, pinched. One eager young man had even burned her palm with candle flame in a desperate attempt to make her produce a sound. Some of those people had tried to be friendly, some pleaded or demanded, some were outright cruel.

The newcomer, though, had no instruments, no bags of any kind with her. "My name is Ferisa," she said. Her face was broad and strong-boned, with eyebrows thick and perfectly arched as if they were two strokes of charcoal. Her hands looked rough, accustomed to hard work, but her clothes were relatively fine. She crossed the room and knelt before Melia, who was sitting in a chair. When their eyes met, the woman—Ferisa—said,

"Hello, little death. I could smell you from the other side of the corridor."

Melia realized the woman wasn't talking to her at all, wasn't staring into her eyes, but behind them.

Then the woman started to hum a tune Melia had never heard before, but which nevertheless felt familiar, reverberating in her bones. Pausing only to take a breath, the woman walked to the fireplace and picked up a burning ember with iron tongs.

Now the pain starts, Melia thought.

But instead of burning her with it, the woman placed the ember in a little censer she produced from her pocket. A faint waft of foul-smelling smoke rose up, entwining with the endless hummed tune.

Melia was curious. This was by far the most interesting method she'd encountered. She wondered if the smoke had some healing property, if it would make her dizzy or nauseous.

It seemed that Ferisa had no interest in Melia. She continued to hum, gently swinging the censer so the cloud of smoke engulfed both of them. It tickled Melia's throat, but apart from that, it did nothing for her. It was a nice show, she thought, but just as useless as the rest.

When the room filled with smoke, the woman laid the censer on the windowsill and knelt before Melia once more.

"Little death, it's time for you to come out."

Something moved inside Melia.

"Little death, come, come, this is no place for you."

Inside Melia's lungs, something crawled, slow and heavy.

"Little death, I welcome you and honor you in the name of our goddess."

The thing in Melia's lungs moved up her windpipe like a giant worm, slimy and cold.

"Come, little death, come." And then the woman came closer and pressed her mouth to Melia's, sucking. The thing moved up through Melia's throat, her mouth, huge and black and cold as the grave. Up and up and up, into the warm cavern of Ferisa's mouth.

Melia gagged and fought for breath as the last dregs of the nightmare slid out of her. The moment the cold was gone, she pushed Ferisa away, disgusted, and jumped out of the chair. "Get away from me," she screamed.

Ferisa swallowed, took a deep breath, and started laughing. "That was quick," she'd said.

~Chapter 11~

Liana

She had to let go of him.

The guards fussed over Amron, his bruises and cuts, and the servants at the palace even more so. In the tumult their arrival caused, he barely managed to catch Liana's eye and mouth a silent "I'll find you" before they led him away.

She was left standing in a torchlit courtyard, surrounded by guards. Not a prisoner, but feeling like it.

"Lock her in the servants' quarters," the captain of the guard barked. "I'll interrogate her later."

Although it was long past midnight, the palace didn't sleep, but the sounds were muted, the lights soft as they climbed up the back stairs, through the narrow corridors, high up to an empty servant's bedchamber under the rafters of the palace, with a slanting ceiling and a single bed in the corner. Some kind soul remembered to feed her, bringing her a fish pie and a jug of water. Liana paced the bare wooden floor for a while in a tight circle, hoping that Amron would come for her, but the night dragged on and he failed to appear. The anxiety that kept her awake retreated before her sheer exhaustion, and sometime around the quietest, darkest hour of the night, she crashed on the bed and slept.

Liana was dozing, propped against the white stag's massive flank, when a rusalka touched her shoulder lightly, and she opened her eyes. The pale face framed by greenish-brown hair was unfamiliar, but the rusalke were like birds, always flocking around her mother—interchangeable, fickle water spirits.

"Come," the rusalka said, "I want to show you something."

Liana patted Snijeg's silken coat. She was waiting for her mother to return, but when Lela wondered off, it could take days—sometimes weeks—before she remembered her half-human offspring.

"Come," the rusalka urged. "It will be fun."

Her mother's retinue had a strange notion of fun. It was mostly hunting and luring hapless animals and humans into clever traps, but sometimes the rusalke would sing, or the leshy would dance, and Liana would watch open-mouthed, awestruck by the beauty no human, or half-human, eye had ever seen and lived to remember.

Liana rose and followed the rusalka through the undergrowth. At six, she was a true forest creature, light and fast, but she didn't possess the rusalka's watery aspect, she couldn't just glide through the branches and leaves, and the speed soon left her breathless.

"Wait," she pleaded.

"Just a little further," the rusalka said. "Come on."

The rusalka lied, as all rusalke did—it was a long way off. By the time they slowed down, Liana was winded, tired, hungry, and too annoyed to pay attention to the faint pop in her ears and a slight change in temperature and light, as if walking from a sunny patch into a shadow on a summer day.

The dirt road lay before them, winding through the trees like a very long slug. The human road. The rusalka stood on it, her tiny, lily-white feet not quite touching it, and urged Liana forward. "Come on."

"No. Mother told me I should never go near the humans."

"Your mother is not here. And I have something amazing to show you." The rusalka smiled her charming smile. "Something you've never seen."

Liana hesitated. Lela had given her a stern set of instructions, but she was too lazy, too disinterested, too absent ever to enforce them.

"Come," the rusalka said. "You'll love it."

Reluctantly, Liana followed her down the road to a tiny village, a handful of cabins on the edge of the forest. To Liana, who slept in the open when it was dry, and inside caverns or massive tree trunks when it rained, it seemed strange that anyone would want to shut themselves inside a small wooden box.

The rusalka led her behind one of the houses and motioned for her to peer around the corner. Holding her breath, Liana looked.

Two girls sat on a dry, sunlit patch of grass. Both were auburn-haired, with faces as round as the moon and tiny rosebud lips, one probably as old as Liana, the other slightly older. Their hair was smooth and clean, free of leaves and branches, tightly braided and tied with red ribbons. They wore proper clothes, dark brown tunics with colorful belts, yellow and green. To Liana, they looked wholesome and pristine like newborn fowl.

Liana had never met any girls her own age and, despite caution and fear, the two little creatures attracted her like sweet honey. They chatted in a language of humans, which Liana understood but rarely used.

Forgetting about the rusalka, about the forest at her back, she made one tiny step towards the girls, quiet and light-footed like a young fox. The girls held something in their hands, two little wooden dolls with woolen hair, dressed in the tiny versions of the girls' tunics. Liana, who'd never had any toys other than twigs and leaves and stones, felt her fingers itch with the desire to hold them.

"Hello," she tried to say, but it came out as a hoarse whisper.

The smaller girl looked up, her eyes widening, and before Liana could clear her throat and try again, the girl let out a shriek so piercing it caused a flock of birds to flee a nearby tree.

Liana flashed a desperate smile, white and sharp on her mud-splattered face.

The bigger girl jumped to her feet, pushing her sister behind her back. "Go away," she said.

Liana sensed the hostility, but these girls were not dangerous, and she just wanted to see them up close, and maybe touch those dolls they held in their hands.

"I'm Liana," she tried again, opening her hands to show she was carrying no weapon.

The bigger girl picked up a stone from the ground and threw it at Liana. She was far too slow and clumsy to hit her, but it hurt nevertheless. The littler girl was still making noise. The bigger one threw another stone, and it made Liana angry. Before the girl could throw a third, Liana rushed at her. The girl was too slow to even realize what was going on—all it took was one push and one yank. The girl landed heavily on her behind, and the doll was in Liana's hands.

"What's all that noise about?" another voice said, a human grown-up voice.

Liana didn't stay to see who it belonged to. She turned and dashed down the dirt road and into the forest. The rusalka was nowhere to be seen, she'd probably slipped away as soon as the trouble began. It didn't matter, Liana knew the forest like the back of her hand.

Or she thought she did. She ran, holding her prize firmly, until the sky began to darken, but she came no nearer to her mother's lair. The trees around her loomed huge and unfamiliar, and for the first time in her life, she shivered with cold. She could hear the forest animals around her, but their chatter was suddenly incomprehensible, a mindless cacophony of chirps and squeaks and howls. She was a stranger in her own forest.

"Rusalka, where are you?" She called the fickle creature. "I don't enjoy this anymore, take me home."

The wind rustled in the leaves, but no water spirit answered the call.

"Snijeg?" She called her companion, the white stag. "It's me, Liana. Come and get me."

Her mother's massive stag never failed to answer her call. She waited for a long time as the air between the trees thickened and the tree roots set traps for her weary legs. Fear crept into her heart. This was the same forest the rusalka had led her out of, any yet it was completely different. She now remembered the strange feeling when she first stepped onto the road, the shift in the light, the chill. If she could only draw aside this curtain of darkness and step back into the warmth, she'd be home. But the forest remained dull and impenetrable, devoid of any enchantment.

In the end, trembling with exhaustion and fear, Liana sat beside a massive oak tree, hugging the wooden doll, tears streaming down her face. "Mother," she whispered, "I'm sorry I disobeyed you. Please help me, I don't know how to get home. Please, Mother."

An owl hooted, and something small and terrified died nearby. A hedgehog stirred in the heap of dry leaves. Far away, a wolf called his companion. But the Goddess of the Hunt had remained silent.

𝕿𝖍𝖊 𝖘𝖔𝖚𝖓𝖉 𝖔𝖋 a key turning in the lock woke her up.

"Amron?" she mumbled, rubbing the cobwebs of sleep out of her eyes.

"No." The captain stepped into the room, in a uniform so crisp and clean it looked ready for a parade. His expression, though, was far from festive. "My name is Darin, I'm the captain of the King's Guard."

Liana uncurled her limbs and rose slowly. The only space where two people might stand upright in the tiny room was beside the door, so she approached him, lifting her head a little to stare at his face. He was only a couple of inches taller than her.

It was uncanny, his face. Weathered by the sun and the wind, with the first wrinkles running across his brow and gathering in the corners of his eyes, but still undoubtedly fetching. High forehead, sharp cheekbones, straight nose, and a generous mouth: It looked like a chiseled bust of a young god, animated by the soft glow of his green eyes and the gentle wave of his chestnut-honey hair.

It was like looking in a mirror—a mirror that distorted her face, aged it, changed its gender, but still reflected it perfectly. Her face, staring back at her.

"Liana," the captain said, his voice raw. "Child."

"Papa," she whispered.

She'd never met him. He'd never returned to Till, never sent for her. She'd been so mad at him; she grew up an orphan, abandoned by her mother, knowing that he was somewhere at court, thriving, ignoring his only child. She'd imagined chasing him down some day and throwing all that fury in his face, demanding an explanation, an apology, some compensation for the lonely, loveless days of her childhood. But then he died and she never got the chance to meet him, and the fury in her heart turned into a wound that could never heal.

That pain threatened to choke her now, as his hesitating arms pulled her into an embrace. There were so many things she wanted to say, a stormy vortex of questions and accusations she wanted to hurl at him. But for now, hearing him say, "My girl, my beautiful girl," was enough.

She refused to cry, though, and so did he. A shared stubborn streak made them separate in an awkward attempt to deny their feelings. He cleared his throat, all formal again; she ran her fingers through her tangled hair.

"What are you doing here? When did you arrive?" he asked.

It was a perfectly reasonable question, but she had no good answer. She supposed there was another Liana, the *real* Liana, tucked away somewhere in Till, unaware of all the uproar about the royal wedding. If her father started asking questions, the other Liana would find herself in trouble, unable to explain why he thought he saw her in Abia.

"I'm not really here," she said at last. "I'm just passing through."

He took a step back. "Did your mother send you?"

"No, I'm here against her wishes."

What was it that she saw on his face? Caution? Fear?

"Are you in trouble?" he asked.

"No, but everybody else will soon be." She gritted her teeth, struggling to say more. Perun had muddled her memories of war, leaving the echoes of its monstrous toll, but erasing the details. "Did you find the Seragians who attacked us?"

"No, not yet." He shook his head. "The city is full of people; they melted into the crowd. The one they left behind had nothing to identify him by. He's in the city morgue, but I doubt anyone will claim him."

"Do you know of any reason why they would attack the prince?" she asked.

"Prince Amron told me they mistook him for his brother at first. If a group of Seragian mercenaries was after the crown prince the day before his wedding to a Seragian princess—" He rubbed his eyes with the heels of his hands, and it was obvious he hadn't slept that night. "The guard controls the whole city, we banned the weapons, we check everyone who comes in, and still they fooled us somehow. I've raised the alarm, the king knows what happened. The Seragian ambassador will be here in the morning."

Would it be enough? When Amron and Liana ran into the night, the trajectory of events changed, the Seragians attacked Amron instead of his brother, and Amril pulled out unscathed. Now every guard in the city was on the lookout for troublemakers. Would it be enough to stop the war?

Stop it? a nasty voice whispered in her head. *If you hadn't arrived, Amron and Amril would have remained at Celandina's the whole night and there would've been no one to attack. How about that?*

"I think you should be as cautious as possible," Liana said, shutting down the voice. "I think the attack will not stop here. There will be blood."

She could almost hear it coming, the red wave, ready to break over the city and leave a trail of bodies behind it.

He narrowed his eyes. "Is there anything specific you might tell me? Anything useful?"

Somebody important will die. Not Amron, no, he survived the bloodbath in Abia, but another royal. His father? His brother? She couldn't remember. "Watch the royal family closely. This is not the last attempt."

His exhaustion hovered on the brink of anger. "That's irritatingly vague, Liana. Give me something I can work with."

She bit her lip so hard she drew blood. "If you fail tomorrow, there will be a war, and it will drag on for years."

He huffed in frustration. "You sound just like them, you know." He motioned towards the sky. "Like one of those veiled, dramatic prophesies that become clear only after the events have played out."

Liana was just as irritated with herself as he was. Why did Perun curse her? She wasn't here to change the course of history, she just wanted to kiss Amron and run away with him.

"I'm sorry, I'm sorry. I'm doing my best to help you." Turning away from him, she walked to the tiny window and looked out, trying to force her brain to give her something useful.

"I know you are," her father said. "But it might not be enough. The prince asked me not to mention your presence, but too many guards saw you, and they gossip like fishwives. By morning, half the city will know Prince Amron was with a strange girl when he was attacked. They'll think you're a spy, and he won't be able to defend you. His position is precarious enough because of the incident with his brother, he doesn't need more trouble."

She shook her head in mute disbelief.

"I can get you out, but you have to go tonight," he continued. "I'll tell the king I interrogated you and found nothing suspicious. Just a simple country girl who was tricked into joining Celandina's establishment and was horrified by the events. I'll send you to Till with a group of merchants. By the time anyone remembers to ask about you in the morning, you'll be miles away from Abia. When you reach home, you'll go back to whatever duties you abandoned to come here, and lay low for a while. I'll take the full responsibility. I can bear it."

It was riskier for him than how he presented it. He must have had enemies at court who would jump at this opportunity to drag him down. After the Seragian attack, his position was even more precarious than Amron's. But he'd mentioned none of that to her.

A wave of warmth rose in her heart: an entirely new and unfamiliar certainty that her father cared for her and wanted to help, even if his plan didn't suit her. "Thank you," she said, "but I can't leave just yet."

"Why not?"

She thought of Amron in that alley, leaning on the wall, catching his breath. Her hips against his, his mouth hovering a hand's breadth above hers. She was so close.

"I need to see Amron again," she said.

He didn't ask why. Instead, he raised his eyebrows and said, "Is that what you call the prince now? Amron?"

A stupid slip. She turned her face away to hide her frustration. "That's none of your business."

"Liana, child, look at me." He stepped around to catch her gaze. "I don't know what's going on, or what you think is going on, but he's a prince of the blood, and he's married. I don't want my daughter—"

"You have no right," she cut him off.

"Excuse me?"

"You have no right to tell me what to do," she said. "You've never been a father to me. I'm sorry I accidentally wandered into your territory and caused you trouble, it was never my intention. But I'm here on my own business, which has nothing to do with you."

He looked as if she'd struck him. "I just want to help you."

Liana knew he was telling the truth. She knew he was trying to do his best in a complicated and possibly dangerous situation. But once she'd opened the old wound, she couldn't prevent it from bleeding.

"Do you?" she asked. "Well, you've had nineteen years to help me, and you did nothing."

"That's not true," he retorted. "My father wrote to me as soon as he found you, I received monthly reports from Till. I never let you out of my sight. And I sent money."

"Did you?" she snarled. "How kind. Did you know my mother banished me when I was six, fed up with those precious few motherly duties she was willing to perform, and barred me from finding her in the forest? A rusalka led me to the first village we came across and just left me there. I was lucky the people who found me were kind, I was lucky my grandfather recognized me. I could have starved, for all she cared. She's never been fit to raise a child. Why did you abandon me?"

The old fury was still there, and it still burned hot.

"I didn't know you existed," he said.

"I don't believe you."

"Do you think your mother shared her plans with me? I was sixteen, dammit, a stupid boy who lost his way in the forest and got waylaid by a goddess. I could hardly understand what was going on, let alone predict she would bear a child. I was shocked, Liana. Your mother is terrifying. I couldn't stay in Till after that, so I ran to Abia and worked my way up the ranks. When my father let me know he found you, I was already so tied up I couldn't leave. I worked from dawn till midnight. I had no wife, no family. I was in no position to raise a child. So I left you in Till, because it was the best thing I could do for you."

Once again, his face was the perfect reflection of hers, pain mirroring pain. It had never occurred to Liana that Lela had hurt him just as much as she'd hurt her, but now it made perfect sense. Humans were little more than pretty pets to her mother. She inflicted pain with a flick of her wrist and walked away without turning back.

"I was a coward, but I was only twenty-one when they found you. I was living alone in a small room not unlike this one.

What would I do with a little girl? And your grandfather did a great job. Look how beautiful and clever you are. I hear Lord Echton holds you in high esteem and the other hunters love you."

Liana turned back to the window, hiding her tear-filled eyes. She would have traded every achievement and every praise in her life for a father who was there for her.

"Look," he said, "if you don't want to stay in Till, come back here when things settle down a bit. I'll help you, you have my word. Just leave now, because I can't protect you."

She wiped her tears with the back of her hand. "I'll leave when my job here is done," she said, catching his worried gaze and holding it. "You're a man of duty. You know how sometimes there's no time for explanations and everything seems illogical, but still you know exactly what you must do? I know what I must do, and you have to let me do it."

"And that thing you have to do, it includes Prince Amron?" he asked with a mild note of disbelief in his voice.

She tried and failed to imagine her father's expression if she told him she'd lived with Amron for thirteen years in this very palace. Such a future would seem impossible from this angle.

"It's not what you think," she said. "You know the prince well, you know what kind of man he is. He hasn't tried to do anything improper, even when he thought I was one of Celandina's girls—which I am definitely not, I hope that's clear."

Her father cleared his throat to hide his embarrassment.

"I just needed a way to approach him, and that was the fastest. I'd almost succeeded in what I needed to do when those Seragians attacked us. Now I need to talk to him one more time."

He was quiet for a little while, studying her.

"I must ask you this, I'm sorry," he said. "This business you have with him, you need to tell me what it is. It's my job to protect him and I need to know if your plans are dangerous. Will he get hurt? Because one attack can be a coincidence, but if something else goes wrong—"

"You don't think I would hurt him, do you?"

"The royal wedding is tonight, Liana. Even one bad coincidence is one too many. If the king has to choose between protecting his sons and believing his captain's daughter, he'll throw you to the wolves."

"The king won't even know I exist, I promise," she said with more confidence than she felt.

"Can you at least wait until the wedding is over?"

"No, it must be now."

He stood before the door, blocking her way out, shaking his head in silence.

"Arrest me for treason if you think I've done something wrong, or let me go," she said. "If you try to keep me locked in here, I swear I'll dig a hole through the wall with my nails."

He shot her a long look, frustration and worry mixing on his face. Then he opened the door and stepped aside. "I'm going to regret this."

She leaned towards him and kissed his cheek. "Thank you, Father."

"Prince Amron's chambers are—"

"I know where they are."

Melia

Melia spent a restless night in her room, dozing off, dreaming of Syr and then waking up to check if Ferisa or Amron had returned, but neither of them showed up. At dawn, a light scratching on the door woke her from a nightmare of bloody blades and bodies hanging by a roadside.

When she opened the door, a little page bowed. "My lady, you told me to wake you at dawn."

"Yes, thank you."

Ferisa's note lay crumpled under her pillow. *Meet me in the cherry orchard at dawn.*

Melia washed her face and, unwilling to call the maids, pulled on a dress she could lace up on her own, braided her hair, grabbed a hooded cloak, and ran into the dim, empty corridor. The sleepy guards leaning on the walls barely noticed her as she rushed past. They must have thought her just another lady returning from nightly adventures.

As she rushed down the stairs, the annoyance at being summoned like a common servant grew in her chest, but she dared not ignore Ferisa, not when she was obviously representing her father. Roderi treated Melia like a clever, well-trained hound: useful and praised as long as it obeyed every command.

The sky above the garden was pale blue, tinted with pink towards the east, and the early morning air had a salty bite to it. Melia passed the orangery, the roses, the exotic trees, and ran on the graveled paths towards the cherry trees tucked in a corner beside a tall wall, their thick green leaves providing a cover from curious eyes. The garden was empty at this early hour, the stone benches freezing cold, the grass covered in dewdrops.

"Where are you?" Melia whispered.

"Here."

A dark shadow stepped out from behind a tree trunk and Melia gasped. Ferisa's eyes were arrowfoil-bright and a bloody gash ran down her left cheek. "What have you done?"

"Oh, you'll hear about it in the morning, don't worry." The corners of Ferisa's mouth twisted in an unpleasant smile. "Your father thought it would be good to stir a bit of trouble before the main event, shaking the smug bastards. A group of Seragian mercenaries attacked Prince Amron last night as he foolishly returned to the palace without his armed escort."

Melia's lungs cramped, refusing to take a breath. Everybody knew the crown prince and his retinue were out last night in Abia, but she was the one who'd confirmed where they were going, she was the one who'd told Ferisa the name of the establishment.

It was all irrelevant at the moment, though. "Is he alive?"

"He's fine," Ferisa said. "He got away."

Melia couldn't recognize this Ferisa. Her companion had been ruthless but clever, a priestess conducting her priestly business behind the scenes. A subtle shadow of death, not this vulgar, garish mercenary. She wanted to ask what had happened after she left Syr, what her father had done to Ferisa, but all she said was, "Why Amron?"

"By chance. We were waiting for the other one."

Melia recognized her father's schemes when she saw them. The falsehood, the thirst for blood, the manipulation—it was all him. Elmar had no power to change this deal, but what if the king believed the Seragians had broken the truce?

The implications of Seragians attacking the crown prince a day before his wedding to the emperor's daughter burst in her mind like blood from a pig bladder. What was she doing here, in this garden, pretending this was just a casual conversation, pretending she could just go back to court and act normal?

It felt so strange, being able to see both sides of the story, and yet being unable to connect them. Like images in a broken mirror. This *is who I am with Amron, and* this *is who my father expects me to be.*

"You should have told me about your plans," Melia said.

"Why? So that you could run to your husband and warn him?" Ferisa retorted. "You forgot to ask who your husband was with."

"I thought you said he was alone."

"No, I said he was without his armed escort." Another smile. "It might be of interest to you that he was snuggling with a girl in a dark alley. A stunningly beautiful girl who screamed like a mad peacock and brought half the guards in Abia upon us."

One of the girls from Amril's party? A whore? That didn't sound like Amron. "I don't care."

"Yes, you do. I know you well, you can't hide your thoughts from me." Ferisa approached her and laid her palm on Melia's cheek. "I don't begrudge you enjoying your husband, little raven. It'll all be over soon anyway."

A sudden urge to punch Ferisa made Melia's hands twitch, but what good would that do? Melia closed her eyes, feeling she'd never woken from her nightmare. "What's next?"

"We wait for your father. The decision is his. But be prepared for violence."

It felt like a game, like some dark fable they whispered to each other. Two desperate women keeping each other warm in the drafty corridors of Syr. A fantasy of revenge devised by two helpless nobodies, whose pain pushed them to dream about setting fire to the kingdom, shaking the great empire. Futile daydreaming, born out of anger. Grand schemes, as empty as her father's halls. And yet.

"Ferisa," Melia said, taking her hand, warm and familiar. Here in Abia she looked as strange to Melia as Melia must have looked to her, but they were still the same people who'd spent so many nights alone in the dark, whispering secrets, holding each other tight. "Amron took me to see the border forts after the wedding."

"So you saw what the Seragians do to us?"

"Yes. No. I talked to the women there." She remembered the dim kitchen, the young woman with her child. "They told me it is not us against the Empire, that the people on both sides of the border are the same—"

"I spent five years on the border, healing people in the villages and forts, helping them pass to the other side," Ferisa cut her off. "And you're trying to explain it to me?"

"They said it was just the soldiers and the brigands. They cared nothing about the king or the emperor—"

Ferisa's hand landed on her shoulder, as if she wanted to shake her. "They're camp followers, bed-warmers, whores. Of course all men look the same to them, as long as they pay them and keep them warm."

"No, that's not—"

"Do you think they understand politics? History? Do you think they understand what honor is, earning their living on their backs and knees?"

"What do you know about honor?" growled Melia.

"Oh, yes, I'm baseborn filth, my lady. You know everything about it, obviously, so tell me, do you think the Seragians did not celebrate when they learned how heavy a blow they'd dealt to Roderi of Elmar? Do you think they didn't toast Rovin's death? Killing their greatest enemy's heir, that must have been a massive achievement. And then seeing his daughter marry into the very family that crawled before them begging for peace? That must have felt like triumph, Melia. They pulled our teeth out one by one. And now they'll come here and watch us helpless and humiliated and congratulate themselves on their cleverness." Her fingers dug into Melia's flesh, but her words hurt more.

"Tell me, when the emperor's daughter steps off her ship today and looks you in the eye and smiles, how will that make you feel?"

Melia tried to blink away the tears, but they spilled from the corners of her eyes, running down her cheeks, where she furiously rubbed them away. "Why are you saying this?" she asked. "I am constantly forced—by you, by my father—to go back and relive my pain."

"What do you mean *relive*? The pain is always here, it never went away."

The sunlight in the garden dimmed and the world slowed down as if it had been submerged in deep water. Shadows rushed to swallow Melia and Ferisa, and when she looked at her companion, Melia saw that she was barely more than a shadow herself. A dark husk; a flaking, hollow shell with nothing but a ball of fury burning inside her chest like a fiery lump of coal. When Melia looked down, she saw that she was the same, a shadow with a blazing heart.

It occurred to her that maybe they were already dead, it was just that their bodies hadn't noticed it yet. They had been infused with so much death that they must have perished a long time ago. Melia never survived her silent sickness, the physicians were wrong, Ferisa was wrong. The body she released from the stupor was just an animated cadaver. And Ferisa, how devout was she to her goddess? How much darkness had she swallowed, how many times had she crossed to the other side, until she became nothing but a burning shadow fueled by vengeance?

Tears now flowed down her cheeks freely and she didn't try to stop them. What were a few salty drops in the dark water that surrounded them?

"There's no going back, no setting things right," Ferisa said. "It's too late for that. All we can do is make them hurt as we hurt. Set this whole evil alliance on fire."

Melia nodded. What choice did she have? It had all been decided a long time ago, when the first man raised his sword in vengeance.

"Your father will be here soon, and then we'll strike." Ferisa cupped her wet face in her hands. "His men are already in their positions, and you—you'll help me deliver the crucial blow. There will be no peace with the Seragians, no wedding, no kneeling before the murderers while our blood still drips from their fingers."

Melia put her hand on the back of Ferisa's neck and pressed her forehead to Ferisa's. They remained like that, in a mute vow, breathing in the same slow rhythm, until the light around them seeped back and the world sped up again.

Dark fog evaporated from Melia's mind and, now certain of her purpose, she saw things with a new clarity.

"The men who were with you last night, has Amron seen their faces? Can he recognize them?" she asked.

"No, they left Abia immediately. They're halfway to Elmar already, and I had my face covered. No one will recognize me."

She was probably right. Few people in Abia knew what Seragians really looked like. All border folk would look the same to them. Dark skin, funny accents, strange clothes seen only on woodcuts depicting border clashes.

"No one will recognize you," Melia echoed. "I wish we could just go away, you and I. Jump over this wall right now and disappear, leave Abia, leave the kingdom. There's so much of the world outside where no one would know or care who we are."

"You'd never leave your father," Ferisa said.

"I would. For you."

Ferisa's eyes were two windows into burning darkness. She nodded. "Two more days. And then it'll be over."

The queen was an early riser, and by the time Melia had made herself presentable and rushed to the royal chambers, the ladies had already gathered, whispering furiously. The queen was dressed in somber sea green silk, her hair braided and covered with a white veil as fine as a spider's web. Melia couldn't decide if she looked paler than usual—her complexion was always pearl white and translucent—but this morning, her eyes were red.

They were gathered in the garden chamber, surrounded by fantastic tapestries depicting plants and flowers with imaginary beasts stalking among them. It was a room for receiving guests, for showing off.

"Your Majesty, the Seragian ambassadress is here," a maid said.

"How dare they show their face at court?" Lenka muttered in the background.

"I hope they're here to apologize," another lady added.

"Shush!" The queen glared at the ladies. "Sit down and pretend to do something useful. I don't want to hear a single sigh from any of you, let alone a comment."

The ladies plopped down on their cushions as one and picked up their books, their sewing and embroidery. Melia kept her fingers busy with a misshapen bit of lace she was unsuccessfully trying to make, but her eyes wandered to the door.

She'd never seen a highborn Seragian before, and although she knew it couldn't be true, her brain still expected to see a slightly upgraded version of the border tribeswomen: dark skin, head wrapped in a scarf, loose woolen coat, baggy trousers.

"Ambassadress Dorosia of Seragia," a servant announced.

The woman who entered was tall, almost a head taller than the queen, and twice as wide, draped in mahogany brocade in a fashion Melia had never seen before. The high-collared jacket with puffed sleeves was cinched at the waist, and the stiff, ankle-length skirt was split in the middle, revealing baggy silk trousers gathered in at the ankle and gold-embossed leather shoes. The woman's face, round and smooth, with a complexion lighter than Melia's, put her age anywhere between thirty and fifty, and her henna-red hair, falling in a long braid down her back, showed no grays.

"Your Majesty." The ambassadress knelt before the queen.

"Ambassadress Dorosia." The queen, sitting in an ivory-inlaid chair, motioned at a cushioned bench before her. "Please sit down."

A lady rushed in and set down a steaming teapot with two painted porcelain cups and a silver tray filled with assorted sweets on a low table between them like a peace offering.

"How is Prince Amron?" The ambassadress's voice was filled with concern, her Amrian perfect.

"Bruised but not injured, thanks to the king's guard." Clipped, cold. "They're looking for the culprits, but their search would be more efficient if you helped us."

"Your Majesty, the embassy's resources are at your disposal." The ambassadress emphasized her words with a light bow. "However, we have no idea who they might be. Since we heard of the attack, my staff has been tirelessly going through the records of every Seragian subject in Abia. They found nothing suspicious. Just merchants and diplomats preparing for the wedding, all vetted by the ministry. Could it be possible that they weren't actually Seragian?"

"A very convenient theory for you," the queen said, pouring the tea, "but no. Their clothes were genuine and so was their language. My son spent six months at the border, he speaks Seragian and knows the local people. These were frontiersmen, Ambassadress."

"Indeed. But were they *our* frontiersmen?"

Melia's heart missed a beat and the queen's cup paused halfway to her mouth.

"You're not suggesting that Elmarrans would dress as Seragians and attack their own prince?" The queen's tone was incredulous, but the very fact that she said it out loud made Melia focus on her handiwork, hiding her face from the queen. "Shall we ask Roderi of Elmar what he thinks about that?"

Queen Orsiana was close, so close.

How had her father persuaded the men to pose as Seragians? Had Ferisa forced them somehow? Drugged them?

"It is in your interest to find them as much as it is in ours," the queen continued. "Our guards did their duty, now it's your turn."

"I am highly motivated to deal with that before the emperor finds out, Your Majesty," the ambassadress said. "But in the meantime, I'm baffled by the party the crown prince organized in that house of ill repute, putting himself and his guests at risk."

The queen gently lowered her cup to the table. "I don't think I have to explain pleasure houses to a Seragian, do I?"

"Not at all. But the prince's behavior seems reckless, impulsive, self-indulgent to the point of endangering others. It's not the first time, either. We are worried about Carevna Aratea's wellbeing."

Melia was close enough to see the queen's lips turn white. "A group of Seragians tried to kill my son last night, and you're worried about the wellbeing of your carevna? I expected a defter spin from you, Ambassadress."

"There's no spin, Your Majesty. The incident with Prince Amron was a vile treachery, and if the culprits are Seragian, they will be executed promptly. I admitted my doubts about them to you, but in public, I will take the blame and apologize, if that's what it takes to appease the king and the city. But I want you to promise me that the incident won't affect the crown prince's behavior to his future wife. The carevna is blameless, and arrives in good faith, hoping to end three centuries of conflict. I need assurance that she will be received as such."

Melia's gaze focused on a fine thread in her lap until she could see every fiber. From the corner of her vision, a red pool of blood spread towards the center and the stench of iron and gore filled her nostrils.

"You have my word that your carevna will be welcomed with friendship and respect," the queen said. "I will treat her as my own daughter, and the crown prince, I assure you, knows his duty. We've worked too hard for this treaty to let one random incident destroy it."

"I agree, Your Majesty. Every Seragian in Abia knows this wedding is of the utmost importance."

The queen's features softened a little. "Let's have some tea, then, and agree no lasting damage has been done."

Melia's hands trembled so hard that needle slid under her fingernail and blood ruined the lace in her lap.

Ferisa was a nobody, that much was clear, even to Melia who barely knew anything about the world. She never talked about her family or home, and only gods knew what wind had blown her towards the border forts and into the path of Roderi of Elmar.

She had a reputation as an herbalist; the soldiers sought her out when they needed arrowfoil for alertness or poppy to ease the pain. She was also a guide, a priestess of the Goddess of Death who eased the passage to the other side. She fit right in among the soldiers who worshiped death.

After she'd given Melia back her voice, Melia was afraid her father would drive Ferisa away as he'd driven away all women from her late mother's retinue. But Ferisa had carved a place for herself deep in the bowels of Syr, where she boiled her herbs and distilled her potions and soon it seemed she'd been there forever. Melia followed her around like an infatuated pup. It wasn't just that Ferisa was a little older, it was that she acted with the utmost confidence of a grown-up.

"Who taught you all this?" Melia asked.

"Oh, I picked it up here and there."

"How did you manage to give me back my voice?" Melia asked.

"It never went anywhere, little raven. It was inside you."

That might have been true. There were so many things buried inside Melia—she felt like a graveyard. Ferisa had simply pushed a hook into the wet earth and fished out a silver string of her voice, leaving everything else inside, rotting in the dark.

Melia learned to talk again to please her father, but rarely did so. Her voice had grown raspy, unmodulated, and using it to break the silence felt like sacrilege. She made herself invisible. She ate as little as possible, she moved without making a sound, she never demanded attention. She perfected her shadowy existence so flawlessly that even her father forgot about her sometimes and left her alone. If he ran into her by mistake, his eyes would widen in surprise, as if he'd forgotten he had a daughter.

When Melia became a woman, it was Ferisa who taught her how to fold the linen rags, who massaged her back and gave her chamomile and fennel tea to ease the cramps. When men started noticing Melia, it was Ferisa who explained what they wanted from her and how to dodge them. Ferisa was a friend, a cousin, an older sister to her, and if Melia's feelings towards her weren't entirely sisterly, she was too confused to explore them.

Then Rovin died and everything changed.

The winter Melia turned nineteen, they brought Rovin home from some insignificant skirmish within sight of the very walls of Syr. Her brother, the heir to Elmar, the apple of her father's eye.

She ran into the courtyard when she heard the commotion. The gray afternoon sky hung low over the rooftops, sucking out the light. The servants were shouting for torches, a page was sent to fetch the physician. "Lord Rovin is hurt, we need help immediately," they cried.

Melia, the only woman in the crowd, pushed towards the cart with two frothing horses still harnessed to it.

"Let me pass," she demanded, but the men paid little attention to her. She elbowed through the pack and jumped on the back of the cart. Cousin Maren knelt there, pressing down a dirty bundle of cloth.

"Don't look," Maren said, but she couldn't take her eyes off her brother.

She'd never been close to Rovin because men and women rarely spent time together in Syr, and Rovin was mostly on the border, fighting. Still, he was her only remaining sibling, after their two brothers died in the crib. The shared experience of the spare, strict childhood spent in Syr bound Melia and Rovin forever with the fierce loyalty of survivors. There was no other person in the world who knew what it meant to be their father's child.

Forcing her eyes away from the wound, she pushed his dark hair off his sweaty forehead. He breathed through his mouth in quick, shallow gulps.

"Rovin," she said, praying that the horror she felt didn't show on her face, "you're home now."

His arm, cold and clammy, caught hers. "Mother," he whispered. "Mother, it hurts."

She blinked, unable to say anything.

"Move." Maren grabbed her shoulder and pushed her away. "We need to carry him inside."

She turned and her father was behind her. His face reflected every last morsel of fear and desperation Melia felt. "Bring him in," he barked. "Move, damn you!"

She ran through the corridors behind them, gathering women with hot water and clean bandages. A whole procession of people led by a black-clad physician, like a harbinger of doom.

The arrow had pierced his gut. If Rovin were on the battlefield, one of his comrades would give him a quick, merciful death with a sharp dagger, and his agony would be over in the blink of an eye. But here in the chambers of the lord's son and heir, high above the dusty plains, nobody dared mention mercy, even though they all knew the outcome. All but Roderi of Elmar, apparently, who paced the room like a madman, his eyes burning, his hands twitching with the desire to tear apart the first person who brought him the bad news.

As a consequence, they all cowardly feigned to fight for Rovin's life, pretending not to hear his desperate cries, his pleas for them to stop. They pulled the arrow out and tried to close the wound that kept opening again, bleeding and festering; they poured bitter concoctions down his throat, which did nothing to alleviate his suffering.

Melia watched them from the corner of the room as they gathered around the table where they'd laid him. With their scarlet hands and blood-spattered clothes, they looked like peasants butchering a pig. Maren held him down while he screamed in agony.

"Stop it, please," Melia muttered softly like a litany, "oh, please, please, stop it, please," but they all ignored her because her father was watching them with murder in his eyes. She wrought her hands in rage and impotence, telling herself after every scream that escaped Rovin's lips: She must do something to stop this torture.

There were men crowded in that room, far more powerful than her: venerable physicians, military commanders, her father's trusted advisors. And yet, throughout that endless, terrible night, they all kept their silence and averted their eyes as her brother thrashed and cried.

In the end, Melia had done what her father refused to do—begged Ferisa for help. "Pray to your goddess," she pleaded, hanging on to the herbalist like a drowning woman. "Make it stop."

And Ferisa made it stop.

A few drops on Rovin's lips before dawn. As the wind howled outside, the shadows moved around Melia and a cold breath touched her neck, the smell of marsh plants filling her nose. Shadows slid through the room and people instinctively moved out of the way. Their voices wavered and were cut off like candle flames in the wind. Time slowed down, and all Melia could hear was Rovin's ragged breathing getting fainter.

Rovin's dark, tortured eyes found Melia's face. "Mother," he whispered. And then he turned his head to the other side. "And you."

A shadow fell across them, cold and dark. From the corner of her eye, Melia could see a creature standing beside her brother, but she dared not look up. Rovin breathed in and let out a soft, gurgling sound. She squeezed his hand and bowed down to kiss his clammy cheek, and then her brother was gone.

The room around her exploded in light and noise, but she refused to let go of his hand while people crammed around her, bringing in torches, raising their oil lamps to see what was going on, trying to push her away. "Do something," her father shouted. "Do something!"

But there was nothing to do, not anymore, and eventually, they all picked up their bandages and bottles, their scalpels and bowls, and scurried away until it was just Melia, and her father, and Rovin's butchered remains between them.

When the first rays of the winter sun crept in through the window, Roderi of Elmar lifted his head and looked at his daughter with cold, dead eyes.

"My last heir," he said.

When Ferisa found her later that day, Melia was huddled like a heap of dirty clothes in the corner of her room, her hands still covered in Rovin's blood.

"You will avenge him," she said, taking Melia's hand.

"Is that what my father wants?"

Ferisa nodded.

Melia didn't know what to say. She only wanted the pain to go away, and she didn't know how to achieve that.

She lifted her eyes above Ferisa's head, to the golden pattern the sunlight had drawn on the whitewashed wall of her room. There was warmth somewhere, and life, far from this endless cycle of death. There were people unburdened by grief and revenge, people who could still feel happiness and joy and hope.

"What if I want something else?" Melia asked, squeezing her callused hand.

"What do you mean?"

She looked at Ferisa's tear-streaked face. "What if I don't want revenge? What if I want to forget about it and get out of here?"

"And go where?" She frowned. "Some soft town in the belly of the kingdom where people know nothing about duty and honor?"

The doors of possibility slammed shut. "No," she said. "Of course not."

"I will help you avenge Rovin. I will go with you all the way," Ferisa said and wrapped her hard, wiry arms around Melia.

It was the only solace anyone had offered her that day, and she took it. She let Ferisa brush her tears away. It was better than thinking about loss and revenge. When Ferisa pulled away from her, Melia framed her face with both hands, feeling a desperate need to kiss her dark eyes, to press her lips to Ferisa's, to taste the bitter arrowfoil on her tongue.

Ferisa stroked her face. "Not now, little raven, you hurt too much. But I promise I will always be by your side."

Melia lay in her arms that night, her face salty from the tears she'd spilled. Ferisa's body was a real, tangible thing in the world of shadows, pulling Melia back into her skin, anchoring her to the moment. Death retreated for a little while, and sorrow hid in the shadows. For one brief, sleepless night, Melia had felt alive.

Liana

It was dawn when Liana left the tiny attic room and went in search of Amron. She headed straight for his chambers on the second floor; she felt a puff of chilly air touch her neck in the warm corridor, and the shadows deepened as if someone had extinguished half the oil lamps. Shivers running down her spine, Liana dashed into a dark alcove and held her breath, waiting to see the cause of the sudden darkness.

A moment later, a young woman turned the corner, her footsteps soft and quick, and walked by Liana, oblivious to her presence. The woman was wrapped in shadows as thickly as the long-forgotten objects in the attic were wrapped in cobwebs. It took several long, shocked moments for Liana to recognize Melia. The icy touch on her neck crawled under her skin and chilled her blood until her heart slowed to a sluggish lurch.

She had seen people touched by Morana's shadow, but never so clearly. Old and sick people nearing the end, a day or two removed from their death. Or sometimes during the war, a blood-curdling shadow foretelling doom. She'd always averted her eyes and kept her mouth shut, for it was a haphazard, unreliable omen, and there was nothing useful she could say or do about it. It had usually been nothing but a short breath of ice, a sudden shift of the light, nothing she could point her finger at.

Melia was different, though. As Liana quietly followed her, the shadows wrapping around her looked gauzy and tangible like a fine cloak woven from darkness. When they reached the open courtyard, Liana slowed down, reluctant to be spotted. Only when Melia turned a corner and no one else appeared did Liana follow her wintry trail. It led her to the main garden, the one situated behind the palace and surrounded by a high wall.

She stopped by the potted oranges and lemons and peered at Melia, who moved fast through the lush greenery. It was easy to disappear among the tall shrubs and winding paths of the garden, so Liana rushed after her until she reached a small cherry orchard in the shadow of the wall. A dark figure stepped from behind a tree when Melia called, and for a heartbeat Liana believed it was a trick, some new spell the gods had put on, for Melia's companion wore the same cloak of shadows as her.

Liana wished she had been taught about divine spells and curses. But she'd been too little when her mother still cared about her, and afterwards, there was no one to teach her.

With so much darkness upon them, they should have been dead, but this was obviously not Morana's goal. No, they both seemed young and healthy and strong. Beneath the shadows, Melia's companion was a striking dark-haired woman. She stood still while Melia paced on the grass.

Liana drew closer, silencing her breathing, becoming invisible as if she were hunting deer in the forest.

"Your father thought it would be good to stir a bit of trouble before the main event," the woman told Melia. "A group of Seragian mercenaries attacked Prince Amron last night."

Something about her voice and the way she held her head rang a bell. Liana had seen her before.

"Is he alive?" Melia asked.

The woman raised one exquisite dark eyebrow and Liana barely managed to swallow a gasp when the realization struck her. It was one of the Seragian attackers, the leader.

What was a Seragian mercenary doing in the Elmarran quarters?

She's not Seragian, you fool.

Liana sank into the tall grass, nauseous. Melia was a traitor. Seragians had nothing to do with the skirmish last night.

The few facts Liana knew about Amron's wife made her think Melia had changed sides after the war started. No matter how hard she searched her memory, she couldn't remember anything that told her Melia had betrayed the royal family before the wedding. And yet, the proof was right in front of her now.

"He was snuggling with a girl in a dark alley. A stunningly beautiful girl," the woman told Melia, and Liana shut her eyes, cursing in silence. She didn't want Melia's focus on Amron, she didn't want her murderous companion following him around.

She had to warn Amron that his wife was a traitor.

"It'll all be over soon anyway," the dark woman said.

Liana had no idea what the Elmarrans planned to do. She hoped Melia would discuss it with her companion, whose name—Liana discovered—was Ferisa, but the women talked about the border skirmishes and politics instead, about the death of Melia's brother and their hatred for the Empire. Listening to them, Liana almost understood the urge to stop the wedding, their rage at the idea that a couple of signatures on a piece of parchment could erase centuries of fighting. What they didn't see—and what Liana couldn't tell them—was that the bloodshed they planned to cause would be far worse than anything they'd seen in the border skirmishes.

Or perhaps they did understand that. As they embraced in the blooming garden, they were little more than shadows, relics of the night, emanating the foul stench of death. Dread rushed through Liana's veins, cold and caustic. This was bigger than her goals, bigger than her desires. This was a game set by the gods, and she stumbled right into the middle of it.

The last time Liana had seen Amron before his death, the last night he'd spent in Abia before leaving to do the king's dirty work, he and Liana quarreled.

It was late, and they were in his room, with its soft carpets and blue tapestries and windows overlooking the sea. It should have been calming, but Liana was not calm, pacing around like a caged lynx. Amron had sent Telani away and was packing the last things—paper, ink, quills—doing his best to ignore Liana's angry sighs.

"I don't understand why you have to go," she said. "If Vairn wants to rebel against the king, then the king should be the one talking to him, negotiating, or fighting, or whatever it takes to solve it."

"For the last time, I'm doing it as a favor, not because he commanded me to." Amron knelt on the carpet, tying a stack of paper with a blue ribbon and shoving it into a saddlebag. "Vairn is an old war comrade. He'll tell me what he won't tell the king. There still might be a peaceful solution."

"You're not the only man who fought alongside that mangy old dog, you're not the only man who knows how to negotiate. You're not entirely irreplaceable to the king. But you're entirely irreplaceable to me."

She was irrational, she had abandonment issues, she knew it. Amron had never given her a reason not to trust him— and she did trust him—but she didn't trust the world. She didn't trust the gods not to play their depraved games and hurt him and take him away from her.

"Liana." He shot her a look of tired tenderness. "He's my nephew and he needs my help."

Family had always been a raw spot for him. To Liana, abandoned by both her parents, his loyalty to the people who shared his blood but didn't always treat him well seemed like madness. Her circle of people was a single dot: Amron. His circle of people comprised half the kingdom.

"You help him all the time. You won the war for him, you

put him on the throne, and it's still not enough. The fighting never stops."

"That's not true, and even if it were, what do you expect me to do? Abandon him? Pretend the problems of the kingdom are none of my business?"

Liana hated the kingdom; she'd gladly see it burn to ashes and crumble into the sea. The kingdom had no decency, no reason, no limits. It was a blind voracious mass that swallowed people and spat out their bones.

They ran in circles, Amron and Liana, fighting about the same things time and again. She had no words to tell him that she was terrified of letting him out of her sight, that out there he was alone under the vast, malevolent sky.

"I'll try to deal with it quickly." He closed the bag and got up. "I'll be back before the autumn rains. Or you can go to Myrit and meet me there."

She hated Myrit, she hated the court. It was filed with people she despised: the bootlickers, the climbers, the back-stabbers. She could never get used to the falsehood of that world, she couldn't understand its rules.

"I'll try," she said, blinking quickly. Tears had treacherously welled up in her eyes, and now they broke the barrier of her lashes and slid down her cheeks.

"Oh Liana, my love, don't."

He approached her: It was a trick, because he knew well she had never been immune to him, and all her resentment would melt at the first touch. Still, she sank willingly into his arms, into the familiar armor of his embrace. The passing of time narrowed to his heartbeat.

"We should go to bed," he said. "I must rise before dawn."

"If you think I'll let you sleep tonight, you're mistaken." She slid her hands under his shirt, the hot skin of his back smooth under her fingers. That part was simple, even when everything else was complicated. Her desire for him had always been raw and immediate, unchanged by time. It was a fluke, a lucky match that smoothed out the rough patches and gilded the good ones.

He carried her to bed, where she guilted him into doing the most wonderful things to her.

Later, after they'd burned away the better part of the night, he said, "Forgive me before I go, even if you think me a fool."

"I'll forgive you if you promise me to come back," she said.

He ran his fingers down her arm, leaving a trail of goose-bumps. "I'll deal with whatever waits for me up north and come back to you."

And Liana had known it was the truth. No matter how much she'd hated it, he was good at what he did. He was a fixer and a solver, and he always knew what to do.

But now, Liana didn't know what to do.

She hadn't seen herself as a particularly stupid person, but kneeling in a shadowy doorway in an alley, trembling with dread, she cursed herself for being a blind idiot. She'd followed the woman out of the palace, and even though Melia's companion tried to be careful, Liana knew Abia too well to be confused by her meandering. She also knew the house the woman eventually entered: It belonged to Roderi of Elmar. The treachery ran deep, all the way to the Defender of the South, the Scourge of Seragia, the border hero. Melia's father.

Liana remembered that the Elmarrans had changed sides and turned against the kingdom, but her meager recollection of the events in Abia didn't include them stirring the conflict. The conversation she'd heard in the garden, the proof that the woman was indeed from Elmar, sent by their lord, changed everything she thought she knew. Elmarrans were responsible for the slaughter in Abia.

The bloody tide of war was rushing towards the festive, careless city, and Liana had nothing but her two hands to stop it. She was out of her depth.

There was a pattern to it, though. Amron had always been the one who planned ahead, perennially worrying about outcomes. He would've seen the trouble looming in the past, he would've understood the futile enormity of her task. He would have warned her.

But of course, he did warn her. *Don't fight the gods*, he'd written. And yet, she had to go and do the exact opposite, because that was what she'd always been doing. Rushing into things without thinking, stirring trouble wherever she went.

All she had been able to think about was getting Amron back. It had never occurred to her that there might be other people around him. People whose destinies she knew, people who would die horrible deaths in the pointless, disastrous war that was brewing right now, before her very eyes.

Telani had accused her of not caring about other people, but that wasn't true anymore, not since her father walked into that little attic room. The pain and yearning she'd felt, the worry she'd seen in his eyes, changed everything. She wanted more time with her father.

If Abia rose against the Seragians, Darin would die. That much she remembered.

No, he would die in any case, because that was how the events in Abia had played out. It was a done thing, it was history.

Except, it wasn't. It was happening now, all around her. She and Amron had changed something already, running away from Amril's party, fighting the Seragians. And now she knew those weren't really Seragians, but Elmarrans. The black heart of treason beat inside the palace. Surely, that meant something?

It occurred to Liana this might not be an already completed fragment of time into which Perun had inserted her, otherwise it would have looked like an illusion, and she wouldn't be able to alter the smallest thing. She would be nothing but a ghost, a powerless spectator of past events. The fact that she had any power here told her this was the present, real and volatile and malleable.

There could never be two presents. The gods couldn't create parallel timelines. They could stretch time or condense it, they could move through it in both directions, but they couldn't multiply it. There was only one timeline.

Which meant all bets were off.

Liana doubled over on her knees, biting into the soft fabric of her sleeve, into the hard flesh of her forearm, to muffle her terrified moan.

There was no other Liana, hunting in the forests of Till, safe and unaware of the events in Abia. There was no victory waiting for her, no hard-won war for Amron in the end, no throne for the heirs of Amris. There was no future life together for Amron and Liana because *there was no set future.*

She howled into her arm like a wounded hound.

Perun had sent her back, and there were no guarantees, no fixed points in the future that were still true. It was all happening here and now, it was all decided at this crucial point, this unfortunate wedding that would change the history of the kingdom. All possibilities were still crammed together, like seeds in a bag.

Her moan shattered into desperate laughter.

It was a trap, Perun had set her up. She had been a naïve fool to believe this was about Amron and her. No, the gods liked to play for high stakes. Thousands of innocent lives, destinies of kingdoms and empires. Nothing was more exciting than a good war: bloody, long, and unpredictable.

There was no such thing as simply getting Amron to kiss her. Removing him from Abia now would mean there'd be no one left to win the war. And the future they'd go to, live through, would be a future of defeat and loss.

Perun could not have done this alone, they must have all agreed on it, the gods, including her mother. Including Morana.

Liana could see the vortex of death before her, starting here at this wedding and ending with half the kingdom burnt to ashes, the imperial army marching across it. People dying or fleeing north, back to the mountains and forests Amris had led them out of, but ill-prepared now, used to soft lives, still hoping that the shattered kingdom could protect them.

She remembered the battlefields. The Siege of Myrit, the city starved to the bones, its lord captured and executed beneath its walls, his wife watching from the battlements. The desperate attack that followed, Amron's forces outnumbered, the knights that Prince Nykodios sent after him, who would've killed him were it not for Liana's arrows. And then the Battle of Syr, the battlefield so horrific that even Liana, hardened from years of fighting, sobbed. Where Amron died and came back, carrying Morana's curse that would destroy him. The victory that cost everything.

Her body was a tight ball of dread on the cold stone, chest bent over her knees, forehead touching the flags, arms crossed over her head.

A light-footed person strolled down the alley, walked by the doorway, paused, and walked back to her.

"Are you all right?" a female voice said.

"No."

"Can you get up? Come, I'll help you."

Liana moved her head a little and saw a pair of leather sandals and a blue linen skirt with a frayed hem. She lowered her hands to the doorstep, pushed herself up. The girl set aside the jug she was carrying and knelt beside Liana.

"Are you hurt? Or sick?" the girl asked.

"I'm terrified," Liana admitted.

"Of what?"

The girl was no older than fifteen, with a plain, well-scrubbed face and dark hair hidden beneath a white cap. She was the smallest of the small fish in this game. If the war broke out and Abia fell, she and thousands like her would die in the streets.

"If you knew for sure something terrible was going to happen, what would you do?" Liana asked.

The girl shot her a long look, taking in Liana's messy hair, her creased dress, her red-rimmed eyes. "I'd try to stop it, I guess," she said at last.

Liana took a deep breath, forcing her lungs to fill with air and her brain to think again. "Thank you," she said. "I'll be fine, don't worry about me."

Throwing Liana one last worried glance over her shoulder, the girl picked up the jug and disappeared. Liana got up, leaning on the wall.

If there was no set future, then everything was still possible. If this was a game played by the gods, if there were stakes, then there had to be different outcomes on the table as well. The one where the kingdom slid into a horrible war. And the one where it didn't.

~Chapter 14~

Melia

The bells outside called the ninth hour of the morning, and Melia rushed back to her chambers to get ready for the ceremonies. But when she reached her corner of the palace, it was crowded with men in Elmarran liveries and she had to push through them to get to her door. Anxiety filled her like icy water and she instinctively tucked disobedient locks behind her ear and smoothed down her dress.

She stepped into her small chamber and closed the door, shutting off the noise outside. A slim figure dressed in black stood beside the window, and in comparison with that solemn, sinister shadow, every bit of finery in Melia's room suddenly looked garish and tasteless, like an offensive attempt to flaunt wealth.

"Melia," her father greeted her, turning away from the window.

"Father." She bowed, remembering too late that she out-ranked him now and he should be bowing to her. He showed no intention to correct her; he simply nodded in return.

He looked older than she remembered, and smaller, in this court filled with tall men. But his physical size never limited the size of his temper, which seemed to fill the room.

"How was your journey?" Melia made an attempt at small talk, her voice cracking.

"Long," Roderi of Elmar said.

"Would you like me to send for refreshments or—"

"No."

One quiet word and she shut her mouth. It didn't matter that she was a prince's wife, it didn't matter they were not in Syr anymore. Her father still had absolute power over her.

"My men are spread all over town, well-hidden and waiting for orders. I insisted on bringing my guard here—some are at the palace, some wait outside Abia. We have over three hundred soldiers."

Melia closed her eyes. She had hoped—no, she had merely tried to force herself to believe—that her father would somehow change his mind. It was not because she liked the court or the people in it; it was simply that she couldn't imagine how any of her father's plans could make life better for anyone. Being around the people here in Abia, normal people, not traumatized by the endless war, taught her that perhaps the most any of them could hope for was a life untouched by the great schemes of vengeful lords.

It was not to be, though, because Roderi of Elmar had arrived in Abia with only one thought on his mind, and it burned in his eyes like black fire as he looked at his daughter.

"Tonight," he said, "we'll end this charade of friendship and goodwill, this humiliation of every Elmarran slaughtered by their blades."

She nodded, looking around the room, wondering how many people were crowded inside the palace, how many ears, how many eyes. Was she being spied upon? Was there a maid, a little page boy tucked behind the tapestries and paneling, listening to her father spew his murderous plans?

Following her eyes, he scoffed. "Don't worry about that, my men surround your chambers like a wall."

The hope she didn't know she'd harbored flickered out and died.

"What…what is going to happen tonight?" she asked.

Her father ignored her question. Instead, he said, "You have one crucial task, and I need you to do it at any cost."

She nodded, terrified that her father would ask her to do something impossible and lethal. But then he produced a tiny velvet satchel and pulled a glass vial out. It was no bigger than her little finger, stoppered with cork and wax.

"Tonight at the wedding feast, no later than the ninth hour of the evening, I need you to pour this into Prince Amril's drink."

"Is it poison?" she asked, without a speck of guilt. She had disliked Amril intensely from the first moment they met.

"No," her father sniggered. "I expect him to drink a lot, as usual. This is just something Ferisa mixed to enhance his intoxication. He will make a fool of himself and embarrass his bride. If someone caught you with this, you could claim you suffer from insomnia and it helps you sleep."

She took the vial and the satchel. It felt like a strangely small task, after all the energy her father had invested in this plot. Putting one loathsome drunkard to sleep—she could do it with an easy heart and clear conscience. But still, she dared to ask, "Is that all?"

"No," her father said. "But don't worry about it. When the ceremonial part ends and the feasting begins, Ferisa will find you."

This sudden closeness, this unpredictable camaraderie between her father and Ferisa, surprised Melia. They used to avoid each other when Melia was still in Syr. Something had changed between them.

Melia searched her father's face, trying to discern his plans. But instead of fury and violence, she found something very different: A faint sheen of devotion illuminated his brow, a wistful, profound expression too close to hope for her liking. Was it Ferisa and her goddess, or was he simply looking forward to his plans coming to fruition?

Melia found his elation more frightening than his dark fury.

"Ferisa knows all your plans?" she dared to ask, keeping her voice carefully neutral.

"Oh yes, she helped me make them while your husband dragged you around the kingdom."

Her father never trusted women, never confided in them. Melia had supposed that Ferisa was just a messenger, but after the attack the previous night, it was clear she was much more. Yet, she had never mentioned it, never warned Melia.

"What is the plan, after tonight?" she asked.

Her father's gaze burned her as if she were a child who had spoken out of turn.

"I thought...I could help if I knew more," she stammered.

"It's too complicated for you, Melia," he said, the corners of his lips twisting into a smile that looked like a threat. "I don't want you to know unnecessary details, as they would only put you in danger."

It might have been caution, but it sounded condescending. She was not some stupid little maid who would blurt out everything to the wrong pair of ears. She'd kept her mouth shut for months, revealing nothing. She deserved trust and respect. But she'd never gather the courage to tell her father that.

"What's going to happen to the royal family if the wedding goes wrong?" she asked instead. Her reason was whispering to her that nothing would happen, this was their territory, they were surrounded by their own guard, by their own faithful people. And yet, her father standing with that smile on his lips was enough to shatter any feeling of safety. "Will there be conflict? Surely, the Seragians are not going to be happy."

"Why do you suddenly worry about the royal family?" her father asked, a glint of suspicion in his eyes. "The king is reckless. He ignores all the sound advice he gets from his guard, so sure of his subjects' love for him. And Prince Amril, well...he's a troublemaker, isn't he?"

Was there a tinge of excitement in his voice? Anticipation? Melia had no love for either the king or Amril; they were both odious, unrestrained, arrogant men. It wouldn't be the first time her father hid the truth from her, and yet his words echoed with so much darkness and chaos that Melia was unable to see her way forward.

"And the others?" she asked.

Her father misinterpreted the fear on her face. "I will protect you," he said. "You will be safe."

His promise was empty, though. There was no safety for anyone in Abia.

Melia struggled to keep her face blank when she entered the king's audience chamber later that morning, walking beside her father. Maps of various parts of the world adorned the walls, displaying exotic flowers and wild animals. Ceremonial weapons and armor stood like mute guards around the room, and precious gifts—jade vases, ivory sculptures, illuminated manuscripts bound between bejeweled plates—sparkled in the sunshine. A sense of calm luxury, of self-assured power, permeated the air.

The whole court was there: the king with his retinue, the queen and her ladies, noblemen and diplomats who'd arrived for the wedding. A lump of bitterness blocked Melia's throat. Despite the turmoil of the previous night, despite the imminent arrival of the Seragian delegation, the king and court still made time to welcome Roderi of Elmar. It was a slap in the face to see this display of goodwill towards her father after they'd been ignoring Melia for months.

Roderi of Elmar, always quick to take offense, scanned the room with his dark eyes. Trained to notice the slightest flicker of discontent, Melia watched him with apprehension. Yet, all she could discern was satisfaction. After condemning everybody in Syr to years of austerity, after making Melia feel guilty for adjusting her gowns to the court fashion, her father seemed to enjoy this opulence. He rolled back his shoulders, stood up a bit straighter, his black figure in stark contrast with the colorful room, but his charcoal silk as fine as any fabric the courtiers wore. It dawned on Melia that his choice of color wasn't solely the expression of grief and mourning. She'd learned a thing or two about colors from Queen Orsiana. Black was elegant, black stood out at court.

"The Defender of the Kingdom, the Hero of Elmar," the king called. "Welcome, Roderi. It's been too long."

Melia winced.

They met in the middle of the room: the tall, golden-haired sovereign, still handsome, but his large frame turning heavy with age; and the Black Lord, half a head shorter, his figure lean, his dun, pinched face a challenge to the king's radiance.

Roderi of Elmar had never seen himself as a hero because he wasn't one. He was the lord of the borderlands plagued by a three-hundred-year-old rivalry. The war wasn't a choice, it was a burden, passed from one generation to the next. And yet, her father had nothing but respect for the Seragians. The Empire was a formidable enemy, a worthy opponent. No, it was his own king that Roderi of Elmar considered loathsome and weak. Melia had spent her youth listening to his complaints about insufficient funds, weapons, soldiers sent to the border, about the soft, privileged life at court, about cowardice and turning a blind eye to the ever-burning fires of conflict in Elmar. In her father's eyes, the unforgivable crime wasn't the Empire's greedy wish to win back their lost province, but the lack of support from the Amrian rulers. They were the ones responsible for Elmar's wounds.

The king and the lord smiled and embraced, and it hit Melia that she despised them equally, for they were both bullies, willing to do anything to get their own way. Wouldn't it be wonderful if someone pushed sharp swords into their hands and sent them out to settle their accounts in the yard once and for all? The whole court and every person in Syr would be able to breathe freely after that.

Melia's face prickled and she looked up to see the queen's clear gray eyes studying her. The angry, rebellious thought in her head, where had it come from? Melia turned quickly, flustered, but the queen merely stepped forward towards the men, breaking their display of goodwill.

"Roderi, welcome," she said, and her voice rang true, although there was a faint note of caution in it. "What news do you bring from the border?"

"It's relatively quiet," her father said. "My scouts tell me the emperor is sending troops to border towns, reinstating the imperial order for the first time in decades. They've long forgotten they're a part of the Empire and it's time to remind them."

"He promised to deal with the mountain tribes as well, before the caravans return in the spring," the king said.

"We all know the Empire has publicly ignored and secretly funded them for decades. They wouldn't have been able to survive there for so long otherwise," Roderi of Elmar retorted.

"Yes, but the emperor won't openly admit to that, will he?" the king said. "Still, the terms are good. I hope you're looking forward to ending the conflict."

A flash of panic glinted in her father's eyes as he said, "I'm not sure I know how to live without it."

The queen frowned. "In peaceful retirement, I hope."

"I'm afraid that might turn out to be wishful thinking, my lady," Melia's father said. "I find it difficult to believe the Seragians will honor the deal. They've already broken the peace."

"We don't know that for sure," the queen said.

"We are working with the Seragians to find the attackers," the king said. "Let's celebrate today, and leave the investigation for later. One incident won't spoil the most important wedding of our lifetime."

The servants arrived with refreshments—dainty bites on silver trays, iced wine, fresh figs cut in half to show their moist red hearts. Melia took a tiny marzipan flower infused with rosewater, but her mouth was too dry and her throat too tight to swallow anything. In vain, she looked for a friendly face in the crowd.

Where was Amron? Ferisa had told her he was fine, but that was infuriatingly vague. Melia was torn between the desire to speak to him to find out how he felt, and the fear of facing him and hiding what she knew about the attack. Everybody around her lied with such ease—her father, Ferisa, ladies-in-waiting— while Melia squirmed and gnawed on herself, feeling she was betraying both sides with her incompetence.

Melia stood in the corner by the window, as far from the queen's ladies as possible, holding the inedible sweet like a fool, wondering how many people would be furious if she ran away now, when a slight commotion drew her eyes to one of the entrances.

Amron appeared in the doorway, perfectly attired in dark blue and silver brocade, his hair neatly tied back, his face composed. She made a beeline for him before anyone else noticed he'd appeared.

"Amron." She touched his arm. "Are you all right?"

He slowly turned his head and she saw that what she'd taken for composure was in fact a carefully arranged mask. Behind it, his eyes were filled with anxiety.

"I'm fine," he said. "I've spent the whole morning with Darin and his men, trying to figure out—"

"Your Highness!" Her father greeted Amron, cutting off his quiet explanation, and suddenly everybody in the room turned to look at them. "I've heard you've had quite a night. Alone against six Seragians? My border captains told me you were good, but this is an incredible feat."

Amron stepped back, creating a buffer of empty space between himself and his father-in-law. "I wasn't alone," he said. "And I would be dead if the king's guards hadn't arrived before the Seragians had a chance to get the better of me."

Melia thought Amron's words would dissuade her father, but Roderi pushed on with an insistence that bordered on rudeness.

"Still, we're all eager to hear the details, if you would be so kind as to share them with us." Roderi grinned. "Your father must be very proud of you."

If Amron heard the sting in his words, he didn't show it. In Melia's brief experience with the royal family, she'd learned that whenever the king measured Amron against Amril, he always found his younger son lacking.

Melia's father turned to the king, waiting for him to say something. But Amron V, so talkative and pleasant a moment ago, now frowned in silence.

"Your Majesty, your son is an excellent fighter, isn't he?" Roderi of Elmar asked.

To onlookers in that room, his words must have sounded like praise, but Melia knew better. He knew how to hit a nerve, how to draw a wedge between people. Roderi of Elmar was lauding his son-in-law to provoke the king.

The corners of the king's lips twitched beneath his golden beard. "He certainly had his share of fighting yesterday," he said dryly and turned to Amron. "You should apologize to your brother."

Amron blanched, pressing his lips together.

"Amril, come here," the king said.

All clamor died in the room. The crowd parted to let the crown prince through. Melia, who'd instinctively hidden away from him, who'd refused to look at him for fear of drawing his unwelcome attention, was shocked to discover Prince Amril's lip was cut and swollen, a bruise marring the corner of his mouth. She had no idea what had happened. Amril was no stranger to fighting, but what did Amron have to do with it?

Despite his injured face, Amril smiled, radiating his charm. "Amron and I can deal with this later, Father." He kept his tone light, indifferent. "In private."

The king ignored him. A soft rustle of silk disrupted the silence as the queen appeared beside Amril. The scene turned so intimate that even the nosy courtiers radiated with unease as thick as a pea soup. Envoys and guests stood aside, aghast.

It was so clear to Melia what her father had done, exploiting the weakness, salting the wound. He was an expert in twisting the blade. Why couldn't everyone else see it?

She felt like slipping behind a curtain and dying of shame, but Amron's pale face anchored her where she stood, so close to him she could feel the invisible tremor running through his body.

"If you were anyone else but my son, you'd be hanged for assaulting the heir to the throne," the king addressed Amron, ignoring the startled gasps from the crowd. "The least you can do is apologize to your brother in public and ask for forgiveness."

"Amril knows why I hit him," Amron said.

To his credit, Amril's cheeks burned crimson as he gave a curt nod. "It was a disagreement, not an assault."

"One does not disagree with a crown prince by punching him in the face."

The king's words were so peevish, so deliberately obtuse, that Melia squirmed. Surely, he could see what he was doing? Humiliating Amron in public for no other reason than daring to touch his belligerent brother, dancing to Roderi of Elmar's poisonous tune. She risked a glance at her father. He stood wide-eyed, soaking in the scene he'd caused.

"He was right to hit me," Amril said, still trying to keep it light, make it sound like a misunderstanding. "I insulted a girl he was talking to."

A girl, Ferisa had mentioned a girl. What did she say? *He was snuggling with a girl in a dark alley. A stunningly beautiful girl.* Is that why Amron had hit his brother? Over some pretty courtesan they both wanted?

She looked at her husband, the toxic jealousy inside her heart goading her to enjoy his humiliation. Was he the same as Amril, chasing after every warm body in a skirt?

Her father was studying her with a greedy half smile.

"You will not mention your whores here at court," the king barked, his face crimson. "I don't care about explanations. Amron hit you and he will apologize for it."

Amril looked sick. Melia's gaze found the queen, silently begging her to do something, to stop this charade. But the queen remained silent, refusing to intervene.

"Get on your knees, now," the king said, "or I'll have my guards make you."

Amron stood still for one endless moment, while Melia and everybody in the room held their breath. She expected him to turn on his heel and leave, she willed him to do it, to be braver than Amril, braver than her, braver than every courtier around them. If anyone could stand up to the king, it was Amron. *Defy him*, she thought.

Instead, Amron blinked slowly, stepped forward, and knelt before his brother. When he spoke, his voice was clear and crisp, pitched to carry. "I apologize for hitting you, Amril. I hope you will forgive me."

Amril looked at the king and opened his mouth to say something, but at that moment the queen turned away from the scene abruptly and marched out, followed by a train of flustered ladies-in-waiting. The movement broke the evil spell that had held the onlookers chained in place, and the crowd dispersed like a shoal of fish before a predator. Roderi of Elmar disappeared in the shadows. Amril touched the king's shoulder and said, "Come, Father, it's done." Even the servants, still holding their trays, scurried away.

In a few heartbeats, there was no one left in the room but Melia and Amron, still on his knees. She wanted to touch him, to say something kind. To say she knew what it felt like to be humiliated, used as a tool, unloved. While she struggled to find the appropriate words, he stood up without sparing her a glance and walked away.

She realized she was still holding the marzipan rose in her hand, now squeezed to mush. Her palm was dyed red.

~Chapter 15~

Liana

Liana jumped over the wall in the back alley. The villa's garden was a jungle of weeds swallowing the few remaining fig trees. The brambles tore at her dress and scratched her skin, and she bitterly regretted leaving her riding boots and trousers at the palace. The nettles burned her as she pushed them out of her path, and sharp, hungry branches grabbed at her hair as she ducked to slip beneath them. No human hand had touched this wilderness in years. It had grown and spread in the perfectly impersonal malevolence of the natural world which only cared for light and food and survival.

The lock to the back door of the villa was too rusted for picking, but a narrow, unglazed window beside the door had shutters with a latch that was easy to lift. Liana slipped into a chamber filled with cobwebs and dust. The darkness swallowed her like a thick, cold sludge, wrapping itself around her limbs, trapping her in its freezing embrace.

Holding her breath, sliding like a fox through a village, she searched the ground floor. A feeling of unease raised the hairs on the back of her neck: the hostile divine magic urging her to flee, to leave this cursed place behind.

The kitchen, the pantry, the storage rooms were all empty, void of any signs of life. In the entrance hall, there were footprints in the dust, leading upstairs. Liana followed them, carefully balancing her weight on each wooden stair to avoid creaks.

Upstairs, a pale, milky light trickled in through the shutters, seemingly unconnected to the bright sunshine outside. Liana paused, listening to the sounds of the house. Nothing moved.

The first door she opened led into a bedroom where the narrow bed had a canopy of cobwebs, and a long-dead pigeon, which must have entered through some hole, lay on the desk. The dust on the floor was undisturbed so she moved on.

The second door opened into a dim room with a clean floor. It was sparsely furnished: a narrow bed, a writing desk, a chair, a chest of clothes. A pungent scent of herbs assaulted Liana's nose, and she noticed another, smaller chest beside the bed. It was open, and filled with satchels and vials. As Liana stepped closer, she noticed a heap of dark clothes at the foot of the bed and a curved blade in a leather scabbard. She knelt down to investigate. The clothes were spattered with blood and the blade was a Seragian yatagan, the same weapon the attackers had wielded. It was the proof she was looking for.

An arm wrapped itself around her throat and an astringent odor filled her nostrils as a rag covered her nose and mouth. She held her breath instinctively. Someone pulled her backwards, throwing her off balance, making her flail her arms in vain, looking for a hold. Forced to choose between breathing and suffocating, she gulped in air though the fabric. A strong, bitter smell engulfed her in its dizzying cloud. Her vision darkened, narrowing to a white spot on the wall, while the arm tightened around her throat, crushing her windpipe.

Then Liana's legs found their footing and she pushed backwards, slamming into the nearest wall. Her assailant yelped and released their grip just enough for Liana to get a lungful of fresh air. Before they had the time to tighten it again, Liana reached backwards, grabbed their arms, and threw them over her head.

As the body hit the floor, Liana recognized the woman Melia had talked to in the garden. She turned as soon as she hit the floorboards and grabbed Liana's ankle, pulling her forward. Liana lost balance, still dizzy from the vapors, but as she fell, she delivered a kick to the side of Ferisa's head with her other leg. The woman rolled towards the heap of dark clothes—and the blade. Liana threw herself in her path and they both grabbed for the yatagan. As Liana reached for the hilt, Ferisa's elbow connected with her jaw. Pain exploded in Liana's head, blinding her for long enough for Ferisa to snatch the weapon and roll away from her.

In a heartbeat, they were both up again, staring at each other from opposite parts of the small room.

Ferisa's eyes, black like two jet beads, shone with arrowfoil frenzy. Liana recognized its bitter odor, she'd seen Seragians use it in the war—it gave them enhanced speed and focus for a while, but burned more energy than the body could produce, turning its regular users to withered husks.

Ferisa didn't look like she lacked energy, though. She was fast, strong, and surprisingly quiet when she moved. It occurred to Liana that she should have come prepared for more than snooping around.

"It's you again." Ferisa crammed the opiate-soaked rag in her pocket, drew the blade, and threw the scabbard behind her. "You fight too well for a common whore. Who sent you?"

Never taking her eyes off Liana, Ferisa locked the door and slipped the key into her pocket; she could afford a short interrogation now. Liana spat out the blood that had filled her mouth. She'd cut her cheek when Ferisa elbowed her. Her head swam, either from the kick or from that blasted rag. One quick scan of the room told her there were no other weapons.

Ferisa was no ordinary opponent. Coils of darkness gathered around her in a slow spiral dance, the mark of the goddess Liana wanted to avoid at all costs. She didn't have to ask Ferisa who had sent her—she knew.

"Do priests now meddle in politics?" Liana asked. "Do you serve your goddess or Roderi of Elmar?"

Ferisa blinked in surprise.

"But she's not a murder goddess, nor a goddess of war," Liana continued. "This is not a divine mission you're on, but a purely human revenge spree for insults real and imagined." It was a wild guess, but it hit the mark.

"You know nothing about my purpose," the priestess said.

"That may be true, but I know everything about the consequences of what you're about to do." Liana spat out more blood. "You think peace is a cowardly solution? You think Elmar has suffered too much to give up so easily? You want the rest of the kingdom to taste blood?"

"Who are you?" Ferisa growled.

"I'm someone who's seen the war you're about to start. The kingdom will bleed, yes, but Elmar will lose everything." Liana's words were slow and deliberate. "You will all die."

Ferisa shot her an unpleasant smile. "Do you think I care about dying?"

"I know you don't," Liana said. "But you're irrelevant, a tool too dumb to see how it's being used. Nobody cares if you live or die."

Ferisa bared her teeth at her. "If you tell me who sent you, I promise to kill you quickly."

"The gods sent me," Liana said in a flash of perfect clarity. "And I'm going to stop the Black Lord."

The time for banter and bravado was over. Liana read Ferisa's intention a moment before the priestess lunged at her, and she jumped back, avoiding the blade. Liana was fast, but in this small, locked room, she was barely fast enough to avoid getting killed. No matter how many times she dodged the blade, she had no chance of stopping Ferisa with her bare hands, not while the priestess's eyes glimmered with arrow-foil and Liana's head was all muddled with poison.

Her heel bumped into something hard, almost throwing her off balance once again. She risked a glance behind her. It was a small medicine chest. She bent down, avoiding another slash, and grabbed it. The precious glass vials clinked when she shook it.

"Don't touch that!" Ferisa cried.

"You want it?" Liana threw the chest at Ferisa, its contents spilling out and falling on the floor, where they burst like overripe fruit. The priestess screamed. Liana turned, pushed the shutters open with her shoulder, and jumped through the window.

She landed in a writhing mass of brambles. The fall kicked the air out of her and the thorny tendrils grabbed her limbs, cutting her clothes and skin.

Above her, Ferisa looked through the window, her face twisted in rage. "I'm coming to get you," she said.

Liana writhed in panic, a rat entangled in oakum. The more she struggled, the tighter the shrub held her, piercing her flesh with its long thorns. A death by a thousand cuts, an agony that was the sum of all the smaller pains assaulting her twitching body. Like a trapped animal, she panicked, hurting herself.

Only when she heard the back door open did she finally pause, cursing herself. She was a forest creature, she knew how to get out of a thicket.

"Where are you?" Ferisa called, a note of amusement ringing in her voice.

Holding her breath, Liana made herself small and lithe, a young lynx prowling through the underbrush. Lightly, she slipped out of the thorny embrace. The shrubs were reluctant to let her go, leaving long, deep scratches on her arms and legs. She winced in pain, but kept moving towards the wall, quiet and invisible. Yet, the faster she crawled, the further away the wall became. Like in a bad dream, moving was an illusion.

A swish of the blade splitting the air warned her to duck. Not fast enough: The sharp steel bit into her upper arm.

"Do you think you can hide from me in my own garden?"

Liana rolled over and delivered a savage kick to Ferisa's knee.

The priestess yelped, losing balance, swinging at Liana and missing her chest by a hair's breadth.

Blood poured down Liana's arm. She cursed, retreating through the shrubs, which suddenly seemed as tall as a maze, blocking her path to the wall. No garden was so large among the crowded houses of Abia.

She was being stupid, thrashing around in panic where she should have been cunning. She blinked quickly, and when that didn't help, she licked the tips of her fingers and rubbed her eyes.

Now she could see.

The priestess charged behind her, but Liana refused to turn, refused to waste her true sight on that creature. Instead, she rushed forward, the path now clear before her. Without slowing down, she jumped and caught the top of the wall. Her arm burned in pure agony, but she didn't let go while her legs scrambled for a foothold. She dragged herself over and fell to the other side, broken and bloody like a deer carcass after a hunt.

Her head, her throat, her back, her arm, the whole surface of her skin hurt, but there was no time to contemplate her injuries because a hand grabbed the top of the wall, and a dark head rose over it.

Liana got up and lurched down the alley, leaving a bloody trail behind. She couldn't outrun the priestess; her only chance was to get out of this quiet corner of Abia and hide in the crowd.

She'd run for her life before, but it had never stung so badly.

Footsteps echoed behind her, her death in hot pursuit.

She broke out of the alley. The street wasn't crowded, but there were people there, giving her strange looks and stepping out of her way. She briefly contemplated asking for help, but no one carried weapons and there were no guards around. They couldn't help her.

Liana ran towards the harbor. The sound of Ferisa's chase disappeared in the growing noise, but still she pushed on, hoping that even a murderous priestess wouldn't be so mad as to rush to the main square on the day of the royal wedding, swinging a bloody Seragian blade.

In the square, Abia celebrated. Liana slowed down. A dozen long tables were laid out in her path, and the people crowded around them to get free food—white bread, fish stew, roast pork, sweet buns. The aroma of sizzling fat, garlic and herbs, and melted butter made Liana's stomach growl but there was no time to eat, no time to listen to the musicians who played on a dais, no time to admire the floral garlands and colorful banners flapping in the wind. She needed to find her father, tell him what was going on.

She stumbled through the crowd in a bubble of anguish that kept people at a distance. They refused to even look at her, averting their eyes as soon as their brains registered something was amiss. An intruder in the sea of happy people, a wrong note in a sweet song. Only small children stared—for a little while, before their parents pulled them away. No one wanted to deal with Liana's bloodied face, her injured arm and torn clothes, the anger and panic in her eyes.

She rushed towards the main gate of the palace. There was no time for sneaking in, no time to search through the maze of corridors: Darin needed to know about the Elmarrans right away. As she approached, two dozen guards poured out of the gate and cleared the crowd gathered before them. "Make way for the king," they shouted.

Trumpets blared, piercing her ears as she pushed through the crowd and slipped behind the guards' backs. All she could think about was getting in and finding her father. The cleared path was just a lucky coincidence, and she stepped forward, meaning only to use the absence of the pressing bodies to reach the gate. Her way was instantly blocked by the guards, though.

A horrified gasp surged through the crowd, followed by the ring of steel as the guards pulled out their swords.

"Wait," someone said.

At that moment the fog that filled Liana's head finally cleared and she saw herself as a seagull flying above the square might see her. The enormous mass of people filling the square, the path leading from the palace gate to the harbor, the guards surrounding the empty space, the white flagstones reflecting the sunshine. And herself.

Why didn't she realize what she looked like? Her dress was torn, the sleeves and skirt shredded to ribbons, her left arm covered in blood from shoulder to wrist. She'd lost her sandals, her feet leaving bloody footprints on the white stone. Her hair was a mass of twigs and leaves, her face and neck battered and bruised. And in her hand—in her right hand— she held the Seragian blade.

"What is going on?" The same voice she'd heard before, demanding, annoyed.

"Sire—" one of the guards said.

"Move."

The guards parted to reveal a tall, bearded, golden-haired man dressed impossibly fine in ultramarine velvet and cloth of gold, the sapphire-and-diamond chain around his neck and the rings on his fingers shining so bright they blinded her. His eyes, deep blue and calculating, took in every embarrassing detail of her appearance, while his right hand rested on the hilt of a sword that didn't look ceremonial at all.

Liana should have thrown herself to her knees, begging for mercy, but her body refused to cooperate. She stared, frozen, at the dazzling figure. Then her eyes slipped to the brightly dressed, bejeweled crowd behind him. Somewhere, a tiny voice in her head screamed at her not to mention Darin, not to humiliate her father before this man, but her eyes still searched for him in the crowd, in vain.

"Do you plan to attack us?" the king asked, drawing her attention back to him.

She looked at him, at herself, at the yatagan in her hand. Why did she have the weapon? Ferisa had had it in the house, she'd cut Liana with it, chased her over the wall and down the streets to the square. Liana's eyes searched the crowd, but there was no sign of the priestess. She looked at her hand again, her fingers snug around the hilt.

She was holding a bloody blade before the king on a day when carrying weapons was punishable by death in Abia. If she kept staring stupidly at Amron V, she'd die.

She threw the blade down, it slid over the stone and stopped before the king's feet.

"This is proof of the Elmarran conspiracy to accuse the Seragians of the attack on Prince Amron. I found this in the house belonging to Roderi of Elmar."

In the silence that followed, the king nudged the blade with the tip of his shoe. "Is that true, Roderi?" he asked.

A black-haired, black-clad man stepped out from the crowd of courtiers. There was nothing particularly frightening about him, Liana was surprised to discover. He didn't even carry the sigil of the Dark Goddess, no smoky tendrils, no cloak of darkness. A perfectly ordinary man, with a forgettable face set in a calm expression with only the faintest shadow of confusion.

"I'd say it was a ridiculous accusation if it weren't so grave, sire." His tone was unperturbed, smooth. "My whole retinue is lodged at my house here and I assure you none of them are Seragian." He lowered his eyes to the blade, lips curving in distaste. "As for the yatagan, I have hundreds of them in my armory at Syr, taken from the dead hands of my enemies, but I don't carry them around."

It took the king less than a heartbeat to decide. "Hang her," he said.

Two guards grabbed her before she remembered to beg for her life.

Someone was thinking faster, though. "My lord!" The queen caught the king's hand, inserted herself between him and the Black Lord. "Mercy, please."

The king flicked his other hand and the guards froze, but didn't release Liana.

"Look at her, she's just a deranged girl, she doesn't know what she's saying. We still haven't found the remaining attackers, we don't know where their weapons are." The queen turned to Liana. "Did someone give you this blade, girl? Did they tell you what to say?"

A gray gaze, sharp as flint, drilled into Liana's head. She nodded, her tongue stuck to the roof of her mouth.

"Spare her and have someone question her. She might give us a clue." The queen's voice was soft, dispassionate, as if she were talking about the weather. Her eyes were glued to the king's face, her hand holding his, her body blocking Roderi of Elmar from approaching him. It looked casual, unobtrusive, a little spousal discussion about life and death before half the city.

"Fine," the king said. "Lock her up."

Just like that, one moment she was dead, the next she was alive again.

The Black Lord scowled, but the king didn't see it.

"Come, my lord," the queen said. "We've wasted enough time."

Oddly subdued, the royal procession moved, pelting Liana with curious gazes as the guards dragged her into the palace yard.

~Chapter 16~

Melia

Melia scrubbed her palm with short, savage movements, but the dye from the marzipan had soaked into her clammy skin and now she had a red-stained hand, like a sloppy child. She savored the shame that went with the thought, the feeling of incompetence, because it blocked the memory of the savage humiliation she'd witnessed.

She found it hard to define Amron's status at court. Admired by the guards and the clerks, well-liked by the ladies, respected by the nobles, and loved by the queen, he was nevertheless ignored or challenged by his brother and openly disliked by the king. Melia, who was no stranger to cold, demanding parents, found this unusual, for Amron was everything the king could have wanted in a son. As opposed to Amril, who frightened and disgusted Melia, but seemed to be regarded as the amusing, generous prince by the courtiers, and was clearly his father's favorite.

Melia felt this injustice keenly, even though Amron refused to acknowledge it even existed. Drying her hands, she considered going to Amron, offering kindness, as he would have undoubtedly offered her if the roles had been reversed, but before she gathered the courage, it was already time to dress for the ceremonies and get on with the endless day. She should have followed the queen when she left the audience chamber, should have been helping her dress, but her father's visit and the scene he'd caused had disrupted her morning schedule. She called the maids to help her dress, but only one girl came—in the chaos of the palace, it was almost impossible to find help.

"My hair is fine as it is," Melia said, assessing the thick black braids pinned to her head with pearl and ivory combs. "Just help me change."

Melia's attire for the ceremony was blue. An underdress of the finest periwinkle silk, light as a breath and smooth as water, and a gown of heavy silk brocade in a vivid shade of ultramarine, with a delicate flower pattern, had all been chosen by Queen Orsiana; she had picked the designs, patterns, and colors. Melia, who had never worn blue, felt strangely cold when she put it on. It didn't compliment her skin; the icy tones killed its natural warmth and made her look sallow. But the gown wasn't there to make Melia look pretty, it was there to make her look regal, and that task it accomplished without a doubt. She had never worn—or seen—anything so fine. If she ignored her harried face in the mirror, if she squinted until it became a blur, she could almost discern a fine dusting of royal grace on her person.

There was a knock on the door, and a little page announced, "Her Royal Highness, Princess Amielle."

Melia took a deep breath and clenched her teeth. She hadn't met Amron's sister yet—she'd left the court when she married—but they were of equal rank now and were supposed to stay together during the ceremony.

"Where is my brother's wife? The queen is waiting for her." An imposing blonde woman walked in, almost as tall as Amron and equally bony, with eyes of the same dark shade of blue-gray and a thick, heavy mass of golden hair. A closer look revealed a slightly finer, more delicate structure of her face and a barely visible hint of pregnancy under the layers of linen and silk. She was more outspoken than her brother, too. "I suppose that's you," she said, her gaze fixing on Melia.

Melia nodded. "Princess."

"Call me Amielle," the princess said curtly. "And I'll call you Melia."

It was a command, not a suggestion. The princess looked around the room, taking in the mess Melia could never force the maids to tidy: the strewn clothes and shoes, open chests, a myriad of bottles and perfume vials, boxes, clasps and pins, combs and brushes covering every flat surface.

"I apologize for the mess," Melia said.

"My brother would hate it."

"Excuse me?" Melia said, not quite sure she heard correctly.

"I said Amron would hate it." The princess stated it flatly, as a simple fact, without mockery or judgment, but also without kindness. "Clutter makes him physically uncomfortable, he can't help it. If he walked into this room, he'd feel the instant pressure to leave. Is that what you're trying to do?"

"No, I—" Surely the princess was joking? "Amron never mentioned—"

A sharp glare pinned her down. "You've been married to my brother for months and you don't know *that*? What do you know about Amron?"

Melia's cheeks heated up. What did she know about Amron, really? He was diligent. He tried to be kind to her. He was intensely reserved. "I know what he shows me," she said.

The princess looked down on her as if she were a slow child. "My brother is unhappy," she said. "And he doesn't deserve it."

It struck Melia that this was the single most infuriatingly difficult morning of her life. So many people demanding more of her than she could give. "In what world do those who deserve happiness get it?" she asked.

The princess chuckled. "Not without spirit, I see. That's a good start. Now, let's go, Mother will be furious if we're late."

While they walked down the corridor, Melia dared to ask, "Have you seen Amron this morning, after the—" She didn't know what to call it.

"The spectacle our father made of him?" the princess asked,

her long stride forcing Melia to run. "No. He's licking his wounds in private somewhere, I'd wager."

"Is he all right?"

The princess paused so abruptly Melia almost stumbled. "No, he's not all right. Would you be?"

"No, I—"

"But that's what our father does. He's done it to all of us, but to Amron the most because the two of them are like two wild dogs who just can't let one another go. Amron refuses to bend and Father refuses to stop trying to break him, and they're both worse off for it." She resumed her stride. "Men and their pride."

No one has ever talked to Melia with such bluntness. "What could I do to help him?"

"Pretend it never happened," the princess said as they stepped into the queen's chambers. "He'll be grateful."

The ladies were just pinning the veil to the Queen's braids with tiny diamond stars. She turned when they entered, beautiful in icy shades of the palest blue, yet her face was distracted and worried. "Someone get a chair for the princess," she said. "You should rest."

"Oh no, I'm fine. We can go if you're ready," Amielle said.

"Stubborn as the rest of them," the queen muttered. "Let's go, then."

A long procession formed in the corridor and descended into the yard, where the king's party already waited for them. Melia looked for Amron in vain—she couldn't spot his golden head anywhere in the crowd.

"What are we waiting for?" the princess muttered, just as an odd silence spread throughout the crowd.

Melia stood on tiptoes, trying to see what was happening at the gate, but the men from the king's retinue blocked her view. Whatever it was, it didn't last long, and the procession moved, meandering towards the harbor. Passing through the gate, she saw a bloody, roughed up girl being held by two guards. For a brief moment, she wondered what the girl had done to deserve such treatment. Then she remembered the royal wedding must have attracted all kinds of madmen and troublemakers, and averted her eyes.

As the bells rang the eleventh hour of the morning, the Seragian fleet carrying Carevna Aratea and her entourage sailed into the Bay of Abia. Melia watched them from a wooden dais, shaded by a blue and gold canopy, crammed in with the members of the royal household. Princess Amielle stood beside her. Amron had materialized behind his brother at some point between the palace and the harbor, perfectly poised and immaculately dressed. She tried to catch his eye, but he kept close to Amril, whispering and laughing in a rare display of brotherly intimacy.

Melia stood on her toes, trying to get a breath of fresh air. The sky was blue as the royal livery, with feathery white clouds sailing fast across it. The day was windy, but it was still too early in the year for the wild gales that lashed the coast in the winter. The three imperial galleys sailed smoothly into the bay, lowered their red sails in a series of fast, precise movements, and rowed into the harbor. Their long, slender hulls cut the waves like sea snakes, with eyes and gaping maws filled with sharp teeth painted on their prows.

"My, my, are they planning to eat us?" Amielle muttered.

The remark was light, without a trace of premonition, and yet Melia felt cold dread spreading through her veins. Despite living her whole life on the border, she had never met real Seragians, seen the true face of the Empire. Up until that moment, she could only imagine them as brigands, scrawny, desperate men attacking in small groups, hiding in the mountains, freezing and starving in the caves and abandoned villages. When her father talked of them, they were nothing more than vermin to be flushed out and destroyed.

She knew, in theory, that the Empire was vast, and that the Elmarran border was just a nuisance for the emperor, one of the many wars that smoldered on the edges of his lands. She knew that those unruly tribes were no more than grains of sand on the imperial map. The conflict that shaped her life, that took away the people she loved most, that had left her empty and dead, and turned her father into a flaring husk of hatred, was just a small, irritating note in the margin of the Empire's history.

Amris the Golden-Haired defeated the Seragians in Elmar three hundred years ago, wiped them off the map, sent them running over the mountains with their tails between their legs. After that, all the Seragians could do was harass the people along the border, sending the most desperate, angry bandits with nothing to lose to pillage and burn. No emperor had tried to lead an army across the border again, to conquer Elmar, to take Syr once more. As a child, Melia was taught to believe it had been so because the Elmarrans guarded the border so well, and the Empire had never dared to escalate the skirmishes into a full-blown war.

Looking at the galleys in the harbor, three out of the three hundred the emperor supposedly had at his command, Melia realized the history she'd been taught was a child's tale. Yes, the Elmarrans fought hard, yes, Elmar was a narrow, deadly strip of desert protected by some very sharp mountains, but it was nothing when compared with the size and might of the Seragian Empire.

Seragians poured out of the galleys as soon as they docked. First the guards in their uniforms, armor gleaming in the midday sun. Then the servants in black and gold liveries, bearing gifts. Then musicians, clerks, diplomats, noblemen—a mass of foreign people, perfectly orchestrated on the stone piers.

They reminded Melia of a clockwork mechanism, they were so smooth, so perfect, so deadly. Their order, their coordination, the sheer beauty of their perfect disembarking surpassed any army she had ever seen. The emperor who commanded such obedience, who had such skill at his disposal, could do anything he pleased. What if he decided to attack Abia from the sea and send an army over the mountains at the same time, with this level of discipline and dedication? What if all the might of the imperial army turned upon this little kingdom? They had no Amris now, no half-mad, half-divine hero whose unmatched talent was to conquer and triumph. Who would defend them now?

Watching the imperial grandeur unfold under the eyes of the whole court and thousands of common people, she could not help feeling overwhelmed. She tore her eyes away from the magnificent guests to watch the reactions of the people she knew. The king, fidgeting on a makeshift throne, looking far more anxious than triumphant. Amril, with an immovable smile plastered on his face, and Amron behind him, pale, with his eyes wide open.

Her gaze then slipped down to where the nobles stood, to the familiar crowd in red and black. Her father was too far away for his expression to be readable, and from Melia's high position on the dais, he looked small. All his schemes, all his anger....In this sweeping historical moment unfolding before their eyes, her father seemed like a puny trouble-maker, a reckless farm boy prodding a sleeping dragon with a sharp stick.

The thought almost comforted her. After all, what could Roderi of Elmar do to spoil this? There were hundreds of guards around watching the crowd. Captain Darin stood on the pier with his men, each one armed to the teeth. Together with the Seragians, they were an army. What could Roderi of Elmar do to provoke them?

Little page boys walked around the dais offering refreshments, and Melia snatched a glass of iced lemonade from the tray. It was so cold her teeth ached.

"Do you think we'll stand here until sundown?" she asked the princess, watching the galleys spit out their precious cargo as if there would be no end to it.

"No," Amielle whispered back. "The wedding's at noon. Look, the bride is coming now."

A ripple went through the Seragians on the pier, and the vibrant mass parted to open a path that led straight from the galleys to the main square and the foot of the dais where Amril stood. It looked like magic, like the sea splitting in two, like sunlight carving a golden road through the waves.

"How are we going to recognize—" Melia started and immediately stopped when a figure stepped on the gangplank of the main galley. She was dressed in white, but a white so bright it made all other shades of white look gray, so brilliant it looked like the fabric was spun out of the light itself. She walked slowly, carefully, and alone. As she stepped onto the pier, a procession of women formed behind her, dressed in the imperial purple and gold. Music followed her footsteps—not loud, brash fanfare, but dreamy strings, gentle as the lapping of the waves and the whisper of the wind.

The crowd in the square fell silent and not a soul moved. You could have heard a pin drop as the Seragian carevna walked to the dais. It was five hundred steps or more, and she took her time, allowing everyone to ogle her attire. The wind picked up the fabric of her overskirt and sleeves, diaphanous and so light it created an illusion of weightlessness. The bodice and the skirt underneath encapsulated her body in heavy satin, shining like polished steel. The belt and the diadem that held her veil were encrusted in pearls set in white gold.

"I expected this," the princess said, "and yet…"

And yet. Melia closed her eyes to protect them from the imperial flare, and her mind wandered back to the weather-beaten stones of Syr, to the empty rooms with worm-eaten furniture and threadbare carpets, to the austerity and the grind of the endless war. Every pearl in that diadem was drenched in blood, and the carevna's wedding dress was just as red as Melia's had been.

As the Seragian procession approached, Amril stepped down from the dais, followed by Amron and a dozen noblemen, including Amielle's husband, Erian of Leven. It became clear to Melia why Queen Orsiana had fussed so much about the clothes for the ceremony, why every fabric, every shade, and every cut had to be approved. A tiny spark of admiration for her flickered in Melia's chest. It was a hard task not to be completely overshadowed by the Seragian women's attire, but Amril and his men managed to pull it off. The crown prince, in a blue so dark it was almost black, was the perfect contrast to his glowing bride.

They met on the square beneath the dais, in a large circle formed by the guardsmen. Even with the diadem on her head, the carevna barely reached his shoulder.

"Welcome to Abia, Carevna Aratea," Amril said in Seragian.

His bride lifted her veil, revealing a heart-shaped face so pale it matched her dress. From where she stood, Melia could see enough to decide she was no great beauty, just a short girl with thick red braids framing her serious face.

"Thank you," the carevna replied in perfect Amrian. "My father the emperor sends his greetings."

Amril took her hand and the procession moved on a carefully planned route that took them through the widest streets of the town, scrubbed until the stones shone for this occasion, and strewn with flowers. Every street corner offered a new scene: landscapes painted so vividly you felt you could step into them, plays and songs, and people cheering. Melia searched for disgruntled faces in the crowd and couldn't find a single one. Food was free for all, and so was the wine, and it looked as if it were really that easy to make people happy, at least for a day.

The procession circled around Abia and came back to the royal dais on the main square, which was now empty and had transformed into the wedding altar. A priestess of Lada, crowned with flowers and dressed in red, waited to bless the union.

As Amril and his bride faced the priestess—their figures perfectly visible from any corner of the square—as they said the words and performed the rites, Melia expected to see something magical happen. Every scene, every move that led from the arrival of the ships to this moment, had been so masterfully arranged. This was the finale. Surely, the gods would give a sign that they blessed a union as great as this.

She prayed for a sign. If the gods approved of this union, then any kind of rebellion was futile. The future of the kingdom had already been decided, and it was peace.

But try as she might, Melia saw no special signs of divine goodwill. Oh, it was beautifully arranged: the golden chalice adorned with rubies that glimmered in the sunlight, the trained alto of the priestess, projecting perfectly over the crowd, the choir hidden behind the dais, with their celestial voices. The crowd surely thought it enchanting.

And yet, all Melia could see was Amril's impatience and contempt hidden behind his beautiful mask. And the bride: She didn't even believe in these gods, they were powerless in Seragia, where their one god, the almighty Sha, ruled with an iron hand and an army of priests. Their promises were as solid as the clouds sailing over the brilliant sky.

Melia's eyes filled with tears; she blinked and the scene fell into colorful fragments like a stained glass window shattered by a gale.

~**Chapter 17**~

Liana

No servants' quarters, no cozy room in the attic this time for Liana. The guards dragged her to the basement of the palace, to a stale windowless hole with nothing but a rough wooden bench and a chamber pot in the corner. They left her no light, no blanket to fight off the chill, no water. When the key turned in the lock and their footsteps faded away, she touched the thick wooden door, trying to find a weakness, but it was in vain. After an hour or so of pacing wildly, raging about her own stupidity, she finally curled up on the hard bench. The precious moments slipped away, wasted. Somewhere above her, the bloody plot had been set in motion, spreading, gaining speed as she trembled in the dark, powerless and forgotten. By the time someone found her, it would all be over.

Exhausted, she shivered on the bench. Her arm had stopped bleeding and already her body was rushing to repair itself, but that just worsened the pain. Her skin burned as if a wild cat had clawed her from head to toes, and her throat was swollen and raw. Yet the physical pain was nothing compared to the self-loathing she doused herself in.

She'd been so unforgivably stupid, thinking she could deal with the priestess alone. She'd stumbled into a trap and made a terrible fool of herself. And what was worse, she'd failed to help anyone.

But what could she have done alone? The idea that she could stop the wheel of history from crushing them all just because she was aware of what was coming was a fool's hope. There was no time for smart plans, for devious schemes, and even if there had been, Liana had never had a head for tactics. All she knew was that Amron was married to a traitor whose murderous priestess was on the loose somewhere in Abia.

She closed her eyes, trying to feel the space around her. Perhaps if she could step behind these walls, there would be a way out.

"Mother," she whispered in a small voice, hating herself for asking for help. "Can you hear me?"

She reached out, touched the stones. They turned to ice under her fingers as a massive wave of black water rushed in, closing over her head. Reeds wrapped around her ankles, pulling her down.

A flash of sharp teeth in the depth and a face she hoped she'd never see.

"No!" she screamed, air escaping her lungs in bubbles.

And then she was back on the stone bench in the cell, her dress soaked in cold water, her feet covered in filthy mud.

She jumped, expecting the freezing claws, but no attack came.

Her dress was dry, her feet clean. The curtain between the worlds held.

She laid back, frightened and exhausted, planning to close her eyes for a moment, when sleep defeated her and pulled her into its dark embrace.

Liana was twenty-two when she first met Amron.

Wrapped up in her daily hunting tasks, she'd cared little about the war raging in the south and less about the delegation coming to see Echton of Till. And yet, when Brano asked who wanted to join the lord on his journey to welcome the important guests, she volunteered.

Early winter had dusted the forest with the first layer of new snow, pristine and brilliant in the weak sunlight. From a gentle hillside, they watched the royal delegation approach, their dark cloaks and blue liveries in stark contrast with the white landscape.

Liana rarely had a chance to see any foreigners in the Brezov castle. Occasionally, there would be a visit from some noble, and a hunt, but none of them ever paid attention to a young huntswoman. She longed to go south—from the dark forests of Till, there was nowhere to go but south—and see the brilliant cities, golden fields, vineyards, and olive groves. The cold never bothered her, but she longed to feel the kiss of the southern sun on her face.

She melted into the trees with the rest of the lord's escort, only to appear before the delegation as they negotiated a slippery bend in the road. Half a dozen men, followed by two dozen soldiers. She imagined they would look like courtiers, or at least the courtiers from the stories and songs she'd heard—dressed in exquisite clothes, groomed, pampered. Instead, she saw a pack of hardened, weary riders—some gray-haired, some bearded, some young and comely—who looked no different from her companions.

Actually, that wasn't true.

She noticed him as soon as he removed his dark hood and the sunlight gilded his hair. There was such a serious, subdued beauty to his face that she couldn't take her eyes off of. She had no idea who he was. A young nobleman among his peers? He felt her burning gaze and his eyes found her in the throng of two groups of riders meeting.

She expected the usual reaction: a lewd, inviting smile, a wink, some kind of overture. Instead, he just widened his eyes and held her gaze for a fraction of a heartbeat before turning away.

"What are you staring at?" Brano asked, laying his gloved hand on her thigh.

The head huntsman had several ideas about Liana's place—among the hunters, in his bed, before a priest exchanging vows—which he never bothered to get her opinion on. His persistence in taking care of her had eroded her reluctance. She'd been alone and lonely, constantly besieged by men who wanted to possess her. She'd tried women for a while, and liked them, but they were no less jealous and possessive. She'd given in to Brano because he'd never doubted her hunting skills. She refused to marry him, though. Her divine sight had never given her a glimpse of the future, but she had a disquieting feeling love wasn't supposed to look like that. No matter how limited her choices were, how vast and empty the forests of Till, Liana gritted her teeth and persisted in her belief that one day she would find a love undeniable and true.

"Who is that man on the left, the blond one on the bay courser?" Her curiosity got the upper hand, even though she knew Brano was prone to jealous fits.

"Some Amrian lordling, no doubt," he said. "Let's get them into the castle and be finished with this."

Liana wasn't finished, though. The ride back was short and her horse knew the way, which was fortunate because her gaze kept returning to the man, who was deep in conversation with Gospodar Echton. It turned out that Brano was wrong: He was no lordling, but the Prince Regent himself, the famed military commander, the king's uncle, and as far above Liana on the social ladder as she was from the mouse living in the corner of her room.

Liana barely remembered the rest of that day—she spent it in a fog, performing her duties like a senseless puppet. Lord Echton negotiated with the prince about sending more soldiers south, about raising the taxes once again to fund the war, about the food he could spare. Liana had seen her first map of the whole kingdom that day, and when the prince showed how far the Seragians had advanced, it seemed to her they were almost at the foot of the mountains. Without an army, the forest and the snow wouldn't be enough to protect Till.

When the evening came, both parties gathered at the great hall, which barely deserved the name. The castle at the border with Leven was old and small, chosen for its insignificance, the perfect spot for a discreet meeting that could turn the tide of war.

The group of hunters sat on the benches around a trestle table in a dim corner with the rest of the soldiers and retinue. On the other side of the cold, smoke-filled hall, the high table looked grand only because of the lords who sat there. They'd reached a deal, it seemed, yet the atmosphere was serious, their heads bowed together in an animated discussion, Gospodar Echton's gray, wiry fuzz and the prince's tawny gold. No music, no entertainment, no merry drinking—the soldiers and the hunters soaked in the tension and drank their beer in silent determination. Even Liana's perfect eyesight had trouble penetrating through the gloom, but that didn't stop her from staring at the prince.

"You haven't touched your food," Brano noticed, pointing at a gray piece of mutton glistening with congealing fat on her trencher.

"My stomach is upset," she said. "I'm going to lie down, excuse me."

The four huntswomen in their group were given a curtain-separated nook with two pallets. Although everybody knew that Brano considered Liana his lover, she chose to sleep among the other women. She claimed it was for the sake of decency, yet she had a gnawing suspicion that the frayed ties which held her close to Brano were ready to snap.

A short, dark man waited at the chamber's door. He had the black, relentless eyes of a terrier which measured Liana up as she approached. She'd seen him standing behind the prince that day, dressed in the blue royal livery. He wore a sword on his left hip and a dagger on his right, and he looked like someone who knew how to use them.

"Mistress Liana, my name is Telani, and I'm a secretary to His Highness," he said. "He'd like to see you."

"Why?" she asked. She didn't mean to be rude, but something about his stance annoyed her.

He raised one eyebrow, pointedly staring at her much-mended hunting garb. "Does it matter why? It's not like you're in a position to refuse."

Gospodar Echton was too old to chase girls, but occasionally he had guests who thought their status allowed them to use the women in the castle as bed-warmers. Liana had always managed to slip out of such situations.

"Is that so?" she asked.

A mocking smile twisted the corners of his mouth. "Don't play coy, I've seen that redheaded ruffian treat you like his property," he said. "But if you think I'm here to procure a piece of warm flesh, think again." He turned on his heel and walked down the corridor. "Come with me or don't."

"Wait!" She followed. "I'm sorry I was rude."

"Most people are rude," he said, marching through the net of narrow passages. He navigated the castle with the perfect assurance of a resident rat. "But my lord is not, so watch your tongue."

They came to a narrow door leading into a sparsely furnished chamber. A bed in a corner, a chest, a desk with a jug of water, a cup, and a leather bag on it. The only clue that someone inhabited it was a fire burning in the fireplace.

"Wait here," Telani said. "He'll come when he's finished with Gospodar Echton."

When he shut the door behind him, Liana snooped around. She found a saddlebag filled with clothes beside the chest. It smelled pleasantly of soap and bergamot, but the touch of the fine wool and linen felt too intimate so she refrained from searching it. Instead, she opened the bag on the desk. It revealed even less—there were a couple of maps of places she didn't recognize and a stash of letters and documents. Liana's grandfather had taught her to read and write, but the letters were all battle reports and documents written in an impenetrable legal language.

Liana put them back and yawned. It had been a long day.

She didn't want to sit on the hard, high-backed chair and lying on the bed would be looking for trouble, so she settled on the faded rug in front of the fireplace. Time trickled slowly, measured only by the crackling of the fire, as the evening slipped into night. Brano was probably looking for her, if he wasn't too busy drinking with his men, and would be irritated if she if she wasn't waiting for him. Anxiety gripped her for a moment before she realized she didn't care one bit about what he was doing.

And the prince, did she care about him? She knew the basic facts, like anyone else: the younger son, the military commander and regent after his brother's death, married to the elusive heiress of Elmar. People spoke well of him, mostly, even though there had always been a dose of resentment for the court. The royals were imaginary beings, creatures of luxury and leisure in faraway palaces; hardly anyone Liana knew had ever seen them. Gospodar Echton didn't count—he was one of the great lords with royal ancestors somewhere down the line, but he was also a grizzled old bear preoccupied with his horses and hounds and the restless brood of children and grandchildren who drained his coffers.

She wondered what the prince wanted from her. The whole setup certainly didn't look like a tryst, and his secretary had denied it—but if it wasn't that, what was it? What business could a prince have with a huntswoman? Curiosity kept Liana stuck to that rug on the floor, even if common sense told her it would be better to slip away and pretend none of this ever happened.

She must have dozed off because the sound of the door opening woke her, followed by light footsteps and someone saying, "Gods, I've forgotten you're here, I'm so sorry."

She turned and the prince stood a few paces away, unbuckling his sword belt, shaking his head. He was tall and lean, broad-shouldered and long-legged. Handsome up close just as he'd been from afar, although she'd seen better looking men. A different quality attracted Liana: a presence more solid than most people, an acute three-dimensionality that bent the world to him. Unlike the insecure men she knew, who were obsessed with their image, with other people's opinions of them, all he projected was a self-contained poise. It pulled her in like a magnet.

"Your Highness." She rose and bowed her head.

He studied her face. "You're Darin's girl, aren't you? I recognized you immediately, you have his eyes and mouth."

These were not the words she'd have expected in a million years, and they kicked the air out of her lungs. "I never knew my father," she said.

"Oh," the prince said, "of course."

The news of Captain Darin's death had reached her the previous summer, and she felt a pang of loss, though it was hard to grieve something she'd never had. His absence had been a constant in her life, unchanged by his death.

"Did you know him well?" she dared to ask.

"Yes. Knew him, liked him, respected him immensely."

She nodded. It was a strange thought: The Darin the prince had known was not the beardless boy her grandfather and other hunters remembered, but a grown man, with a life she knew nothing about. She wanted to find out more, but she wasn't brave enough to ask.

"Please sit down." He offered her the chair, and she almost refused, mortified by the thought that he would remain standing, but then he sat on the heavy wooden chest and she reluctantly accepted.

"Echton tells me you're a superb hunter and the best scout he has."

She blushed at this praise, wondering whether he knew about her mother. Very few people did: her grandfather, Gospodar Echton, and—obviously—her father. Had Darin mentioned the Goddess of the Hunt to his prince? Was there something deeper than curiosity in his eyes?

People were intrigued with the touch of the divine when it came neatly packed inside legends, but in reality it frightened them. Liana had always hidden the more uncanny of her abilities and worked hard to justify her skills. She stayed in the background, leaving the praise and glory to others, happy that most men's interest never went further than her looks. She knew deep inside that if they ever realized Liana could beat them at every challenge, they'd hate her. More than hate her, actually; they'd find a way to hurt her.

Was the prince interested in her divine blood?

She studied him as he absentmindedly rubbed the golden stubble on his jaw. Dark circles of exhaustion framed his eyes, and he stifled a yawn. He didn't look like he was fishing for the uncanny.

"Is there something I can do for you?" she asked, hoping he wouldn't demand some kind of divine miracle.

"Oh no, quite the opposite." He paused, measuring his words. "Your father left no will and gave no instructions, but he told me about you, and I believe it was intentional. I owe it to him to make sure you are all right."

"All right?" She bit her lip, wondering what Brano, what any of her companions would think about this situation: a prince of the realm checking if she were all right. She almost laughed at the improbability, but she swallowed it at the last moment. The prince wasn't joking. His words were serious, weighted with the power of the royal command.

"Is there anything I can do for you?" he clarified. "You have a secure position in Lord Echton's household, but perhaps you want something better? I can't offer much, with half the kingdom in flames, but if you want to join my mother's household or find a noble husband, I can help."

Embroidering or bearing children, were these the only options? She reminded herself that the prince didn't know her and was trying to be generous. Paying a debt to her dead father.

But it wasn't some indifferent kindness that she saw on his face, nor a tedious obligation. His look was keen and intense, surprisingly warm beneath his steel glaze. A whiff of personal interest lay at the bottom of it. For the first time in her life, she was flattered by a man measuring her up.

No, not flattered. She was intrigued.

"Take me with you," she said abruptly, the words spilling from her mouth before her brain had the time to check them. "Let me join your retinue."

His eyebrows shot up. "There's nothing but war where I go now. With Echton's help, we hope to break the siege of Myrit and push the Seragians back towards the coast. It will be months of campaigning, and I'm not even sure we stand a chance." He rubbed a knuckle across his lower lip. His hands, elegant and long-fingered, were marred with chilblains and callused from fighting. "I shouldn't be saying this, please don't pass it to Echton."

"You think we don't stand a chance?"

He shook his head. "That's just exhaustion speaking, ignore it. I'll find a way to outmaneuver them." He shot her a tired smile. "Mind you, allowing you to join me is no favor. It's more like a punishment."

"I don't mind," she said. This was no time to be humble. "I'm the deadliest archer you'll ever see, and I can track and hunt down any animal or human without them ever noticing me. I'm sure I'll be useful to you."

"You're no soldier, though. Would you rather risk your life down south, would you rather risk being caught and tortured by the Seragians or bleeding out slowly on a battlefield than ride through these forests? Gods know I need every ally I can get, but if your father were alive, he'd be furious with me for dragging you into mortal danger instead of making sure you had a good, peaceful life."

Would he understand if she tried to explain it to him?

"This is not a good life," she said. "This is a small life, secluded and meager. I am twenty-two and I feel all my options here are exhausted. My father went south and I want to follow him, but not to become a lady-in-waiting or someone's wife." She let out a mirthless chuckle. "I couldn't hold a needle or soothe a child if my life depended on it. No, I want to go and fight." She looked into his eyes. "I want to go where you go."

A long silence followed her words, yet she felt something important had been communicated between them in that small room. All rank had been stripped away for a short instance, all the disparity in power evaporated. Two young people making plans, nothing more.

At last, he nodded slowly. "Fine. I'll tell Echton you're coming with me." He rose and she jumped to her feet. "Is that all?"

She wanted to say yes, she opened her mouth, but her voice faltered. The idea of going back to her quarters, of answering her companions' questions, of accommodating any mood Brano might choose to burden her with, seemed unbearable. The world she'd inhabited a couple of hours ago fell to pieces like an old, worn-out shirt, impossible to put back on.

His eyes studied her face while his fingers traced the embroidery on his collar. He seemed so serious and utterly composed, and yet…

"I don't know," she said at last. "Is it?"

It was risky and rash and downright impudent. He hadn't given her a single inviting signal, the faintest hint of desire. She could have been embarrassing herself.

Still, they remained looking at each other until he cleared his throat and said, "Am I reading this completely wrong? Because if I am, you're free to go, and all I've promised stands."

She took one step towards him, then another. She had to lift her head a little to see his face. His body gave off heat and a faint scent of bergamot and leather.

"You're not reading it wrong," she said, dizzy with daring. "Also, it has nothing to do with the previous conversation, my plans, or your perceived debt. It just is."

Liana had never seduced a man before. She never needed to. It had always been them chasing her, extorting a more or less enthusiastic response. It dawned on her now that she'd never really wanted any of them. Not like this, not with this wild urge to shatter his poise, get under that smooth surface and wreak havoc inside, light him up like a bonfire and make him cry out her name.

"It will be outrageously inconvenient," he said. "And possibly demeaning and ruinous for you."

She let out a raspy laugh. "I'm not some precious lady; the only reputation I need to protect is tied to the tip of my arrow. I'm free to do what I want, and what I want is this."

She laid her hands on his shoulders, the sleek wool, the hard bones. A faint blush colored his cheeks and his breathing quickened as his arms slipped around her waist, drawing her close. This slow fire of excitement in her stomach, the solid certainty of being in the right place, was new. Slowly, his lips found hers, an inquisitive brush growing into a kiss, hard and deep. She pushed her hips against his and closed her eyes.

A wave of icy water washed over her, sharp teeth biting the soft flesh of her mouth, hard hands gripping her body. Liana kicked blindly with all the strength she could muster.

The hands released her and she fell to the cold stone floor of the cell.

"That was a delicious memory," Morana said. "Shame it never happened."

The Goddess of Death stood before her, shrouded in silvery light, her long black hair moving although there was no wind to pick it up. She smiled at Liana, her mouth filled with sharp teeth.

"Get away from me," Liana whispered.

"You should be careful what you wish for." Morana's eyes were deep like two wells, the golden glow in them only a faint flicker in an endless night. "Your past is no more and your future will never arrive. You're stuck here, helpless and out of your depth, and if you make one more mistake, he'll die."

"Why do you care? You hate him."

Morana's laugh was a deep, chilling sound of stones grinding underwater. "As I said, the past is gone. I have no quarrel with him, his slate is clean."

"You have no reason to help me, to help us." Liana struggled to rise, but her legs wouldn't carry her. She landed heavily on the bench.

"You still think Perun will help you?"

"We have a deal," Liana said.

"Has he ever done you a favor? Has your own mother ever done you a favor? Helped you in any way?"

"I can work with what they've given me."

The goddess laughed again. "When you figure out what they've done to you, call me. I'll be waiting."

"I don't understand."

"Use your brain." The goddess laid her hand on Liana's brow. "Wake up."

~Chapter 18~

Melia

Melia had never seen such a feast. The great hall of the palace looked like a summer garden, a colorful image of opulence and splendor. The soaring ribbed vaults reminded Melia of the branches of the ancient trees in the legendary forests of Virion, while the evening light that filtered through the tall stained glass windows bathed the hall in a jewel-like glow. Garlands of blooming roses, fragrant lilies, and dark ivy decorated the walls, framing the tapestries depicting chivalry and romance. Seragian imperial banners—purple, black, and gold—hung together above the dais with the golden sun on the blue field of the House of Amris.

The scent of flowers and beeswax filled the air, while candles in silver holders gave off their warm light. Massive chandeliers hanging from the ceiling shone like trapped stars, casting shimmering patterns across the polished stone floor. Long banquet tables gleaming with silver and crystal stretched the length of the hall. Gentle music filled the air, rising to the vaulted ceilings.

Melia felt small and insignificant and quite displeased with herself.

Her eyes followed the new couple. Amril had turned on

his charm, and not a single soul could catch a glimpse of his violent moods beneath his radiant good looks. His sapphire eyes shone with goodwill, his generous mouth was curved in a disarming smile, despite the cut and the bruise that marred it. He held his bride's hand, guiding her through the crowd, pausing often to whisper something in her ear.

And the Seragian carevna, the long-awaited emperor's daughter? As far as Melia knew, the emperor had a dozen wives and at least thirty legitimate children. What made him and his horde of advisors choose this somber redheaded girl? She glided through the mass without touching anyone, like a cloud of pristine white vapor, and weighed every scene before her with an ice-blue gaze.

The court had forced Melia to acutely feel her own lack of beauty. She'd been terrified of the possibility that Amril's wife would be some stunning, enchanting princess who'd outshine every lady-in-waiting. In fact, Princess Aratea could hardly outshine Melia herself. Without the glorious jewels surrounding it, her homely, freckled face had little charm.

"What do you think about the carevna?" she asked Princess Amielle, who still walked beside her as they entered the great hall.

"She doesn't reveal much, but that's to be expected," the princess replied. "At least she's not too young. I was afraid they'd send a child."

The carevna looked about Amril's age. Fresh enough, no doubt, but far from girlhood.

"Wouldn't a younger girl adapt more easily?" Melia asked absentmindedly.

"Would you adapt more easily if you were younger?" the princess retorted.

It wasn't a real question, but Melia still considered it. How far back would she have to go to stand a chance of becoming a sleek, scheming court lady? Before Rovin's death? Before her mother's? Or perhaps she'd always been hopeless, from the moment she slid out, bloody and terrified, into this world.

The bride and groom climbed on the dais and reached the high table, where two gilded thrones with red velvet cushions awaited them.

"A kiss! A kiss!" someone shouted, and the whole crowd picked it up.

Amril waited for the call to grow into a mighty roar and then pulled his bride close and gave her a long, intense kiss.

Melia averted her eyes, sickened by Amril's duplicity, by the self-assurance of the Seragian porcelain doll, by the senseless cheering. Who did the crowd cheer? The cruel, reckless prince kissing the enemy.

Amron materialized beside her and she looked up, hoping foolishly for some hint of affection or at least camaraderie. But he was a hypocrite like the rest of them, righteous and untouchable in his armor of ice all through the long succession of speeches and congratulations, the prattle about the wish for peace, the union between the kingdom and the Empire, the historical deal. Lies and self-interest.

She remembered the women in the kitchen of the fort, feeding their children with stale scraps, hoping their men would return. Her stomach turned at the sight of the first course, the hake and mussel soup topped with parsley and olive oil. It felt like ridicule.

Her father was right about one thing: The court cared nothing about those living—and dying—in the borderlands.

A bleak spell of loneliness wrapped itself around her like a wet cloak.

"Amron, will you not look at me?" she asked softly.

He sat with the perfect, cold composure of a statue, every lock of his hair held in place by a gold coronet, every crease on his clothes perfectly symmetrical. When she'd imagined him before the wedding, this cold perfection was what she'd seen in her mind. Now it looked unnatural, as if someone had taken the real Amron and replaced him with a hostile stranger.

"Leave it, Melia," he said.

Someone from the lower tables proposed a toast to the

bride and groom at that moment, wishing them a fruitful union, and they all obediently raised their glasses and drank.

"Did I insult you somehow?" she asked.

He shook his head, refusing to answer.

"Amron." She gathered the courage to touch his arm. "What have I done?"

He inspected his hands, refusing to look at her. "Gods know I don't ask for much." His voice was so quiet she barely heard it. "I don't ask for love or respect or even obedience, but I do expect loyalty from my wife. And this is not loyalty. What your father's been doing is the opposite of it."

"I cannot control my father."

"I know that. But you can control yourself. You can decide whether your loyalties lie with him or with me. And you can tell me what he's planning to do."

The music fell into dissonance, the lights dimmed, and Melia's hands turned very, very cold. With the utmost care, she laid her silver spoon beside her untouched bowl of soup.

"I don't know what you mean," she said.

"This morning, the scene at the palace gate."

She almost asked what scene—with all the events of the day, the short disturbance had slipped her mind. Then she remembered Amron hadn't even been there. What was he talking about?

The soup was taken away and the next dish was brought in: a massive fish baked in salt. Melia hated fish.

"That poor mad girl who threatened your father?" Melia tried to recall the girl's face, bruised and sprayed with blood, surrounded by wild locks, as the guards dragged her away. Was she important for some reason?

"The girl who brandished a Seragian blade," Amron said, "and accused your father of attacking me and conspiring to destroy the peace treaty."

A Seragian blade. Melia looked across the vast hall: Ferisa still sat beside her father. Two dark-haired people bowed over their wine glasses, chatting. They almost looked like a couple.

How many Seragian blades had there been in Abia before

the carevna's arrival? And how many of them belonged to Roderi of Elmar?

"Surely, everybody at court knows that my father is a war hero, the protector of the kingdom." Her voice came out high-pitched like a child's. She cleared her throat. "The king himself said so this morning. To think he would conspire with the Seragians is sheer madness."

"Is that what I am, then? Mad?"

Melia swallowed, her fists balled, hidden among the layers of fabric in her lap.

"Why would you believe some barely coherent street urchin?" she asked.

Amron pressed his lips together, and it suddenly dawned on Melia that he knew the girl. The wine she'd drunk rose to her throat in a sour tide, threatening to spill over her dress, the tablecloth, and his fine velvet. She swallowed it down with effort. Was it the same girl who'd faced the attack with him?

Melia breathed through her nose, too afraid to open her mouth. Ferisa was the one who had the weapons, who was supposed to keep them in her father's house. What were the chances that some little whore had followed Ferisa, survived the encounter, and managed to bring the blade before the king?

"Who is the girl?" she asked.

"It doesn't matter who she is, but what she said."

"It matters to me." The cloying smell of food, candles, and flowers made her dizzy; the alcohol sloshing in her empty stomach loosened her tongue. A lonely, unimportant, unloved wife. "Why do you care for this girl, Amron? Is she your mistress?"

"No."

"Then what? Tell me, I want to know." Whiny, pleading.

His mouth reduced to a pale line of anger. "What is your father scheming? What kind of evil has he brought here?"

"No greater evil than you already harbor. You're a hypocrite and a liar, just like the rest of them."

She must have raised her voice, because people turned to look at her. The fish on the platter stared at her with one cloudy, baked eye, mocking her uncouth jealousy, her inept qualms.

"Excuse me," she muttered and fled.

As she pushed through the crowd of dancers and onlookers, she thumbed the little vial safely hidden at the bottom of her pocket. Surely, a sleeping draft was not an attack? It was just something to embarrass Amril, to make him look ridiculous in his bride's eyes.

But why would she help her father do that? She turned back to Amron, on the brink of telling him everything, but her husband was already talking to the carevna, all the anger gone from his face. A golden head and a fiery auburn, close together; he said something that made her laugh in earnest, she laid her hand on his arm. A rusty nail of jealousy pierced Melia's chest as he led the carevna to dance.

On the opposite side of the high table, her father talked to the queen. Melia didn't want to go to him, but he drew her like a magnet until she found herself hovering at the edge of the conversation.

"I could take so many things personally, Roderi, but I don't," the queen said. "Especially things of this magnitude."

"Then you're a better person than me."

Melia veered away from them, repelled by the familiarity, afraid of overhearing more. She wished she'd eaten something, but all the food looked overly elaborate, hostile in its richness. She grabbed a piece of bread from an overlooked basket and nibbled on it, unwilling to go back to Amron, reluctant to have anything to do with the ladies or the nobles she didn't know. Not only did she feel lonely and embarrassed, but she was also mortified by the possibility that someone might want to talk to her.

Princess Amielle, who'd been her companion earlier, set beside her husband, Erian of Leven, looking radiant as he held her hand. No room for Melia between them. A happy marriage, or at least an intimate one. Amron danced with Aratea, her hand on his shoulder, her eyes glued to his face.

The remains of the fish were cleared away, and the guests drank some more. Melia wanted to run, but she couldn't.

Where was Ferisa? She had to ask her about the girl with the yatagan, about her father's plans. About her vanishing when Melia thought she finally had a friend at court.

More people were dancing than sitting now, and Melia panicked at the thought of barging among them, clumsy, unsophisticated like a waddling duck, embarrassing herself. She spotted Ferisa at the edge of the crowd, looking stunning in red silk, her dark eyes burning, her cheeks flushed. As beautiful as any of the ladies, no trace of the hedge healer about her, and far more royal than Melia herself. Melia should have resented this smooth transformation, this radiance she herself could never have achieved. Yet, her heart could only admire Ferisa for it.

She rushed to Ferisa with praise on her lips, just as a man materialized before her, putting his arm on Ferisa's shoulder, whispering something in her ear with casual familiarity.

"Not here. Later," Ferisa said with silky voice, her eyes wide-open, red lips smiling, the invitation on her face so obvious it cut Melia like a lash.

The man turned, revealing a sharp profile, golden beard, cold blue eyes. The king, nodding at Ferisa with a smile.

Melia melted back into the crowd before Ferisa could spot her, baffled and hurt. She'd never presumed she knew all of her friend's secrets, but Ferisa was rapidly turning into someone Melia couldn't recognize.

She was sick of the wedding, tired of the endless day and craving the oblivion of sleep. Her father and Ferisa could clearly manage on their own, they didn't need her puny help. She scanned the crowd, looking for the best escape route.

Someone caught her arm.

"Dance with me," Amril said. "Your husband stole my wife, it's only fair that I steal his."

"No, please, I'm—"

"I'm offended that you're so unhappy at my wedding," Amril said, his grip tightening. "Your expression is like a drop of lemon juice in a cup of milk, it sours everything."

His fingers dug into the soft flesh of her arm. Why was he even looking at her? It was his day, his triumph. He looked like the perfect, golden, fairy-tale prince. Why did he need his brother's lackluster wife?

She tried to smile, but it had no effect on Amril. His hand moved to the small of her back, pressing.

"Of course I'm happy for you," Melia stammered. "And I wish you and your bride all the happiness in the world. If you saw a frown on my face tonight, it wasn't because of your wedding."

Amril was not easily thrown off when he sniffed a weak spot. "What was it about, then? My brother's been sulking all day, but that's expected. He's humiliated himself publicly twice in as many days."

Behind him, Amron said something to the carevna, and she chuckled. Another stab of jealousy to Melia's heart, watching the bride in Amron's hands, gliding with elegance despite barely reaching his shoulder, with a sweet smile on her unforgivably homely face.

Still, it wasn't the Seragian princess that she worried about.

Her thoughts must have been obvious, because Amril asked, "Is Amron making you unhappy again?"

She thought of the loyalty Amron had demanded of her, and then she thought of the mud-splattered girl the guards had dragged away.

"That girl yesterday," Melia said, "what was so special about her?"

Her words lit a spark in Amril's eyes, and Melia knew she'd said exactly what he wanted her to say.

"Nothing. Except that my brother is infatuated with her. You see that bruise on my face? That's because of her. He's fallen hard."

"He denies it." A weak whimper.

"Of course he does. But he's my little brother, I've known him since the day he was born, and I've never seen him so smitten before. He's not like me, I fall in and out of love twice a week, but Amron is serious about it. I'd be worried if I were you."

Did Amril just enjoy saying the most inflammatory, hurtful things he could think of?

Melia couldn't do it, she couldn't dance and smile and talk to him and pretend his words didn't cut her. "Excuse me," she said for the second time that evening, and tore herself out of his grasp with such force she collided with the couple behind her. Blushing, she fled. Reaching the high table, she noticed Amril's half-full glass on the table, unattended. It was almost too easy to slip the vial between her fingers and pour its contents into his wine.

Out, she wanted to get out. But someone cried, "It's time for bedding!" and the crowd swallowed her again.

~Chapter 19~

Liana

Liana woke to voices coming from behind the door.

"I have agreed with Captain Darin to bring the girl up for questioning now."

Amron.

"My lord, the king's orders are that only he can—"

"Do you want to go up to the great hall and ask him? I can wait."

"No, my lord. Please—"

"Then stand aside. If my father has objections, he can take them up with me in the morning."

Liana was already on her feet when the door opened and Amron peered inside.

"Come quickly," he said.

As she passed through the door, he threw his cloak over her, swathing her in the warm velvet that smelled of him. The two guards stood aside to let them pass, hands on their hilts, suspicion mixed with reluctance on their faces. Still, they didn't have the audacity to draw a weapon on a prince.

As they rushed through the net of dark passages, she asked, "Is Captain Darin waiting for us?" dreading her father's reaction.

"No, he doesn't know I'm here," Amron said. "I bluffed, counting on the fact that a couple of sleepy night guards who'd rather be gambling than standing in a drafty corridor wouldn't have the gall to stop me."

Her chilled body objected to running, but she kept up with him, barefooted on the smooth wood of the back corridors. "Who told you I was here, then?"

"My mother."

Liana didn't ask how Queen Orsiana knew she was the same girl Amron had dashed off with, or why she thought it was important her son knew what had happened to her. In the few brief interactions Liana had had with the queen, she'd always acted with purpose, even if that purpose wasn't always clear to those around her.

They were climbing up the servants' stairs to the second floor. "Where are we going?" she asked.

"To the only place where I can hide you at the moment."

His chamber. Despite the exhaustion and fear and hurt, she felt a spark of excitement at the thought that they would be alone. They ran through the familiar passage built in the wall and slipped through the door, behind a tapestry, and into a room with a solitary candle burning on the desk.

A sense of familiarity washed over Liana. It wasn't the same room he'd used when they lived together, but it was undoubtedly his, nevertheless. Crowded, but organized, filled with the books and art he loved, his scent lingering like a ghost of his presence. It felt like home.

Amron lit several more candles, letting warm light wash over the room. He was still dressed in his ceremonial garb for the wedding—he must have rushed to her as soon as he'd been free to leave. She draped his fine cloak over a chair; it would be a shame to ruin it.

He turned to look at her. "Gods," he said. "What happened to you?"

There was a small mirror on the washstand. It showed her a woman she barely recognized: tangled hair, dress torn to ribbons, dirty face splattered with blood, a nasty gash on her arm.

"Are you hurt?" he asked.

"It's just cuts and bruises." She examined the wound on her arm: Ferisa's blade had cut deep, yet it had already started closing without being sewn shut. "I heal very fast."

"It would be wise to clean them." He opened the door, exchanged a few muffled words with someone standing outside, then returned to her. "Sit down, please."

She picked a simple wooden chair, unwilling to leave traces of mud on fine fabrics.

"Your father told me about you," he said.

She wondered how a father who barely knew her had introduced her to the man she loved. "How much did he tell you?"

"Only the important bits."

The bit about her mother, too—she saw it on his face. Yet Amron was discreet almost to a fault, as always. Despite the obvious curiosity, he didn't pry, aware that divine blood was not the wonderful magic the legends portrayed it to be, but a dangerous curse.

"He couldn't tell me how a girl who'd never left Till before could travel across half the kingdom alone, without money or protection. And, more importantly, he couldn't tell me why you were here in Abia." He poured some water from the jug into a porcelain basin and brought it to a little round table near Liana's chair. He put a sponge and a towel beside the basin. "Here, this will do for now. Wash yourself, I won't watch." He walked to the window. "I thought you'd tell him more than you told me at the party, but all he knew was that you wanted to speak to me again."

Liana removed her torn dress and thin linen shift. The water was warm, the sponge soft. She rubbed off the worst of the grime from her face, then proceeded to wash her body, dripping on the fine carpet. The water turned brown with streaks of pink.

"I wasn't sure what I was supposed to say, back then. I only knew things would go wrong at your brother's wedding, so I came to warn you."

"Does that have anything to do with your divine gifts?"

It was still night outside, behind the glass panels. A black moonless curtain dotted with stars. If Amron could see the reflection of the room—and Liana—in the window, she didn't mind one bit.

"Yes, although not in the way you might think."

"Can you see the future?" he asked.

There was no set future, she'd figured out as much and Morana had confirmed it. Still: "I can see possible outcomes and they are all quite bad," she said.

She dried herself with the towel and, deciding her clothes were unsalvageable, wrapped herself in it. It barely covered her from breasts to hips. "Do you have a hairbrush?"

"Beside the bed."

She ran her fingers through her thick locks, removing the twigs and leaves, and then brushed her hair until it fell in shiny waves that reached below her waist.

"You can turn now," she said.

He turned and narrowed his eyes. It was an oddly piercing gaze, going through her and beyond her. "I don't know how, but we know each other quite well, don't we?" he said.

"Yes." A whisper that barely slipped past her lips.

He took one step towards her, then stopped, ridiculously regal in his blue silk brocade. His shadow danced on the wall behind him. As he studied her, his fingers touched his neck distractedly, and slid under his gossamer-thin linen shirt, following his collarbone. It was an invitation he was unaware of, an intimate, absent-minded gesture she'd seen him make when he wanted her. It was an opening.

"How is that possible?" he asked.

The sight of his exposed throat distracted her. *You are mine,* she wanted to tell him, *I've had you a thousand times and I want you a thousand more,* but caution sealed her lips. Still, what she couldn't say with words, she could express with a touch.

She closed the distance between them and took his hand. "You hate to be touched by strangers," she said, "and yet, my touch feels good."

His breathing turned ragged as he gently pulled away. "I don't think this is wise."

Light as a feather falling, she placed her other hand between his collarbones, where his fingers had lingered a moment ago. A pink flush swept over his neck and face. Her fingers slid up and around, to the back of his head, into his hair, twisting the long, silky strands. "And if I pull here—"

He shivered, yielding to her tug. Letting his breath out, he opened his mouth a little, and she thought, surely, this would be the moment he'd kiss her. Instead, very slowly, he touched the silver locket nestled between her breasts. "What's in there?" he asked.

Her eyes glued to his face, she fumbled with the clasp and opened it, revealing the lock of golden hair coiled inside.

"Whose hair—" he started, and stopped. He wasn't the only man with that particular shade of dark Amrian gold, and yet it was perfectly plain that the lock was his.

She shut the locket, watching him closely as confusion and desire fought in his eyes.

"Amron," she said.

And then someone knocked on the door.

He shook his head as if waking from a dream, and went to open it. He exchanged a few words with someone standing outside, and when he turned, closing the door, he had a bundle of clothes in his arms.

The moment was gone, she saw it clearly, and the uncanny recognition that had cracked his shell and made him show his desire evaporated into thin air. He was back to his old self: restrained, careful, hiding behind good manners.

"I got a little carried away a moment ago. I apologize if I made you uncomfortable," he said.

"You didn't," she said, but there was no going back to intimacy, not when his mind was already on different things.

"I got you a uniform, it's the least suspicious thing I could get at this hour. My mother has female guards; in a palace this crowded, no one will question you."

He laid it on the chair and turned away from her once

more. There was nothing left to do but put it on. At least it was practical and it had trousers, high-waisted and tied at the ankles, along with a shirt and a short tunic with the royal emblem. A leather belt—without the sword, unfortunately—and a pair of leather sandals came with it. The whole ensemble fit her surprisingly well, almost as if Amron knew her exact measurements. Or had spent more time watching her than she was aware of.

She plaited her hair. "Do you have something I could tie it with?" she asked.

He rummaged through his drawers and came up with a satin ribbon, royal blue like her uniform. "This should do," he said.

It might have been a coincidence, but more probably, it was some god's idea of a joke. Liana trembled as she touched the ribbon, an exact copy of the one his last letters to her had been tied with.

Somewhere beyond the divine curtain, two days and seventeen years away, he was dead, gone from the world, unattainable to her. A sense of desperate urgency overcame her, the need to grab his wrist, pull him close, and kiss him roughly. But that wouldn't do. The deal was for him to kiss her, not the other way round.

"Is everything alright?" he asked.

It was a matter of life and death, she was supposed to weigh her words carefully, consider the gods' game, the stakes, the people involved, the possible outcomes. She ought to have strategized, even if she'd never strategized before. But standing close enough to him that she could feel his warmth had robbed her of any tactic she'd believed she had.

"What if you could step away from all this right now?" she blurted out.

"Step away?" His gaze cooled down. "What do you mean?"

"Leave all this behind, the court, the struggle, the impending conflict, all that burdens you, all the unhappiness."

"Leave it how? Board a ship and sail away? Run into the woods?" A wan smile twisted his mouth.

"It's a little more complicated than that," she said. "And a little more final. Like stepping into another world, similar to this one, but also different. A world where you knew me once and could know me again."

The invitation turned the impossible to possible, and she could almost hear the pieces of the puzzle clicking into place for him, the inexplicable intimacy, the details she knew about him, the immediate feeling of belonging, of fitting together like two halves of a life maliciously broken by the gods.

"It would be just the two of us," she pointed out, although she was sure he'd figured out as much. "And I don't know what that world would look like." *Ravaged by the war you failed to stop.* "But we'd have each other."

His gaze was intense, curious, and seeing he hadn't refused it immediately gave her the courage to continue.

"I know you've wondered what it would feel to be ordinary, just a normal man unburdened by the royal duties, the demands of the court. To make your own way in the world, without the privilege you were born into, without the demands made by others, without the rigid list of expectations you have to fulfill. It would allow you to see what you are really made of."

He averted his eyes to hide the hunger in them. It was a futile move, because she'd always known it was there. It ate him from the inside, the thought that all his achievements had stemmed from his privilege, from the fact that he'd been born as the king's son. Even though every person who knew him could've told him that his kindness, courage, diligence, had nothing to do with his status, and that he worked as hard and fought as bravely as any of his clerks and soldiers, there was always a part of him that wondered, *what if?*

"It would allow you to shape the world around you with nothing but your sword, your quill, your tongue, and see how far you could get."

His gaze hovered above her head, faraway and hazy, seeing the strange cities, the unexplored seas, the endless wonders of the world. "I'd love that very much." A whisper so soft the silence swallowed it immediately. The sharp yearning written on his face revealed that he wanted it as badly as she wanted him.

Kiss me, she thought, *kiss me and we'll be off. The rest of the world may take care of itself without us.*

The rest of the world.

Amron rubbed his eyes as if waking from a dream and raked his fingers through his hair, disturbing its sleek neatness. "What about everybody else?" he asked.

She could never lie to him, and he would never forgive her if she did. "They would remain here."

"And face the conflict, the bloodshed you warned me about?"

She nodded.

"If you know anything about me, then you know I'd never leave them to face it alone," he said. "So whatever it is that you're offering, I first need to know what I would be running from."

His rebuke wasn't harsh, but it made it look as if she wanted to turn him into a coward who'd left his family to fight alone and abandoned his duty. She couldn't tell him that his duty would ride him into the ground, squeeze every last drop of blood from him, and get him killed at some insignificant backwater he'd be dragged to on the king's whim. His duty would never let him turn into the man he wanted to become because it would always demand too much. His duty would crush every dream he had of the peaceful life with her and rob them of years of happiness.

And even if she told him all that, he would still choose his duty over his personal interests because that was written into the very core of his being.

Suddenly feeling the weight of her bruised, exhausted body and her impossible quest, she crashed down on the hard chair and buried her face in her hands. "I'm so tired," she said. "And I desperately need a drink."

"I'm sorry, I should have asked you sooner." He produced a silver flask from some invisible pocket. "Take a sip of this first."

She took a hearty gulp and liquid fire filled her mouth. It was the fig brandy he always carried with him, the one which could pull you back from death's door.

While she savored the warmth spreading through her body, he poured two cups of rosehip tea from the silver teapot on his desk and offered her one. "This should help you feel better."

It was warm and fragrant and it did make her feel better.

"Before we get distracted again, or attacked, or separated, I think you should tell me everything from the beginning, because this feels like putting together a broken plate in the dark—every shard is sharp enough to draw blood, and I can't see the whole. I wish Darin could be here to hear it all, but our time is running out. The moment my father remembers to look for you, I'd better have a good reason for stealing you."

Where should she begin? With the things she could remember, the things that were true.

"It begins with my parents, Darin and Lela," she said. "I'm sure that, being Amris's heir, you know how rarely the couplings between gods and humans produce children, and how erratic those children's gifts are. My blood comes with certain advantages: speed, stamina, strength, hunting skills second only to my mother's. I heal fast and age slowly. I'm good at seeing people for who they really are, and seeing divine touch in the world." She paused. "I'm telling you this so that you know I'm not some powerful, divine creature, just a very good huntress with some talent for divination."

He nodded, but didn't interrupt her.

"Now comes the difficult part, the part where I need you to trust me." She closed her eyes. "We've met before, and when I say *before*, I mean when you were twenty-six and I was twenty-two years old."

The twenty-three-year-old Amron sitting across from her raised his eyebrows, but instead of claiming it was impossible, he merely asked, "How old are you now?"

"Two days ago, I was thirty-six. Now?" She shrugged. "I can't tell. I'd be nineteen if I were still in Till, but I'm here instead, so…"

The lack of shock on his face reminded her that he had a mother who was far more versed in dealing with the uncanny than Liana. He must have heard a fair share of the queen's stories in his childhood.

"Am I right to assume that you knew the forty-year-old me, then?" The incredulity in his voice was not tied to the fractured time, but to his age. No one at twenty-three could imagine themselves at forty. "How was I doing?"

You were dead.

She didn't say it, for what good would it do? For the first time in her life, she lied to him by omission and glided around his question. "I can't—and won't—tell you anything about that future, because it's not real, it exists only in my mind and nowhere else. The gods cursed me with it, and then left me here."

"So…the things that happened there won't necessarily happen here?"

"I don't know," she said. "Maybe. But what I do know is when I met you, the kingdom was at war with the Seragian Empire, and that war started here, in Abia, at your brother's wedding. When I found myself at this moment in time, I thought there was a reason the gods put me here."

"To stop the war?"

"To stop it, to make it worse, to save someone, to kill someone, who knows?" *The battlefields, the blood, the kiss that would lead into a war-torn future.* "But I don't care what they intended. I want to stop it. They muddled my memory, so I had to piece all this together from the hazy fragments and things I've learned here."

He pinched the bridge of his nose. "So, Amril's party, everything you said there, and the fight afterwards, you were trying to warn me?"

"Yes."

"Why me, though?"

It was her turn to raise her eyebrows.

"Oh." He blushed again. "How well do we know each other, exactly?"

"Fairly well." Despite the grief, the bad news, the complexity, she paused to enjoy the sweetness of the moment, his eyes resting on her, the questions he dared not say aloud.

His soft laughter broke the tension. "I've had my share of

strange encounters with women, but this one beats them all. I almost wish this was a prank by Amril to set me up with a girl."

"Your brother is not that imaginative."

"No, he isn't." His laughter fizzed out. "Something else bothers me, though. If you were still in Till when Amril got married, how do you know the war started here?"

"Because it's common knowledge. I don't know the details, you're right about that. That's why I ran around like a mad-woman, whispering strange warnings to anyone who crossed my path."

"But the things you said to my father this morning, they were precise." He frowned.

There it was: the moment for the hard truth.

"Yes." She hesitated. "Things have changed in the meantime."

He'd never talked about his wife when they were together. Liana had asked a few tentative questions in the beginning to see where they stood, to assess the risk of falling head over heels for someone who was, technically, still married. But Amron had refused to discuss Melia. *It's over, she's gone and she's never coming back*, was all he'd said.

"At dawn, after talking to my father, I went looking for you," she said. "I saw your wife in the corridor and something felt off, so I followed her. She met with a woman in the garden, a woman wearing a Seragian uniform."

"Melia met with a Seragian woman in the garden at dawn?" Incredulity rang in his voice.

"No, I said the woman was in a Seragian uniform. She was Elmarran, though. And she was one of the attackers from last night. Their leader, actually. I recognized her voice."

He sat very still, looking at her.

"The woman's name is Ferisa, I found out. Perhaps you've met her?"

A brief, barely visible nod.

"I followed her out of the palace, through the streets of Abia, and into the house that belongs to Roderi of Elmar. I found the yatagan there, and got these cuts and bruises. She knows

I know about her now, and she's after me. I ran to the palace, I didn't know I'd encounter your father. I was stupid enough to let the guards catch me with a weapon in my hand. I tried to warn the king, but Roderi of Elmar was there, and I looked like a madwoman and spoke like a raving prophet… I should have been more subtle. I think no one believed me."

"My mother did," he said softly.

"And you?" she asked. "Do you believe me?"

He stood up and walked to the window, his figure sharply outlined against the darkness behind him.

"It's bothered me for months, the Elmarran reaction to the peace treaty. Their contempt, their quiet displeasure, their failure to acknowledge it. I was confused at first. I saw so much death at the border that I thought they would surely welcome peace. They deserved it more than anyone else in the kingdom." His voice trailed off, swallowed by the night outside. He shook his head. "I was wrong, and my father was wrong too, misjudging human nature. Roderi of Elmar doesn't know how to stop fighting, how to forgive and forget. What he wants after all those years of fighting is not peace, but revenge."

She'd heard this reasoning a long time ago, in a battlefield tent, but she didn't interrupt him. He had to figure it out by himself.

"Revenge against the Seragians, yes," he continued, "but even more than that, revenge against the people who forced him to make peace with the Seragians." He turned away from the window. "Against us."

"Your wife is a traitor," Liana said.

"I know."

Commotion in the corridor disrupted his quiet words. Voices, shouting. Fists banging on the door.

"Prince Amron, you must come, now! It's your brother!"

~Chapter 20~

Melia

Melia wondered if her own wedding night had looked anything like this from the outside, to the guests who'd celebrated while anxiety raked her guts.

The crowd of giggling young women led the bride upstairs. The queen's ladies, the Seragian escort: no one Melia usually associated with, but now their bubbling excitement pulled her into their chirping flock. The wish to disappear, to melt into the background, to crawl into her bed and forget about the awful day, disappeared as Princess Amielle caught her hand.

"You don't want to miss this part," she said.

"I've never seen it before, not from the outside." Against her better judgment, curiosity seeped into Melia's voice.

"It's your duty. You're a royal now, you must witness Amril's wedding night, in case someone tries to claim the marriage wasn't consummated." Amielle winked; she wasn't entirely serious.

"I doubt anyone would dare to claim such a thing." Melia chuckled, but in the back of her mind, a sharp shard of memory cut through the mirth. Amron putting his clothes on in haste, leaving her alone in the cold, empty marital bed in Syr to contemplate her flaws all through that long night.

She winced, but the princess wasn't looking at her. Her bony, long-fingered hand held Melia in an iron grip, pulling her through the brightly lit corridors to the royal chambers.

On the other side of the carved wooden door flanked by the two royal guards, it seemed the feast at the great hall had been a mere prelude to the real party. There were tables laden with food and drink in the antechamber. Not the greasy, heavy, show-off dishes and strong wines that were served downstairs, Melia noticed, but exquisite, dainty bites that smelled exotic and looked divine, paired with iced pomegranate juice and elderberry wine. A girl in Seragian dress played a soft, sweet tune on a lute while the women chatted and laughed.

"This looks very cozy," Amielle said. "I remember my wedding in Myrit, Amril and Amron got me tipsy and told me so many dirty stories I couldn't stop laughing when Erian entered the room. He thought I was laughing at him, poor soul." The princess grabbed two glasses from the table and handed one to Melia. "Did Amron live up to your expectations on your wedding night? He can be awkward around the people he doesn't know well."

"He was…very accommodating." Melia blushed.

She looked desperately for something to save her from the conversation. The queen's ladies surrounded Melia like a flushed, rowdy mob, filling her with discomfort. She'd never learned how to work a crowd, how to charm people, chat politely. The ladies closed their ranks against her—a few acknowledged her with a brief nod, but most of them simply went on ignoring her like any other day.

She was saved by the carevna's arrival. The emperor's daughter glided between them, flanked by her escort. Melia found herself staring at their elaborate silks, transparent gauze, and layers of intricate gold jewelry on their chests and wrists. Once more, she felt like her idea of the Empire had been childish, ignorant. She knew *nothing* about those women and their lives.

They formed a procession that followed Aratea from the anteroom to the bedchamber, quiet and filled with fragrant flowers, with a massive canopied bed with the sheets already turned down.

The queen's ladies were eager for the disrobing ceremony, with all the teasing, pulling, and more or less accidental pinching it involved, but the carevna's own women took her gown off so swiftly and deftly that no one had the chance to step in. Fast and silent, they decked her in a gossamer-thin white shift, which they covered with an embroidered, lace-trimmed white wrap. Aratea's hair, brushed and braided into a simple braid that reached the small of her back, was shockingly red on the pale background.

Aratea turned to the queen's ladies and said, "Thank you so much for your help. I have presents for all of you." She signaled to her women. They brought beautifully carved wooden boxes and guided the ladies back to the antechamber, emptying the bedroom.

"Please stay," Aratea said to Melia and Amielle. "I'd like to think we're sisters now."

It felt frightening, this open invitation. This familiarity was so strange to Melia, who'd never had a sister. Meeting her eyes in the mirror, Aratea shot her a pale smile. "I can tell I'm not the princess any of you expected."

Melia blushed, but Amielle said, "We refrained from speculation."

In the brief silence that followed, Melia studied her own hands, trying to ignore the other Melia locked inside her head, the one who wished nothing but death on all Seragians, the one who'd laced Amril's drink with gods knew what. She convinced herself that Amielle and Aratea certainly had secrets of their own, and she was no worse than them. No Amrian princess, no Seragian carevna, ever harbored any love or friendship for the lords and ladies of Elmar.

"So what can you tell me about Prince Amril?" the carevna said.

What was it with the princesses and their bluntness, Melia wondered. She kept her gaze on her entwined fingers, afraid that if she looked at Aratea, she might blurt out that Amril was a conceited, spoiled, insecure bully who sought adoration but offered nothing in return.

Amielle saved her.

"You might have heard he's difficult, and I won't deny it. But I assure you my brother's heart is in the right place and he knows how important you are."

Melia admired Amielle's skill at saying something true without saying anything important. Unwilling to add anything, she picked up a glass of cold pink liquid, fruity and fragrant, that fizzed on her tongue, leaving a faint trace of alcohol.

Aratea narrowed her eyes. "I've been taught that the men in your kingdom are barbaric, uncouth and uneducated in the art of communicating with women. You leave the art of seduction to chance, the lovemaking to a mere physical act."

Melia almost choked on her drink. Making men feel good was for courtesans and the wanton ladies of the court, not for royal wives, wasn't it? Thinking about it now, she realized all that Amron ever tried to do was make her feel good. "You were taught those things?"

"I was taught all manner of things, but I'm not sure my husband will appreciate any of them."

Melia had spent months feeling sorry for herself, hating the life at court, unable to let go of her past. But, looking at the Seragian princess before her, she felt a pang of shame. Aratea was more foreign than anyone here, in a country where she had no one and everything was different, and where many still considered her an enemy. And she didn't marry the patient, considerate prince; she married the other one.

"I think it's best to stay silent and observe until you can judge the situation," Amielle said, her laconic manner reminding Melia of Amron. "I'm sure you've also been taught how to do that."

Melia felt the barb in Amielle's words, but she nodded nevertheless. It was a wise piece of advice, and useful. Amril might have been rash, aggressive, self-centered, but he wasn't stupid. The Carevna of Seragia was not some girl he could harass and insult. He wouldn't dare, not after the most difficult negotiations in history.

No matter how he felt. No matter what Melia had put in his drink.

Aratea was a little older than Melia, and she seemed poised and refined, but when the door of the antechamber opened and the noise of male voices filled the air, a spark of panic flared up in her pale blue eyes.

"It's time," Amielle said. "We must leave you now."

Don't resist him and he'll have nothing to break. But those were not the words one said to a bride on her wedding night, so Melia kept her mouth shut and gave Aratea a long look of sympathy. "Good luck," she whispered.

The carevna nodded and sipped from her glass. She was probably too sober to face Amril.

The atmosphere on the other side of the door had grown wilder. The ladies were joined by the men from the prince's retinue, and there was no shortage of flushed faces, messy clothes and ruffled dresses, and hands sliding to touch hot skin under the pretense of dancing. As if the idea of what was about to happen in the royal chamber had inspired everybody else to seek their own fulfillment once the formal part was over.

"I'm leaving now," Amielle whispered in Melia's ear. She touched her rounded belly. "This thing drains all my energy. I'm going to faint if I don't lie down."

Melia couldn't object to that. Still, as Amielle was leaving, she muttered, "And what am I supposed to do here on my own?"

She searched Amril's party, looking for Amron in vain. Her husband was nowhere in sight, leaving Melia at the mercy of the hands reaching for her. Usually, her plain looks and cold manner protected her from unwanted advances, but on a night like this, when everyone was more than a little drunk, she was just as coveted a prize as any lady-in-waiting. A young man caught her wrist and pulled her into his lap. She elbowed him in the stomach, her eyes on the crown prince.

Was Amril behaving any differently than usual?

He stood in the middle of the crowd, draining a cup, looking his unruly, wild self.

"Careful, my prince, alcohol destroys virility," a lady said and laughed.

"It's not the wine that makes men limp in your presence, Ramina, but your shrewish tongue," a young nobleman retorted.

Amril was swaying gently, his flush turning an ugly shade of purple. Melia regretted that she hadn't asked Ferisa what she'd put into the concoction, because he surely wasn't displaying signs of fatigue and sleepiness. On the contrary, she noticed the bright spark of arrowfoil in his eyes, the agitation of a soldier getting ready for battle.

She turned her back to the crowd and took the vial out of her pocket. A solitary drop lingered in it. Melia was no expert in potions, but she had spent enough time in Ferisa's den to recognize the smell of the herbs she often used, to tell her potions apart.

She shook the drop into her palm and sniffed it. Arrowfoil, yes, for energy and aggression. But also lobelia and vervain. She licked the drop.

Oh, Father!

Powerful emetics, both of them. It was too late to do anything about it, though.

And why should you do anything about it?

"Bring me wine!" the prince ordered.

She didn't care for Amril, and he didn't care for her. He'd crush her like a cockroach if he thought she stood in his way. He'd sacrificed every inch of Elmarran soil, every drop of blood the Elmarrans spilled, for an advantageous marriage with a Seragian princess. He deserved no consideration, no help.

The golden prince. Behind his mask of bravado, he was probably as nervous as his bride. He'd bedded tavern wenches and ladies alike, more than anyone could count, but the woman waiting for him in the royal bedchamber was not like them. Every noblewoman knew from the earliest age that her body was not her own. It was interesting to see a prince realize that. Amron had known it—and fought against it on their wedding night—but he had the luxury of being the less important prince.

In the other room, even if it was for this night only, that composed, plain young woman whose body was Seragian territory and a vessel for imperial will held just as much power as Amril.

And thanks to Melia, he would perform badly.

The songs had turned bawdy, and the court ladies reached for the prince's clothes, giggling as they disrobed him. He was laughing, but his laughter had no joy to it as the hands that had known his body before now untied, unclasped, unbuttoned, and pulled off the layers of fine fabrics roughly, impatiently, and without any wish to caress. The cruelty was shocking but not surprising if one remembered how Amril had treated them. This was a payback for his wandering hands, his demanding grasps.

Amril flinched and cried out in pain. Disheveled and undressed to his shirt, he pushed the ladies away hard, breaking the unspoken rules of the wedding-night disrobing. One stumbled, one would have fallen if a courtier hadn't caught her. They protested, but Amril ignored them, raking his fingers through his locks. A fine film of sweat lay on his brow.

The two imperial ladies-in-waiting guarding the bedchamber watched the spectacle with distaste. The crowd's feeble attempts to invite the carevna to show herself were ignored, the language barrier suddenly an impenetrable obstacle.

"Go and make us proud!" some drunken fool cried.

Amril's bloodshot eyes searched the room and fixed on Melia. "Where's my brother?" he asked.

Where *was* Amron? It was not his habit to shirk his duty like this, even if he was angry, even if this crowd bewildered him. Amril so rarely relied on him, but now Amron's absence loomed like a missing tooth, like a rug pulled from under one's feet.

The truth was, in that roiling sea of sycophants, he was the only person capable of reining Amril in, and Amril knew it.

Faster than she expected, Amril crossed the room and grabbed her arm. "Where is he?" He shook her so hard her teeth chattered.

"I don't know," she stammered, frightened by the wild glint in his eyes.

"Someone find him," Amril ordered.

He looked sick, yet everybody pretended not to see it. Goaded by his friends, he let go of Melia and stepped towards the bedchamber.

"She's in for a treat," a lady said behind his back, her voice dripping poison.

"Show her that move, you know, the one that makes the girls moan."

A choir of exaggerated moans echoed in the background. Amril swayed on his feet and shook his head like a wounded boar preparing for the final charge.

"Conquer the Empire for us!"

Melia kept her expression frozen, afraid to show her disgust lest they turn on her.

"Open the door," Amril said.

If Amron had been there, perhaps Melia would have repented and begged him to stop his brother, to take him to some private corner and let the potion run its course. But Amron wasn't there, and even if his erratic behavior frightened her, she had no means of stopping Amril.

The Seragian ladies opened the door, and Amril walked through them like a man heading to his execution.

The noise in the antechamber fell to hushed whispers, cushioned by the soft melody the lutenist strummed. The lust was postponed for a little while, the erratic, nasty revelry temporarily brought to heel while the royal business was conducted in the next room.

What were they waiting for? For Amril to walk out with a triumphant smirk on his face? For some physical proof, like a bloody sheet?

Melia felt sick.

"Any moment now," one of the ladies whispered, "he never lasts very long," and all her companions burst into muffled fits of laughter.

But there was only silence on the other side of the door,

silence for so long that the men grew uncomfortable and the women bored. Those intent on seeking their own pleasure snuck out, and the crowd dwindled, leaving only the curious and the unfortunate.

Too many scents mixed in the air—food, flowers, perfume—and it lay thick and heavy on Melia's shoulders, choking her. Her father was far away, yet she felt his fiery gaze burning the back of her neck, his hot, hungry breath behind her ear. And Ferisa, damn her, what was she doing? She used to be Melia's friend, her anchor, not this malevolent creature seeding destruction wherever she went.

If only Amron were beside her. Even though it was too late to save the night, they could retreat with dignity. Melia stifled a yawn, looking at all the food that lay forgotten on the tables, all the bottles filled with bright liquid, the ice slowly melting, wishing she knew how to drink herself to oblivion and wake up in some other place. Or some other time, where Ferisa's potion had been nothing but a sleeping draft, and Amril snored gently in his wedding bed while the carevna read a book beside him, wondering how long it would take for the most stubborn guests to take the hint and go away.

The course of the night had already been decided upon, though. Voices rose on the other side of the door, breaking the uncomfortable silence. Pleading, then a high-pitched yelp, something heavy stumbling, hitting the door. A cry, "No, don't—" and then the door opened so violently it almost tore its hinges.

The carevna flew through the doorway, landing on the carpet in the middle of the room. The Seragian women screamed, rushing to her. Amril stood on the threshold, swaying wildly, his bloodshot eyes staring at the antechamber but seeing nothing.

Pushing away the ladies, Aratea cried, "What are you staring at? Help him!"

The prince fell to his knees, head bowed, hands hitting the carpet, and threw up a stream of red liquid.

Melia screamed, and she wasn't the only one. The ladies shrieked, and Amril's friends woke from their stupor, ran to him, pulled him away from the mess. A lady with a wet cloth ran to wipe his face, someone poured a glass of water and tried to lift it to his lips. The prince shook them off and turned to his wife.

Supported by her ladies, Aratea looked like a ghost, red hair pouring over her shoulders, white nightgown ruined. She stepped towards the prince. "Amril, you're unwell," she said.

The glistening puddle on the floor was dark red, but it was clear to Melia, who'd seen enough blood spilled for a lifetime, that it was only wine.

The prince opened his mouth to say something and instantly doubled over, a red tide rushing out of his mouth again. When it ceased, he lifted his head, wiping his mouth with the back of his hand, and said, "What have you done to me, you bitch?"

The words were nothing unusual for Amril, for the rash, crass, unrestrained prince who didn't have to weigh the words that passed his lips. In taverns and at court, everybody cowed before him, lashed by his reckless tongue, the people who could restrain him fewer than fingers on one hand.

Still, the words he could carelessly throw at his friends or lovers meant something else when hurled at his Seragian bride.

Like silk parting before a sharp blade, the remaining people split into two groups: the Amrian courtiers gathering around Amril, and the Seragian ladies backing off towards the bedchamber with their mistress.

"Can you say that again, please?" the carevna said, her Amrian formal, clipped. Despite her wild hair and the stained nightgown, she looked every inch the emperor's daughter.

"What did you put in my drink?" Amril said, too immersed in his shocked fury to restrain himself and apologize.

Melia, hovering in the shadow of a curtain, looked towards the door, hoping that someone outside had heard the commotion and that guards were on their way.

"Are you accusing me of trying to poison you?" Aratea said slowly, every word pitched to carry.

"Isn't that what you Seragian cowards do?" he retorted.

That sobered some of the men around him. Hands pulled Amril back, into a cloud of urgent whispers, but it was already too late. In the bedchamber doorway, the carevna exchanged a few words in Seragian with her women, too fast for Melia to understand. One of them produced a heavy silk wrap and wrapped the carevna in it, covering the shameful stains.

I did this. This is my doing.

A ridiculous thought.

And yet, there was nothing ridiculous about Aratea as she laid an icy gaze on her groom and his friends. "I understand now what you think of me," she said, "and I understand that, in spite of all preparations, you might not have been ready for the wedding. All I can do now is retreat and seek advice from the Seragian ambassadress."

Not waiting for a reply, one of her ladies shut the bedchamber door, leaving the rest of them crowding around the prince in a sour-smelling room.

No one knew what to do next; they stood in a frozen tableau around the prince until footsteps thundered in the corridor and Amron ran in, followed by a handful of guards.

"Amril." Amron rushed to his brother, knelt down beside him.

The two men who held the crown prince let go, not even trying to hide the relief on their faces.

"Where's Aratea?" Amron asked his brother.

Amril shook his head.

The door of the bedchamber creaked open, but instead of the carevna or one of her ladies, Captain Darin stepped out, stern and impeccable as always. The atmosphere among the courtiers changed, a sudden silence following the chaos.

"The princess requested my men to escort her to the Seragian embassy," Darin said.

"Have you slipped into my wife's bedroom behind my back and allowed her to leave?" Amril lifted his head, his face pale with greenish shadows.

"I think it's probably for the best, my lord. Just for tonight."

Whispered conversations filled the room as Darin's men herded the guests towards the door.

"She poisoned me," Amril said, sullen like a boy.

"You deserved it," Amron muttered, and amazingly, unexpectedly, his brother cracked a sour smile.

"You've come here to gloat, haven't you?"

"No, I've come to fix this. Come." With Darin's help, Amron dragged Amril up. "The physician is on his way. Do you have the cup you drank from?"

"I drank from many cups."

"Of course you did." Amron motioned one of Amril's men over. "Help the prince to bed. Clean him and let him lie down."

"I'm not drunk," Amril said. "I've been drunk many times before, and this is different. Someone poisoned me."

"I know," Amron said. "But I don't think it was your wife."

Amril paused on his way to bed. "Who was it then?"

"That's what I'm trying to find out. In the meantime, as soon as you feel you can stand on your own, rush to the Seragian embassy and apologize to Aratea."

Amril frowned, but allowed himself to be led away.

"I'm going to find my father, he needs to know what's going on," Amron told Darin. "Send two dozen guards to the embassy and watch over them until dawn. I'm afraid something might happen."

"I'll go there myself," Darin said.

Amron nodded, while his gaze searched the room, stopping—finally—on Melia. "A word, please," he said.

The relief of seeing him drained as a tide of panic filled her veins. "Where were you?" she asked.

He ignored her question. "It was you," he whispered.

"I don't understand," she stammered.

Amron grabbed her shoulders. His grip wasn't rough, but it was firm as he gave her a brief shake. "It was you who put something in his drink, wasn't it? Down in the great hall, while he was dancing?"

She winced.

"I haven't told Amril or Darin yet, but you must tell me what was in there." His thumbs dug beneath her collarbones. "Is it dangerous? Is it going to harm Amril?"

"No." She shook her head violently. "It's not dangerous, I swear."

"Why did you put it in his drink? Who gave it to you?"

She shook her head, tears blurring her vision.

"It was your father, wasn't it?"

"He said it was just a sleeping draft."

"But it wasn't, was it?" he asked. "This is arrowfoil, I smelled it on him, and something else, you saw how sick he is. What was in there?"

"Arrowfoil, lobelia, vervain, that's all I know, I swear." She was crying hard now, even though he'd let go of her. "It just made him sick, nothing else. He'll vomit everything he drank tonight, but he won't be harmed."

He took a step back. "Melia, what is the point of this, what does your father want? His men pretending to be Seragians, attacking me in the street? Poisoning my brother on his wedding night? Does he think we're going to break the peace treaty over this?"

"He can't forgive the Seragians. He won't forgive," Melia said.

"Nobody is asking him to forgive. But this? This is treason, and I have to go to my father and tell him about it."

The broken shards inside her head connected briefly to form a picture of utter chaos. Her father's actions and their consequences. "No, Amron, please, he's going to kill him."

Amron paused, weighing the options. "He's going to find out one way or another. By morning, Darin will piece it together. Whatever your father intends to do, he needs to stop."

But all she could think about was the king's cold, harsh gaze, his complete unwillingness to show mercy. "Don't betray him, please, I'm begging you."

Amron rubbed a spot between his brows with his index finger. "I suppose nothing irreversibly bad has happened yet. There's still time to fix this." He laid his hand on her shoulder again, gentler this time. "Go to him, go now. Tell him to leave

Abia immediately, go to Syr, and bury himself there in the red dust until everybody forgets about him. And then come back to me. I won't mention you, I won't reveal what you've done. We'll explain Amril's behavior somehow, apologize to the carevna, and the wedding will proceed as planned."

"Will you forgive me?" she asked.

"You are my wife." He squeezed her shoulder briefly. "Go now, hurry, before this escalates."

Liana

Amron ran and Liana followed him to Amril's bedchamber. It looked like a street brawl, not a wedding celebration. Amril was on his knees, restrained by his friends, looking sick, a puddle of vomit soaking into the carpet before him. The ladies of the court cowed in a corner, one was sobbing. There was no trace of his Seragian bride.

Invisible in her uniform, Liana retreated to the shadows in the corridor. Guards marched in, then her father rushed out without noticing her, followed by stunned courtiers who scurried away, pretending not to see each other.

Amron talked to his brother in the voice he used to calm down skittish horses and belligerent soldiers. For the second time since Perun dropped her in Abia, Liana was on the brink of believing that the damage could still be absorbed and Amron could still make everything right.

Then Melia came out, turned her head left and right, failed to notice Liana, and dashed down the corridor. Liana wanted to run after her and break her treacherous neck like a twig, but then Amron stepped into the corridor and said, "Liana?"

"You let her go," she said. "You know everything I told you was true, and still you let her go."

Behind him, servants entered the royal chambers to clean the mess. Amron motioned her to follow him to a quiet alcove, out of their sight.

"I'm going to see the king now and I want you to come with me," he said.

"But your wife—"

"She's gone to tell her father to get away from Abia right now, shut himself in Syr, and never show his face again."

"In spite of his treason?"

Amron looked tired in the pale light as he massaged his temples as if staving off a headache. "It's been mostly ineffective so far. The attack in the alley, your skirmish with that woman, Amril's drunken escapade. Nothing irreversible or catastrophic. Tomorrow morning, Amril will be his most charming, humblest self when he apologizes to his wife, and what his charm can't fix, my mother's diplomatic skills will. Darin and his men will guard Abia against anyone who still wants to break the treaty. And my father—I hope—will do the reasonable thing and hush everything up."

"And you'll just let Roderi of Elmar go, unpunished?"

"The alternative is worse. If we admit we let a traitor wreak havoc among us, the Seragians will think us weak, or they will think we did it on purpose, and the peace treaty will be dead in the water. And if my father publicly accuses Roderi of Elmar of treason and proves his guilt, he'll have to punish him. He'll execute the Defender of the South to appease the Seragians. The whole Elmar will be up in arms in a heartbeat."

Liana saw reason in his words, but the injustice burned her like acid. "And your wife?"

"My wife will be my worry."

Liana's heart sank. Always reasonable, always loyal. Why couldn't he be rash and furious, for once in his life?

"Come, we need to find my father," he said.

It was only a short walk to the king's quarters, but when they reached them, a guard shook his head when Amron asked to see his father. "His Majesty is not in."

"I see." Amron nodded. "Is he where I think he is?"

"I'm sure Your Highness knows where to find him."

"Did he take any guards with him?"

The guard shook his head. "He never does."

A mixture of annoyance and resignation ran over Amron's face, and Liana was certain it wasn't directed at the guard.

"Let's go," Amron said. "We need to find him."

Liana didn't ask where they were going—she could guess. They passed the queen's quarters and turned into a shadowy corridor. Amron stopped before a narrow door, took a deep breath, and released it slowly. If the king was doing what Liana supposed he was doing, it was no wonder that Amron was hesitating. Still, he raised his hand and knocked.

The door remained closed.

Amron knocked again, harder, and this time a muffled female voice said, "Who's there?"

"It's Amron. I need to speak to my father, please. It's urgent."

The door opened a fraction, just enough to show a lovely female face surrounded by chestnut waves. She rubbed her eyes. "I was sleeping, I'm sorry."

"Lenka, is my father here?"

"No." She shook her head. "He promised he would come tonight after the feast. I waited for him, but then I fell asleep."

"Do you know where he might be?"

"No. Is he not in his room?" She addressed Amron with little deference, as if she'd known him for a long time.

Liana had never bothered with the inner workings of the royal court, but someone once told her—mistaking her for Amron's mistress—that being a royal mistress was a job. This young woman probably treated it as such, with practical, efficient self-interest.

"No, and the guard told me he was with you." Amron frowned. "Lenka, when you talked to my father tonight, did he seem strange? Was there anything odd?"

The lady twisted a long curl around her finger, thinking. "I don't think so. He was tense about Amril's wedding, but he was just his usual impatient self. He hardly ever shares anything with me." She raised her eyes to Amron's face. "Is there trouble?"

"Perhaps." Amron shuffled in the doorway. "Did he seem interested in someone else? Some other girl, a guest taking his fancy?"

The king's mistress didn't seem offended by the suggestion. "You know what he's like—if he wants something, he gets it." She frowned. "I heard him mention the orange garden, though, to someone. I don't know who it was."

"A woman or a man?"

"What do you think?" Lenka bit her lower lip, plump like a cherry, and her eyes switched to Liana, studying her in the weak light. "And who's your new friend? I haven't seen her before. I know you like them rustic, but this might be too coarse even for you."

Liana bit her tongue, reminding herself that the arrow wasn't meant for her.

"That's none of your business," Amron said. "Thank you for your help, Lenka. I'm sorry I woke you up."

She pouted prettily but didn't persist. "Well, good night then," she said, threw one last incredulous glance at Liana, and closed the door.

That left Liana and Amron alone in a dim corridor.

"He might have returned to the feast," Liana suggested. "People will be dancing and drinking in the great hall till dawn. Perhaps he was in the mood for company."

"No, when the king leaves, he doesn't return." Amron pinched the bridge of his nose, thinking. "If I order the guards to find him, they'll raise the alarm, and Darin has his hands full with the Seragians as it is. If my father went for a quiet meeting in the orange garden, or—gods forbid—a tryst, I'll end up looking like a massive, incompetent fool."

"Could he be in the garden, taking a quiet walk, then?" *Or fornicating among the potted citruses, more likely.*

"I don't know. He does whatever he pleases. Perhaps he's alone somewhere, perhaps he's meeting someone, who knows. Oh, damn." A faint note of desperation slid into his voice. "If Darin figures out it's the Elmarrans before the king can hush it up, Abia will burn."

"Find Darin, then, and worry about your father's preferences later," she said.

"If I tell all this to Darin, he'll understand what I'm doing, but he won't have any choice but to go after Roderi, and I won't have the authority to stop him." He shook his head. "Gods, I wish my father were predictable for once in his life."

The palace was nothing like a forest, but still, Liana was a huntress and a tracker, and the prospect of hunting someone down made her heart beat faster. "Come on, we won't solve anything by standing here," she said. "Let's check the garden, we have nothing to lose."

Garden was too generous a word for the terrace filled with oranges, lemons, and other citrus trees in large pots glazed in white, blue, and yellow swirls. Cascading jasmine covered the walls, providing the illusion they were surrounded by nature. A small, dolphin-shaped fountain in the center provided a soft background murmur which couldn't disguise two quarreling voices.

Amron touched his lips with his index finger, sliding silently around the massive pots, Liana at his heels.

The quarrel turned into a struggle, followed by a curse and a cry. Amron ran.

A figure sat on the gravel, pressing his belly, blood leaking through his fingers and dripping on the gravel.

"Father!" Amron fell to his knees beside the king.

From the corner of her eye, Liana saw the other figure running between the trees. She recognized the shape, the movements, in an instant, and dashed after her.

"Liana, don't!" Amron called. "I need help."

Trembling with frustration, she watched Ferisa slip over the wall, and then she rushed to Amron, who was pressing the wound on his father's belly with a bundle of cloth.

"Raise the alarm! Let the guards bring the physician here," he said.

"No!" his father ordered. His breath was ragged, his face deathly pale in the moonlight, but his voice was stern and clear. "Sit beside me for a second."

"Father, you must—"

"Don't argue with me, boy. Sit down."

Without further arguing, Amron sat on the gravel.

"How did you find me?" the king asked.

"Lenka told me where you were, I came to tell you that Roderi of Elmar…"

"…Is a traitor. I know."

"What were you doing here, then?" Amron asked.

"I thought I could get to Roderi by reasoning with her. More fool me." The king coughed weakly. "Where's your wife?"

"I sent Melia to tell her father to run from Abia and hide in Syr. We can't let the Seragians know he's behind it."

"You want to hide the treachery?"

"Yes."

There was a long pause.

"Did you conspire with your wife and father-in-law to bring your brother down?" the king asked.

"No!"

"You've always been jealous of Amril. That strange attack yesterday—how convenient that you weren't hurt."

"Father, you can't believe—"

"And your wife, skulking around, reporting to her father. This is all your fault for dragging them here. What's your plan? Tell me."

"Stop it!" Liana growled. And then she turned to Amron. "Get your mother, now!"

Pale with shock, he opened his mouth to argue, but she cried, "Go!" and he ran.

"It's you," the king said, studying her face. "I should have guessed. Will you finish what that bitch started?"

"You're drunk," Liana spat.

He tried to grab her arm, but Liana was stronger. She caught his wrist and removed his hand. "Your Majesty, you're drunk," she repeated, calmer, "and wounded and confused. But Amron is loyal to you and is currently doing everything he can to stop the conflict. If you can't see that, you should be seriously worried about your judgment."

The only answer was the king's fast, shallow breathing.

"All Amron ever wanted was for you to acknowledge how damn good he was at everything you threw at him," she added, even though she knew it was futile.

And then voices echoed among the trees, footsteps on the gravel, and Amron appeared, followed by the queen in her nightgown with a pale lilac shawl wrapped around her shoulders.

"You need a physician," Queen Orsiana said, her voice leaving no room for argument. "But discreetly. Let's get you to my room. Amron, please."

Unwilling to spin wild accusations before his wife, the king allowed Amron to prop him up. Liana stepped to the other side to help him.

That morning in front of the palace, the king had cut an impressive figure: tall, strong, and terrifying. In the moonlit garden, he was a pale ghost, a heavy middle-aged man hanging between them like a drunk thrown out of a tavern.

As Amron moved forward, the king grunted, his eyelids fluttering.

"Walk now, please," the queen said.

The three of them stumbled across the terrace and into the corridor. The cool draft revived the king somewhat, and his legs found purchase on the stone flags, lifting some of the weight off Liana's shoulders. The sour odor of his sweat mixed with alcohol offended her nostrils, and the unwanted proximity of his body made her wish for a good scrub. Not to mention the repulsion stemming from his treatment of her that morning. But Amron needed her help, and she was going to help him.

The two guards in front of the queen's chambers, a woman and a man, opened the door without a word, pretending they didn't notice the king. They'd obviously seen him at his worst before.

"Come in, come in." The queen rushed them through the door and into the antechamber, where the sleepy lady opened the bedroom door for them.

It was the room Liana had slept in for the last thirteen years, complete with the massive four-poster bed, the green brocade curtains, and the floral tapestries. She missed her step, tripping on the edge of the carpet, almost pulling the king down. Queen Orsiana jumped at her side, steadying her. The queen's hands were cold and surprisingly strong.

"It's fine, you're safe here," she said so softly only Liana could hear, and then she ordered, "Lay him on the bed."

Liana helped Amron drag his father and lay him down. The velvet on his belly was ripped, the small hole surrounded by a barely visible circle of dried blood. Belly wounds were dangerous, but this one didn't look immediately lethal. Unless…

"Orsiana," the king said. Propped up by pillows, his blond hair matted, his face deathly pale beneath his beard, he didn't look like a drunk anymore—he looked frighteningly frail.

"Amron." Queen Orsiana sat beside her husband, and it took Liana a long moment to remember Amron and his father shared the same name, and that the queen was talking to her husband. The queen's hands slid down his body to the rip in the fabric. "You're wounded. Oh, I'll fetch the scissors, we need to cut the fabric away, wash the wound. Call for physicians."

But the king caught her wrist. "Orsiana, no. There's no point, it's already too late."

"What do you mean?"

"The blade was poisoned," Liana said softly. Three pairs of eyes turned to her, the uninvited guest, the ghost in the room. "Elmarran poison."

"How does it work?" the queen asked.

"Makes you go numb," the king replied before Liana had opened her mouth. He was struggling to breathe. "I can feel it spreading through my body."

The queen gently pulled her hand out of his grasp and stroked his face. "What did you do?"

"I tried to reason with Roderi, but he sent his woman instead. It doesn't matter now." The king paused to take a sip of the water the queen offered him. "We need to talk in private."

Amron caught Liana's hand. "Come," he whispered. "We should wait outside."

They closed the door behind them. The antechamber was empty, lit by a single oil lamp. Amron sat on a bench beside the window and hid his face behind his hands. Liana stood frozen, weighing the possibilities, her fingers itching to touch him, her brain telling her he might not welcome it, might not even want her to witness his anguish.

In the end, her heart won, and she sat beside him, wrapping her arm around his shoulders, keeping her touch light, ready to retreat at the first sign of rejection. Words were futile and hollow in a moment like this, but still she said, "He didn't mean it."

He remained stiff for a while, a cold stone effigy closed off from the world. But then he turned, wrapped his arms around her, and sank into her embrace.

"I should have told him about my mistrust of Roderi earlier, but that would have put Melia in a terrible position."

"I don't think he would have believed you anyway," Liana said.

"You're right. He would have brushed it off, just like he brushed off all my doubts about Elmar and this match."

His breath felt warm on her skin, his head heavy on her shoulder. She breathed in the familiar scent of his hair, her hands welcoming his sharp bones, his hard shoulders. She closed her eyes, pushing away the world around them, focusing on the perfect simplicity of breathing, the synchronized rhythm. Inhale, exhale.

The night around them writhed in agony, yet here, inside these rooms, there was nothing but silence. Liana might have dozed off for a moment, because the next thing she felt was a light touch on her shoulder.

"It's time, he wants to see you," the queen told Amron.

He separated himself from Liana, cold rushing in to replace the warmth of his body. Standing up, he smoothed the creases on his clothes in a gesture so automatic he probably wasn't aware of it. His face was bone white, stunned.

"I'll give you a little while, and then I'll fetch your brother," his mother said. "I've already sent Deana to find Amielle."

He nodded, threw one long look at Liana, and was gone.

The queen stood with her arms crossed, hugging herself against the night breeze.

Liana had met the queen when she'd first joined Amron. She'd never been hostile to Liana, not in the way mothers-in-law sometimes were, possessive of her precious son, jealous of the love he gave her. She'd accepted Amron's choice, despite the fact that Liana had no family, no standing, nothing to offer but herself. And yet, there had been a rift between them, because Queen Orsiana always thought about the kingdom first and Liana found that monstrously cold.

In fact, although she was mortal, Queen Orsiana seemed more godlike than the gods to Liana. She had their scope, their comprehension of the immensely complex structure of the world in her head, as well as the ability to focus on the smallest detail when it was necessary, but she had none of their frivolity, their aimless capriciousness. She was compassionate and understanding, and yet perfectly ruthless to the ones she loved the most when her goals demanded it. Like Amron, but harder. And like him, she could see the divine touch.

The queen's clear gray gaze rested on Liana—curious, careful. "He's in love with you," she said so softly it was like a feather falling on a pillow, "though he doesn't know it yet."

Liana sat very still, a mouse before an owl. She waited for the queen to say more, to judge her or demand an explanation, but she turned on her heel, saying, "I need to find Amril," and disappeared into the darkness, leaving Liana alone with her thoughts.

The king was dying.

If the king died, the war would be inevitable.

Every step she'd taken, every choice, proved to be futile. History swerved a little, but it returned to its course in the end. Liana desperately ran through the options in her head. What if Melia did what Amron had asked her to, what if she begged her father to run? Could it change anything? Probably not, for Roderi was not trying to hide his intentions anymore—this was open rebellion. He'd attacked the king. And if he accused the Seragians, if he managed to spread the lie fast enough...

The queen returned with her elder son. Amril's face still had a greenish hue, but he moved swiftly, proceeding directly to the bedroom, only shooting a distracted look at Liana and not really seeing her in her uniform.

Amron walked out as soon as his brother entered, looking even more distressed than before. His eyes were red, though no tears slid down his cheeks. The queen put her hand on his shoulder.

"I'm sorry," she said.

He shook his head. "I'm a fool," he said in a faraway voice. "I always thought, if I tried harder, perhaps he would finally see me, he would finally—" Pain cut his voice to a ragged whisper.

Liana faded into the shadows, an intruder, an unwelcome witness. Amron wiped his eyes with the back of his hand.

"He loves you, as much as he can love his complete opposite," the queen comforted him.

"You're far too generous," Amron said. "After all he's done to you."

The queen took a step back, lifted her head to look her son in the eye. "You're free to judge him for how he's treated you, but you should leave me out of that equation. Our marriage was our own, for better or worse."

"He promised to love and respect you."

"And what makes you think he didn't?" The queen raised her hands and cupped her son's face. "You're the cleverest of all my children, and yet you can be so dumb sometimes. His absence was a gift, a blessing. Do you think I wanted his unrelenting, demanding attention all the time? Do you think I wanted one dangerous pregnancy after another until I died? Would you do that to a woman you loved?"

"Mother—" He tried to turn his head, but she held it in a firm grasp.

"Your father is a hard, complicated man, and he's made many mistakes in his life, but our marriage is not one of them, and I won't have you hate him for it. I didn't raise you to be so narrow-minded."

Amron blushed and looked away. "Point taken," he said, as his eyes found Liana in her nook.

Liana expected embarrassment or anger, but all she saw in Amron's face was relief.

"Mother, this is Liana, Captain Darin's daughter."

"The girl with the Seragian blade, yes," the queen said. "Come closer, child."

Queen Orsiana's hands were cold and gentle when she laid them on Liana's cheeks. "You look like your father, but there's more to you than that, isn't there?"

Liana shot a glance at Amron. He couldn't have told her anything about Lela, about the war, about their future, there had been no time. And yet, the queen knew.

"Can you help us?" the queen asked.

"That's why I came," Liana replied. "Though…" Her gaze darted to the bedchamber where the king lay dying. "It might not be enough."

"If I ask you to do something, if everything else fails, will you do it?"

There it was, the divine trick wrapped up as an innocent question. Liana knew about deals, knew about bargains. She hesitated.

"Not for me," the queen said so softly only Liana could hear. "For Amron. That's why you're here, right? Will you do it for him?"

What was she supposed to say? "I will," she confirmed, and felt the words bind her stronger than chains.

Amril stumbled out of his father's room at that moment and grabbed Amron, pulling him away. "Where's your wife? Why did you send her away?" His anger shattered the atmosphere, mixing fury with grief.

"To tell her father to run away."

Amril took a swing at him, but Amron was faster, dodging the blow.

The queen caught Liana's arm, pulling her back. "Don't interfere."

"Did you plan all this with Roderi and your wife?" Amril growled.

"No. I thought she wanted to embarrass you and spoil the wedding. Not this."

"I don't believe you," Amril spat. "All you've ever wanted was to take my place."

He lunged at Amron again, but Amron pushed him away. "Use your wine-soaked brain for once in your life. If you give him chaos, he'll use it against you, and then you'll have worse problems than Elmar."

"He tried to kill Father."

"Yes. And despite that, he's not your biggest problem."

At that moment, a young woman ran into the room. Tall, lean, and blonde, she looked so much like Amron there was no need to ask who she was.

"Where's Father, what's going on?" she asked. "Are you two fools fighting?"

"You need to go in," the queen said.

"We all need to go in, I'm not wasting his time if what Deana said was true," Princess Amielle said. "Amril, Amron, the Seragian embassy is under attack, Erian just got the news. Someone is spreading rumors that the Seragians have killed the king and are planning to take the throne. The guards are there, fighting the mob."

"We need to go there," Amril said, but the queen caught his arm, stirring him towards the bedchamber.

"Not you," she said.

Amron turned towards Liana, his eyes uncertain. He lingered on the doorstep, the last of his family. "I'll come as soon as I can."

"Stay with your father," Liana said. "I must find mine."

Melia

Melia ran.

The night outside was lit by hundreds of torches, the streets crowded with people. In the flickering light, their grinning faces looked like masks of terror, their lurching, inebriated movements and twisting shadows like monsters descending from the black sky to swallow this town and everybody in it.

She couldn't tell if Abia was celebrating or writhing in agony as panic pushed her through the crowd, where hands grabbed at her fine dress and men wrapped their hungry hands around her waist, slid them between her thighs, their breath sour and hot, the stench of desire and wine choking her. She clawed at their faces, twisting out of their arms furiously, running on, even though she knew it was too late.

It had already been too late when she arrived in Abia. When she married Amron. When her brother died.

Her father's house at the end of the winding alley, hidden behind the high wall, was—for once—lit up and crowded. The guards at the entrance recognized her, and she ran through the door to find herself in a hall filled with men. She recoiled, sick of the crowds, when a hand grabbed her shoulder.

"Ah, you're here. Finally," Ferisa said. "How did it go?"

Melia could barely recognize her, this woman dressed in sleek black silk, filled with a sinister light. When did she change to this? When had she stopped being the lowly priestess and death-guide who'd wormed her way into her father's household and become this suave, bloodthirsty thing? Finding a lonely, desperate, motherless girl wandering the corridors of Syr must have seemed like a gift from the gods. A path to Melia's trust and her heart, and ultimately, to her father's ear.

"The crown prince is ill and the carevna fled to the embassy. I guess that's exactly what you wanted to achieve." Melia narrowed her eyes, focusing on Ferisa's chin. "You have a speck of blood here. Whose is it?"

Ferisa rubbed her jaw and smiled instead of answering. "Come, your father will want to see you."

Roderi of Elmar sat in his office, giving orders to half a dozen men, but he sent them all out with a flick of his wrist when Melia stepped in.

"Father, I need to talk to you in private," she said, nails biting into the soft flesh of her palms.

Ferisa turned to leave, but Roderi of Elmar said, "Stay." And then to Melia: "Ferisa knows all my plans. Whatever it is, I want her to hear it."

His glare peeled away layers of Melia's skin until she was nothing but a soft, vulnerable worm twisting before him. Still, from some unknown well in her heart, she pulled the courage required to say, "Father, you must run immediately."

He lifted his eyebrows, feigning confusion. "And why would I do that?"

"Because Amron knows you're a traitor, but I begged him to give you the chance to retreat to Syr before the king finds out."

Unlike Ferisa, her father wore no sleek silk. He was in chainmail, and instead of making him panic, Melia's words provoked a bout of grim, mirthless laughter.

"Oh, I wouldn't worry about the king," he said.

Melia had no sixth sense, no special feeling for the uncanny, yet her blood turned cold and a feeling of finality akin to the moment when the soldiers brought her brother home came over her.

"Father, what have you done?" Her voice betrayed her, fading into a ragged whisper.

"You didn't think this was some game to drive the Seragians away and spend the rest of our lives under the boot of the king and his ilk, did you?" her father said. "This is a rebellion, Melia, and it won't end until all of the royal cowards are gone."

"And the Empire?"

"Back to where we should have been, were it not for this cowardly treaty: at war."

The great, courageous, warlike Roderi of Elmar couldn't see it, he really couldn't. Perhaps because Melia was a blind spot, a disposable thing to him, a blunt tool to distract his enemies. The war with Seragia would be nothing like the border skirmish in Elmar. The emperor wasn't distracted this time, he wasn't uninterested. The whole blasting focus of the imperial gaze was on Abia, because this was *personal*. Because, unlike the Black Lord, the Emperor of Seragia cared about his daughter.

"Don't do it," she whispered.

Her father was already saying something to Ferisa when she uttered the words. He paused, turned to her. "What did you say?"

She should have said *nothing* and scurried out, like always. But she couldn't stand the stench of death that had been following her everywhere, she was tired of the endless bloodshed, endless grief. And therefore she threw herself on her knees before her father, under Ferisa's incredulous gaze, and begged.

"Please, no more death, no more blood."

"Is that what your spineless husband has taught you?" He grabbed her chin and forcefully lifted her head. "To be a coward? To run away from your enemies?"

"I want no part of it," Melia said. "I'm done."

"You'll be done when I'm finished with you." He shoved her so hard she crashed into a cabinet. "When they pulled you out of that heap of corpses, I praised the gods for saving my child. Had I known they'd take Rovin instead, I'd have left you to rot."

Ferisa, who used to be her friend, who used to comfort her in the bleak loneliness of Syr, now made no move to help her. Instead, she put her hand on Roderi's shoulder in a sickeningly intimate, plainly possessive gesture, and said, "It's time to let Abia know the Seragians have killed the king."

The king?

What have they done to the king?

Melia fled the room. As she climbed the stairs, she heard her father giving instructions to his men. "Spread the word that the king is dead and the Seragians are to blame. Lead the mob to the embassy."

From the stairs leading to the first floor, she watched the grim-eyed guards leave the hall, armed to the teeth, the noise of grinding metal and harsh voices making her tremble. She scurried up, running blindly until she found a dark, empty room, where she huddled in the corner.

It didn't help; the tide of death still found her, as it always had. A black wave of grief and loss washed over her and filled her with darkness, followed by sights and sounds she couldn't ignore, no matter how tightly she covered her ears or shut her eyes. They played out in her head, relentless, unending.

Rovin in his last moments, delirious with pain, begging for mercy.

And that older, cursed image that had haunted her since childhood, which she could never place. The dead horse on a dusty road, its entrails spilled, the stench of shit and blood, the screaming in the background.

It was important, it was *crucial*, it refused to let go. She was always too afraid to go back to that moment, to allow herself to be pulled into the vortex of death. For years and years, she had been too afraid to remember.

When they pulled you out of that heap of corpses, her father had said.

And Melia remembered.

The riders had materialized out of the whirling cloud of dust tinted red by the setting sun. Melia only saw them because she had nothing better to do than look out of the carriage window. Her nurse was dozing, head thrown back at an awkward angle, a thin line of dried saliva in the corner of her mouth. Mother and Teya were whispering about the upcoming arrival of some delegation to Syr and Father's expectations and the difference between southern and the northern hospitality. Melia didn't understand half of it, and that's why she was watching the arid hills outside, counting the stunted trees, hoping to see some interesting animal.

The hot wind lifted clouds of fine dust that scratched one's throat and got into every crease and pore. One moment, there was nothing before Melia's eyes but the barren landscape, the next, a group of horsemen was riding at full speed towards them.

"Mother," Melia said. "There are men coming."

Her mother ignored her, fervently discussing something with Teya. So Melia elbowed her nurse, provoking a sleepy grunt, and tried again: "Riders are coming."

Her mother shot her a quick glance. "Don't interrupt us, please."

The approaching group was close enough now that Melia could see individual riders. No uniforms, just dust-colored wool that made them almost invisible. And small, fast desert horses, known for their sturdiness. The setting sun gleamed on the steel in their hands. Melia's curiosity now gave way to suspicion that something might be wrong.

"Mother!"

"Melia, stop it! There's no one around—"

Shouts from their escort cut her off. Horses neighed, and the carriage plunged ahead. One of their soldiers shouted through the window: "Hold tight."

Melia's nurse woke up with a cry. "What?"

"Brigands," Melia's mother said, a thin crack of uncertainty spoiling her perfect poise. Beside her, Teya's golden face paled to sickly yellow.

The carriage sped up on the uneven country road, rattling and creaking. Melia's teeth chattered, biting her tongue. The taste of blood, hot and metallic, filled her mouth. She whimpered.

"Oh, gods!" The nurse pulled Melia close and tucked her under her arm like a hen tucking chicks under her wing. "Close your eyes, dear, don't look out."

Melia shut her eyes and buried her face in the nurse's soft flesh. But even with her ears covered, she couldn't block the shouting from outside. The carriage flew, shaking them like marbles inside a box.

"What are we going to do, my lady?" Teya moaned.

"Nothing," her mother said, clinging to the edge of her seat. "Our men are proper soldiers, armed and trained. These are just some desperate outlaws, looking for easy prey."

The shouts outside turned into screams, from both men and horses. Something hit the side of the carriage, hard. It veered, throwing Melia and her nurse towards Mother and Teya, bones scraping, heads hitting the thinly padded sides. The clash of steel outside rang in her ears, together with curses, cries, and sounds she'd never heard before: the crunching, wheezing sounds of people getting cut to pieces.

The carriage skidded, leaning to the left so sharply Melia was certain they would turn over. One wheel hit a rock, the carriage swayed wildly, throwing the passengers to the other side; it slowed down and stopped. Melia lay beside he mother, shaken and bruised. She grabbed her mother's knee, the first solid part she could reach, and her mother's bony arms wrapped around her. Melia's heart thrummed in her ears as her mother squeezed her hard in a silent warning to be still and quiet. She lay where the impact had thrown her, too shocked to think clearly.

It was all happening too fast for her to understand. Yet, she needed no explanations to know something very bad was coming. Like a mouse in its hole, she could smell the cats prowling outside.

The women disentangled their limbs in panicked silence. Her mother cradled her head, wincing in pain, and Teya's arm was twisted at a wrong angle. The priestess was crying, but she pulled herself back to the seat without a whimper. Melia's nurse was breathing hard through her mouth, the whites of her eyes flashing in the dim interior.

When the noise on the road died down, Melia hoped for one desperate moment that a friendly face would look through the window and tell them they'd continue their journey immediately. But the silence stretched out, and the women in the carriage held their breath.

Then the door opened. The dying light outside outlined the black silhouette of a man. His face was in shadow, but his clothes revealed he was not one of their soldiers. He said something in a language Melia did not understand. Her mother replied something sharp and cold. When she used that voice, people usually trembled before her and bowed their heads, but this rider reached inside the carriage, grabbed her mother's arm, and pulled her out, throwing her in the dust. A cry escaped her lips as she hit the ground.

The man threw more words at them in his gravelly language and Teya translated: "They want us to get out."

Melia's legs refused to obey, but her nurse picked her up and carried her out. Her skirt felt unnaturally cold in the wind; she realized she'd pissed herself.

In the red light of the sunset, blood looked black. It had already soaked into the thirsty dust, leaving only shadows under the bodies of their men—silent, unmoving, their limbs bent at odd angles, mouths open in silent screams. Wind brought the stench to Melia's nostrils: blood and sweat and shit. A horse lay in the middle of the road, its belly cut, intestines glistening like a nest of snakes.

When she saw that horse, Melia's fear became a solid thing, a lump of ice inside her chest. With absolute cold lucidity, she realized they were going to die.

The men made the four of them stand at the edge of the road. Her mother, in her fine black wool shot with gold, held her head high and watched the brigands with her dark, angry eyes. Beside her, Teya, in her priestly reds, cradling her injured hand, trembled and whispered, "My lady, tell them who you are. You're a million times more valuable to them alive than dead."

The men searched the carriage, pulling out their luggage, opening the chests full of silks and wools, throwing them into the dust. One man got hold of a small chest filled with coins; he plunged his dirty hands in and let the gold trickle through his fingers, laughing at the shiny stream. The men tied the things they liked to their saddles and stuffed them in their bags, leaving the rest scattered around the carriage.

"Roderi doesn't negotiate with Seragian scum," her mother replied to Teya. "He hangs them on the crossroads. So shut up and hope they take the gold and leave."

One man reached under the carriage seat and pulled out a leather folder. Seeing that it was just letters and documents, he threw it in the dust. The wind picked up the papers, lifting them in the air. Another man, who was stuffing silk scarves into his saddlebag, reached out and caught one sheet. He didn't read the writing, he probably couldn't, but he looked at the seal and then at Melia's mother. He called another man, then a third.

Melia watched their faces with impassive curiosity. They were weather-beaten, burnt by the sun to dark walnut, lined by the wind, covered in dark, scraggy beards. Abruptly, they stopped laughing and admiring their spoils. Instead, they gathered in a tight circle, their faces contorted in anger and alarm, speaking fast and gesticulating towards the women.

Melia's nurse prayed softly, a senseless litany of words, a drone of an insect caught in a jar.

A man approached her mother and asked her something, pushing the seal under her nose. Melia recognized the sound of her father's name, garbled by the strange language, repeated over and over again.

Her mother shrugged and shook her head.

"Roderi? Elmar?" the man repeated.

Roderi of Elmar, Melia's father, who defended the border of the kingdom and hanged Seragian outlaws at crossroads.

Her mother's lips were a thin, hard line. The man pulled out a knife and put it against her throat. "Roderi?" he asked once more. A drop of blood trickled down her mother's smooth skin. The knife pressed deeper.

Melia's mother closed her eyes and a single tear escaped her lashes.

"No," Teya screamed. A futile bout of courage pushed her forward in an attempt to grab the man's hand. But before her fingers touched him, another rider grabbed her by her hair and pulled her back. A flash of steel and she fell to the ground, blood gushing out of her neck, soaking into the dust.

"Teya!" Melia's mother moved, but the man who held her was faster. He opened her throat in one smooth move, and she fell beside Teya, blood spurting through her fingers, wrapped in vain around her neck, unable to stop the deadly tide.

Melia opened her mouth but no sound came out.

"No, please, no." The nurse pulled Melia back and held her tight, wrapping her in a cloak. "She's a child."

Melia buried her head in the dark folds, the image of her mother bleeding to death etched on the insides of her eyelids. The dark eyes wide open in horror and disbelief, the mouth gasping for air, the red fingers grasping, twitching.

The air moved behind Melia as blades slashed through it: cold and then searing hot. Her nurse screamed, and warm, sticky liquid poured over Melia, soaking into her clothes. They fell to the ground together. Sharp stones bore into Melia's back while the soft, heavy flesh smothered her from above. Blood poured over her face. She tried to wipe it off, but her arms were trapped under the convulsing bulk of her nurse's body.

She closed her eyes, wondering how she'd know if she were dead.

Much later, Melia heard voices.

It was dark and very cold, the wind lashing over the empty plains. She was unable to move her body. Something dark and heavy immobilized her completely, allowing her barely enough space to fill her lungs with small gulps of air. Her eyelashes were sticky and crusted. She blinked slowly, tears rinsing her eyes, blurring her vision. Orange flames hovered in the air, hooves crunched the gravel. Curses and shouts.

At first she thought the robbers had returned to finish her off. Then she realized she understood what the men were saying, though it made no sense. The panic and fear in their voices. The sound of her mother's name. And "Seragian brigands, this far from the border."

Two pairs of hands lifted the dead thing off Melia and pulled it away. When somebody grabbed her under the arms, she whimpered. They let her go immediately. Fingers touched her neck.

"Over here, give me light!" a man cried. "The girl is alive."

A scream burst out of Melia's mouth as she remembered. She'd died that day, her soul had fled her body among the carnage, beneath the still-warm pile of bodies whose blood soaked her clothes, her hair, and fed the ravenous red dust beneath. She had died, and all that was left was this empty husk, this puppet of a woman, this weapon her father had sharpened and plunged into the heart of the court.

The fact that she hadn't seen the scope of her father's plans, that she hadn't meant to start a war, was irrelevant. She wanted to flee from the stink of blood, from the shadows of death in Syr, and all she'd managed to do was to bring them here.

She was the poison, the miasma spreading the sickness, the deathbringer. She should have had the decency to die and stay dead.

She curled into a tight ball of pain on the dusty carpet. If the king was dead, if her father—or Ferisa, more likely—had done something to him, then the war was inevitable. And more than that—Amron would know his father had died because he'd shown mercy to Melia. She had no courage to show her face before him, no right to ask for help.

She was helpless and useless as always.

Unless....She couldn't go back to the palace, she had no power to quell the bloodthirsty crowd. But the Seragians still didn't know it was all Roderi's doing. If she found a way to talk to the carevna, she might still prevent a war.

It was a mad idea, a monstrous idea—betraying her father to the Seragians.

She rose from the threadbare, faded carpet—everything her father touched disintegrated—and approached the washstand with a hand-sized, blurry mirror in a wooden frame. She knew well the angular, haggard features: the eyes surrounded by dark circles, the narrow, crooked nose, the lips chapped from biting, the wiry black hair escaping the braids. And yet, for the first time, the person who looked back at her wasn't a homely stranger. For the first time in her life, Melia saw her mother's echo in her own face. Her mother, who was beautiful and strong, and more than an empty shell, a mindless tool in Roderi's hands.

"I am not helpless," she told the reflection. "I am not his puppet."

All her life, she'd been taught that Seragians were bloodthirsty monsters. They'd killed her mother, they'd killed Rovin. In return, her father killed them, in an endless circle of violence that brought no release, only increased the pain. Hurting the enemy couldn't heal her own wounds, it could only turn her into a creature of darkness, a harbinger of death.

Melia was sick of darkness, sick of death.

She turned on her heel and ran out of the house, into the turbulent streets of Abia.

Liana

At dawn of the third day, Abia was in turmoil. The city slid from hangover straight into rage. Flower garlands and colorful standards still adorned the streets filled with armed people carrying torches. All semblance of peace seemed like a naïve illusion now, a fool's dream.

Liana ran, angry tears streaming down her face. All her work had come to nothing, every attempt to push history off its course shattering like a crystal chalice hitting a stone floor. The people of Abia were rioting against the Seragians, their anger fueled by the lies spread by the Black Lord, their fear based on the endless smoldering conflict on the border, the centuries of rivalry.

It was impossible to close a festering wound: Sewing it tight only made it pulsate and swell until it exploded, raining blood and pus on the festive town.

The pink glow of the summer dawn spread over the eastern sky as she ran towards the Seragian embassy, praying to the fading stars above that there was still something she could do to stop the carnage. Two streets away from the embassy, the crowd thickened, a press of bodies pushing forward blindly like a mudslide. Liana threw herself into the thick of it, slipping between people where she could and elbowing forward the rest of the way until she saw the imposing stone mansion. Its high, rusticated walls and ground-floor iron grilles suddenly looked not nearly sturdy enough.

The wooden shutters on the upper-floor windows were closed, letting out nothing but random, thin streaks of light, revealing that there was somebody inside. The massive wrought iron gates were shut, and if there were any Seragian guards behind them, they didn't show their faces.

The neighboring houses sat dark and still behind their ornate facades, their owners probably cowering in the dark while waves of angry people splashed against their walls.

The mob, idiotic as it always was, didn't quite know what to do. The leaders, the ones who had spread lies in taverns and on the streets, the ones who'd whispered about Seragian blades and poisons, still hadn't shown their faces. The people grumbled and pushed forward, but the dark, silent shadow of the embassy offered no challenge, confusing them, placating their rage temporarily until they switched places with the fresh blood pushing down the street.

Before the main entrance to the embassy, there was a splash of royal blue. Darin and his men, standing in a semicircle, guarding the Seragians.

"Stand back," Darin shouted. "Go home! The Seragians are not a threat. All you've heard are rumors and lies."

Liana pushed forward, ignoring the punches and curses. A man slid his hand between her legs, grabbing her crotch with hard fingers. She barely managed to find his face in the crowd, shiny eyes, alcohol-fueled leer. Without missing a step, she grabbed his middle finger, pulled it backwards, and snapped it like a twig. She ducked behind the next man and heard a wail that was soon drowned out by the roar of the mob. She stepped on toes and elbowed stomachs without remorse, breathing through her mouth to avoid the stink of too many sweaty bodies crammed together after a night of feasting, and propelled herself forward like a fish swimming against the current.

She was still wearing the uniform, and even though it didn't help her much with the crowd, when she broke out of the mass, the first two guards who spotted her reached out and pulled her into their circle. She counted twenty heads, and Darin. Not nearly enough.

"Go home!" her father was saying to the crowd. "There's nothing here."

The guards hadn't drawn their weapons. All that kept the people from rushing at the embassy gate were the royal uniforms and the power of Darin's voice: calm, authoritative. He wasn't a particularly big man, but he had the air of a leader used to giving orders and being obeyed. He projected it into the crowd now, and they—knowing well who he was—paused, faltered in their anger. He was keeping them away from the embassy by the sheer force of his will.

Inside the uniformed circle, Liana hesitated, unwilling to break the spell. Telling the guards that the king was dying and that the Black Lord was probably planning the next attack would weaken them, leave them exposed to the mob. And yet—how long could her father's fragile spell last?

If he noticed her, he didn't turn. His gaze was locked with the mob. "Go home, good people," he said. "Abia is safe. We'll be guarding the embassy, no Seragian will leave unless we let them."

Liana wanted to help him, but didn't know how except to stand there and stare down the crowd. Beads of sweat formed on the foreheads of the guards beside her as they breathed hard, stinking of fear. And yet, not a single one of them panicked; they all stood behind their captain, ready to fight the mindless mob at his command.

"Go home," he said, his voice placating, hypnotic. "We'll stay here. And the king will speak to you in the morning."

She felt their fire dampen. The angry roar at the front died down, melting to a mere buzz that spread down the street towards the edges of the mob. The people in front of her blinked and turned to their neighbors, looking sheepish, as if they'd just been found sleepwalking. The only thing that prevented them from turning on their heels and walking home was the mass of people behind them.

"Father," she reached out, touching his shoulder.

"Liana?" He turned, his face ashen under a fine film of perspiration. "What—"

A female voice cried from somewhere near the embassy, "The king is dead."

Everyone froze. Liana stood on her tiptoes, trying to see who was speaking. She was too short. Still, she could guess who spread the doomed news: a dark-haired woman with black eyebrows and burning eyes, spewing lies and hatred all over Abia.

"Where are you going, you cowards?" Ferisa shouted. "The king is dead, the Seragians killed him. And the king's guard, the very men who swore to protect him with their lives, are now protecting the Seragian scum."

For the briefest of moments, Darin froze, uncertain of how to deal with such a monstrous accusation. When he came to, he cried, "Lies! The king is at the palace, all is well. Go home."

Too late. The dispersing mass pulled back together, the barely banked flame flaring up again.

"If all is well, why is the Seragian princess here at the embassy? Why did she run away from the palace?" The crowd shifted, and now Liana could see Ferisa, surrounded by the Elmarran guards. The time for hiding was over, apparently—this was a direct challenge. "Let's drag the traitors out and ask them!"

The Elmarrans pulled out their swords. The ring of steel cut through the noise, hushing it. In that lull, which lasted a mere heartbeat, Liana looked at the faces of the king's guards, of the people in the crowd. Those who still had their wits about them realized it immediately: This was the tipping point. Wide-eyed, horrified by the press of angry bodies around them, they searched for an escape and found none. They were all in it now, whatever happened, while the hundred-headed mob-beast decided what to do next. This was the last moment when some semblance of peace still reigned, when pausing, regrouping, dispersing, and avoiding bloodshed was still possible.

Then history put its merciless thumb on the scale and the beast roared in bloodthirsty fury. Somewhere behind the diaphanous curtain of the dawn sky, the gods turned their eyes towards Abia, eager for a sacrifice.

"Attack the embassy," Ferisa said. It wasn't even a shout, but it spread through the crowd like wildfire.

The king's guards drew closer to the gate; Darin pushed Liana behind him as he drew his sword.

"Stand back!" he shouted.

The mob surged forward, the first lines panicked and resisting, suddenly realizing they were facing the guards' blades, but the back relentlessly pushed forward, mincing everything in its way.

"We're going to die," one of the guards whispered.

There was nowhere to run: They were trapped between the heavy, barred gate of the embassy behind them and the angry mob coming at them. Liana looked at her father, his back rigid with determination, his hair darkened with sweat, and she wished she could say something: that she was sorry she'd squandered this chance to meet him, that she'd failed to give him useful information, that she was proud to be his daughter.

But any distraction now could kill him, so she braced herself for the wave that was coming, refusing to look into the sky or think about divine tricks.

At that moment, the shrill sound of trumpets cut through the roar, followed by screaming, the clash of steal, the beat of ironshod hooves on the cobbles.

The crowd writhed in panic, everyone trying to get out of the way, pushing, kicking, climbing over the bodies. Behind them, a band of horsemen—a dozen or so—in royal liveries, followed by more guards, cleared the street with their truncheons. Leading them, pushing through the crowd on a mean-looking bay stallion, still in his ceremonial clothes, was Amron.

Liana's heart skipped a beat: This was the Amron she recognized. Fearless, determined. The men around her started breathing again, sheathing their swords. Her father's eyes focused on her the for the first time since she'd arrived.

"I'd strangle you for risking your life like this if I weren't so happy that you are unharmed," he said. "What are you doing here?"

"I came to tell you something." She stood on tips of her toes to reach his ear. "The king is dying," she whispered. "This is an open rebellion, led by Roderi of Elmar."

He nodded, his face revealing nothing.

"Prince Amron knows everything," she added.

At that moment, Amron reached them and dismounted.

"Amril is at the palace with the queen," he told Darin. "The city gates are secure. I sent Tilen to Roderi's house with a dozen horsemen, though I doubt he's there. Two dozen men guard the docks and the approach to the Seragian ships. There's unrest all over the city, but it's mostly bands of drunkards who don't know what's happening. Nothing like the situation here at the embassy."

He talked to Darin, scanning the soldiers and the crowd, not looking at Liana, and yet his hand found its way to the small of her back. It rested there for a few moments, in mute reassurance, and then retreated before anyone noticed. Liana looked for grief or despair on his face, but there was none—whatever he felt for his father was hidden now. He was the man she remembered from the battlefields and long marches: calm, composed, self-assured.

"We must find the woman, Ferisa," she said. "She was here with the Elmarran guard, pushing the crowd to attack the embassy. She can't be far. You must stop her before she causes more damage."

Amron nodded. "I'll hunt her down. How many men does she have with her?"

"I didn't see more than a dozen," Darin said. "But more could have been hiding in the crowd."

Amron looked around. At that moment, the street was filled with the blue liveries of the king's guards, and horsemen were guarding it on both sides, but Liana knew they still had too few men to face the threat. Abia was a porous town, filled with dark alleys, shortcuts, and hidden passages—there was no saying who waited in the shadows.

"I'll leave the horsemen and the guards with you," Amron said. "It is of the utmost importance that nothing happens to the embassy today. I'll go after her alone. Stealth might be better here than numbers."

"Not alone," Liana said. "I'll go with you."

Darin frowned, and she expected him to call them mad, tell them to go back to the palace and hide behind its walls. But instead, he just nodded. "I'll send a message to Prince Amril, to let him know what happened and be on the lookout for Roderi and his servants, and remain here with my men." His eyes lingered for a moment on Amron's face, and then on Liana's, and suddenly she was certain that he'd seen Amron's hand on her back, that he knew what was going on between them. Still, all he said was, "Be careful. Guard each other's backs."

A sound, faint as a whisper, made Liana turn her head towards the embassy. All her senses, human and divine, flared up, honed by the years of archery, the long days spent hunting. Somewhere behind the curtain, a divine hand threw the dice.

"Watch out!" she cried and pushed Amron down, throwing herself on top of him.

A volley of arrows rained from the roof of the embassy.

Someone screamed. And when she turned and looked up, her father fell to his knees with an arrow in his chest.

~Chapter 24~

Melia

There was no approaching the Seragian embassy, not from the crowded street that led to the main entrance. In the distance, a flash of red and black: her father's guards spreading rumors and lies, inciting the mob. Ferisa was there, too, poison flowing out of her mouth. The air stank of burning resin and fear.

Melia didn't want to see the writhing mass of bodies rolling towards the embassy, didn't want to hear their chanting, didn't want to feel their rage. She had her own black pit, and if she joined those wretched people, the darkness inside her would explode, swallowing everyone in her way.

No, she was sick of rage and despair.

Abia was a maze of streets, houses, gardens, and courtyards. Melia turned a corner, and then another one. The street was quiet, the windows dark under the pre-dawn sky. Fifty paces or so was probably enough: No street in Abia lay parallel to another, but Melia guessed she was somewhere near the back of the embassy. Most of the houses had nothing but sinister facades and barred gates turned towards the street, but one had a garden wall.

The wall was high, but its stones were rough, with gaps wide enough for her feet to find purchase. She prayed no one would spot her—no nosy neighbors peering from behind the curtains, no late revelers or early birds stumbling upon the improbable sight: a woman in full court dress, blue silk, silver embroidery, white veil with gold pins, climbing over a wall like a thief, her skirts rustling, rough stones snagging the fine fabric.

She hauled herself over the wall and landed on the grass, hoping there were no guards waiting for her. Nothing moved but the leaves gently fluttering in the wind. Somewhere in the distance, the crowd roared. There was a narrow staircase leading up to a terrace with a well. She climbed up: From there she could see the embassy roof. Over another wall, to the terrace of the neighboring house, down the stairs into the courtyard, onto the roof of the stable, and over yet another wall and into the garden of the embassy.

A hand grabbed her as soon as she landed, a cold blade kissing her throat. "What do you want?" a voice whispered in her ear.

She stood very, very still, until her heart stopped beating like mad. "I mean no harm," she whispered. "Please, I'm unarmed."

The hand pushed her hard and she fell on the gravel, scratching her palms.

A young guard in the Seragian uniform stood above her, a dagger in his hand. "Is this how you're trying to sneak in now?" he asked. "How many of you are there?"

"I'm alone," she said, "and I have important news for the carevna."

The guard seemed agitated—who wouldn't be in those circumstances?—but he was trained well enough to listen and look. He must have noticed her dress, her jewelry, her pleading tone.

"I am Princess Melia, Prince Amron's wife, and I need to talk to the carevna urgently. She knows me. Please tell her I need to see her."

"Come," the guard said, his tone noticeably more polite than before. He helped her get up and steered her, holding her elbow, towards a small door in a deep nook.

When he knocked, a small spyhole slid open.

"Princess Melia is here to speak with Her Imperial Highness," he said.

The spyhole closed.

"Is that a yes or a no?" Melia asked.

"We need to wait."

She leaned on the wall, trying to clean the dirt from her scratched palms. They burned as she pressed them to the cool silk of her skirt. For some reason, she remembered playing with Rovin when they were very small, running after him and falling, scratching her hands and knees. She wailed then, and she felt like wailing now, not because the pain was great, but because she felt equally helpless and frustrated.

She eyed the guard in the weak light; he was younger than her, growing his first pitiful mustache. And yet, he gripped the dagger like he meant to use it, and she was certain he would have cut her throat had he believed she posed a threat. How weird it was, this readiness to kill a complete stranger for no reason other than following orders.

Would she kill him just because he was a Seragian, an enemy, a soldier bearing the collective guilt for her mother's murder, for her brother's death, for her miserable life? Could she hate him?

She dug deep into her heart, remembering the brigands, the curved blades, the blood soaking into the red dust, but all she found was grief. What did her mother's murder have to do with this hook-nosed, sad-eyed boy who probably drew the short straw and had to stand here all night? He was nothing to her, least of all an enemy. He wasn't the one who'd made her life miserable, who'd destroyed every possibility of happiness, every semblance of home for her.

No, her quarrel was solely with her father. The Seragians had nothing to do with it.

Finally, a key turned in the lock and the door opened. "Come in," a voice said.

Melia stepped over the threshold, leaving the boy guard behind. It was the first time she set foot on the Seragian soil, but there wasn't much to see: a dark corridor and one of Aratea's ladies holding an oil lamp.

"It is you," the lady said, her Amrian slightly accented. "I thought it was a trick."

"No tricks," Melia said. "Just me."

She followed the lady through several maze-like passages, climbing narrow stairs that smelled of pine and dust. They emerged in a set of rooms which, even in the weak light, looked perfectly strange.

There were no tapestries on the walls; instead they were painted with the most complex, colorful floral and geometric ornaments. The floors were covered in soft carpets and there were no chairs, only cushions, low sofas, and little exquisitely carved tables. The smell of caramelized sugar and cloves permeated the air.

"We must search you, my lady, I hope you understand."

Melia nodded as two more women dressed in soft gray shirts and trousers, with daggers at their waists, appeared from the shadows. Their hands were gentle but relentless as they searched through the layers of Melia's clothes and the corners of her body. They finished with washing her scratched hands in lemon-scented water that stung her damaged skin, and then rubbed some soothing lotion onto them.

"The carevna will see you now," the lady said.

Melia walked through a carved door into a lavishly furnished room, with an untouched bed in the corner, two shuttered windows, and no personal belongings strewn about. It was lit by a single lamp placed on a low table. The emperor's daughter sat on a cushion, writing a letter, alone. No musicians, no ladies, not even the ambassadress to keep her company.

Aratea's hair was tightly braided and covered with a dark scarf; she'd taken off the exquisite wedding nightgown and was dressed in sensible Seragian clothes—wide pants gathered at the ankle and a soft silk blouse the color of ripe plums. In the shifting light, with a quill in her hand, she looked serious and composed, like a chronicler noting down the events that had happened many years ago.

The carevna lifted her pale eyes to Melia. "I could feign surprise, but that would be insulting for both of us, I think," she said.

Melia swallowed hard and nodded. Her planned opening words disappeared from her head.

"Please sit down." Aratea motioned at the pile of cushions on the floor. "Did your father send you? Is he ready to negotiate?"

Melia crashed down on a pillow with an embarrassing lack of grace. Too cowardly to ask what the carevna knew about her father, she said, "No, I came here all by myself to beg you to reconsider your marriage to the crown prince. He was not himself tonight, because of me, because my father poisoned him."

"Oh, that?" Aratea did seem a little surprised now, her auburn eyebrows shooting up. "That's irrelevant. Already forgotten."

"So you're not going to ask for an annulment over it?"

The carevna shook her head, a faint shadow of a smile appearing on her lips. "You are a great lord's daughter, a prince's wife, you should know how those things work. Do you think that's possible? An annulment because of your husband's treatment of you?"

Amron had never treated her roughly, but if he had, there would have been nothing for her to do, except maybe talk to the queen and ask her to intervene.

"Believe me, that was not the worst thing that happened to me during the wedding, nor the worst thing I expected to find here."

Melia had already felt like a fool when she realized how her father had used her, now she felt like a bigger one. Of course none of his plans had been aimed at the annulment, it was just a distraction. She nodded. "There are worse things coming, though. The crowd surrounding the embassy— that's not spontaneous, that's my father's work. He's rebelling against the king, and he's accusing you for everything that happened. He will not stop until we're at war with each other again."

Aratea acknowledged her words with a light nod. "Tea?" she offered.

"Thank you."

Melia watched as Aratea poured the dark liquid from a painted teapot into a translucent cup and accepted it, breathing in the fragrant aroma. They both sipped in silence for a little while.

"I know very little about politics, and most of what I know is wrong," Melia said. "But am I a fool to sit here and think I have no reason to hate you? Does my opinion matter at all, or are we just pieces on a board, moved by some invisible and infinitely powerful hands?"

The carevna smiled into her cup. "Big questions for small hours. May I tell you a story?"

"Please do." Although the night wasn't cold, Melia enjoyed the warmth of the tea spreading through her limbs. It calmed her burning nerves.

"There was once a girl born to every imaginable luxury: the most beautiful surroundings, superb care, the best teachers. Yet, as it often happens, the girl took all those brilliant things for granted and soon she got bored with her golden cage and its exquisite amusements. While her brothers went out into the world, she could only read about faraway places and daydream about visiting them.

"For some reason, the one place that intrigued her the most was a small, rough kingdom at the edge of the world, with rowdy people and turbulent history. She learned everything she could about it—the language, the customs, the legends—feeling sorry for herself because she knew she would never see it.

"And then an unprecedented thing happened, an unheard-of offer of a position in that forgotten corner of the world. The girl's sisters—the more beautiful, more accomplished, more sophisticated princesses—all refused it with horror and disgust, claiming they'd sooner take their own lives than sail to that backwater. When the girl's turn finally came to give an answer to their father, she surprised them all by wholeheartedly accepting. After all, it was her only chance to see the world."

The carevna took a sip of tea, while Melia stared at her, transfixed.

"So you see, I chose to come here with my eyes wide open," Aratea continued. "Our envoys miss very little, and what they don't see, our merchants report back to us. The news, the gossip, the ugly truth. Prince Amril—I know every angle of his character, every important moment of his life. When he looks in the mirror, he sees less than I see when I look at him. And your husband—I bet I know more about him than you do."

Melia almost laughed at such overconfidence—Amron showed so very little of himself to the world—but she only gave Aratea a noncommittal smile.

"I'm not bragging, you understand, I just want to point out I know what I need to know."

"Then you know all about my father, I suppose," Melia said.

"Your father," the carevna said, "is a liability. I understand his resentment and his grief, and the reasons why he doesn't want to accept this treaty."

Aratea, the clever, pampered princess, in her glorious costumes and gilded rooms. Melia doubted she knew anything about grief, anything about despair, anything about the black rage fueling Roderi of Elmar. Oh, one could write it all down on paper—so many years spent fighting, so many deaths. But no writing could convey the smell of blood when the sun burned the red stones of Syr, the shadows gathering in the corners, whispering about wasted lives, her brother's screams as he begged for death. What could this girl with her milky complexion and flaming hair know about feeling like an empty husk, skin fragile as old parchment, bones made of petrified dust?

Melia didn't understand politics because politics comprised maps and letters, deals and tricks, and endless words stripped of meaning. It was a dance, a game the rulers played while people bled into the red dust.

"We warned the king about your father, and the king claimed he had him under control. Perhaps he thought it because you were at court by that time, but he was wrong."

"Did you know about my father's intention to blame it all on you?" Melia asked.

"Not initially, but the moment our ambassadress realized the Seragians who attacked your husband weren't Seragians, it became clear."

Melia nodded. "What are you going to do about it?"

Aratea picked a sugared orange peel from a glass plate and nibbled on it. "Do about it? There's nothing I can do but wait."

Melia looked at her in disbelief. "But—surely, you don't want the citizens of Abia to believe the Seragians were behind the attacks?"

Aratea chuckled. "I couldn't care less what the citizens of Abia believe, they're not my problem, but the king's. He's either going to regain control in his own city and harness one of his rebellious great lords, or he isn't."

There was a strange sense of detachment radiating from the carevna, as if a cool glass panel stood between them. It was all impersonal to her, Amril poisoned and raging, the people rioting at her gates, as if she were a mere spectator, not the main player.

"And what if my father won't be harnessed? What if the rebellion spreads and the city burns?" she asked.

"Then it will burn," Aratea said. "I'd hate to see a city as beautiful as Abia burning, but that won't be my fault."

Melia, who had no special love for Abia, felt a pang of irritation. "Aren't you afraid?"

Aratea looked at her with eyes so cold Melia wondered whether it was her nature, or some consequence of the imperial upbringing. "I am terrified, but what would be the point of showing it? I'm not mad, I don't want to die, I don't want the mob to break into this house and tear it down. If they attack, we'll defend ourselves. But I came here understanding the risk, understanding this is a savage, bloodthirsty place that will probably see me as an enemy. I walked into it just like my brothers walk into battle—out of duty, seeking glory, ready for sacrifice."

It sounded very noble to Melia, and very hollow. There was no glory in death, no honor. There wasn't even any dignity in it. Just pain and gore and nothingness.

"However, if the king doesn't stop the riots, and if I'm forced to run from Abia, or even if I die, my father will respond in the manner he sees fit."

"With fire and steel?"

"With fire and steel."

Melia lowered her gaze to her hands, fingers entwined so hard they turned white. She was more damaged than any person she knew, and even she was unable to see the events through such a cold, calculating lens.

The glazed windows and heavy wooden shutters couldn't keep the noise of the mob from seeping into the room, and it drew Melia in like a hypnotic chant. The people outside were fools, but Melia was no less foolish for sitting inside this sweet-smelling room strewn with soft cushions, trying to negotiate with an enemy who saw her as an insignificant speck of dirt on the parchment of history.

"Which outcome would you prefer?" she asked the carevna. Where there was no mercy, all she could appeal to was self-interest.

"I'll accept any outcome that my father chooses," Aratea said.

"Yes, but which would you prefer?"

Aratea's glaze was smooth, without any cracks, but Melia knew everybody desired something, even if it was only a quick death. She was an expert on fathers who controlled their children, on people used as tools, on destinies that outgrew the person who carried them, and she knew that deep down, in the darkest corners of one's heart, it was all nonsense. People wanted what they wanted, no matter how much they lied about it.

What do you want, Melia?

Not now.

"What do you want?" Melia insisted.

Given the confused expression on the carevna's previously calm face, she might have been the first person to ask her that question.

"I don't…" Aratea's voice trailed off. Her small, pearly teeth bit into the soft flesh of her lip. "I want a place in this world that is my own. I want to remain here and travel this kingdom and see the places I've only read about. I want power that does not come from my father."

Melia nodded, keeping her mouth shut, waiting.

Aratea wrapped an unruly lock of hair around her finger and tucked it back beneath the scarf. "Is this some kind of a trick question? Because you know well there's nothing I can do. There's nothing you can do, either. We can only wait."

"No." Melia shook her head. "I'm done with waiting. You believe the world revolves around your father—I used to think the same about mine. They're so powerful, the masters of life and death, so huge they fill your whole horizon. But that's a deception. The world is full of people, and every one of them has the power to change the course of events."

"Is that what you like to think of yourself?" Aratea retorted.

Melia let the insult slide. "I'm not asking you to help me, nor asking you to do anything that you're not already doing. Keep waiting a little longer."

"Waiting?"

"The king's guard is out there, defending the embassy, and they won't let any harm come to you. All I'm asking is for you to wait it out, wait till the riots run their course, don't use them as the reason to run back to your father. Abia will come to its senses, I'm sure, and I'll… I'll stop my father somehow, I promise." She had no idea how she would do it, but she kept the uncertainty out of her voice. "You've made your choice to come here and wed Amril. Stand by that choice now, please."

Aratea looked at the shuttered window in silence while the mob roared outside.

"Perhaps we don't have much in common, except the ambition of our fathers and this family we both married into," Melia said. "But that's enough, because when I think about where I'd rather be when all this ends, that place is not Syr. I was wrong to call it home, it was never a home to me, just a place where my father abused me and would abuse me again if I returned.

"There is some freedom here. Not much, but enough to allow you to breathe. You are a clever woman, you will know how to use it."

Aratea's face didn't show emotions, or at least any emotions Melia could read, but the long pause told her the carevna was thinking about it. She was tempted to offer friendship—they were married to brothers, after all—but it sounded false in Melia's mind. She'd never known how to make friends.

"Fine," Aratea agreed at last. "I'll wait in Abia as long as I can, and I'll give Amril a fair chance. Is that what you want?"

Melia nodded, letting out a tiny sigh of relief. She was wondering what the appropriate goodbye would be—should they shake hands like men who'd just made a deal?—when shouts exploded in the corridor. The ambassadress barged into the room without knocking.

"Fire!" she said. "They set the roof on fire!"

Melia caught Aratea's eyes and mouthed a silent *please*.

Aratea nodded. "Get everyone down to the courtyard. Don't fight the king's guard or the mob if you can."

"And you, my lady?"

"I should get back to the palace."

~Chapter 25~

Liana

Darin fell to his knees, clawing at the arrow in his chest. Liana knelt beside him, grabbing his hand. There was no pulling the arrow out, it had to be pushed through the flesh. Blood sprayed out in a bright arc, unstoppable.

The guards swirled around them in a wild vortex of panic. Shouts, the thunder of running feet, hooves, the crowd roaring, Amron's face a pale dot among the blue uniforms.

She opened her mouth and the word she never wanted to utter again broke out. "Mother!" she cried. Her fingers raked the air until there was a hint of resistance, a gossamer fabric tearing beneath her nails.

The swirl of colors around her sped up, the noise grew—and then it stopped.

The crowd, the smell of smoke, the screaming, the cobbles under her knees, it all disappeared. Only silence remained, interrupted by birdsong and the wet, mossy smell of the forest. Dappled sunshine flickered on the clearing surrounded by magnificent oaks.

She still knelt beside her father, arms wrapped around his torso, blood soaking them both. The forest green of his eyes was clouded, his chest barely moved.

A woman walked out of the thicket, dark-haired and young and sharp-faced like a bird of prey. A translucent green dress wrapped her body like smoke.

"Help him," Liana begged.

Lela paused at the edge of the thicket, her eyes fixed on Darin. "I never cared to see the ravages of time on him," she said. "But let this be a lesson to you, Liana. Humans grow old, and humans die. Just like this." She snapped her fingers and the illusion vanished.

"No, damn you, no!" She was screaming when Amron pulled her back from her father lying on the cobbles. The deafening noise in the street swallowed her screams.

"Let us help him, Liana, move."

There was barely any maneuvering space in the crowd. The guards formed a tight protective circle around their wounded captain. Behind them, the world was on fire.

One guard forced the end of a leather belt between Darin's teeth while another broke the arrow shaft. Darin roared. Two more men held him as he thrashed in agony.

"He'll die! He'll die!" Liana wailed.

Amron wrapped his arms around her. "They know what they're doing, let them help him."

She writhed in his grip, trying to break free, overcome with the pure, desperate need to fight someone, to hit something solid.

"My lord, you can't stay here!" someone shouted.

The roof of the embassy was burning. Those hit by the first volley were swallowed up by the crowd, clogging the street once again. The mounted guards, several of them injured but none as badly as Darin, were forced to retreat. The flames, the arrows, the press of people drove their horses mad. Rage, fear, and confusion vibrated in the air like a swarm of angry wasps.

The arrows still rained down from the roof into the screaming crowd. The Seragians made no attempt to fight the traitors who climbed up there. Inertia, indifference, or a plan to stand aside while the king's guards died defending them?

It didn't matter in the end. The greatest empire in the world, entirely unhelpful or deliberately obstructing.

They retreated to the shadow of a neighboring building.

"I wish I could just let them burn, damn them," Amron said, exhaustion seeping out of his words.

Liana didn't care anymore, the fight had drained out of her. Her father lay still as the guards pressed a piece of cloth to the wound, wrapping his shoulder. "We need to get Darin out of here."

"You go with him. I must stay here. If I don't stop the fire from spreading, the whole city will burn." Amron stepped away from her. "Water!" he shouted, gathering the guards around him. "Get the buckets! Organize the chains to the fountains! Find a ladder!"

Liana knelt down beside Darin. His eyes were closed now, and he lay still, his breathing shallow.

She thought people had lost their last specks of common sense when they rushed towards the fire instead of running away from it, but then she realized they were indeed carrying buckets and water, making a long human chain down the street. Treason was an imaginary threat, but fire was a real, immediate one, and the Abians knew how to face it, even in the midst of the rebellion.

She looked up towards the burning roof—no archers could hide in the spreading blaze, but the danger was still out there.

The guards made a stretcher for her father.

The arrows stopped as the fire crowned the roof with bright red flames. Where were the Elmarran bastards? They weren't up there, and they weren't in the street, facing the king's guard. Yet, they certainly hadn't evaporated into thin air. They were wreaking havoc somewhere, pushing the restless city into rebellion.

"Amron!" she called.

At that moment, the gate of the embassy opened, and a crowd of people—guards, servants, ladies—rushed out, coughing, faces covered with scarves. They poured into the street, but the people cared little for them now, their focus was on the blazing roof.

"Where are the others?" the guards asked as the Seragians wiped soot and sweat off their faces. "Where's the carevna?"

All they got were shrugs and confused looks. "She got out," someone said. "Didn't she? We saw her running."

Thick smoke poured through the door of the embassy and through the cracks in the shutters.

A handful of guards prepared to carry their captain back to the palace. Two men lifted the stretcher, the others formed a cordon around them.

"How many exits are there from the embassy?" Amron asked a sooty woman whom the others followed.

"Just this one, it goes under this wing into the main courtyard, and all the exits from the building lead there."

"Where is the carevna, then?"

The woman hesitated.

"Ambassadress, please. I'm trying to help," Amron said.

The woman nodded. "There is a back garden, surrounded by a wall. It's possible to climb over it and get to the neighboring gardens. Perfect if you don't want to be seen leaving the embassy."

Amron looked up to the blazing roof. "There's no time to go around. How do you get to the garden?"

"Turn right in the courtyard," the woman said, "through the big arch, down the corridor, turn left, and there's a short flight of steps leading to the door. It will take you to a small terrace above the garden."

"We must go," the guards carrying Darin said.

Liana said to Amron, "You can't go through the building, it's on fire."

He was already tying a wet rag around his neck. "There's no time." He scanned the rest of the guards. "Who's coming with me?"

Four men ran to him, dousing their clothes with water and pulling scarves and rags over their mouths. He turned to Liana. "Get Darin to the palace safely. I'll see you there."

She didn't want him to go into the fire without her, but her father needed her more. Or perhaps she was just reluctant to abandon him, as her mother had done.

Amron and the guards ran into the darkness filled with smoke, and she forced herself to head in the opposite direction, following the guards carrying the stretcher.

As they pushed through the crowd, a commotion rippled through it from the opposite direction.

"Move," someone shouted. "Make way for Prince Amril!"

Liana kept her head down, pushing forward. Sharp as a hawk's, Amril's eyes found her in the crowd. The guards rushed to report to him, but he waved them away, pinning Liana down with his cold blue gaze.

"This is all because of you," he said loudly enough for the guards to hear. "If you hadn't dragged my brother to that dark alley and provoked the attack, none of this would have happened."

And then he turned away, shouting commands, ignoring her completely.

~Chapter 26~

Melia

The smoke was thick and acrid, making Melia's eyes water and her throat burn. She could barely see Aratea running before her.

"We must reach the back exit." Aratea coughed, catching her breath,

They ran down the narrow stairs and smoke-filled corridors, deep into the dim bowels of the building, retracing Melia's footsteps several hours before, to the low door leading to the terrace.

The first thing Melia saw in the fading light of the evening was the young guard lying in a pool of blood, his throat slit.

The second was Ferisa.

It had been a fever dream, Melia and Ferisa.

She'd never heard of two women living together as lovers and partners, but then—she knew so very little about the world anyway. It never stopped her from daydreaming, though. In her austere room, on the thin mattress, between threadbare sheets, in the safe nest of Ferisa's embrace, she'd dreamed of vast blue seas and grassy plains framed by the snow-peaked mountains on the horizon. She imagined strange cities, golden domes glittering in the sunlight, lush gardens filled with the chatter of birds, proud stone towers jutting into the sky. She dreamed of people, their skin dark as ebony or white as snow, in bright silks and soft furs and hard leather, their languages as incomprehensible as birdsong. She dreamed of Ferisa and her braving the world together, living by their wits, sharing meals by a campfire, exploring chaotic markets filled with wonders.

She was infatuated—with the woman, with the taste of forbidden fruit, with the idea of freedom.

Her brother was dead, her father was sliding into madness, and Syr was a trap, a mausoleum, a monument to death.

"Run away with me," she said. "Let's leave this place, never to return. There must be so much world outside, so much happiness to snatch from the boughs of fortune."

Ferisa let out a deep, throaty laugh that made Melia's skin prickle. "Where would we go, little raven?"

"Anywhere but here," Melia replied. "There must be a place you've always wanted to see."

Ferisa turned to her, propping herself on her elbow. She was smiling, but her eyes were burning with that hard, angry fire Melia had learned to dread. "With what money, what horses, what guards?" She ran her hand down Melia's hip. "You've lived your whole life sheltered here, behind these impregnable walls. You think your lot is hard, but let me tell you—the outside world is harder."

The outside world wasn't filled to the brim with death, Melia wanted to say, but how did you say that to someone who spooled death out of thin air every day and wove it into the shimmering red-and-black fabric of loss? Instead, she said, "I'm not afraid of the outside world, not if I'm with you."

"Brave words." Ferisa's smile was a crescent moon hanging in the starless sky. "But I wouldn't be so rash. You've lived here, behind these walls, your whole life. You're the heiress, the lord's only daughter."

Melia pressed her lips together so hard it hurt. Ferisa should have known that being the Black Lord's daughter meant nothing in terms of comfort or safety. True, she wasn't hungry or homeless, but she wouldn't wish the brutality of her existence on anyone.

"You never had to sleep on the hard, cold ground, with the wind lashing you all night," Ferisa said. "You've never had to leave everything behind and run for your life because some crooked innkeeper accused you of theft. You've never gotten beaten within an inch of your life because some man didn't like what you said. No, little raven, the outside world is not a good place for a woman without protection."

"I'd still go," Melia whispered stubbornly, holding on to her pillow, a makeshift raft on the ocean of heartache. "I'd go with you, because this is no life."

"You say that now, but you're about to marry a prince. You'll change your mind when you become a pampered court lady."

"Damn you, Ferisa." Melia's eyes filled with tears. "Why would you say that?"

Ferisa let out a languid laugh. "I'm teasing you, little raven. No, you're not a court creature, I guess."

"I don't want to marry a prince and go to court," Melia said.

"I'll follow you." Ferisa's solid, calloused fingers stroked Melia's face. "You'll do what you must and I'll stand by your side. And when it's over, we'll run away together. I promise you that."

"Hold the carevna," Ferisa ordered.

"No, stop!" Melia cried, but nobody paid any attention to her.

The guards grabbed Aratea between them, lifting her like a doll, and pulled her towards Ferisa, standing like a spirit of vengeance in the small garden. Dressed in black, dark eyes burning on a ruthless face, she looked so much like Roderi of Elmar it was uncanny. Gone was the compassionate herbalist who'd first come to Syr, gone was the death priestess capable of mercy, of spiritual insight. All that was left was this avatar of war.

Melia couldn't recognize her, but still she ran to her side.

"Ferisa! Please, stop."

She reached for Ferisa's arm, but Ferisa merely shook her off like a tiresome pest, her eyes fixed on Aratea.

Melia refused to be ignored. She stepped in front of Ferisa, reaching for her face. "Ferisa! Whatever you're doing, stop it now, please."

Finally, the burning dark eyes turned to Melia. "Stay out of it. You've done your duty, you brought the carevna where I wanted her, but you must leave the rest to me now."

Disheveled and furious, the carevna pierced Melia with her icy eyes. "Is that why you came to the embassy? To burn it down, to trap me? Was everything just a pretense?"

"No! I didn't—"

Before Melia could explain, Ferisa gave a sign to the guards to drag the carevna away from her.

"Why are you doing this?" Melia asked. "This is not what we wanted, this is not what you promised me."

"Pillow talk and childish dreams which evaporated fast in collision with the real world," Ferisa retorted.

"This is not the real world, this is the chaos my father deliberately created. Is this how you want to live for the rest of your life? Didn't you have enough pain and death in Syr? How much war is going to satisfy my father? What do you think?"

"What would you have me do?" Ferisa asked. "Say no to him? Say no to my goddess?"

Melia looked around, to the fire rising to the darkening sky, to the bound Seragian princess, to her father's guards, to Ferisa, who'd once cared for her. "Help the carevna reach the palace and leave the rest to the royals to sort out. And then just walk away, from my father, from Abia, from the war. I'll follow you."

"After all this time, little raven, you still harbor that fantasy?" Ferisa's voice was almost gentle. "The carevna is our path to the revenge your father has dreamed of."

The revenge? The whole kingdom at war? "What has my father ever given you to make you follow him like this? All he does is demand—obedience, sacrifice, pain."

"He promised to marry me."

Melia stumbled backwards, horrified. Ferisa and her father? Never a trace of warmth between them, of understanding, of mutual liking—not so much as a speck of interest. If anything, they had always despised each other, avoided each other's presence. How could it be?

"I thought you hated men," she whispered, feeling like a stupid child.

Ferisa smirked, deeming her unworthy of an answer, and turned to the guards. "Let's go!"

"No! Wait." Melia reached once again for Ferisa, but she pushed her away.

"I'm not going to hurt you, Melia, but stay out of my way."

"Ferisa!"

There was nothing to do but watch them drag the carevna towards the wall. The garden had no exit: They had to climb.

In a cloud of smoke, stinking like fire demons, a group of the king's guards burst through the door of the embassy and, without a single word spoken, rushed after Ferisa's men, the sound of their footsteps muffled by the roar of the fire.

Melia only saw them because she was looking in that direction. The Elmarrans had their backs turned, and by the time they realized what was going on, the guards were already upon them.

"I thought you went to talk to your father."

A hard grip on Melia's shoulder, Amron's angry eyes on a soot-smudged face.

"He didn't want to talk to me. But I persuaded Aratea to wait and give Amril another chance…"

There was no time to explain. Escaping the bloody melee, Ferisa grabbed the carevna and pulled her to her chest like a shield. She bared her teeth at Amron. "Who did you come to save, your wife or the emperor's daughter?"

Amron pushed Melia behind him, a sword in his hand. "Surrender," he said to Ferisa. "You can't win this one."

At the wall, the Elmarrans were still fighting Amron's men, and losing. Ferisa cut a fine figure in her black suit, tall and wiry, with a blade in her hand, but she was an herbalist, a hedge witch, a poisoner, not a soldier. Melia couldn't understand what mad bout of bloodthirst had made her pick up a sword and go out in the streets, looking for conflict. It was an act—a lethal, senseless act. Did she do it to impress Melia's father? To create the illusion that she had command?

"Let her go," Melia cried as Aratea struggled in Ferisa's grip, kicking and biting. "She didn't do anything, she was only trying to help. Take me instead if you want a hostage."

Ferisa ignored it. She brought her sword to Aratea's neck. "Stop struggling, it's poisoned. One scratch and you're dead."

"And how do you plan to climb the wall with her?" Amron asked.

"I'm not," Ferisa answered, "there's another route. And if you try to follow me, I'll kill you just like I killed your father." She pulled Aratea towards the burning building.

The moment she disappeared through the smoky entrance, Amron ran after her, Melia at his heels.

Inside, the heat singed her hair and skin. The stone stairway wasn't burning, but it was filled with black smoke. She could see nothing but Amron's boots before her.

Surely, no one could get through it alive.

She pressed a handkerchief to her nose, but the smoke still burned her throat and made her head spin. The heat was unbearable. Melia fell to her knees, unable to go on. Amron was nowhere to be seen, his footsteps swallowed by the roar of the fire.

"Help," she whispered, certain that no one would hear her.

A hand shot out from the darkness and pulled her forward. She stumbled, struggling to get on her feet. She made the mistake of breathing in; it was like swallowing liquid fire.

Someone picked up the rag she'd dropped and pressed it over her nose. "Breathe slowly," the carevna said.

"Where's Ferisa?" Melia rasped.

Aratea motioned deeper towards the center of the building. "In the yard, Prince Amron caught up with her."

Melia crawled forward, but the carevna grabbed her. "Don't be a fool, we must go back."

Before Melia could shake her off, the corridor leading to the terrace collapsed behind them in a fiery cloud. No time for anything but pure panic: Melia's body sprang forward, her legs breaking into a run, her hands grabbing Aratea, pulling her along.

There was no roof to collapse in the courtyard; there had to be some air there. The arch, filled with light, beckoned at the end of the corridor, the roar of the blaze behind them, the wisps of Melia's hair flying about her head, catching fire. She anticipated bursting into flames like a dry twig, or the whole building swallowing her like a massive pyre. Despite her lifelong closeness with death, every fiber of her body rejected it as she dashed through the unbearable heat.

The carevna ran with her, aiming for the smudge of daylight nearly erased by the black smoke. Holding hands, they leapt out.

The fire, the burning embassy, the stone-paved courtyard, the heat all vanished. Melia and Aratea landed on the hard, frosty ground. A windswept, snowy plain stretched to the end of the horizon, where it melted into an indifferent gray sky. A single dead tree stood a few paces away from them, black branches reaching up in a futile prayer.

Ferisa stood under the tree, as black and barren as its ancient trunk. Her long curls had escaped the braids and coiled around her head in a raven cloud lashed by the wind.

Amron stood before her, his sword unsheathed but pointing down, his gleaming hair the only touch of color in the desolate landscape.

"Throw it down," Ferisa said, only it wasn't Ferisa, it wasn't her voice, it slid into Melia's head without traveling through the air. "Kneel and I'll give you what you want."

"You have no idea what I want," Amron said.

"Oh, you stupid boy." The goddess laughed. "I can hear your heart beating the sweet amphibrach of her name: Li-A-na, Li-A-na, Li-A-na."

"Stop it!"

Morana fell silent but the beat reverberated through the landscape, rattling Melia's bones. She told herself it didn't hurt. It didn't.

"Kneel and you can have her," the goddess said. "Take her out of my sight and I'll forget about you for a while."

"No," he said.

The goddess stood perfectly still under the tree; only her hair moved in the wind. "You've always been a fool, Amron of the House of Amris. A brave fool, but a fool nevertheless."

Amron stood stubbornly against the wind, and Melia waited for something terrible to happen. Surely, one didn't refuse the gods and live to tell the story?

"This is not the last time we speak," Morana said.

He turned his head away in mute rejection. It was a mistake: In a blink, the goddess dissolved, leaving a dark shape in her wake. Ferisa stood where Morana had been a moment before.

Flames exploded all around them.

Ferisa charged at Amron without making a sound. He saw her move: One moment he was standing before her, the other he was a blur of blue and gold, faster than Melia's eyes could follow. He charged at Ferisa, ramming into her, throwing her off balance. The sword flew out of her hand.

Melia could hear the crack when Ferisa's head hit the flagstones. The building was collapsing around them. Aratea pulled Melia's sleeve, but Melia wrenched it back without sparing her a look.

"Amron please," she screamed, "don't hurt her."

Amron grabbed Ferisa's sword and threw it into the flames. "Run!" he shouted at Melia and Aratea. "What are you staring at?"

The carevna obeyed, dashing across the burning courtyard towards the main entrance, still free of the rubble. But Melia couldn't follow, not with Ferisa lying there. She ran to her and cradled Ferisa's head, looking for injuries. Her skull wasn't broken and she was awake, if stunned.

"Help her get up," Amron said. "And be quick about it."

She thought he'd run after Aratea, but he stood there, waiting.

"Come, I'll help you up," Melia said softly to Ferisa. "We must get out." All the anger and betrayal faded away when old instincts kicked in, the familiar shape of her shoulders in her arms, the scent of her hair, the fire in her dark eyes. It didn't matter if the world was burning around them, Melia still owed her this much. "I'll convince Amron my father forced you to do this, as he's forced all of us. Just trust me, please."

Ferisa got up, nimbler than Melia expected her to be. She pulled Melia close and whispered, "I'm sorry, little raven." Then she reached for her boot and pulled a stiletto out of a hidden sheath.

Amron was looking towards the exit, head turned away from them. Ferisa tore out of Melia's arms, running.

"Amron!" Melia screamed.

He turned just as Ferisa reached him. The flash of metal aimed at his torso, the blade in its upward arc. Surely, there was no chance she could miss.

"No!" Melia screamed.

Amron's hand shot out, grabbing Ferisa's wrist, breaking the perfect trajectory of the blade, turning it inwards. His body pivoted in a fluid, almost dancing movement, using Ferisa's momentum to spin her, twist her around, and bury the blade in her chest.

~Chapter 27~

Liana

The guards picked up Darin, lying still on the stretcher, and carried him away from the chaos. Whatever they thought about Amril's accusation and Liana's role in the attack, they kept their mouths shut. They knew she wasn't one of them—the uniform couldn't fool them—but they also knew both Darin and Amron trusted her, and that seemed to have been enough. They barely looked at her—between the mob and their captain's life hanging on a thread, there was little time for gossip and accusations.

Yet, Amril's words bore into her mind like a drill. What if he was right? What if Liana's escape with Amron did change history, but instead of pushing it away from the war, it had pushed it towards the war? If they hadn't escaped Celandina's house, perhaps the attackers wouldn't have found anyone to ambush. There would have been no reason to accuse the Seragians of anything. That attack had set a whole chain of events in motion.

Perhaps every step she'd made since landing in Abia led towards the inevitable conclusion. In trying to run away from the war, she had led everyone to it. Liana, the divine tool of destruction.

She willed herself to stop the unsettling thoughts, knowing the tricks the gods loved to play on people's minds, but it was futile. The third day was leaking through her fingers, the afternoon slipping away, her bargain weighing heavily on her. Yet, what else was she supposed to do? She couldn't make Amron shirk his duty, and at this moment, his duty was to do everything in his power to prevent conflict. There was no room for intimacy of any kind. No matter what moment in history she stepped in, no matter where in their shared life she was, the war separated them just as it always had, their bodies divided by cold steel and burning embers.

She failed at so many things because, as usual, she'd forgotten to calculate in people behaving as people—irrational, scared, angry. She knew the importance of the moment, the complexity of the multitude of the threads meeting at this point, this wedding in Abia, and yet she'd believed she could simply extricate Amron without the whole structure collapsing into a burning tangle.

She had failed to prevent the king's stabbing, she had failed to prevent her father's injury, she had failed to help Amron in any meaningful way.

The guards carried their captain quickly, pushing through the city caught up in the throes of unrest. The crowds on the streets had thinned. The more cunning among the citizens had gone home, closed their shutters, and barred their doors. The downside, however, was that those who'd remained on the streets were probably looking for trouble, carrying their ill intentions like burning torches.

History rushed towards the bloody finale.

Keeping her head low, holding the edge of her father's cloak, Liana let out a quiet groan that melted into bitter laughter. Who did she think she was? Some deity with the power to turn the course of history at the tips of their fingers? Some legendary heroine that shaped reality according to her wishes?

She was nothing but an accidental bastard, a divine offshoot that got lucky against all odds. Her improbable connection with Amron, those fifteen years of his unrelenting love for her—*that* was an anomaly, a thread of history gone rogue—not the war.

The war was inevitable, Amron's love for her was not.

But looking at the bloodstains on her father's cloak, black in the lengthening shadows, she cursed herself for being such a weakling. Her father would never give up the fight, no matter how bad the odds were, and neither would Amron. They would do whatever was in their power to stop the terrible tide; they would go down fighting.

She wouldn't give up—for them.

The guards rushed through the darkening streets, reaching one of the back entrances to the palace. A low wooden door, a long corridor, and the guards' quarters, the same as they'd ever been. They'd all but forgotten about Liana as they laid their captain on a pallet in the guards' infirmary. In the flickering candlelight, Liana caught the deep worry on the men's faces, but they didn't linger; the city was burning, their duty awaited them.

She tucked her hand under Darin's cloak and wrapped her fingers around his, warm and calloused.

A hand on Liana's shoulder. "Stand aside, we'll take care of him." A firm female voice, a stern, serious face. "Scissors! Water! Needle!" the woman called, and a flurry of people materialized around Darin.

"He's my father," Liana whispered, but no one heard her. They cut him out of his uniform, pushed the arrow shaft through his flesh, cleaned the wound, and sewed it shut. They moved quickly and with competence, the stern woman directing them. And yet, frustration bloomed in Liana's chest, aimed at her own uselessness, her own ineptitude. She was wasting time, not helping her father, not helping Amron.

"I heard he was injured," a soft voice said behind Liana's back.

She turned: Queen Orsiana stood in the shadows, like a solitary ghost. Liana tried to step aside, to bow, but the queen caught her hand. "Don't. Just tell me what happened."

So Liana told her about the embassy, the fire, the arrows. The queen listened in silence, watching the women as they bandaged Darin's chest, paying her as little attention as they did Liana. Only when they finished did the stern woman turn to the queen, greeting her with a nod. "He's lost a lot of blood, but the arrow missed his heart. If he pulls through the night, he might live."

"Thank you, Nila."

When the women retreated, rushing to help some other unfortunate guard, the queen approached Darin and laid her hand on his brow.

Liana followed her reluctantly, unsure what to do.

"Darin is a good man," the queen said. "It's not my place to tell you how you should feel about him, considering everything, but you need to know he's always cared about you."

Liana swallowed the bitterness that rose in her throat. "It's entirely possible to love a man but hate his choices," she said.

"Indeed. But sometimes all choices are bad."

"I don't know him well enough to judge him," Liana said. "When he learned of my existence, he never sent for me, not even when my grandfather died and I had no family left. He sent money and occasional letters. He was a stranger to me, and I to him. And yet…" The queen's gaze was curious, kind, her silence encouraging Liana to speak. "I've always held a place for him in my heart and now, when I finally have the chance to fill it, I fear it will be wrenched away from me."

Liana paused, surprised at her own words, shocked at the ease at which they came out before this quiet woman. She hadn't planned to talk about her father at all.

"Love is complicated," the queen said. Laconic as the statement was, it was also true.

The grown-up Liana understood the impossibility of Darin's choices, but the child in her still hurt. This was not the moment for rational explanations, though—for inspecting the outcomes and judging in hindsight. What they both needed was her forgiveness.

She bent down and kissed his clammy cheek. "It's fine, Papa. I understand," she whispered in his ear. "I love you."

He didn't open his eyes, but his eyelids fluttered, and she was almost certain he'd heard her.

She turned to the queen. "Thank you. But I suppose you're not here to offer me comfort."

"No," the queen said. "I'm here to beg."

Upstairs, it was eerily silent in the small study the queen led her to.

Somewhere behind the locked doors, in Queen Orsiana's bed, the king lay dying, and yet, there were no servants running around in panic, no black-clad physicians with their stinking vials and bloodletting tools, no efficient women with needles and bandages, no priests praying. In the soft light, Liana noticed the queen's eyes were rimmed with red.

"I'd pray for Darin if I thought it would help," she said before Liana had the chance to open her mouth. "But I trust Nila and her women more than I trust the gods."

Wrapped in her pale lilac shawl, the queen leaned on the delicate desk inlaid with mother-of-pearl. She looked like a very small snowbird, trapped inside a jewel box. Liana had to remind herself that she was neither helpless nor fragile.

"I'm sorry I dragged you here," the queen said. "I need your help."

Liana's heart sank; she'd expected this moment ever since she and Amron found his father. The queen had told her she would ask something of her.

"I came to beg you to talk to your mother."

The queen words were a punch in the solar plexus. Liana recoiled, her face a mask of revulsion.

"No, your father didn't tell me about her, I figured it out a long time ago. And even if I hadn't, you're so obviously hers it shines through your skin. Your aura is emerald green and it smells of forest and blood." The queen's eyes were two shards of flint, cold and sharp. "And even though I know you've lived in Till, I don't think that's where you came from just now. You're like an arrow flying, there's a purpose to your being here."

Liana nodded. It was pointless to lie.

"And that purpose is Amron," the queen concluded.

In some ways, the queen's frightening clarity was liberating, like a knife cutting away rotting flesh. There were things Liana couldn't say out loud—not even to Amron—because they were too mad or too terrifying. But the queen, with her mirror-like eyes and a body that seemed constructed of paper and light, looked barely human, like some ancient prophet. She looked as if she could absorb any divine joke Liana might throw at her.

"He was mine, for a long time," Liana said. "Then I lost him. Then I begged the gods—" Liana pressed her hand to her lips, hope and dread and grief threatening to explode her heart. "When you love someone, I suppose you are ready to do whatever it takes."

Neither of them were sitting down, the queen still leaning on the desk, Liana standing in her dirty sandals and blood-spattered clothes on the soft teal carpet. The queen was shorter, but when she approached Liana and took her grubby hand with her cold white fingers, Liana felt she had to look up to meet her gaze.

"If this were just about the king, I wouldn't dare ask. What is my grieving heart compared with the whole kingdom? But this is not about him." The queen's hands were smooth, silken, yet her grip was hard. "If he dies, we all die. I've seen it."

They'd all died the last time, Liana wanted to say, all but Amron, and he...

"Amron too," said the queen. Light as a feather, final like a stone sinking on the bottom of a lake. "But you already know that, don't you?"

She didn't know it, not this time round. She could have hoped his luck would hold once again, but even if he survived the beginning, there would be no Liana waiting for him in Till, to follow him, to join him in every battle. To save his life, just as he had saved hers, time and again.

"I did all I could do to prevent the slaughter, but history doesn't budge," Liana said. "I failed at every turn and the events rolled over me like a cart rushing downhill. I don't know how to stop it."

Somewhere in the palace, the king was dying. Somewhere in the city, Amron was running through a burning building to face the Elmarran blades. Somewhere in the streets, Roderi of Elmar was pouring his poison. And hundreds of miles away, in some exquisite room, in some sunlit residence filled with birdsong, the Emperor of Seragia was biding his time, moving ivory figurines across the map of the world.

"You need to ask the gods for help," the queen said.

"You just said you trust your physicians more than you trust the gods. If they can save my father, perhaps they can save the king."

"No." The queen shook her head. "You know how that poison works."

She did. Still, she said, "I asked my mother to help my father this afternoon, and she refused. The gods won't answer me. I'm sure they'd listen to you sooner than they'd listen to me."

The queen shook her head. "I tried. I begged and offered bargains and sacrifice, but they won't listen. Once, I was useful to them, a tool in their hands that rewrote the history of this city, but that task is long finished, and they have no interest in me now. I have nothing left to give them."

"I have nothing left to give them either," Liana echoed. "I forced my mother to listen to me once, for Amron's sake; she didn't come willingly and she didn't offer her help freely. I forced her. And then I struck a bargain, and bet everything I had on it. And now I'm going to lose." She rubbed her tear-stained cheeks. "It was impossible, of course, all deals with the gods are rigged. But I was desperate and he was…" Her voice wavered.

"Dead," the queen said.

Liana nodded. "And now there is no one left to help us."

The queen walked to the window overlooking a garden. Inside the walls of the palace, the evening seemed peaceful, the gentle breeze carrying the scent of flowers and the salty whiff of the sea. Only a distant rumble, like a thunderstorm far on the horizon, reminded them of the turmoil in the streets.

"Whatever my sons do down in the city, it won't be enough if the king dies. There'll be no persuading the people that the Seragians are blameless. And by the time the emperor hears about it, the peace treaty will be out of the window, and the only possible response to the events here will be another war. Amril and Amron, they can win the fight in the streets, but only you can win the fight against death."

It was so obvious now where it all led. Yet, Liana struggled against it. "I can't. Nobody can. I tried and failed."

The queen turned back from the window and crossed her arms over her chest, like a humble petitioner. "Try again. Please."

Her gaze was too intense to bear. Liana averted her eyes, studying the tapestry filled with silver fish, the silver candelabra shaped like an octopus, the white marble fireplace with delicate flowery carvings.

Liana's time was almost up, only one night remaining. And even if she could somehow drag Amron out of the burning city and make him forget the rebellion spreading around them, even if it was possible to make him kiss her, what would the outcome be? Certain war and uncertain future, and Amron, who would never forgive her such a move.

She'd offered it, back in his room. He rejected it.

The only thing left now was the attempt to save the peace treaty, against the odds. Even if it cost her everything, at least she would lose knowing that Amron was safe. It was worth the sacrifice.

On the queen's desk, yellow roses floated in a crystal bowl filled with water.

"I'll do it," Liana said. "But I need to be alone."

The queen nodded. "Thank you."

When she left, Liana scooped up the roses and threw them in the empty fireplace. Then she bowed low over the water, the tip of her nose almost touching the surface, closed her eyes, and whispered, "Morana, I'm here." Fingers gripping the edge of the desk to prevent them from shaking, Liana slowly submerged her face.

The curtain between the worlds ripped as the cold snatched her in its grip, the icy vortex pulling her down into the gloomy depths. She sank like a stone, heavy and frozen, crushed by the immense pressure of the water above.

"Breathe, you stupid girl. There's no water here."

Liana opened her eyes. She stood in a massive chamber filled with shifting greenish light and the sound of waves somewhere overhead. A whiff of water reeds, of rotting plants, reached her nostrils. In a blink, the goddess appeared before her.

"You've figured it out, haven't you? The rigged deal?"

Liana had always thought Morana was the most terrifying of all the gods, but standing before her now, there was little difference between her coiling hair, her deathly white face, and Lela's merciless gaze and predatory growl. All gods were terrifying. All gods lied.

"I don't lie." When her mouth was closed, Morana looked like a thin middle-aged woman with black, serpentine hair. But when she talked, she revealed rows of needle-sharp teeth, like a hungry moray. "I am the ultimate truth." The Goddess of Death grinned.

Liana winced but refused to step back. "You told me to call you."

Morana nodded.

Liana breathed in slowly. Perhaps the gods could wipe the slate clean when it suited them, but Liana wasn't so generous, not to the one responsible for Amron's death in the first place. It was hard, very hard to look at Morana's pale, grim face and not hate her.

"I made a bad deal. A rushed, desperate deal. And now I'm going to lose, and I will join my mother's hunt, never to return to the mortal world, and I'll never see Amron again, in this life or the next." Despite her best efforts, tears welled up in her eyes. "And to make matters worse, the war seems to be inevitable now that the king is dying. When I leave this place, it will sink into a fiery chaos. Queen Orsiana thinks I should negotiate with my mother but Lela won't listen to me. You're the last one I can turn to, although I can't see why you'd be willing to offer anything to me."

Liana lifted her eyes to the impossibly high arches above her head, covered in glittering fragments that might have been a mosaic or fish scales. Although there was no water around her, she felt she was at the bottom of a lake. She tried to compose her thoughts, but bitterness seeped into her words as scenes of battlefields flashed through her mind. "So much death, so much grief. Oh, how they're going to worship you, your name will be on thousands of lips every day."

The goddess stood perfectly still, yet her hair and gown moved, as if floating around her. "You are as shrewish as your mother, I see. A little humility would serve you well, considering you've come here to beg."

Liana bit her lip so hard the skin broke under her teeth. Sharp pain cut through the fog filling her head. "I am begging you to help me," she said.

"And yet you resist me with every bone in your body."

Liana wanted to turn away then. She was sick of divine games, sick of their tricks.

"Not so fast," the Goddess of Death said. "Tell me what you want."

A flash of anger, a spark of desperate resistance. "I want to stay here, with Amron." The words flew out of her mouth, and even if it was possible to take them back, she wasn't willing to.

The corners of Morana's mouth lifted in a toothy smile. "That's not what the queen asked of you."

"No. But you asked me what I wanted, and I want that. Can you do it?" Liana paused, sensing the chains of a bargain forming out of thin air. It was dangerous to say your wishes out loud in front of the gods, but to make this wish come true, she was ready to give anything the goddess asked for. "Can you?"

"No," Morana said after a long pause. "I cannot undo the deal between you and Perun. Other gods' bargains are beyond my reach."

Liana's heart sank. "Then why tell me to call you at all? If there's nothing you can do?"

"Oh, I can do many things," the goddess said.

Liana took a deep breath and exhaled slowly. If she couldn't stay with Amron, perhaps she could ensure he survived even if she wasn't there to protect him. Perhaps the queen was right after all, and the only way to stop the war was to save the king. "The king is dying," she said. "Can you spare him?"

Morana's grin grew wider. "Now you're getting closer."

It had to be enough to stop the war. "Spare the king," she said. "And tell me your price."

The long black coils of hair reached towards Liana, like tentacles ready to wrap themselves around her. She stood still, staring into Morana's eyes, black with golden swirls inside them.

"Three days," the goddess said. "I'll grant the king three more days."

"That's not....That's not enough."

"And yet, that's my offer," the goddess said. "Take it or leave it."

Would it be enough? Perhaps. Just to stop the Black Lord, to get Amril back to his wife.

"And what do you want in return?" Liana asked.

Morana stepped closer. "I take life, I don't create it. To give it to the king, I need to take it from someone else."

"Who...?" The image of Darin lying on the pallet, his face white as chalk, his shoulder bandaged, flickered before Liana's eyes. "No, not my father. You can't take him!"

"He's already at my door. It's a bad bargain for me, he's got less than three days to live."

"No! Leave him alone. Take them from me, take those three days from me, I don't care," Liana cried.

"Oh, but you have many more than three left," the goddess said.

A cold wave of fear washed down Liana's back. Of course it wasn't so easy. "How many, then?"

"Not a single day," Morana said. "And all of them. What I want is your divine nature in exchange for the king's life."

Liana didn't even know she could be separated from one half of her being, but it hardly mattered anymore. If she had to live without Amron, she didn't want a long life. And her mother would hate it so much, having a fully human daughter plodding after her.

"My divine nature in exchange for three days of the king's life," Liana said. "I agree."

~Chapter 28~

Melia

Amron picked her up and ran through the fiery nightmare towards the exit.

Melia thrashed and sobbed, trying to break his steely grip, ready to burn alive just to avoid being touched by him. A violent bout of grief for Ferisa clutched her chest—not for the woman who lay in the courtyard filled with burning rubble, lit by the blaze she'd kindled, but for Ferisa as she had been when there was no one else but the two of them. For the hope she'd had, that the worst of her father's plans could still be undone. For herself, who'd opened her heart just once, only to be betrayed.

She beat her fists on Amron's chest, sobbing without tears in the infernal heat, feeling her hair crackle. He stumbled, wheezing, then ran on into the thick smoke under the arch. They shot out of the burning embassy as something\crashed behind them. Outside, in the gathering darkness lit by flickering flames, no one paid any attention to them. People were rushing, carrying buckets of water, trying to prevent the fire from spreading to the neighboring buildings and swallowing the whole street.

Amron dropped her unceremoniously as her last punch landed on his shoulder. "You should've told me all of it, from the beginning," he rasped. "I would've helped you."

Someone pushed a pail of water towards her, and she dipped her head in it, drinking, then poured it over her head. "Murderer," she spat at Amron as soon as she got her voice back.

He froze, speechless.

Wild recklessness overtook Melia, the feeling she had nothing to lose. "I loved her," she said. "I would've left you for her in a heartbeat. Do you understand that?"

Water plastered his hair to his forehead, covering his singed brows; his lips were chapped, the skin peeling off. He swayed, his usual cool poise shattering. She aimed to hurt him, but his eyes only looked exasperated.

"Do you think I care about that?" He grabbed her shoulders and shook her. "How was that more important than a conspiracy to burn this kingdom to ashes? Melia, we'll all be dead before dawn if this doesn't stop *now*." He shuddered and removed his hands from Melia's shoulders, taking a step backwards. His eyes traveled the length of her, hard and unforgiving. "It's useless, you'll never be on my side." He shook his head as a shadow of dejection ran across his face. Then he turned on his heel and pushed his way into the crowd.

She didn't follow.

She knew, she *knew* Ferisa wouldn't have stopped until one of them was dead. She had been beyond reason, beyond any leverage Melia had once had on her. It didn't matter, though. The threads that bound them were stronger than betrayal, stronger than death.

She pushed through the crowd in the opposite direction, wishing to be as far away as possible from Amron, from the embassy, from the flames that devoured Ferisa. Sobs raked her body as she ran, yet nobody paid any attention to her. She was just another distressed, grieving woman on the streets of a bleeding city.

Abia was a battlefield tonight; the stage her father had set, and she'd helped him do it. Armed people ran through the darkness, guards on horseback, mobs with knives and clubs. Someone sat bleeding in a doorway, nursing a broken arm.

As a band of king's guards rushed down the street, she pressed herself against a house to avoid being squashed. In the torchlight, she saw a tall man with golden hair, but it wasn't Amron, it was his brother, shouting orders as they passed. She pulled a rag over her face, waiting for the darkness to swallow them.

The world she knew was falling apart, and she had nowhere to go. Curling up in some dark spot seemed like an attractive idea, and yet her body kept moving. *Out,* she thought, *out of here.* Out of Abia, out of this damned kingdom, there had to be something more out there. Perhaps there were ships in the port willing to sail out? She still had her jewelry, she could pay for a passage. She could still run away and start a new life, anonymous, free.

She pushed towards the harbor but the damned city was a maze, set to trap her like a wild animal until she threw herself at the walls, smashing her bones, bruising her flesh, bursting like an overripe fruit, bleeding over the white stones that never cared for her, a stranger, an enemy.

Tonight, all the paths led to the main square, to the chaos of fire and steel blurred by her tears. No matter how many times she turned, her feet always took her there, a puppet on a string, propelled by a force she couldn't fathom. Men and their swords, her father and his hatred, the war and all its dead, a mountain of bodies, surging up into the sky.

Her mother in the crowd, her face ashen, dark curls soaked with blood, reaching out for her with a skeletal hand. And Rovin, surrounded by blades, screaming in never-ending pain, his wound open and festering with the dark rage that fueled the conflict. And Ferisa, finally, in that vortex of faces, still burning, her skin peeling off her charred flesh, her hair a torch, her eyes two embers in blackened sockets. She opened her arms, inviting Melia to her fiery embrace. Perhaps it was better this way, to perish, even if it meant endless torment. At least she wouldn't be alone.

The desert wind, high and sharp like a woman's wail, filled her ears, drowning the cries and the clash of steel. *Ferisa, wait for me, I'm coming.*

A hand gripped her shoulder and pushed her aside. "What are you doing here, stupid girl? Run home!"

She was sucked back into the crowd, nostrils filled with the stink of blood and offal. Angry screams rose from the square, the blaze of torches painted sharp against the night sky. Blue uniforms of the king's guard, black and red Elmarrans, and the sea of other people, fighting without any semblance of strategy.

The chaos boiled before the main gate. Melia tried to turn, but the suffocating press of bodies pushed her towards the fire and the blades. She desperately elbowed the people around her to get a breath of fresh air, moving forward, forward. The mass was a live, brainless, writhing thing. Where one body was pushed away, two sprang up to replace it, closing all escape routes. There was no turning back now, only plowing on, towards the fires, the clamor, the voices. The golden head—Amril again—screaming something, his voice swallowed by the noise. And a man in black armor, towering above the crowd.

She knew him.

It was all coming together now, the pieces of the nightmare finally forming a picture. Her father, on a horse, in front of the palace, torchlight on his face like the blaze of doom.

She pressed through the throng, oblivious to the pushing and punching, ignoring the pain.

"Clear the palace of the Seragian traitors," Roderi of Elmar cried while his men attacked the king's guard. The predator posing as a defender.

The mob roared, at least those who could hear him. The others were scrambling in the dark, punching, stabbing, getting trampled. Locked in a dance with Death, even though they didn't recognize the tune.

"We'll never let the Seragians take the kingdom," the Black Lord shouted. He raised his hand towards the group of king's guards surrounded by the mob, Amril among them. "Where is the king? What happened to him? Have you conspired with the emperor to put his daughter on the throne?"

"No!" Amril cried, but his words were swallowed by the furious roar.

"When you wake up tomorrow, you won't have an Amrian king ruling you, but that Seragian wench, sent by her father to bring you to heel."

If Melia could reach her father, what would she do?

The tide of bodies lifted her and spat her paces away from the Black Lord. *All you do is lie*, she wanted to say to his damned armor, to his merciless eyes, to his insufferable smirk. But who would hear her, who would believe her?

"Capture the traitor!" her father ordered. "We'll force him to open the palace gates for us and show what he's done to the king!"

Melia cared nothing for Amril and his haughty Seragian bride; she had no compassion left for the sniggering courtiers and cruel ladies, for Amron's sister with her scathing words and his cold, cold mother. The palace was nothing but a place of torment and sorrow for her, a stillborn life that never took a single breath. She had been nothing but miserable there.

And yet, the idea of her father getting what he wanted was unbearable: the slaughter, the endless war, the eyes of Seragia turning upon this corner of the world, its proper armies, not the starved border brigands marching over the plains of Elmar, crossing the White Mountains, driving their blades into the soft belly of the kingdom. There was no way—*no way*—her father could win. But then, he had never fought in order to win, he'd fought for the love of conflict. To feed the rage and spread the pain.

Amril disappeared beneath the wave of Elmarran guards, his men driven up against the wall, trampled by the mob, killed by her father's lies.

"Tear down the gate!" her father roared.

Melia looked up to the top of the wall, to the palace roof lit only by the moonlight—but neither were built for defense, and if there were archers there, they didn't want to shoot blindly into the rolling mass of people.

The sturdy iron and wood of the gate endured the pressure until someone dragged a wooden beam to the square and the men used it as a ram. Every strike reverberated in Melia's bones until the heavy cedar gave in. The massive gate broke with a thundering crash and the current pulled Melia into the courtyard of the palace.

A group of guards stood in the yard, in a pool of torchlight, their swords unsheathed. Melia's heart sank when she saw the man leading them. *Amron.*

"Stop!" he cried in that clear, commanding voice of his, but there was no miracle this time, no charm to hypnotize the mob, they were too far gone in their madness.

The mass hit them like a tidal wave. Melia screamed his name in horror, but her voice was swallowed by the noise. They were going to die, they were all going to die.

Somewhere, her father roared in triumph.

And Melia, the frail, hollow-boned Melia, no heavier than a straw doll, surged with the crowd, like a leaf carried by the current.

At that moment, light flared on a balcony on the second floor of the palace—a dozen people with torches stepped out. Trumpets blared, cutting through the roar and the clash of metal. A familiar tall figure appeared in the light—the unmistakable golden hair and beard, the bulk of his royal presence.

Like an explosion, awareness spread through the crowd: shouts, cries and then sudden, stunned silence as all the heads looked up. All but Melia. She turned and slipped among the unmoving bodies toward her father.

"I am alive," the king shouted.

Roderi of Elmar pressed his lips together, an unmistakable sign of rage. Resisting the urge to duck behind the armed men and melt into the night, Melia stepped forward and caught the reins of his horse.

"There is no Seragian conspiracy," the king cried from the balcony. "It's all lies!"

"Father," Melia said. "Father, listen to me."

"Come meet the carevna," the king said. "She had to escape the burning embassy tonight, you should go there and help put the fire out, not linger here. The palace is safe, I promise you."

Surrounded by the king's guard, Amril pushed through the crowd until he reached the circle of torchlight beneath the balcony. When the guards moved, Melia saw Aratea was with him, a little worse for wear. Holding her husband's hand.

Roderi of Elmar watched the scene, his face a storm cloud.

"Father, Ferisa is dead," Melia said, gripping his reins.

He refused to look at her. Jumping down from his saddle, he yanked the reins out of Melia's hand and handed them over to one of his men.

"Father," she tried again. "Please, stop this, there's no point anymore. They know what you did."

"Go home!" the king ordered the mob.

Everybody in the crowd was looking up, everybody but Melia and her father. And she suddenly knew where she'd seen this scene before.

> *An unfamiliar courtyard. The flagstones were slick with blood, the people around her pushing, fighting, crying for help in the flickering light of the burning buildings. Amron stood before her, smeared with blood and ash, with a bemused expression on his face. Her eyes slipped down to his hand pressing his belly, black blood pouring through his fingers, soaking into the blue silk he wore, dripping on the flags. He opened his mouth to tell her something, but no sound came out as his legs folded and he fell.*

Her father pushed forward through the crowd, and Melia ran after him.

Amron stood beside his brother and the carevna, his sword back in its scabbard. The guards were all looking up as the king addressed the crowd. The Black Lord reached beneath the folds of his cloak. He was aiming for Aratea, but Amron must have seen the movement and turned, pushing her behind him.

Too late, Amril and the guards lowered their eyes, only to see the flash of steel in the torchlight. In that moment, Melia finally caught up with her father, overtook him, threw herself before him. Before the blade.

Liana

"**Mother, mother, quickly!**" somebody called.

Liana opened her eyes in the queen's opulent, candlelit study. Her face and hair were soaked, but no water had touched her clothes. A vague memory of making a deal with the Goddess of Death flickered at the back of her mind, causing a bolt of panic, yet nothing about her seemed different. She was still the same Liana, wasn't she?

You're still on Perun's time, you fool. It hasn't run out.

There was still a chance.

"Mother?" Amron's sister peered in, her face haggard but smiling. "Where is the queen?" she asked just as her mother rushed in through the other door.

"Amielle, what's happening? Why aren't you with your father?"

"Because he's arisen and asking for you. Come!"

The queen shot a brief look of gratitude to Liana before her daughter dragged her out.

Liana, still dazed and slow, got up and followed the trail of noise to the antechamber where the king stood perfectly whole and wholesome, goddamned radiant in the sea of gray, panicked faces.

"There's fighting in the courtyard," a guard said. "Roderi of Elmar and his men are wreaking havoc, accusing Prince Amril and Princess Aratea of assassinating you. The city is in turmoil, the citizens are demanding to see you."

"What? I'll personally flay that lying bastard."

Fighting?

Liana didn't give a damn about the king and his plans, but if there was fighting down in the courtyard and in the square, then Amron was somewhere near, and perhaps there was still time before dawn to quench this rebellion, to stop the Black Lord. To get a moment alone with Amron.

She rushed downstairs. The main door leading into the great hall was shut and barred, but that meant she simply had to go around, through the empty guards' quarters, across the practice yard, through the stables, and out on the other side. Just in time to see the crowd cheering the king who stood on the balcony, resplendent and obviously, undeniably alive—at least for the next three days. It would have to be enough to wrap up the wedding, to remove the Elmarrans, to ensure that Amril succeeded smoothly.

Amril and Aratea stood in the courtyard in a pool of torchlight, disheveled, bruised, and covered in soot, holding on to each other like two shipwrecked sailors. A shadow of anger marred his face, a twist of disgust hid in the corners of her mouth, but they'd both been raised for this and they endured, facing the crowd. It crossed Liana's mind that she'd rather be dead than trapped in their marriage, but then, they probably deserved each other.

And then finally, *finally*, the Seragian guards showed up— the useless, calculating, perfectly trained troops who'd waited to see which side would win before helping the king's men deal with the last Elmarrans, pushing them into a corner of the yard. Now that the mob had lost its bloodthirst, they posed no real threat, surrounded and outnumbered. Their lord, the monster she'd cursed so many times during the long years of the war, lay face-down on the flags, hands tied behind his back, two guards standing over him. His teeth were bared, a rabid dog ready to bite, frothing. The rest of him, though, looked as small and insignificant as a desperate drunk who'd broken too many bottles and had to be restrained. Knowing what the king's justice looked like, Liana expected his head to grace the walls by tomorrow morning.

The wave of rebellion broke against the walls of the palace; the ancient stones held out against the fury of the mob. Now there was nothing left but some confused people who cheered because they felt they had to, and some defeated soldiers.

"Go out in the city and spread the word that everything is all right," the king commanded. "And then go home. My men will take care of Abia."

It was a promise and a threat, and the mob understood it perfectly well, dispersing with their tails between their legs.

Yet Amron was nowhere in sight. Was he still at the embassy, fighting the fire? Surely, it had been conquered by now; there were no flames rising in the sky above the city. Was he somewhere in the streets, driving the last rebels into the sea, clearing Abia of traitors and warmongers? Liana was ready to run out blindly, to search for him until her time ran out, when the strange, mournful sigh of a wounded creature reached her ears and she spotted a flash of gold in the dark under the arcade.

She approached haltingly, fearing he was hurt. Then she heard his voice.

"Stay awake, stay awake," he said. "I'll get help."

"No." A whisper. "I don't want—"

"Don't you dare die now."

In the chaos and darkness, no one had noticed him, no one was searching for him but Liana. He was on his knees, doubled over.

"Amron?" she whispered.

He cradled someone in his arms. A head, with a mass of black hair, shoulders, female torso, one arm hanging, touching what Liana thought was a black pool of shadow but now realized was blood.

With much effort, Liana's eyes picked out the features of the face, half pressed to Amron's chest. It was Melia.

All the hostility and years of subdued jealousy drained out of Liana.

"I'm so sorry," she said. "Amron, I'm so sorry."

"Liana, is that you?" He lifted his head. Tears had carved white lines in his soot-smudged face. "She's wounded, she needs help."

"Shall I run to the infirmary and get someone?"

"No, not in the palace, it's too risky." He shook his head. "I know who might help her. She has a surgeon."

Before Liana could ask who he meant, he got up, holding Melia in his arms.

"Clear the way," he told Liana, but there was little need. The back exit they used was deserted, the people in the alley already shuffling home, minding their own business. Amron marched on until they reached the locked door of a villa, the same one Liana had knocked on two days before.

"But…this is a brothel," Liana said.

"Yes, and they have a surgeon at hand, and know how to keep a secret. Knock, please."

They waited a long time before they heard footsteps and a narrow strip of light poured out of the slit. "We're closed," a voice said.

"Tell Celandina it's Prince Amron," he said. "If she helps me, I'll owe her a favor."

"I'll be right back."

They didn't wait long this time. More footsteps, and the door opened to reveal a familiar face.

"Your Highness. And *you*." A shadow of displeasure darkened Celandina's pretty face when she recognized Liana. "And…who do you have here?"

"Someone important to me, wounded in a fight. I need you to help her," Amron said.

If Celandina recognized Melia, she did nothing to show it, nor did she ask superfluous questions. She led them in, ordering the girl following her to call the surgeon. They entered a small room, spare but pristine. Amron laid Melia on the bed. Her eyes were closed, her breathing shallow.

"Oh, this is bad," Celandina murmured, "stomach wounds don't heal well."

"I know," Amron said. "But we must try. She saved my life tonight."

A lick of cold air touched the nape of Liana's neck. *Saved his life?*

A surgeon ran in, holding his bag, followed by the girl, carrying water and bandages. Celandina lit every candle in the room. In a heartbeat, they were all busy around Melia, cutting away fabric, cleaning the wound, stopping the bleeding.

"Steady now," Amron said, holding Melia's hand, although she showed no sign of hearing him.

Liana was left standing in the shadows, a useless bystander. *Melia* had saved Amron's life, not Liana. "Amron." The words rolled like gravel in her mouth. "Is there anything I can do?"

He barely spared her a look. "No, you've done more than enough. I must help Melia now." His fingers were entwined with Melia's as the surgeon took a scalpel out of his bag. "I'll find you later."

And she had no heart to tell him there would be no later.

She walked out of the villa and back towards the palace light-headed, her ears buzzing. The final image of Amron—dirty, distraught, beautiful—was etched on the insides of her eyelids, refusing to be washed away by her tears. The square was almost empty now but for the guards and casualties. The rest had slunk away to their dens. Tomorrow, they would wake up bruised and hungover, with a nagging sense of shame they'd try to forget as soon as possible. They'd be good citizens, cheering the Seragian carevna and Amril, accepting the transition of power when it inevitably happened in three days' time. Their lust for blood had been sated, the sacrifices to the gods made. Abia would wipe this stain off her white cloak and continue to live in peace and prosperity.

Somewhere in the palace, Darin slipped in and out of consciousness, dreaming feverish dreams of the northern forests and the feral goddess who ruled them, but he was alive. He'd be there when the princes needed him, as would Queen Orsiana. The Seragian emperor would find the royal family united, and the treaty would hold.

It was, in all measurable ways, a victory.

And yet, it tasted like ash in her mouth. Amron had chosen Melia because she needed him more, because it was the right thing to do. Liana fought to suppress the tears that filled her eyes as she headed towards to the Northern gate. She was done with Abia, done with history, done with the kingdom. She'd given all she had to give, and it wasn't enough to get her what she wanted the most.

She walked through the familiar streets, now filled with trash and rubble and people hurrying home, and bid a silent goodbye. It had been her home, after all, and it wasn't its fault that it had demanded so much. She'd chosen to tie her life to Amron, she'd chosen to challenge the gods. The city was just a high stake in that game.

The massive Northern gate was closed, but a few guards stood there, watching over the restless city.

"Let me out, please," she said.

They lifted their torches to get a look at her, a tired woman in a bloodstained uniform of the king's guard, and found no objection to her plea. They unlocked the small door, and she stepped out of Abia for the last time.

It really didn't matter where she went next, so she chose a nice tree by the road and sat down, her face turned towards the east. When the first light of dawn appeared above the mountains, and the thick, white fog rolling down the slope materialized into a white stag, Liana gripped the silver medallion containing the last remaining proof Amron had ever loved her, and closed her eyes.

They had gone to Myrit soon after the war, back when Liana's curiosity still got the upper hand over her disgust, and she'd allowed Amron to drag her to court.

The court was a smaller affair then, mostly political: The lords who'd survived the war gathered around the young king and his regent, vying for scraps of power. Yet, Myrit was a proud city filled with ambitious people, and even though it had suffered greatly, rebuilding it quickly was a matter of stubborn defiance. After all, for those who were not overly preoccupied with human suffering, war offered opportunities of renewal and growth.

And so Liana found herself in the former palace of the Lords of Leven—now the royal residence—polished to its former glory, all colorful marble, scented woods, and intricate tapestries laid in a maze around blooming gardens and murmuring fountains. The war had made people a little reckless, a little wanton; faced with their own mortality, they lusted after every pleasure life could offer them. They were all young, too, the new generation, the fighting generation, the winners, rushing headlong into the future so that they wouldn't have to look behind them and see the carnage, the ghosts, the grief.

Amron shone at court. After years of blood and grime, of chainmail and leather, of sleeping in tents or worse, he was back in his element, in silk and velvet, in marble halls, under blazing chandeliers. Touched by glory, gilded by victory, all eyes on him.

Liana struggled to keep up. Her share of glory was by no means insignificant—she was revered, her courage praised, her beauty admired. But she was a novelty, a fragment that didn't fit in, and that showed soon enough. She had no house, no family, no connections in the intricate network of people who ruled the kingdom, except for the old Gospodar Echton, who treated her with absent-minded cordiality. She showed no talent for politics, she had no wish to use the fact she had a direct approach to the most powerful man in the kingdom for her own advancement. She was a nobody; she was no lord, no lady, no wife, no princess. The regent's paramour, the wild northern warrior girl: She was an anomaly they couldn't, or wouldn't, wrap their heads around. The men mostly tried to bed her: They found her stunning even though she was outside the court's fair—frail—pale aesthetics. But the real reason behind their advances was to challenge Amron's power, to find his weak spot. The women mostly despised her.

The women—ah, the women! There were few of them around during the war, this class of women: thoroughbred, powerful in their own right, privileged. No place for silk and sighs and poisonous whispers on the battlefield. But as soon as the fighting was over, they crawled out of the woodwork in their brilliant gowns and dazzling jewels, ready to climb the new ladder of power that was being built in the halls, corridors, and bedchambers of Myrit.

They flocked around Amron. Liana watched their smiles, their covert touches, their relentless flirting. She'd never been entirely free of jealousy, but there was amusement in it too, a game she and Amron played, entirely comfortable after years of sharing everything. To sometimes bring in someone new for a night or two, when they both felt intrigued enough.

It was a dangerous game at court because sex was a currency there, a stepping stone to power. Therefore, no one important. A lady-in-waiting whose skin was smooth as satin and who'd never kissed a woman before, a dark-eyed guard Liana devoured while Amron sat in the shadows. Rare, short-lived treats.

Isetta should have been as insignificant as the rest of them, a younger sister of a minor lord, pretty with her black hair and blue eyes and fresh face, but nowhere near as beautiful as Liana. She was besotted with Amron—all the women were—and they danced and drank and laughed together, and Liana was warming up to the idea of her pale limbs and cherry-tinted mouth in their bed, when something happened. A disruption, an anomaly.

Instead of batting her eyelashes at Amron or accidentally brushing his ear with her lips as she whispered sweet nonsense, she talked to them. About nothing serious at first: Abian poets at his grandfather's court, the Seragian ivory chests in the royal collection, the silk patterns the weavers of Myrit imported from the south. Friendly chat, but it left Liana painfully out of her depth. She had no formal education, no courtly upbringing. She knew how to track man or beast through the thickest woods, how to dress a wound or choose the fastest horse at a glance, how to train a hound or kill a man without making a sound. But this was a different world now, and those skills, admirable as they had been, were useless. She lacked refinement and, at twenty-seven, she was acutely aware she could never catch up with the people whose courtly manners were their second nature.

When Isetta pulled a lute out of some corner and Amron wrapped his arms around her to teach her an old folk ballad, the wave of jealousy that hit Liana was so strong she got up and left, afraid she would make a scene.

She took a long walk to cool down, but it brought her no relief. Then she shut herself in the bedroom and sat there, steaming in agony, replaying the moment when Amron's fingers slid around Isetta's wrist over and over again in her head.

"No," she said later that night, when Amron came to bed. Alone, thankfully.

"What?"

"Not Isetta. I don't want her."

"Fine. As you wish." He made no attempt to change her mind as he removed his clothes. He only said, "I thought you liked her."

"I did." For once, she refused to be distracted by his body, by the linen slipping over his pale skin and hard muscles. She felt querulous. "But you liked her even more."

He paused to shoot her a confused glance. "What do you mean?"

She couldn't tell if he was being naïve or playing dumb. "You fit so well together. She's your match: pretty, noble, educated, refined. I saw her brother looking at you, calculating. A man like you needs a wife, after all."

"Liana." He sat down abruptly, astonishment draining his face of color. "You can't believe that."

"I'm not the right partner for you," she said. "They all see it. No one dares to say it to your face, not yet, but I'm a burden to you. Good enough for tents and battlefields, but ridiculous here in the palace. You need a wife who will bring you connections and power, who will be your ally."

"I see you've joined the ranks of those who think they know what is best for me," he said, only a faint line in the corner of his mouth revealing his anger. "But you should know better, Liana, you really should. Have I ever done anything to make you feel you were not enough?"

"No, but—"

"Do you think I would ever, *ever* agree to another political union, after all I've been through?"

She shook her head, all words gone from her mind.

"I can't marry you now because the kingdom is still bleeding, and such a willful, defiant act could tear it apart. But that doesn't mean I will marry anyone else, for any reason."

He sat on the edge of the chair, gripping the armrest so hard his fingers turned white. She'd rarely seen him this furious, this hurt. But still, she couldn't get rid of the claws that pierced her heart.

"Seeing you here, among these people, your people…I couldn't understand why you chose to be with me. Why do you want me, Amron?"

"Because I love you, you fool." He jumped out of the chair, raking his hair into a disheveled mess. "I love you, isn't that obvious?"

"Love has never been essential in a relationship, not for someone your rank."

He winced as if she'd slapped him. "Oh that is cruel, Liana. You're slashing deliberately now."

"Why did you choose me?" she insisted. "There are so many women out there more elegant, clever, and educated than me. Kinder, gentler, sweeter. Women who would make it their only goal to make you happy."

"How terrifying," he said.

"Why me?" she asked again.

Amron paused his exasperated fidgeting and regained his poise with considerable effort, sitting down beside her.

He laid his hand on her knee: Touch—clear, explicit—had always been his language of love. The warmth of his fingers penetrated through the thin linen of her nightgown. Her heartbeats measured the time, silence stretching before them as he struggled to find the words.

"Because you see me," he said at last. "You don't care about rank or power. All my life, people have wanted me because of what I am—a prince, a doorway to privilege—but not you. You see me for who I am, and you like what you see, and that is incredibly liberating. I have no better mirror than your eyes.

"I don't want a woman who would mold herself according to my wishes, I want a woman who loves me on her own terms. I want to be myself in private, just like I want you to be yourself. And you are entirely yourself, Liana—bravely, brazenly yourself, like a cat who doesn't give a damn about the rest of the world. Don't get dragged into this courtly mire, into their stupid, volatile rules, their mercenary ways. Do you think any of those women care about me? They just want a prince under their thumb.

"You, on the other hand, want nothing from me, but *everything* of me, and I'm happy to give it. Every breath, every heartbeat, every last drop of blood, for as long as I live. And once when I'm gone, it won't diminish you in any way. You'll still be your beautiful, fearless, unadulterated self."

~Chapter 30~

Melia

Being dead wasn't so terrible.

The Seragian ship had sailed out on the morning tide. Salt wind cooled her cheeks as she sat on the deck in the shadow of the massive, wind-filled sails. Watching Abia disappear in the distance filled her heart with ache: the last connection to her old life, melting into the horizon.

Her health was still fragile—the encounter with her father's blade was a close call. Close enough, in fact, to kill Princess Melia of Elmar. She touched a bundle of documents in her pocket for reassurance: She had a new name now, a new future before her.

It was an unexpected gift, and she planned to enjoy it.

The surgeon who'd never introduced himself had sewn her shut, and the pretty, stern woman who called herself Celandina nursed her in a small room in an unfamiliar house. Fever gave Melia nightmares of her flesh burning, of blazing embassies and funeral pyres. Death sat at the foot of her bed every night, wearing Ferisa's face.

"Take me with you," Melia begged.

"No, little raven, it's not your time," Death who was Ferisa said.

Then one morning she woke up and Amron was sitting beside her, no trace of burns on his face, his hair reverted to its glossy splendor.

"You're dead," he told her.

"Excuse me?"

"Officially, I mean. Dozens of people saw your father stab you. I testified later that you tried to run away, collapsed in an alley, and died. The body was never found, but Abia was in so much turmoil no one paid it too much attention. My word was enough."

"And my father?"

"Executed in the main square. The nine Elmarran guards who attacked the embassy were hanged, the rest of them banished. The Empire is appeased, the carevna happily reunited with my brother."

She averted her eyes, focusing on a square of sunlight on the white wall. The news should've hurt, but somehow the words coming out of Amron's mouth dissolved like smoke. All the death and fury and grief were the burdens some other Melia had carried. This Melia—the dead Melia—felt more alive than she had in years.

"What am I supposed to do now?"

He didn't answer immediately. Silence filled the room, broken by a lonely bird keening in the garden.

"Pick a new name, go someplace wonderful." He smiled, but his eyes remained serious.

It sounded deceptively, stupidly simple. But then, wasn't that the exact thing she'd been dreaming of all these years?

"And you?"

"I'm going to Elmar, to snuff out the last flames of the rebellion." The sunlight gilded his pale complexion, and she remembered their first night together, the gentle touch, the quick retreat. "You saved my life, I saved yours. There are no debts between us, you're free to go."

The truth was sharp-edged and cold, like an ice blade.

"I wish I could've loved you," she said.

"I wish I'd been a better husband." His kiss was long and sweet, the warmth lingering on her lips when he moved away. "Goodbye, Melia."

Liana

The white stag stood in the middle the road. Plumes of milky vapor rose from its nostrils, while the dawn light wrapped the magnificent animal in a luminous cloud.

It was Liana's turn to keep her side of the bargain, and join Lela.

"Snijeg." Liana approached and stroked its silken coat. "Old friend. None of this is your fault."

The beautiful animal nuzzled her cheek.

"Take me to my mother."

She climbed on its broad back and Snijeg broke into a canter, Liana gripping its antlers. The air around her thickened like molasses, resisting her body, pushing back as they gained speed.

"Snijeg, what—"

The stag leaped. Liana crashed into something hard, the impact throwing her off Snijeg's back.

She cried in pain and surprise as she hit the ground.

"Snijeg?" she called.

The stag had vanished. In vain, Liana tried to follow, to pull aside the curtain between the worlds. Her fingers found nothing but air.

"Pathetic." Her mother stepped through a wisp of fog. "You're not five anymore, you know how to cross."

"I can't." As the words slipped out of her mouth, the realization hit Liana and she burst out laughing. "I really *can't.*"

"You stubborn, willful girl, what are you playing at?"

The expression on Lela's face only increased Liana's frantic mirth. "Look at me, Mother. I'm mortal. Completely, irrevocably mortal."

"Impossible," Lela snapped.

"Ask Morana."

Lela opened her mouth, doubtlessly to hurl another insult at her, but then her divine eyes recognized the truth, and disgust twisted her features. "You could've lived forever, and you threw it all away for a man. You'll curse that choice once you grow old and sick."

"Always so kind to me, Mother." Liana laughed so hard tears ran down her face. Or perhaps the tears had nothing to do with the laughter. "If I never see you again, it will be too soon."

With a look of cold repulsion on her face, the goddess disappeared, leaving nothing but a cloud of silver vapor behind her. Liana was left sitting on the empty road.

Behind her, the deep, clear sound of the bell pierced the silence. The Fat Odo above Abia's Northern gate was striking the hour of dawn. She took a deep breath, and a splitting headache bloomed between her temples.

She had no divine blood left.

She rose slowly, expecting her body to fall apart, but it turned out that being mortal didn't feel much different from being half divine. If she'd lost her speed and stamina, she couldn't tell by standing up and rubbing her bruised shoulder. Her eyesight was still good, her teeth were all in her mouth. She checked her hands, they looked the same— long fingers, short nails, archery calluses. She touched her face, tracing the salty residue of tears. Without a mirror, it was hard to determine if she looked any older. Her skin was taut, smooth under her fingers.

"You've chosen a fine moment to become vain," she muttered.

She was filthy, still wearing the same guard uniform she'd spent the last two days in, sprayed with blood and smudged with mud and soot.

As the sun rose over Abia, the first travelers and carts started moving in and out of the city, the traffic slow but picking up. She stood at the edge of the road, wondering what she was supposed to do.

No divine gaze to lay on her shoulders like a cold burden, no expectations, no scheming. She was utterly unimportant now, free to go wherever she pleased, do whatever she wanted with the rest of her life.

She threw one last look at Abia. The familiar walls looked welcoming, pulling her home. The guards at the gate, chatting with the people, the archers patrolling the walls, the standard flying above their heads.

Liana gasped as sunlight illuminated the standard. The golden sun of the royal house and the silver fish of Larion. There was just one person in the whole world allowed to fly it. Had they forgotten to remove it? No, that was unthinkable.

When was she?

Liana rushed towards the gate. The guards frowned at her appearance, but the royal uniform apparently still meant something, because one of them asked, "Do you need help, sister?"

It would have been so easy if she could just ask who ruled the city, but they'd think her mad. She said, "No, thank you," and rushed into Abia.

The streets looked almost the same as she remembered them—the houses, the courtyards, the gardens—but something felt different. She couldn't quite put her finger on it until she went deeper towards the center and saw there were more shops, more taverns. It looked busier, richer, the houses all brushed up, the streets spotless. Like a drawing of Abia where some imaginative artist had added a bit of shine to make it prettier. She walked into a tavern she didn't know, but which looked busy even at this early hour. The tables were occupied by merchants and tradesmen drinking beer and eating hot pies whose smell made Liana's stomach grumble. She reached into her pocket and found a handful of silver coins, more than enough for a pie and a drink. She waved over a passing girl.

"A pie and a beer, please."

The girl took in her appearance and frowned.

"I can pay." Liana took a silver coin and pushed it into the girl's hand.

When her food and drink arrived, Liana caught the girl's wrist. "Wait, please. I've been away for a long time, I need you to tell me a few things about Abia."

"I'm in a hurry," the girl protested until she saw another coin in Liana's hand. "What do you need?"

"I want to know how happy you are with the ruler of this town."

The girl lifted her eyebrows, obviously thinking Liana was pulling her leg. "I don't think about that," she said.

"Humor me. What do you think about your lord?"

"Prince Amron, you mean? He's good, I guess." The girl shrugged, eager to get away.

Liana's heart stopped in her chest. The standard and the name—it was too much to be a coincidence.

"And Prince Amron, he is the king's…?"

"Brother," the girl said. "Of course."

"Ah yes. King Amril and Queen Aratea, right? How long has he been on the throne?"

"Seventeen years. I was born on the day of his coronation." The girl shot her a gap-toothed grin as someone called for more beer. "Look, I must work. If you want to talk, I can call the tavern keeper."

"Just one more question, please. Prince Amron, is he married?"

The girl shook her head. "He's a widower." And then she pulled her hand from Liana's grip and dashed away.

Seventeen years.

Liana suppressed the urge to run straight to the palace and shout his name in the courtyard. Seventeen years since Amril's coronation, seventeen years since his father's death. Which meant the year was 361 and she was right back where—when—she'd left. Except, Amril was on the throne, and Aratea with him, which meant the war with the Empire had never happened.

She crumbled the steaming pie crust on her plate, trying hard not to cry in a tavern.

They did it, they stopped the war. The years of fighting, of death and destruction, never happened. No wonder Abia looked so prosperous. History had taken a different turn, and seventeen years later, this was a different world. A world where Amron ruled Abia in peace, where he didn't have to run errands for his royal nephew and hold the broken kingdom together for him. A world where the king never sent him on a doomed errand, a world where he hadn't died.

Her hands shook as she stuffed the food in her mouth, focusing on chewing, swallowing, breathing. Not crying, definitely not crying.

Hope was the most dangerous, the most cruel of all feelings, and she didn't dare, she didn't dare...

Liana finished her meal, leaning on the table like a drunken sailor. Her limbs felt impossibly heavy, her legs had forgotten how to walk.

He was alive, and close, and all she had to do was...what?

Would he even remember her? He'd known her for three days, three confused, catastrophic, traumatic days. It would be no wonder if he'd deliberately forgotten them.

She rose and stumbled into the street.

This Amron was not the same Amron she'd known, that was certain. His life had been dramatically different—seventeen years of different choices, different events, different people. Seventeen years without her. No historical turmoil to erase rank and throw them together, no years of hardship to bring them close. Would he even like her?

You didn't come this far to run away like a coward. Face him and find out.

Outside, the town was in full morning rush. The scent of warm bread wafted from the bakeries as women hurried with baskets filled with fruit and vegetables and young men lingered in squares, gossiping and teasing the maids who filled their jugs at the fountains.

There must have been a Liana-shaped hole in Amron's life. Who'd filled it? Some accomplished noblewoman who read poetry in bed and kept his high visitors amused? Some clever courtesan who kissed him hard and kept him awake in the long winter nights? Some random girl he fell in love with simply because she was there?

Men had it so much easier. They could duel their opponents and no one would bat an eyelid. What could women do? Poison them?

As she rushed towards the palace, Liana's fingers itched with the need to strangle this entirely imaginary woman who shared Amron's life. She went in through the main gate—enough people were crowded there that even her blood-spattered uniform attracted no attention. In the courtyard, she veered away from the entrance to the great hall and turned towards the stables instead. She considered going down to the basement, scrubbing up quickly, making herself presentable, but so much time had been wasted, she could not waste a moment more. What was the point of a pretty dress if he didn't care about the person wearing it?

She passed the first floor with relative ease, but from there on, it got complicated in the mid-morning flood of people filling every corridor. What the guards might overlook, the maids certainly wouldn't.

Where would Amron be at this hour? Definitely not sleeping, he was an early riser. Working, probably, in his private study or his official one, or somewhere on the first floor with the clerks, or receiving people in the great hall, or even somewhere outside, with the merchants or councilors. But he wouldn't be alone there, and she needed to see him in private. Which meant only one place—his room.

The one he'd always liked? The one with blue tapestries? Through the servants' corridor, turn right, open the door…

"What do you think you're doing?" A voice behind her back and the unmistakable jab of a dagger somewhere in the vicinity of her kidneys.

She hadn't heard him, she hadn't smelled him, she hadn't felt him. All her instincts were as blunt as a wooden sword.

"I need to talk to Prince Amron in private," she stammered.

"Really? Why? Who sent you?"

She knew that voice. Deep, rasping, drawing out the vowels. "Telani, is that you? Let me go, damn you, I'm not here to hurt him."

A long pause. Then, "Turn around slowly and keep your hands where I can see them, or I'll stick this dagger in your gut."

She did as he ordered. It was indeed Amron's secretary, his dark eyes distrustful as always, his nose still broken, his mouth a scowl. But he was clean-shaven for once, and wearing black velvet and…was that a gold chain around his neck? Was that *embroidery*?

"I'm so glad he found you," she said. "You look swell."

"Have we met?" And then, surprisingly accurate: "Liana?"

"Yes. But…how did you know?"

"Because I spent two miserable years of my life searching for you." The fact that he'd recognized her didn't make him any friendlier—quite the opposite. "Talking to every sheepfucker and dim-witted woodsman in Till, riding for miles through the snow with the hunters, dragging that redheaded imbecile who called himself your fiancé out of some cheap whorehouse, only to find nothing. No trace of you; vanished into thin air. Your father was mad with worry, and my lord…you were *missed*. Where have you been?"

"It's a very long story," she said. "Can I see him please?"

He scrutinized her appearance, from the tangled hair and dirty uniform to the dust-covered, sandaled feet. "A wash first, perhaps?"

It was a reasonable suggestion, but the time for reason had run out. "Now, please. It's urgent."

Telani rolled his eyes. "Fine. Follow me."

They walked down the corridor to Amron's study. Telani went in alone and came out a few moments later. "He'll see you now." And then he grabbed her arm. "If you perform your disappearing act again or do anything else to hurt him, I'll never stop hunting you."

She shook him off. "Don't be jealous, Telani, there's enough of him for both of us."

The study looked almost the same when she stepped in. The man standing beside the desk in the pool of morning light, dressed in somber shades of teal and gray, was different, though. There was a slight roundness to his face she didn't remember, emphasized by the absence of worry lines at the corners of his mouth. For once, he looked fresh instead of harrowed. His stance was different, too, more relaxed, missing that permanently edgy awareness of a fighter. The eyes, however, were the same: keen, sharp.

"It *is* you," he said.

"I heard you were looking for me." The soft carpet and the thick tapestries swallowed her voice.

"I promised I'd find you later, didn't I?" His gaze remained glued to her face. "You look exactly the same as the last time I saw you. How is that possible?"

She took a deep breath. She'd made him believe her before, she could do it again. "Because the last I saw you was just a few hours ago," she said. "Seventeen years ago."

He blinked. "I don't understand."

Stepping closer, she caught her long braid and pulled it over her shoulder, lifting its end towards him. "Look, it's still tied with that blue ribbon you gave me."

His fingers examined the crumpled satin, then slid up to touch the hand that held it.

"I would've come sooner if I had the choice," she said. "But what was seventeen years for you was one night for me. I'm sorry, I'm so sorry. It's a long and complicated tale."

His hand was wrapped around hers now, gentle but firm, as if he expected her to run away. "I'll gladly listen to every detail you want to share with me. Will you stay here? Can you stay here?"

"I think my running days are over." She offered him a pale, woeful smile as she lifted her head. "I'll stay if you want me."

There were so many words they needed to exchange. The story of gods and war and loss, of relentless hope and love. The story of family, of his mother and siblings and nephews and nieces, of Liana's father, of betrayal and sacrifice, of abandonment and acceptance. And then there were the practical things, too, the question of her status, of other women who might or might not have been there, of marriages and relationships and the mundane details of everyday life.

But none of it mattered now, as he stepped closer to her, letting go of her hand only to slide his arms around her waist and pull her in. If it felt a little rushed, a little awkward, it was because their minds still struggled to catch up with the inexplicable strangeness of it all. Their bodies, however, refused to be tricked by time and absence. They remembered what to do.

She cupped his face: the angle of his cheekbones, the line of his jaw fitting the curve of her palms perfectly. *I know you,* the touch said, *you're mine.* Her fingers slid down his neck—feeling his wild heartbeat—and under his shirt, to the hidden spot between his collarbones.

A sharp intake of breath, lips curved in a smile of recognition of a memory he couldn't have had, and yet its promise made him gasp.

"I've waited so long for this," he said. And then he bent down and kissed her.

Acknowledgments

Writing a book is a lonely job, but publishing isn't. So many people helped me and encouraged me on my short but nerve-wracking journey to bring this book to you. I'm grateful to my excellent first readers, whose comments made this book much better: Cécile Cristofari and Andrea Tatjana. Antonia Rachel Ward has been a friend, a dear colleague, and a trusted editor since the first story I've published. Bori Cser has not only read my work, she has also listened to my bad jokes and complaints about the industry with angelic patience. Diana Fox shared wisdom and kindness when I needed them most. I'm grateful to my team at Dark Matter INK, and especially to my editor, Maddy Leary, who has been wonderful to work with and helped me polish my words until they shined.

Writing community has always been good to me—writers really are the best colleagues one can wish for. Kate Heartfield, Lucy Holland, Ed Crocker—thank you from the bottom of my heart. Florence Chien, you understand my obsession with art. I'm immensely grateful to my street team, who generously gave me their time and support, and to my fellow Codexians, who taught me how to be a professional.

In Croatia, I'm grateful to my amazing publisher, Morana, who restored my trust in the industry. The unsurpassed crew of

Morina kutija and the amazing team of The Isle of Wonders—thank you for making me feel at home.

And lastly, my eternal gratitude goes to my family, who sacrifice a lot to give me enough time and space to write. Without you, none of this would be possible.

—Jelena Dunato, October 2025

About the Author

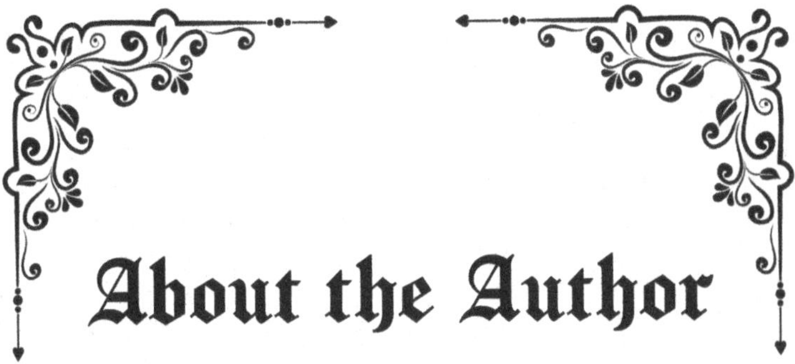

Jelena Dunato is an art historian, curator, speculative fiction writer, and lover of all things ancient. She grew up in Croatia on a steady diet of adventure novels and then wandered the world for a decade, building a career in the arts. Her stories have been published in *Beneath Ceaseless Skies*, *The Dark*, *Haven Spec*, and *Small Wonders*, among others. She is a member of SFWA and Codex. She is the author of novel *Dark Woods, Deep Water* and novella *Ghost Apparent*. She lives on an island in the Adriatic with her family.